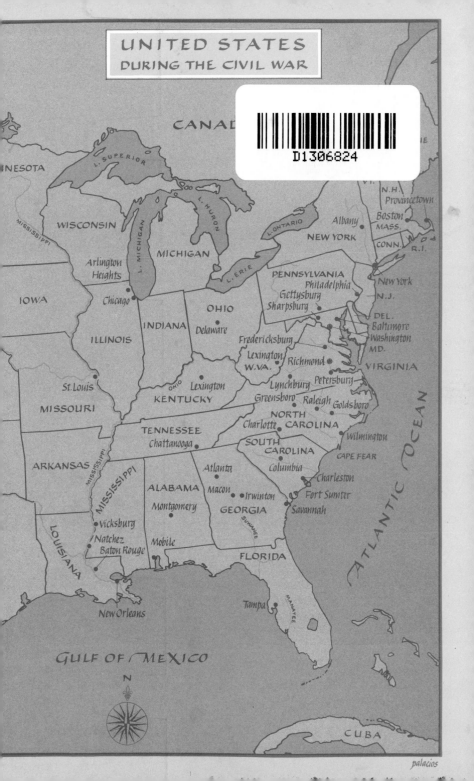

THE
PASSIONATE
REBEL

BOOKS BY FRANK G. SLAUGHTER

The Passionate Rebel
Devil's Gamble
Plague Ship
Stonewall Brigade
Women in White
Convention, M.D.
Code Five
Countdown
Surgeon's Choice
The Sins of Herod
Doctors' Wives
God's Warrior
Surgeon, U.S.A.
Constantine
The Purple Quest
A Savage Place
Upon This Rock
Tomorrow's Miracle
David: Warrior and King
The Curse of Jezebel
Epidemic!
Pilgrims in Paradise
The Land and the Promise
Lorena
The Crown and the Cross
The Thorn of Arimathea
Daybreak

The Mapmaker
Sword and Scalpel
The Scarlet Cord
Flight from Natchez
The Healer
Apalachee Gold
The Song of Ruth
Storm Haven
The Galileans
East Side General
Fort Everglades
The Road to Bithynia
The Stubborn Heart
Immortal Magyar
Divine Mistress
Sangaree
Medicine for Moderns
The Golden Isle
The New Science of Surgery
In a Dark Garden
A Touch of Glory
Battle Surgeon
Air Surgeon
Spencer Brade, M.D.
That None Should Die
The Warrior

UNDER THE NAME C. V. TERRY

Buccaneer Surgeon
The Deadly Lady of Madagascar

Darien Venture
The Golden Ones

THE PASSIONATE REBEL

Frank G. Slaughter

DOUBLEDAY & COMPANY, INC.
GARDEN CITY, NEW YORK
1979

ISBN 0-385-14336-2
Library of Congress Catalog Card Number 79-6980

CONTENTS

BOOK ONE

MOBILE

The right eye of the young woman bracing her superb body against the mainmast of the British brigantine, *Pride of Bristol,* was pressed against the eyepiece of the telescope in her hand. In turn, the polished brass barrel was directed upon a sleek vessel, with the Stars and Stripes of the United States Navy flying proudly from its staff, rapidly overtaking the *Pride of Bristol* from the southeast. With side wheels churning at full steam, the course of the second ship would soon take it across the bow of the old sailing vessel, forcing the *Pride* to heave to or be rammed. Few of the crew moving about on the deck below paid much attention to the other ship, however—or to the tall form of Captain Pennington Darrow, who was perched in the crow's nest atop the mainmast high above the deck, watching tensely the course of the overtaking vessel.

The crew could hardly be blamed for any lack of attention to the situation in which the broad-beamed old brigantine found herself late on this April afternoon in 1861, though. From any angle, Maritza LeClerc was a far more intriguing picture in the afternoon sunlight than any ship. Tall for a woman, Maritza resembled one of the figureheads carved of wood that had adorned the prows of Yankee square-riggers for more than two centuries, as they searched the world's seas for whale oil with which to light the lamps of New England—with the exception that *she* was very much alive indeed.

The brisk afternoon breeze, common here along the southern Gulf Coast, molded the light brown fabric of Maritza's dress against her body, outlining it in all its almost amazon beauty. At twenty-five, she was a worthy scion of a race of Southerners sublimely conscious of their *noblesse oblige,* plus, in her case, the French title of countess legally acquired by marriage to the late Count Étienne LeClerc.

Distant cousin of at least two United States senators, Countess Maritza LeClerc, nee Slidell, had quickly learned to hold her own in the diplomatic world, to say nothing of the give-and-take of business involved with managing her husband's considerable estate during the year of his final illness and the six months since his death. Bilingual, like many Louisianians, even before her considerably older husband took her as a bride to France and his château in the beautiful Loire Valley near Paris, she had represented abroad the interests of the Slidell family of Louisiana and Mobile, plus her own large plantation in Alabama near the port city. And now that war between the United States of America and its southern portion seemed imminent, she'd become a passionate rebel against northern domination as well.

Looking up at the tall figure clinging to the top of the mainmast and cupping her hands about her mouth, Maritza shouted to the tensely observant Pennington Darrow: "Do you think they will try to stop us, Captain?"

"They'd better not. This is *still* a British vessel, even though we're loaded to the decks with Enfield rifles and ammunition."

A distant boom sounded from the pursuing United States warship and seconds later a round shot sent a small geyser skyward roughly a quarter of a mile from the stern of the *Pride of Bristol*.

"I thought you said they wouldn't fire on a British vessel?" Maritza observed a little sarcastically.

"That's the U. S. S. *Montgomery*. I took a cruise on her the summer between my third and fourth years at the Naval Academy. They're probably pretending to mistake the Union Jack for the flag of the Confederate States of America." Penn Darrow closed his telescope and, scampering down the rigging with the agility of a monkey, dropped to the deck beside Maritza.

"What are you going to do?" she asked.

"We'll hold our course for Mobile Bay—with your permission as owner. You can see the mouth there on the northern horizon."

"Isn't that dangerous—with explosives aboard?"

"The captain of a U.S. warship isn't likely to be stupid enough to anger the British into recognizing the infant Confederacy as a nation by attacking one of Her Majesty's vessels, even a rotting old tub like the *Pride of Bristol*. Besides, Alabama had already seceded before we left England, so Fort Morgan at the mouth of Mobile Bay should be in the hands of the Alabama militia—though whether they can handle the cannon is another matter."

"What would you do in the place of yonder Union commander?" Maritza asked.

"Send a search party aboard if he can stop us. Once he found that we're loaded to the Plimsoll mark with rifles and ammunition, he'd have a legitimate reason to take us into a Union port."

"Can he do it—stop us, I mean?"

"He's got cannon and we don't," said Penn Darrow laconically. "Besides, one of those shots he's dropping all around us could go through this old hull as if it was made of paper."

"Then you're still optimistic?"

"I have to be. Everything I've got is tied up in this cargo."

Maritza turned her glass upon the shoreline, still several miles distant on the northern horizon. The squat outline of Fort Morgan on the eastern side of the channel into Mobile Bay looked massive enough. The dark mouths of the cannon protruding from the gun ports also appeared quite capable of blowing the *Montgomery* out of the water.

"I'd say Fort Morgan looks formidable enough," Maritza observed, "and the Union ship will soon be in range if it keeps on."

"I doubt if it will," said Pennington Darrow.

"For once we agree," Maritza told him. "I met Lord Russell in London and I don't see him launching England into war over one half-rotten merchant vessel."

"We'll soon find out," Penn Darrow said with a shrug. "You're more recently from Paris than I am. Do you think France might join England, if it comes to a war between Britain and the United States?"

"My guess is that Napoleon III would be happy to see that happen," said Maritza.

"Why?"

"Slavery has already divided the United States to where it's not really much of a competitor for trade, either with England or France. A weak and divided nation—or even two countries— between Canada and the Rio Grande would fit right in with Napoleon's plans for moving into the Western Hemisphere by way of Mexico."

From the rapidly closing warship came the boom of a second shot, landing only a few hundred yards from the *Pride of Bristol.*

"That Yankee captain must have realized we're going to make a race for the safety of Mobile and the guns of Fort Morgan," said Penn Darrow. "Fortunately, the deepest channel into Mobile Bay passes practically under the guns of the fort."

Unslinging the telescope from the lanyard around his neck, he crossed the deck to the wheel and glanced at the charts spread out before the steersman. "I came into Mobile on a warship once while I was at the Naval Academy—before I was tossed out near the end of the senior year for having a girl in my room after 'lights out,'" he told Maritza. "If we can get across that bar, we are safe."

"I see some spray near the middle of the opening." Maritza had followed and was standing beside him looking down at the chart. "Is that where the bar is located?"

"Yes," he told her. "Whatever channel there is, it's probably narrow and shallow but the broad beam of the *Pride* cuts down her draft. One thing's for sure, we won't have time this afternoon to anchor outside and wait for a bar pilot to guide us through the channel."

"What you're saying is that we've got the triple hazard of a Union gunboat trying to stop us outside the bar, plus a channel that may be too shallow for us to negotiate and gunners at that fort who may not really know how to handle those big cannon."

"I couldn't have put it better," he agreed.

"This looks like a poker game," she observed. "And it's your turn to bet."

"You're a cool one, all right," Darrow conceded, "but I'm risking a ship and ten per cent of a valuable cargo—"

"Which you'll lose if that Yankee captain out there scares you into heaving to."

"While you stand to lose the fortune you've got invested in the arms below deck," he reminded her, "which is considerably larger than my ten per cent."

"I've already placed my bet, Captain." Maritza closed her telescope. "I've got a bottle of fine French cognac; cross that bar successfully into Mobile Bay and we'll broach it to-night—after one of Celestina's dinners—in my cabin."

II

Maritza was awakened by a shaft of bright sunlight pouring through the open porthole of her cabin, from which Celestina, her personal slave who was more of a companion than a ser-vant, had just pulled back the curtain. Designed originally for the owner, the cabin was naturally the most luxurious on the ship; the berth large enough for two people sleeping close to-gether.

"What time is it, Tina?" she asked, swinging her legs over the edge of the broad berth and stretching luxuriously like a drowsy cat.

"Nine o'clock. Cap'n Darrow left the ship two hours ago. Said he was going into Mobile to see 'bout where we can dock and also to make arrangements for selling the rifles." Celes-tina's tone was cool but Maritza didn't notice; she was review-ing in her mind the exciting series of events that had followed Penn Darrow's decision to try coaxing the *Pride of Bristol* across the bar at the mouth of Mobile Bay and her promise of supper in her cabin—plus a bottle of cognac—if he succeeded.

The race for the channel mouth had been exciting. Ordering all hands, except the helmsman, into the rigging, Darrow had climbed rapidly back to the crow's nest. From there, he had personally directed the setting of all sails on the old brigantine, sending it plowing northward through the low chop in the Gulf of Mexico toward the entrance into Mobile Bay. For a while it seemed that they might make it alone to safety, since the *Pride* carried a massive spread of sail and the wind was freshening steadily, as the red ball of the sun sank lower into the western horizon. The captain of the *Montgomery* was obviously an experienced seaman, however, and black smoke quickly began to gush from the tall stacks, as more coal was thrown into the fireboxes to set the side wheels churning ever faster. As the space between pursuer and pursued steadily shortened, Maritza watched the still distant fortification anxiously.

"I can see a lot of activity at Fort Morgan now," she called up to Penn Darrow. "They're going to do something."

"Pray it's for us and not against us."

To obtain the best view of the fort, Maritza was standing in the very bow, ignoring the spray from the cutwater just below her. Nor did she flinch when she was drenched as the bowsprit dipped and rose in the steadily increasing chop from the freshening wind and the thin dress revealed every line of her magnificent body. Behind her the throb of the taut square sail, driving the old vessel on toward the bar and the narrow break marking the channel, was like the low-pitched beat of an African jungle drum.

Darrow's position atop the mainmast was the riskiest perch on the whole ship, Maritza knew. Should the *Pride of Bristol* go aground in the channel, he would be catapulted as if by a giant slingshot to his death in the raging breakers. He ignored this threat of personal danger, however, shouting orders as the sails were set and even swinging across the yards once to cut away the lines from a broken spar before the splintered ends of the wooden timber could rip open the great square sail.

In the end, it was intervention from another quarter that saved the *Pride of Bristol*. Watching the activity on Fort Morgan, Maritza saw one of its guns suddenly belch smoke and flame, although it was a fraction of a second later before she heard the sound. For a perilous instant, it seemed that the heavy shell, plainly visible as it hurtled through the air, was aimed at the *Pride of Bristol*. Then she saw it arc into the

water, sending up a tremendous geyser directly in front of the
Montgomery in the universal warning to heave to or stand
away.

Momentarily, as the column of water sent skyward by the impact of the huge cannon ball hid the other vessel from view,
Maritza dared to hope the projectile might have struck the
Union warship. Then, as the water fell back in a wall of spray,
she saw that it was still intact. The captain of the *Montgomery*
was quite conscious of what the warning shot from the shore
battery meant, however, as the staccato shouts of orders clearly
indicated. Side wheels churning frantically, canvas flapping, the
man-o'-war changed course. It charged past the *Pride of Bristol*
so close that Maritza could easily see its ensign dip in a gesture
of acknowledgment by the captain that he had been out-
maneuvered in the grim game played out here almost at the entrance to Mobile Bay this spring afternoon.

After that dramatic scene the hour remaining before full
darkness fell had been something of an anticlimax. With the
Montgomery now headed away from land and no longer a
threat, Penn Darrow had guided the old merchant ship through
the channel into Mobile Bay with depth to spare. He had not,
however, tried to negotiate the sometimes tricky thirty-odd-
mile-long channel leading to the docks of Mobile itself. Instead,
he had anchored the *Pride* for the night about halfway to the
city, well out of the way of passing ships.

The promised dinner that evening had been prepared and
served by Celestina with complete perfection. By the time Penn
Darrow poured the last drop of imported brandy—considered
since antiquity the most effective aphrodisiac of any vintage—
Maritza's pulse had already begun to quicken. Though whether
from the brandy or the obvious glow of desire in the eyes of the
handsome man seated across the small table from her in the
cabin, she could not have said.

"To us!" She remembered the final toast, when the last of
the bottle had been poured into fragile wineglasses Celestina
had managed to resurrect from somewhere, before leaving the
cabin with the dishes on a tray. As she lifted her glass to touch
his before drinking, Maritza remembered wondering whether

she'd be able to resist the impulse—made a hundred times stronger by the burning light of desire in his eyes—to yield.

"If I'd known you'd be so foolish as to spurn the handsomest man to come your way in almost a year, I wouldn't have let that billy goat of a first mate butt me most of the night," said Celestina, still on a note of disgust.

"What else did you expect of me? After all, I *am* a widow."

"Of six months—and you haven't enjoyed a man for more than a year, since Count Étienne had his stroke. He'd be the first to tell you that's too long."

Maritza had no secrets from the octoroon who had been her slave, companion, and closest friend since she was twelve. Both startlingly beautiful, with the tawny, feline beauty of a pair of tigresses, they were roughly the same age, twenty-five. And with less than an eighth part of Negro blood, Tina had shared all but the most intimate moments of her mistress' life.

The two girls had gone to Paris together, when Senator John Slidell—whose ward Maritza had been after her parents' death— decided that she, with near royal blood in her veins from both her French mother and her Spanish father, deserved a mate higher in the social and financial scale than an Alabama cotton planter. Slidell had no trouble either in arranging a marriage for her at eighteen with Count Étienne LeClerc, twenty years older but still vigorous and handsome.

"What a waste of fine French cognac." Tina was still grumbling as she laid out the filmy French lingerie Maritza had brought from Paris. "If Captain Darrow knew how to handle a woman as well as he knows how to handle a ship, I'll wager you wouldn't have slept alone last night."

"It was *my* choice." Maritza was pulling the nightgown over her head. "What's funny?" she added when Celestina suddenly laughed.

"At least you've learned to undress with more grace than you did on your wedding night. Count Étienne spent a half hour coaxing you out of your shift."

"How did you know that?"

"Castle bedrooms have large keyholes but few keys," said Tina with a toss of her head. "I had to spend the rest of the night with Édouard, the butler, as a reward for giving me the keyhole with the best view—but it was worth it."

"You slut!"

"Pretty is as pretty does. From what I remember of that night, you were an apt enough pupil, once you got the hang of it."

Maritza couldn't help laughing. "Coming from you, that's praise indeed."

Tina was pouring water from a bucket into a large metal tub in the center of the cabin. "Just because I had the misfortune to be born with a touch of the tarbrush, while you're the bastard of a rich Spaniard and a daughter of French nobility, doesn't make me any less of a woman than you," she said sharply.

"Forgive me." Maritza was instantly contrite. "You know I didn't mean it that way."

"Come get in the tub then. I need to wash some of our clothes today."

Crossing the room, Maritza paused before a fairly large mirror fixed in the midst of a set of drawers built into the cabin wall. With her shining mass of golden hair, the aquiline features with the faintly olive tint in her skin from her Creole and Spanish heritage, the full breasts and the slim tapering thighs, she knew she was beautiful almost beyond the dreams of any lover.

"Stop admiring yourself and get into the tub," Tina ordered imperiously.

"I wish I could wash my hair."

"We'll have to do that another day. If you're going to be the American correspondent for *Le Pays,* you'd better get busy writing the story of how we were fired on by a U.S. gunboat and barely escaped with our lives."

"You're right," said Maritza. "That storm in mid-ocean made us lose two weeks and Monsieur Claudet will be expecting to hear from me. I can probably mail the account from Mobile tomorrow."

"Captain Darrow will see that it gets sent; he's the kind of man who does what he sets out to do." Celestina laughed, her good nature restored. "Except bring you to bed—and I wager he'll do that before we get away from here."

Maritza didn't deny the possibility. In fact, the very thought quickened her pulse and brought a faint pink tint to her nude body. Slipping down into the warm water and letting it caress her like a lover's touch, she shivered with pleasure when the slave scrubbed her breasts gently with a washcloth.

"Captain Darrow's hands on these could have done more than make you shiver," Celestina observed as she moved on to Maritza's torso. "I'll wager he could hold down any reluctant maiden with the spring steel in those legs of his—if she were such a fool as to resist him."

III

Maritza was sitting outside in the deck chair that afternoon, enjoying the late April sunlight and finishing her story for *Le Pays,* when Penn Darrow returned from Mobile in a ship's boat rowed by four sailors.

"You look tired," she told him as he came up the ladder and over the rail. "Come into my cabin and I'll have Celestina make you some rum punch. A vendor came by in a boat this morning selling fresh fruits and vegetables."

"That sounds like nectar from Mount Olympus," he said, following her into the cabin. "The port is jammed with ships and cotton, but most American vessels are afraid to make a run, with the *Montgomery* hanging around outside the bar. I've been haggling with port authorities most of the day, trying to get them to let me bring the *Pride* upriver and dock in the middle of town."

"Why would they object to that?"

"For one thing, they're afraid a Union sympathizer might manage to cause an explosion. What we've got under the hatches could demolish half the docks in the city."

"This is secession country," Maritza objected. "Why would

anybody want to blow up a shipload of munitions bound for the Confederacy when they need them so badly?"

"As I said, somebody who sympathized with the North."

"But who would do that this far south?"

"More than you'd think. A lot of people who don't own slaves are against slavery."

"But the controversy is over states' rights."

"Just now, states' rights and slavery are synonyms to most Southerners," he explained. "Besides, not everyone's quite so passionate in their rebel spirits as you are." He accepted a tall glass of punch from Celestina and took a deep draught from it. "Umm! This is good, Tina."

"What did you decide?" Maritza asked.

"They finally agreed to let me sail the ship up the bay tomorrow morning to a spot several miles south of the city, where there's a good anchorage. Actually, that isn't such a bad idea because then the munitions can be loaded directly onto the shallow-draft stern-wheelers that will carry them upstream to Montgomery, if the Confederate government buys them."

"Aren't they the most logical purchaser?"

"Logical, yes, but they'll still probably want to haggle. The militia commander in Mobile would like to have them, too, but he can't handle a transaction of this size financially, so he sent a telegram to Montgomery. The answer came back before I left that they're sending down a buyer from the Confederate Quartermaster Department. Just to keep the bidding spirited, though, I passed the word around to some speculators that the rifles will still be auctioned off. You ought to get that price of thirty-five dollars apiece you've got your heart set on. And with a profit of twenty-five dollars per rifle, plus what you get for the other munitions, you're going to be a rich woman, Countess."

"You won't come off so badly yourself, with ten per cent of the gross going to you. Not that you don't deserve every cent of it for refusing to heave to yesterday afternoon when the *Montgomery* started firing on us."

"By the way," he said, "I learned why the *Montgomery* was willing to chase us practically under the guns of Fort Morgan.

President Lincoln has ordered a blockade of all Southern ports."

"How could he do that?"

"The Confederacy and the Union are at war."

"War!" Maritza almost dropped the glass of punch she was holding. "When my foster uncle, John Slidell, was in Paris about six months ago, he said that would never happen," she protested. "The North has no stomach for fighting and, even if the Yankees start a war, the South could whip them in a month."

"That was before Abraham Lincoln was elected President and before the Confederates captured Fort Sumter in the port of Charleston about two weeks ago."

"Fort Sumter's only another grubby fortification. When Étienne and I were there a few years ago, it wasn't even garrisoned."

"It still wasn't until just before the capture. Then Confederate cannon were emplaced to fire on Fort Moultrie, where the U. S. Army garrison was, and the Union officer in charge—a Major Anderson—moved his troops to Fort Sumter because it was easier to defend. *That's* when the fireworks started."

"When did you say all this happened?"

"The first Confederate cannon fired on Fort Sumter April 12 and the garrison surrendered April 15."

"Surely it would have been better to starve the Yankees out. Then the South wouldn't have had to bear the onus of firing the first shot and starting the war."

"That would have been the logical move," Darrow conceded, "but the troop commander in Charleston seems to be quite a fire-eater. He decided to become famous overnight."

"Who was he?"

"A General Beauregard."

"Cousin Pierre!" Maritza cried. "Why, he's nothing but a windbag!"

"Windbag or not, Beauregard used his cannon to huff and puff until he blew Major Anderson and his troops right out of Fort Sumter. That, of course, left Abraham Lincoln no choice

except to declare that a state of war exists between the Union and the Confederacy."

"How many Southern states are involved?" she asked.

"Seven, so far; they're expecting Virginia and North Carolina to join any day. Lincoln has ordered the United States Navy to block all Southern ports, but that means spreading the number of vessels the Union has very thin. Only one ship, the *Montgomery,* is protecting the coast from the Rio Grande to Mobile Bay."

"Has there been any more fighting?"

"Beauregard has been too busy making speeches and receiving compliments for that, but the day after Sumter fell Lincoln called for seventy-five thousand troops. He, at least, means business."

A sudden light burned in Maritza's brain. "That makes our cargo of Enfield rifles almost as valuable to the Confederacy as gold, doesn't it?"

"Just what I told the purchasing agent for the Alabama militia companies being mobilized in Mobile, but most of them are too busy having fancy uniforms made to consider needing any weapons yet. Unless I miss my guess, our Enfields will wind up in the Confederate capital at Montgomery, where a former senator and Secretary of War is President of the Confederate States of America."

"Jefferson Davis!" Maritza cried. "I know him and he's certainly not a man to try to split the country in two, just to prove he could do it."

"I agree," said Darrow. "Davis was Secretary of War while I was at the Naval Academy and that was his reputation even then. Nevertheless, the Confederacy and the Union are at war."

Maritza shivered. "Étienne told me something of what war is like; he was an officer in the army of Napoleon III until he was mustered out because of a fever. If President Lincoln has called up seventy-five thousand troops, the whole South will eventually be drawn into the fight."

"You can always claim French citizenship by marriage and remain neutral," he reminded her.

"I'm a Southerner by birth, so I have no choice except to be on the Southern side," she said proudly. "I do intend to pretend neutrality, though, so I can write for *Le Pays* about Northern atrocities. Which reminds me," she added. "I need to get into Mobile and mail the report I've been writing all day to my editor in Paris. The French people are intensely interested in everything American."

"I'll take care of it for you first thing in the morning when I go back to Mobile," he promised. "There's a rumor going around that Jefferson Davis will embargo shipment of cotton abroad."

"Why would he do that, when cotton's about the only thing the South can export?"

"The cotton brokers I talked to are betting Davis hopes to make England and France recognize the Confederacy as a nation in order to get cotton for their looms and spinning jennies. The price on the docks is dropping all the time and as soon as we get this cargo of munitions sold, I want to load the *Pride* with cotton and head for England as fast as I can. That is, if you agree."

"I not only agree but I may be able to furnish the cotton," she said. "Celestina and I will go ashore with you tomorrow morning so I can hire a buggy and drive out to the plantation I own about ten miles from Mobile. My solicitor here has been leasing it by the year to a cotton grower whose land adjoins mine, but the price of this year's lease hasn't been paid yet and I want to find out why. If it doesn't come through immediately, I'll have a cotton crop of my own to sell."

"I'd offer to go with you but I need to talk to a few more cotton brokers," Darrow told her. "There're plenty of boats for hire at the dock, though, and you can easily get one to bring you back aboard tomorrow afternoon when you get back from the plantation."

IV

About ten miles from Mobile, Maritza pulled the buggy she had hired that morning to a stop beside a field of cotton that extended as far as she could see. After the shaded, sandy road, where Spanish moss hung from great water oaks to make a tunnel through which the rutted track ran, the brightness of the sun on the open field made a glare that hurt their eyes, in spite of the lush green carpet of cotton plants already half knee high.

"We're home, Tina!" Maritza cried when a summer breeze rippled the leaves of the plants lightly, sending a wave of shimmering green across the field. "After the war's over, I'm coming back here and build me a house with tall white columns and plant acres of azaleas and camellias around it. I'll raise tall sons who'll go to Congress and maybe to the White House. And daughters so beautiful they'll turn the heads of all the young men in the country."

"You've got the money for it already," said Celestina practically. "Why not do it now?"

"I've got a job to do—and a husband to find."

"Cap'n Darrow would be glad to father all the sons and daughters you want."

"When he comes back from sailing a cargo of cotton in England, I think he's going to accept a commission in the Confederate Navy," Maritza objected.

"And maybe get killed! You mustn't let him do it."

"How could I stop him—if I tried?"

"You've got the money—and the political connections. Why don't you buy him a desk job in Montgomery, Richmond, or wherever the government is going to be located, then he'd be handy for breedin' purposes."

Tying the reins to the whipstaff socket, Maritza climbed down from the buggy to run through the cotton field, ignoring the wetness of the dew on her stockings and the hem of her frock.

"My father and mother loved this place!" she cried. "And I love it just as much."

"Oh! Oh! Here comes somebody," said Celestina, then her tone changed to one of warmth and excitement. "It's Moses, your foreman, Miss Ritza!"

"So it is." Maritza ran toward where a tall black man with graying hair and a whip coiled around his neck had brought the horse he was riding to a halt and was dismounting.

"I'm home, Moses!" she cried. "Home for good!"

"Mawnin', Miss Ritza." The overseer's tone had little warmth. "Mawnin', Celestina."

"What's the matter with you, Moses, talkin' like we're strangers?" Celestina demanded indignantly. "You been listenin' to that stuff Abraham Lincoln's spoutin' up in Washington?" Now that she was back home, Tina's speech was taking on the slurred accent of the native patois once again.

"Moses used to carry me piggyback when I was a little girl, Tina," said Maritza. "He couldn't hold anything against me." She looked up at the tall Negro questioningly. "Could you, Moses?"

The black man's mouth worked painfully, as if he were moved to say something unpleasant and was reluctant to do so.

"I guess mah feelin's was hurt, Miss Ritza," he managed to blurt out finally. "None of us on the plantation ever thought you'd sell the lan'—and us, too—'thout even comin' home to tell us why."

"I didn't sell you, Moses!"

"Mind you, ain't none of us got nothin' 'gainst the major—he's a cunnel now." The words were tumbling out now in a rush. "He's kept us all together, too—"

"One minute, Moses," said Maritza. "Did you say sell?"

"Yassum. Not more'n a month ago, Cunnel Mann came back from Montgomery specially to tell us he was buyin' the plantation from you. He's a good man—"

"I haven't sold the plantation, Moses. And I don't know any Colonel Mann or even what you're talking about."

"You ain't sold the lan'—and the slaves that's worked it since yore mammy and pappy used to come out here from Mobile?"

"No, Moses."

The bewilderment of the big Negro overseer was evidenced by the frown that creased his forehead. "You swear to that?"

"Take that back, Moses," Tina snapped. "You know Miss Ritza never told you a lie."

" 'Scuse me, ma'am. They's a lot about this I don't understand."

"And a lot I don't understand either but I haven't sold the land or any of you," said Maritza firmly. "In fact, when the war's over I'm coming back here to live. Right now, though, I'm going to see my lawyer in Mobile and find out what the hell's been going on."

It was almost three when Maritza and Celestina passed through a gateway of filigreed iron with a sign on it that read, "ANDERSON & ANDERSON, Attorneys at Law." Inside the small courtyard, fragrant with the smell of jasmine and morning glory, they took a stairway leading up to the office of Mr. Thomas Anderson, Jr.

The lawyer's parents had come to Mobile from Boston before the American Revolution and remained, entranced by its beauty. The family still retained its New England ties, however, by regularly sending at least one son out of each generation North to study law at Harvard College before returning to undertake the legal profession. Thomas Anderson, Sr., had been Maritza's own father's solicitor when he was alive and, with the son, handled the investments of half the great families of Mobile.

"Maritza!" The lawyer came into the outer waiting room, as soon as the visitors were announced, greeting her with both hands extended. "Or shouldn't I rather say, Countess LeClerc?"

"You've known me long enough to be on first-name terms, Tom," said Maritza. "I think you may remember my companion, Celestina."

"Of course. With so much beauty in my office at one time, I can hardly believe my own eyes. You have my sympathy in the death of your husband, Maritza. The firm of Anderson & Anderson handled a number of transactions for Count LeClerc in this area."

"I know," said Maritza. "That's why I came to see you today."

"I'm sure you'll be interested to know that my oldest son, Thomas III, is studying law at Harvard College," said the lawyer. "He will return home to practice with me in another year, unless President Davis carries out his intention to draft young men into the Confederate Army."

"Most people I talked to, where I rented a horse and buggy this morning, seemed to think the war will be over long before that," said Maritza.

"I'm not as sure as they are," said the lawyer. "Perhaps because our family came from New England originally and I spent a number of years in Boston studying law. I know how pitifully few resources for manufacturing are found in the South compared to what already exist in the North. But, anyway, I'm glad to see you decided to return to Mobile. After you sold the plantation—"

"I haven't sold the plantation, Tom."

"But I have a deed in my safe signed by you; it was sent to me by a Monsieur Philippe LeClerc. I believe he's your late husband's nephew and heir."

"Only to the château—to keep the name and the building in the family. I still own the plantation here."

"But I recognized your signature myself on the deed from one to the property that my father drew up, when your late husband gave it to you after receiving it as part of your dowry."

"Can I see the deed you're talking about?" Maritza asked.

Anderson hesitated. "Colonel Richard Mann left it with me for safekeeping, as many others here in Mobile do."

"You said I signed the deed, which I certainly did not," said Maritza firmly. "That, quite obviously, gives me some previous rights in this transaction."

"You're right, of course. I'll get the deed." Going to a large safe in the corner of the office, Anderson removed a folder and brought it over to the table where Maritza and Celestina were seated.

"Isn't that your signature?" he asked, pointing to the bottom of the page. "And you can see that it transfers the property to Monsieur Philippe LeClerc."

Maritza stared at the document with unbelieving eyes. The name written at the bottom of the sheet was undeniably hers—and equally undeniably in her own handwriting. Yet she could swear that she had never signed the paper.

"Perhaps you remember now," Anderson suggested. "In the business of settling your husband's estate—"

"I never signed this paper, Tom," she said firmly. "It's a forgery."

"But the property description is exactly the same as the contract of gift between your guardian, Senator Slidell, and Count Étienne LeClerc that was part of the dowry settlement."

"That would be easy for Philippe. A copy was undoubtedly in Étienne's papers." Maritza's voice was still a little hoarse from the shock of seeing a signature that appeared to be hers but which she had never made.

"An expert forger I knew in Paris told me a great deal about how they work," said Celestina unexpectedly. "Philippe Le-Clerc wouldn't hesitate to hire someone to duplicate Madame's signature. He hated her because he was afraid she might bear Count Étienne a son and deprive him of the title."

Anderson gave Tina a startled look. For a slave to speak out in such a manner and, what was more, to accuse a member of the French nobility of being a forger was obviously beyond belief.

"How could you ever prove your signature is a forgery, Maritza—that is, if it really is?" the lawyer asked.

"If you knew Philippe LeClerc as we do, Tom, you'd know that this is just the sort of thing he wouldn't hesitate to do. But, like you, I wonder how we could ever be able to prove it."

"I think I can take care of that," said Celestina calmly. "Would you let me see the deed again, please, Mr. Anderson?"

"I'm afraid there's no denying the validity of the signature," the lawyer said as he slid the paper across the table to Celestina. "After all, the countess has even identified it herself."

"You saw what *appeared* to be her signature." Celestina had turned the sheet over and was running her fingers with a stroking motion gently across the bottom. "Actually, it's a forgery—and not a very good one at that."

The lawyer mopped his forehead with a handkerchief. "To prove that, you'd have to be a magician."

"Not quite," said Tina. "Would you give me a sheet of onionskin paper, sir, and the softest pencil you can find?"

"Of course." The lawyer fumbled in his desk and came up with a sheet of very thin paper and a soft black lead pencil. "But I don't see—"

"You will," Celestina assured him calmly as she placed the thin paper against the bottom of the back side of the deed and began to stroke gently across it with the pencil. The other two leaned closer and, while they watched, a look of astonishment came upon their faces. Beneath the swiftly moving pencil, Maritza's signature began to appear—but in a darker color than the shading and reversed—literally a mirror image.

"Good God!" said the lawyer. "Given a bona fide signature, anyone could forge a duplicate of it."

"It's simple," Celestina explained. "You take any document with a real signature on it, like the deed to the château *Madame la Comtesse* signed over to Philippe LeClerc. Then with a metal stylus you trace the signature on the document you wish to forge, pressing hard enough to leave an imprint on the second sheet. When that imprint is gone over with pen and ink, you have what appears to be a true signature on the forged document."

"Has the purchase price for the plantation been paid, Tom?" Maritza asked the lawyer.

"I have Colonel Richard Mann's check in my safe. It's going to Philippe LeClerc on the next ship for Paris."

"I hereby denounce this deed as a forgery and if this Colonel Mann insists on trying to go through with the sale I'll take him to court," she said. "Can you tell me where I can find him?"

"In Montgomery. He's in the Confederate Army—the Quartermaster Department."

"I'll see him myself when I get to the capital a few days from now," she said. "Meanwhile, though, you can hold his check.

I'll take the forged deed and Tina's demonstration of how it was done to show him."

"Colonel Mann is an honorable person, Maritza. If your signature was forged—and there doesn't seem to be any doubt about it—you'll have no trouble whatsoever from him."

"What about the money for this year's lease?" she asked.

"It went to you in France in January. The check came back from the Banque de France endorsed by you."

"After being cashed by Philippe LeClerc with the aid of his forger, no doubt," said Maritza. "But I suppose it's too late to do anything about that."

V

Penn Darrow returned to the *Pride of Bristol* shortly after a hired boatman deposited Maritza and Celestina at the foot of the boarding ladder. He looked tired and a little depressed. Maritza was sitting outside on the deck, enjoying the evening breeze after the drive through the hot spring air to the plantation and back, and the session with her lawyer.

"If I didn't have female passengers aboard, I'd be out there swimming in the bay," he confessed.

"Tina and I would be doing the same if we were alone," Maritza assured him.

"You swim then?"

"Very well. Étienne dammed up a small creek to form a lake in an isolated part of the estate. We often swam there."

"Women's bathing dresses are so cumbersome, I don't see how you ever stayed up."

"Ours weren't," she said laconically. "By the way, a doctor from Apalachicola not far from here invented a machine for making ice—"

"I've seen them."

"I remembered that there was an ice-making plant in Mobile and stopped on the way back to the ship to buy a block. Tina's cooling some wine if you'd like to share that and a light supper with us on deck."

"You just saved my life," he told her. "I'll be back out as soon as I can go to my cabin and wash up."

When Darrow returned, Celestina had set up a small table and two chairs on the forward deck. A bottle of wine was also cooling in a water bucket filled with chipped ice beside the table. Using the corkscrew hanging from the edge of the bucket, he opened the bottle and poured some wine into a glass, handing it to Maritza. When she nodded approval, he filled both glasses and put the bottle carefully back into the ice.

"You said this afternoon you would tell me about a new plan of yours," she reminded him. "This would be a good time while Tina is broiling a snapper I bought for our dinner."

"As good a time as any," he agreed. "But like the best-known plans of mice and men—"

"Maybe I can help."

"I thought I'd found a way to make some money carrying cotton to England, if it doesn't take too long to sell these rifles and ammunition."

"It sounds like a good idea. What's holding it up?"

"The brokers demand payment before the cotton leaves the dock."

"That does pose a difficulty," she admitted. "Your ten per cent of the cargo's value wouldn't go far in buying a shipload of cotton."

"I figured to have enough for the down payment and expected that the broker would lend me the rest to be paid to his agent in England. The trouble is that businessmen in England don't seem to know exactly how Lincoln or Davis are going to handle the sale of cotton."

"And, anyway, the interest rate the brokers would charge you would take half your profit."

"That's the way the game's played in these parts but the stakes still aren't to my liking," he said with a shrug. He gave her a sudden quick look. "Why the inquisition?"

"I was just thinking that you could save a lot of money by taking a partner who could finance the deal."

"You?"

"Who else? We pool our assets to buy the cotton for cash and get a better price."

"My ten per cent of the price you get for the Enfields might pay half—"

"You'll not be paying for *any* of it—or interest on your share," she assured him. "All I ask is that you get a fully loaded ship safely to England, sell the cargo, and deposit my half of the profit in London with my solicitors."

"I'll sign a document to that effect," he said promptly. "Just have your lawyer draw it up the way you want it to be."

"A simple handshake should be enough." She held out her hand and he gripped it momentarily before she withdrew it.

"You're on, partner," he said. "If you were in charge of the Alexandria Line before Washington, instead of your cousin Pierre, who's on the way there from Charleston, according to the newspapers, I'll wager that Abraham Lincoln would already be preparing to flee Washington."

"Have you decided what you'll do with your ten per cent of this cargo and half the cotton?" she asked.

"I'm thinking of becoming a privateersman," he confided.

"A what?"

"When the South seceded, the U. S. Navy remained under control of the Washington government, so the Confederacy has no ships of war. They can have them built in European shipyards, of course, but the Union will fight them all the way— diplomatically. Meanwhile, there's a swifter way of interfering with Northern commerce."

"How?"

"In one of the Scottish shipyards I can buy a swift, screw-driven sloop that's almost completed and arm her with a couple of long-range four-and-a-half-inch guns. All I need then is a letter of marque from the Confederate government to start harrying Union shipping."

"Sinking unarmed vessels?"

Darrow laughed. "The captains will heave to quickly enough, once I threaten to put a cannon ball through their hulls below the water line. Nobody will be hurt but the Yankee owners—and then only in their pocketbooks."

"What will you do with the ships you capture?"

"Put a prize crew aboard them and send them to Rio to be sold."

"Why Rio de Janeiro?"

"The scuttlebutt in Mobile is that the Brazilian government will soon recognize the belligerent status of the Confederacy and other South and Central American states will follow. By the time I get back to England, buy the privateer I want, and outfit it, there should be plenty of ports open to my prizes. With a fast steam- and sail-driven sloop, I can run rings around any lumbering Federal merchant vessel on the seas and probably leave most U.S. warships astern too."

"*If* you can raise the money to buy the sloop," she reminded him. "Certainly no banker or shipbuilder in Scotland or England is going to take a chance on such a risky deal."

"Someone's always willing to gamble, if the stakes are high enough. And in this case, they are."

"I agree," she said crisply. "When you leave Mobile, you'll carry a letter to my solicitors authorizing them to turn my share of the cotton venture over to you."

"By God, Countess!" Rising, he seized her around the waist with both hands and danced her across the deck. "We're going to make a great team."

Maritza was certain he was going to kiss her—and wasn't at all averse to the prospect. Celestina, however, arrived at that moment, followed by the ship's cook carrying their dinner on a large tray. It was a typical southern seacoast meal: a large red snapper broiled over live coals and basted in butter; luscious red yams baked over the same coals, then hollowed out and mixed with butter; fresh green beans split in the French manner and cooked barely enough to make them succulent; plus hush puppies—delicious balls of corn meal, eggs, and soda with tiny bits of sliced onion, cooked to a dark brown crust in deep fat—plus, of course, the chilled wine.

For a while there was little conversation; the food was too delicious, the wine too cold and refreshing to be allowed to change its temperature. Finally Penn Darrow leaned back in his chair and inhaled deeply.

"You must have found Celestina serving the gods," he said. "She'd bring her weight in gold from any buyer familiar with her accomplishments."

"You haven't savored all of them yet—and I'd better not catch you trying!"

"From what I've seen so far, you can take care of yourself," he assured her, "and so, I imagine, can Celestina. I've an idea that you'd never obey any man."

"I agreed to when Étienne and I were married and even turned all my worldly goods over to him," she said. "Fortunately, he promptly deeded the plantation near here back to me."

"Not many husbands would have done as much."

"My guardian, Senator John Slidell, practically pushed me into marriage seven years ago to get me out of competition with the daughters of his friends in the New Orleans marriage market, but I've never held that against Uncle John," she said. "Étienne gave me the title, but more important, he guided me through the most difficult change—from girlhood to womanhood."

"For which any man who may one day be privileged to hold you in his arms will no doubt be in debt to him forever—including, hopefully, myself."

She turned to look at him in the soft moonlight which now enshrouded the deck. "You're very handsome, Penn Darrow, and any woman would be honored to have you admire her," she said. "But I came back home to help the South and act as correspondent for *Le Pays* so the people of France can have a true picture of what's happening here. Don't expect me to come swooning into your arms like a schoolgirl mooning over a lover, just because you happen to be handsome and physically stimulating."

"Is that a warning against further hope?" His eyes were bright with a light which, in spite of her words, stirred an answering warmth in her body.

"You can take it that way—or as a challenge to possible success one day." Then she added: "I spent much of the time you were away yesterday writing a description for *Le Pays* of our brush with the U. S. S. *Montgomery*. Now I need to get to Montgomery itself as soon as possible. How long do you think it will be before we can sell the cargo?"

"Day after tomorrow—with luck. The purchasing agent from Montgomery telegraphed that he'd be here that morning and, with the South definitely at war, the decks will be awash with profiteers seeking to buy the Enfields and resell them to the government at a substantial profit. My advice is to keep them on the leash, at least until we know what Jefferson Davis' purchasing agent is going to offer."

"Will the Confederate agent be able to pay in gold?"

"From what I learned in Mobile, the states that seceded not only seized Northern forts and harbor fortifications but took all the money in U.S. mints, post offices, and other Federal repositories as well. Our job is going to be to get as much of that gold as we can into our pockets and then exchange it for cotton. If all goes well, Countess, I've an idea you'll come out of this war even richer than you'll be when we sell the cargo day after tomorrow."

"I hope so," she said. "When it's over, I'm going to build the finest house in Alabama on my plantation near the city."

"And until then?"

"Everybody knows the main theater of fighting between the North and the South will be Virginia, at least until our side can take Washington and drive toward Philadelphia and New York, causing the North to sue for peace. If I'm going to be an effective correspondent for *Le Pays,* I need to go where the action will be—"

"If you were in the shoes of General Pierre Gustave Toutant Beauregard," he assured her, "I've a notion you'd already be building a pontoon bridge across the Potomac to storm Washington."

"It's not a bad idea."

"As a military strategy, perhaps not. But that's not the way Jefferson Davis has said he wants to conduct the war, according to the newspapers I've read since we got to Mobile. He intends for the South to defend itself and make Abraham Lincoln the aggressor."

"Surely attacking Fort Sumter was aggression."

"Not the way Davis and his advisers see it. They claim that Lincoln's sending ammunition and supplies to Major Anderson at Charleston, without an actual declaration of war, amounted to firing the first shot."

"And you men accuse women of being devious," she said on a note of anger. "How unfair can you be?"

"*Touché,*" he admitted. "But since we're going to be in business together, it's a stimulus to know that a hidden fire burns within that lovely body, needing only the touch of a man's hands to fan it into flame."

"Not just any man, Captain," she corrected him loftily. "The ones I grant that privilege must meet my standards—and I warn you that they're high, very high indeed."

"And I, *Madame la Comtesse,* accept the warning." He bowed low but the light in his eyes warned her once again that here was no Parisian dandy to be led around by the nose. "Also the challenge."

"Which reminds me," she said. "You know a great deal about me but I know next to nothing about you except that you're a born seaman and claim to have been tossed out of the U. S. Naval Academy because of a romantic indiscretion."

"Indiscretion, yes—but hardly to be called romantic; the poor girl was worn out by then. Actually, I'd enjoyed far more cooperation from my mother's personal maid in a grove of pecan trees behind the slave quarters."

Maritza laughed. "In France they call it *le droit de seigneur,* but it was the same over here. Since you grew up inland, though, I wonder why you ever went to sea at all."

"I am the first sea dog in my family," he conceded, "which makes me out a romantic in one way, I suppose. When my father and grandfather came south from New England in the early 1800s, they bought land about a hundred miles up the Alabama River. Our sawmills were far above the rise and fall of any tides but as a boy I used to ride rafts of lumber downstream as far as Mobile. That voyage was thrilling enough to make a boy of twelve long for more, and when I saw the tall masts of ships in the harbor waiting to be loaded, I knew I'd one day go to sea. When I was old enough I was lucky to get an appointment to the United States Naval Academy and was doing fine, until the little incident I told you about ruined my career in the Navy."

"But certainly not as a Confederate naval officer," she reminded him. "The South is going to need trained officers for its ships. You could rise rapidly if you decided to join."

"As master of a fast privateer, I hope to do a great deal more for the South than as an officer in a navy that doesn't exist," he said. "Besides, the idea of continuing our partnership —and hopefully one day making it permanent—is far more challenging."

VI

On the day of the auction Maritza rose early, ate a leisurely breakfast, and dressed carefully.

"Lawd, Miz Ritza!" said Tina. "You dressin' up like you goin' to a ball."

"I'm going to make us rich, if all goes well this morning. And after Captain Darrow sells a load of cotton in England a month from now and buys us a privateer, we'll be even richer. Now stop talking like a slave."

"I is one, ain't I?" Tina's dark eyes sparkled with mischief.

"You know perfectly well I've offered to set you free more than once. Hand me a sheet of paper and a pen and I'll prepare a writ of manumission right now. You can start receiving a salary tomorrow."

"And let you have the right to fire me whenever you want to?" Celestina asked indignantly. "Long as I'm a slave, you gotta look after me. That's the law."

"I could still sell you in the brothels of New Orleans. Beautiful octoroon slaves bring a fortune."

"You can't sell me neither," Tina retorted as she began to

tuck up the waves of Maritza's golden hair beneath a smart bonnet from the most famous milliner in Paris. "The day your momma bought me to be your maid—"

"Companion."

Tina shrugged. "Anyway, I was crying and my mammy—"

"Mammy!" Maritza's eyebrows rose. "Your mother was the mistress of the richest banker in New Orleans, besides being one of the best-dressed women in the city. The only reason she sold you was because you were beginning to look so much like your real father, she was afraid the banker would realize she had another lover on the side. Besides, she knew you would be educated and treated well, as long as you belonged to me."

"Well, anyway, I was crying and you put your arm around me and said, 'Don't worry, Tina. You and I are going to be like sisters and I'm never going to sell you.' So there."

"All right," said Maritza, as the thump of a river vessel against the side of the ship and a sudden increase in the hubbub of male voices from the deck outside announced the arrival of still another potential buyer for the cargo. "Take a peek out there and see whether that wasn't the Confederate purchasing agent from Montgomery who just arrived."

While Maritza was applying the faintest touch of rouge to her cheeks and emphasizing her already long lashes with a dainty small brush dipped in mascara, Celestina went out on deck. When she returned, her eyes were shining with excitement.

"Lawd! The deck's full of men! The one you're looking for just got here on a river steamer, too. Captain Darrow's treating him like he's something special—and he sho is." Celestina's eyes rolled expressively. "Six feet two, if he's an inch, and wearing a dress uniform. I'd hop into his bed any time he wanted me."

When a tap came on the door Maritza called, "Come in," and threw a small cape around her shoulders against the breeze on the deck outside. Penn Darrow, too, was dressed to the nines—black jack boots, spotless doeskin breeches, a white silk shirt with a prodigal ruching of lace at the collar and cuffs, and a shiny black sailor's hat. He whistled softly at the sight of

Maritza and his eyes began to glow with a distinctly un-businesslike light.

"The flock is outside, Countess," he said, offering his arm. "Ready for the fleecing."

"*En avant, mon capitaine.*" Taking his arm, she stepped through the door onto the crowded deck, while Celestina followed carrying, as her mistress had instructed, an empty wine bottle stuck into the pocket of her apron.

The sun was shining brightly on the forward deck, where more than a dozen men had gathered, and Darrow escorted Maritza to a point of vantage in front of the foremast. A case of Enfield rifles had been opened there for inspection by prospective buyers.

"Your attention, please, gentlemen," Darrow announced. "May I present Countess Maritza LeClerc, owner of the cargo?"

"Colonel Richard Mann, Quartermaster Department, Confederate States of America, Countess." The look of admiration in the tall officer's eyes was one Maritza had seen many times before so she couldn't understand the sudden leap of her pulse. "I believe we owned neighboring plantations near Mobile," he added.

"I still own mine, Colonel Mann. Shall we discuss it after the sale?"

"If you wish." He rejoined the half dozen men gathered around the case of Enfields.

"Major Thaddeus Moore of the Alabama militia." Penn Darrow introduced a short, plump man who was also in uniform. Maritza acknowledged the major's bow while Darrow continued until everyone else—a captain from the Louisiana Zouaves and three civilian speculators—had been introduced.

"Thank you, gentlemen," said Maritza. "As you can see from the case which has been opened, these rifles are fresh from the Royal Small Arms Factory in England, with the seals on all except this one still unbroken. Those of you not completely familiar with the British Enfield rifle will be interested to know that the American Springfield is patterned after it and that the two are therefore quite similar."

"Except that the English have been making both short and long versions of the Enfield for years, while most Northern munitions factories are still geared up to turn out only smoothbore flintlocks, plus the 1842 percussion musket," Colonel Mann observed.

"Thank you, Colonel," said Maritza. "Since the Enfield has a caliber of .577, I don't have to tell experienced military men how much more accurate it is than the .69-caliber smooth bore with which many of the Union troops are still armed. The minié ball fired by the Enfield makes it far and away the most accurate weapon now manufactured in large quantities anywhere in the world," Maritza continued. "If you'll look inside the rifle barrel you can see the grooves that give the projectile a spinning movement. When the minié ball expands on being fired, these grooves lock in on the lead of the bullet to make a tight fit, preventing the escape of gas and loss of pressure which characterizes the Sharps. A trained soldier using an Enfield can kill at one thousand yards, while loading and firing at least three times a minute. Are there any further questions about these weapons?"

When no one answered, she announced: "The sale will be to the highest bidder. He will have till sundown this evening to deliver the purchase price in gold or in the form of a draft on a recognized bank. Only after the price has been delivered will the purchaser be able to start unloading the cargo. Do I hear a bid?"

"Twenty dollars each," said one of the speculators immediately.

"Twenty-five," said Colonel Mann.

"Twenty-six," said another speculator but Major Moore topped him with "Twenty-seven."

"Twenty-eight," said Mann, and a third speculator raised the bid by a dollar.

"Thirty," said Colonel Mann and Major Moore simultaneously.

"We seem to be at a stalemate," said Maritza. "Please load one of the rifles from the open packing case, Captain Darrow."

Darrow was obviously surprised by the request but did not

argue. Biting off the end of a paper-covered cartridge containing the powder, he inserted it into the rifle barrel and rammed it home. Next he placed a small cloth square, the wadding, over the powder and shoved that, too, into place before dropping the minié ball in and ramming it home.

"You can see how easily the Enfield is loaded, gentlemen," Maritza observed. "Put the percussion cap in place, please, Captain Darrow."

Still obviously mystified by her intentions, Darrow complied. "Now hand me the rifle, please."

Celestina had been standing just behind Maritza. At a nod from her mistress, she stepped forward and tossed the empty wine bottle she was carrying about a hundred feet beyond the rail into Mobile Bay. There it floated, bobbing up and down in the slight chop given to the surface of the river by the morning breeze.

Lifting the weapon, Maritza sighted quickly and pulled the trigger. The faint snap of the hammer against the percussion cap on its small tube at the stock end of the barrel was followed by a sharp crack as the powder charge was ignited. An instant later the bottle floating on the surface disintegrated at the impact of the rather soft lead of the minié ball, the fragments sinking immediately.

Maritza handed the Enfield back to Darrow, resolutely ignoring the pain in her right shoulder where the heavy weapon had kicked back on firing. "As you can see, gentlemen, in the hands of a trained marksman, this weapon can be very accurate. You will also note that the powder cartridge and the percussion cap have not been damaged on the voyage from England, nor was there any perceptible leak of gas at the breech. Do I hear any further bids?"

"Thirty-five dollars." Colonel Mann's voice was tinged with awe. "If our soldiers in the field can learn to shoot half as well as you do, Countess, we'll capture Washington before the summer ends."

"Thank you, Colonel." Maritza wrinkled her nose a little at the acrid smell of burned powder coming from the open end of the rifle barrel Penn Darrow was holding. "Do you wish to make another bid, Major Moore?"

The Alabama militia agent shook his head sadly. "I was authorized to go only as high as thirty dollars, Countess."

"Then the shipment is sold to Colonel Mann for the C. S. A. Quartermaster Department," said Maritza. "If you will hand over the specie, Colonel, you may have your men start transferring our cargo to the river steamer you brought with you. Meanwhile, Captain Darrow and I will be pleased to entertain you in my cabin at luncheon in half an hour. Good day, gentlemen, and thank you for your co-operation."

VII

Colonel Richard Mann touched his lips with a napkin after finishing the luncheon and the glass of brandy served by Celestina to Darrow, Maritza, and the Confederate officer in her cabin. "That attempt on the part of your late husband's nephew to sell me your plantation by fraud is one of the most dastardly acts I've ever heard of," he said after listening to Maritza's account of her visit to Mr. Anderson's office.

"Knowing Philippe, I should have expected something like that," she said. "Fortunately, Celestina knew a forger in Paris and recognized how it was done."

"I shall stop by Tom Anderson's office this afternoon and tear up both the deed and my check," Mann promised, "but I hope you will continue leasing the plantation to me."

"By all means," said Maritza. "We'll forget the rent check for this year, too, since Philippe has already cashed it in Paris by forging my signature. In return, I hope you will tell us something of what has happened since my cousin General Beauregard opened the war by capturing Fort Sumter."

"Your cousin, madam?" The colonel was obviously startled.

"I was born of Spanish and French parentage but my parents were killed when I was quite young," Maritza explained. "As a little girl, I was the ward of Senator John Slidell and lived part of each year in both New Orleans and Mobile, the home of my father's people. The connection with General Beauregard is through him. I was married to Count Étienne LeClerc when I was eighteen. The LeClerc estates in the Loire Valley in France near Paris are large and it was there that my late husband taught me to ride and shoot."

"He did a noble job," said Mann. "How long have you been a widow?"

"About six months. After my husband died, I naturally decided to return to the land of my birth, even after seven happy years in France. Which, I suppose, makes me what I hear Mr. Lincoln has termed a 'rebel.'"

"Fortunately for the South, a rebel who did not return to your homeland empty-handed. Those ten thousand rifles you just sold to the Confederate Army will soon be shipped northward for our soldiers to use in taking Washington."

"How long do you think the war will last, Colonel?" Penn Darrow inquired.

"If the South can move fast, before the troops Abraham Lincoln has called up are trained and properly armed, the war could be over in a few months, in spite of the Yankee superiority in numbers and in manufacturing. You see, when Fort Sumter fell, the whole United States Army numbered only about sixteen thousand men, most of them scattered in the West holding Indians in check, or garrisoned at coastal forts since taken over by the Confederacy."

"Just how many states form the Confederacy now?" Maritza asked.

"Seven at this writing, Countess: South Carolina, Georgia, Alabama, Florida, Mississippi, Louisiana, and Texas. As I was leaving Montgomery, word came that the Virginia State Convention has voted to secede and will hold a referendum on May 23. No one doubts which way the voting will go and North Carolina state troops have already seized Fort Macon, which is some indication of the sentiment there."

"I met President Davis years ago at my uncle's plantation in Louisiana and I saw him several times after that when he vis-

ited there," said Maritza. "He always looked to me like a sick
man."

"The President's health is fragile but his courage, even in
pain, will ignite the fervor needed by the South and make the
people realize we are really at war."

"I must say that I've seen little of the grim determination
here that is going to bring victory," she commented.

"That's because we are too far from the scene of action," the
colonel explained. "The government will soon move to Richmond and from there President Davis can direct the attack on
Washington personally, even though General Beauregard is
now in command of the Alexandria Line of Virginia troops
within sight of the Capitol in Washington."

"Frankly, I could never see my cousin as anything except a
pompous ass, Colonel," Maritza confessed. "But, then, I
haven't seen him in seven years and perhaps he has changed."

"Has President Davis started issuing letters of marque, Colonel Mann?" Penn Darrow inquired.

"Not yet. What do you have in mind, Captain?"

"When I get back to England with a load of cotton, I'm
thinking of buying a fast sloop to use in blockade running and
privateering. My training at the U. S. Naval Academy was in
fighting ships so I feel that I could function satisfactorily as a
captain of a privateer."

"You may be right—at least for a while," said Mann. "When
General Beauregard captured Fort Sumter two thirds of the
U. S. Navy was in foreign ports. Even when they return they'll
not be able to guard all the shipping New England manufacturers will be wanting to send to England, France, and Spain. A
few prizes could make you rich and you'd be helping our Cause
by preventing the movement of war supplies from abroad to the
troops Abe Lincoln has called upon the Northern states to provide."

"Captain Darrow and I will be partners in the privateer venture, as we are in this one," Maritza explained. "When I get to
Montgomery, do you think President Davis would issue us a
letter of marque for a venture in that field?"

"With General Beauregard your cousin, Senator John Slidell

your sponsor, to say nothing of your acquaintance with President Davis and my own small influence in government affairs, you should have no trouble, Countess," he assured her. "Besides, since your late husband was a French nobleman, you probably know some political leaders in Paris. President Davis hopes to persuade France to join our Cause, still another item in your favor."

"I was presented at the Court of Napoleon III, and on one occasion even served as a lady in waiting to Empress Eugénie," Maritza assured him. "Actually, too, my husband was being considered for a high diplomatic assignment in the Second Empire before he caught an untimely fever and died."

"Then you owe it to the Confederacy to put your knowledge of France and French politics at its command as soon as possible, ma'am," said Mann. "Once we capture Washington, our leaders believe both France and England will join our side. The spinning jennies and looms of neither country can operate very long without Southern cotton."

"There's talk here in Mobile of an embargo on shipping cotton from the South," said Darrow. "Can you tell us whether there's any substance to the rumor?"

"There's substance. I don't agree with the idea but some advisers to President Davis have hatched such a scheme." Mann's voice took on a note of anger. "We cotton growers are dead against the proposal, of course."

"But why would the South embargo the shipment of cotton to Europe, when we'll be needing money so badly?" Maritza asked.

"Those who favor an embargo argue that, if England in particular is denied Southern cotton, Queen Victoria will recognize the Confederacy as a new nation and England will trade freely with us."

"Knowing what I know about politics in both countries, recognition could take years," said Maritza. "You have no idea, Colonel, how much trouble I had obtaining permission from Earl Russell—who really rules England with Lord Palmerston in the name of Queen Victoria—to buy the shipload of Enfields you've just purchased."

"Thank God you were successful, ma'am," said Mann fervently. "But then Russell would have had to be made of stone to refuse such a beautiful woman her every wish."

VIII

With the cargo of munitions safely transferred to a pair of shallow-draft river steamers Colonel Richard Mann had thoughtfully brought with him from Montgomery—more than a hundred miles upstream on the Alabama River—loading the cargo of cotton Penn Darrow purchased with his own and Maritza's money went on apace. Since the *Pride of Bristol* would be carrying no munitions, its British registry protected it from the United States blockading fleet on the return voyage to England. Meanwhile, there was nothing for Maritza to do but read newspapers and write dispatches for *Le Pays* about the American situation to be mailed before she took a river steamer for the provisional Confederate capital. During a visit to Tom Anderson's office she learned that Richard Mann had been as good as his word and both the forged deed to her plantation and the bank draft in payment for it had been destroyed.

"You mustn't leave Mobile before the May Day fete," Anderson said when she told him she'd soon be going to Montgomery.

"I'd forgotten it." Maritza's face brightened. "Do mummers still parade down Government Street and on to Bienville Square as they did when I was a girl?"

"Some things never change and the passion for celebration at any excuse in Mobile is among them. You must attend."

"I'll see whether Captain Darrow plans to sail before then," she said. "I promised him I'd see the *Pride of Bristol* safely through the channel and out into the Gulf. He seems to think I'll bring him good luck."

"You're very fond of Darrow, aren't you?" Anderson inquired.

"Of course. If his courage had failed at the sight of those

cannon balls from the *Montgomery* dropping around us, I'd have lost almost everything I own."

"The Darrows are a fine old family." The rather pointed note to the lawyer's observation didn't escape Maritza's notice. "They have vast timber holdings in the central part of the state."

"If it's matchmaking you're at, I'm not planning to marry again soon, Tom," Maritza said with a smile.

"It's something to be thinking about," he insisted. "Mobile—and Alabama—lost you once to Count LeClerc in France. We don't want that to happen another time."

"I'll probably marry again—eventually. I hope to build a home on my plantation and have at least a boy and a girl, too. But first I've got the truth about an unjust war to report to the French people and that might mean a lot to the Cause."

"Your Spanish heritage comes through one of the oldest lines in Mobile and your French one goes back at least that far in Louisiana. Having you here at home again will mean a lot to the people of Mobile."

The loading of the cotton was completed on the last day of April and supplies for the voyage were all laid in. As Penn Darrow was directing the stowing of the last bale in the hold, Maritza stood at the edge of the main cargo hatch watching until he finished and climbed hand over hand up the line from which the final bale had been detached. Swinging across the hatch opening, he dropped to the deck beside her, virile, alive with energy, and, as usual when working in the hull, stripped to the waist.

"We're ready to sail," he announced.

"Celestina and I have our baggage ready to be taken ashore but tomorrow is May Day," she told him. "The people of Mobile are celebrating it as usual, so why not give everybody a day off before you sail—including yourself?"

"Are you going to the fete?"

"If you'll take me. It's one of the happiest occasions of the year, when the French and Spanish heritage of the city gets all mixed up with the American and the West Indian to make a true melting pot."

"You're on! I haven't really had an excuse to cut loose since we left Bristol. But only on one condition, mind you."

"What's that?"

"Let Celestina go ashore with the crew so I'll have you to myself."

"Fair enough. That's certainly the way she'd want it."

May Day dawned clear and hot. Much of the crew had gone ashore the night before and stayed over to enjoy the earthy pleasures afforded by the teeming dockside area of a city that had become one of the world's largest cotton shipping ports. The rest, with Celestina, were gone too when Maritza came out of her cabin about eight o'clock.

Wearing a light muslin dress with no stays and a minimum of petticoats, she carried a small bonnet and parasol against the noonday sun but this early in the morning had let her golden blond hair fall free in rich waves to her shoulders. Penn Darrow was in white planter's garb—linen trousers with a ruffled silk shirt open at the collar and a broad Panama hat. He whistled softly in admiration when Maritza came out on the deck.

"You'll put the local belles to shame, Countess, and I'll be the envy of the male populace," he said as he helped her over the rail and down the short boarding ladder to the gig floating beside the ship. "It's a good thing May Day wasn't tomorrow, though. I've an idea we'll have a good breeze from the northeast to fill the sails by morning."

"I made arrangements yesterday at a livery stable to hire horses for Tina and myself to ride as far as Cedar Point," she told him. "That's as near as we can get by land to the mouth of the bay without a wide detour but we can at least see you through the channel from there."

"When I see the reflection of the sun from the brass barrel of your telescope, I'll know it's you and can be sure we're starting under a good omen," he told her.

"Is there any prospect of your being stopped out there beyond the bar by the *Montgomery?*"

"The commander at Fort Morgan reported by semaphore

yesterday to Major Moore that there's no sight of any Union warship in the Gulf. No doubt the Union captain figured it would be a waste of time to stop a ship of British registry loaded with cotton anyway."

They had reached the docking area and Darrow left the gig tied to a public pier, while they took a hack to Bienville Square in the center of the city. It was already alive with people in all sorts of costumes and fantastic masks. The influences of Spain, France, and the West Indies—all of which had contributed greatly at one time or another to the culture and customs of Mobile—were visible everywhere.

At a sidewalk cafe they breakfasted on shirred eggs and roe, strips of salt herring sliced so thin they were like crisp bacon, hot buttered biscuits and currant jelly, topped off with coffee laced with apricot brandy.

"How did you happen to be from Mobile when your guardian, Senator John Slidell, is from New Orleans?" Darrow asked as they were sipping the coffee and enjoying the colorful scenery moving through the square.

"This was my father's home; he was of Spanish descent and owned both a plantation outside of town and a house off the square. It had a lovely balcony and a wrought-iron railing from which I remember watching the festivities at May Day."

"Your mother was French, wasn't she?"

"Yes. She met my father in New Orleans and committed the unpardonable sin of falling madly in love—although she was already married to a respectable man—and running away to Mobile with my father."

"Then you were . . . ?"

"A bastard? Yes, you can say it; I don't mind. It took over a year for my mother's marriage in Louisiana to be officially annulled so she and my father could be legally married here in Mobile, where I was born. You'll find the certificate on file at the courthouse in New Orleans."

"How old were you then?"

"About two. I have a faint memory of two people who were very happy together and who must have loved me very much because they made me happy too. Not long after they were legally married, they were both drowned during a hurricane while trying to cross a swollen river to get home to me. Uncle John Slidell and my father had been close friends and, when the will was read, everything was left to me with Uncle John as my guardian. I lived here with a maiden aunt, who's dead now, but moved back and forth between Mobile and New Orleans until I was married to Étienne at eighteen."

"Didn't the family object to your marrying an older man?"

She laughed. "By the time I was eighteen they were anxious to get rid of me. Nobody likes seeing the family skeleton appear several times a year. Besides, I was always rebelling against the restrictions Creole families put upon their daughters."

"Is that why you married so early?"

"It probably had something to do with it, although, as I told you, the family was glad to get me out of the competition. Fortunately, Étienne realized that I was still something of a child, married when I was barely eighteen—"

"And to a man much older than yourself."

"With another that might have made a difference," she conceded, "but not to him. Étienne was the sort of man who is forever young. I'll always be grateful to him for showing me the way from girlhood to womanhood."

A sudden burst of music reached their ears and, pushing back her chair, Maritza climbed upon it while Darrow steadied her, acutely conscious of the body his hands were almost touching through the thin fabric of her summer dress.

"The parade's starting to form!" she said. "Look over there on the other side of the square."

Heading the parade was an undulating paper serpent of many colors, stretched over a framework of wood and borne by roisterers whose feet alone showed beneath it, giving it much the appearance of a block-long centipede. Behind the centipede came a band of musicians with strings, horns, drums, jugs, and every other conceivable instrument. The whole brought forth a bedlam of sound with not much more than a faint resemblance to music, but everyone was happy and gay as the parade wound in and out through the streets surrounding the central square. There a tall maypole had been raised with ribbon streamers attached, ready for the traditional maypole dance that would climax the celebration late that afternoon.

Behind the musicians came troops of dancers, wearing huge masks in every imaginable shape, real and unreal, cavorting in the sheer enjoyment of the occasion.

"Let's join them!" Maritza cried, jumping down from the chair.

Stopping to buy masks—a silky-haired cat's face for her and a wolf's head with bared teeth for him—they joined hands and began a spirited sailor's hornpipe that soon had all the dancers leaping in rhythm with them. Accompanied by gargoyles, sprites, demons of every form, plus an occasional angel, the happy procession continued on its meandering way. It was followed by groups of acrobats, puppeteers, and other performers, who would be entertaining later for a price in empty buildings or tree-shaded areas which each group selected as its personal theater. Finally, when the procession reached the square again, Maritza fell into a chair outside a sidewalk cafe, fanning herself with the wine card.

"I'm thirsty enough to drink a gallon of something!" she confessed.

At Penn Darrow's gesture, a waiter appeared with a tray on which stood two frosted glasses of punch, made from limes, sugar, and potent West Indian rum. Maritza finished the first and hardly noticed when another was put before her, so absorbed was she in the color and gaiety that had turned Bienville Square into a tree-shaded bower filled with celebrants.

So the day went, with snatches of this succulent refreshment and that. Oysters fresh from the bay. Clam chowder Southern style with tomatoes, diced potatoes, and clams dug that same morning. Green turtle soup and key lime pie. All washed down with rum punch and an occasional glass of multiflavored brandy and other beverages.

Darkness was already falling when the winding of the maypole was completed. Maritza staggered a little as she tucked the end of the last ribbon into the pattern at the foot of the pole, to the accompaniment of a wave of applause from the crowd that still filled the small square to overflowing. Her head whirling, she clutched Penn Darrow's arm and leaned against him, laughing.

"All this gaiety and the drinks are too much for me, I'm afraid," she admitted. "You'd better get me back to the ship where I can sleep it off, if you're going to sail tomorrow. Make it quick, too, or you'll have to carry me aboard."

In a hack bound for the pier where the gig was tied, she did go to sleep, slumped against him with her head on his shoulder. But she roused up when he carried her from the hack to the small boat tied to the end of the long dock.

"Row, row, row your boat," she began to sing as he sculled the gig toward the dark silhouette of the *Pride of Bristol* anchored in the stream. When she insisted that he join in, he was stimulated enough by the combination of her beauty and the potent drinks they'd been sampling all day to sing lustily too. Boosting the still chanting—and decidedly inebriated—Maritza up the boarding ladder, Penn guided her across the foredeck and propped her against her cabin door, while he went back to secure the small gig that had brought them from Mobile.

Oppressed by the cloying heat of the night, Maritza staggered across to the rail and looked down at the surface of the bay beneath. The water looked infinitely cooling and, still half dazed, she quickly unbuttoned the top buttons of her frock and pulled it over her head, tossing it back on deck. Loosening petticoats and stepping out of them, she rolled down her stockings, kicked off her shoes, and pulled off her bodice. Muslin drawers, too, dropped to the deck, leaving her body clad only in a shift which went the way of the other garments.

Coming around the forward housing, Darrow was startled to see her climb the rail and poise there for a moment. A lovely nude figure, she looked like a dryad who had left her tree for the river, then plunged into the dark waters rippling against the prow of the rugged old ship in the slow current of the bay.

He wasted no time determining just how well she could swim. Although the current here was not strong, it could still carry her well away from the ship in minutes, placing her in danger of drowning before she reached something to which she could catch hold. Shedding his own garments as rapidly as possible, he dived over the rail but, when he came up, found her treading water some ten feet away, laughing and splashing.

The shock of the cool water had sobered her and when she felt the tug of the current against her body she instantly realized the danger she might be in. Swimming strongly, she moved in the direction of the bow where the anchor chains leading down to the bottom afforded a handhold as protection against the pull of the current. Penn followed and they reached the chains at the same moment, clinging to them while the current swirled about their naked bodies.

"Why the hell did you do that?" he demanded, though it was hard to be angry long at somebody whose lovely head and breasts were revealed as she held onto the anchor chain.

"I was hot and the water looked cool. Besides, I'm a good swimmer."

"I'll grant that, but it was still a foolish thing to do, when you had no way of knowing just how swift the current might be."

"I guess I was drunk but that's all your fault, too, for getting me that way." Then she laughed. "I'll bet that's what you intended to do all the time: get me drunk and then take advantage of me. Come on now, wasn't that your idea?"

"A man would have to be made of stone not to want you."

"Then what's keeping you?" she challenged as she let go of the chain and started swimming for the boarding ladder. "Or has the water cooled your ardor?"

She was climbing up the ladder, a lovely nude figure in the light of the three-quarter moon, when he, too, reached it, climbing up so rapidly that his arms closed about her as she stepped on deck. When she turned, his mouth found hers without effort and, without breaking the contact, he lifted her in his arms. Striding across the deck, he pushed open the door of her cabin, kicking it shut behind them as he crossed the room to the bed, ignoring the fact that both of them were dripping wet.

IX

A shaft of dawning sunlight poured through the porthole beside Maritza, striking her eyelids and stimulating her into wakefulness. She still lay half in Penn Darrow's arms, as she had most of the night and into the early hours of the morning. Exhausted by the explosive rapture of their coming together again and again, the ardor for which she had teased him had at last been finally spent and both had slept. They were still nude, however, and, recalling last night's rapture in drowsy memory, Maritza made no move to pull up the sheet. A slight movement as she settled into a more comfortable position awakened Penn.

"Hello." He pushed himself up on one elbow, the better to see her in the bright sunlight that was now beginning to fill the cabin. "What are you doing in my bed?"

"It's mine—and you're the intruder."

"Shall I leave then?"

"Not for a little while. It's only just after dawn and I think everybody aboard is still asleep."

"I feel sorry for every other man in the world this morning," he confided.

"Why?"

"Because he can't have you. I can even see your heart beating, so now I know all there is to know about you."

"No man can do that, but you're nearer than anybody else ever was."

His index finger had been tracing a circle around the turgid nipple of her left breast as they talked, marking the point where the darker skin of the areola merged with that covering the remainder of the lovely swelling. Reaching up suddenly, she took his head between her hands and guided it down until his lips closed about the nipple he'd been caressing. When his tongue rasped softly upon the suddenly erect flesh, she moved and, with a thrust of her knees, swung his body over until she could hold him between her thighs, receiving him into her embrace—and into her body.

Soothing their ardent flesh, she held him closely, binding them together in an embrace that brooked no lessening in intensity until, on a cry of undiluted ecstasy, relief came with explosive finality.

When Maritza awakened the second time, she saw Penn dressing himself in a corner of the cabin where his clothes had been laid out crisply across a chair. The sun no longer shone through the porthole over her berth, although the protecting shutter was still open, and from outside came the roll of thunder and the occasional flash of lightning.

"What's happening?" she inquired drowsily.

"That wind from the northeast that I mentioned last evening is rising fast. It could be the harbinger we've been waiting for."

Beside his on the chair she saw her own neatly arranged clothing, although she remembered strewing it along the deck as she had discarded everything so hastily last night before diving from the rail.

"Apparently Tina came back sometime this morning," he said with a wry smile. "Seeing the state of things between us, she must have picked up our clothing from the deck outside and brought it in."

Maritza sat up and stretched with a prodigious yawn. "As soon as you're dressed, get out of here," she told him, "so I can take a bath and dress myself."

"You'd better be quick about that, too, unless you're willing to come with me to England on the *Pride*." He came over to stand beside the berth where she was sitting and leaned down to kiss her. "I want you, Maritza, want you more than anything I've ever wanted before."

"Enough to marry me?"

"Of course. Come with me and we'll find a priest the minute the ship touches land."

She studied him for a moment and saw nothing except truth there. The offer was tempting, too, for she knew it would be easy to fall in love with him. Marriage, however, was not in her plans for the future—at least not at the moment. And since they were to be business partners, there should be plenty of opportunities to learn more about him beyond the fact that he was remarkably handsome, as well as an even more remarkably proficient lover.

"Someday I'll probably take you up on that offer," she told him. "But now—"

"Why not now? You obviously love me."

"Simply because I let you sleep with me—what sleep there was?"

"Of course not, damn it! If ever two people were made for each other, we obviously are."

"That mating will make our final union all the sweeter then." She reached up to pull his head down and kiss him before pushing him away, when he instinctively started to follow up on her action.

"Go out and start hauling up the anchor or something," she told him. "You've a war to fight and I have the task of helping lure England and France into supporting the Confederacy."

"Damn you!" he said from the door, but without rancor. "How can you show a man a glimpse of heaven and then shut the door in his face."

X

The sun was at its height above the southern horizon when Maritza and Celestina, the freshening breeze from the northeast belling out their riding dresses, toiled up the slope of a commanding sand dune on the western shore of Mobile Bay. Behind them, the horses they had ridden from the city were tied to a low bush.

"I haven't been on a horse for over a year," Celestina grumbled. "My tail feels like you've been beating me."

When they came to the top of the sand dune, both exclaimed with pleasure at the beauty of what they saw. To the south, easily visible when Maritza unslung the brass telescope that hung around her neck by a lanyard, was the mouth of Mobile Bay, with the squat outline of Fort Morgan visible on the east side and the lesser height of Fort Gaines on the west. Spray was rising where the wind-driven seas broke over the bar to form a hundred small rainbows, coalescing and separating into a phantasmagoria of colors and images that seemed hardly part of a mundane world.

Farther inland, along the low-lying shore of the bay, tall palms leaned against the brisk northeast wind, looking like giant feather dusters cleaning the sky. Below them a low rim of shrubbery, the bushes blown into bizarre shapes by the wind, was broken every now and then by the somewhat higher silhouettes of cabbage palms. Lower still were the ungainly palmettos, while here and there a fruit tree—somehow managing to maintain a foothold where all else was sand and water—was in full bloom, a striking splash of color in the afternoon sunlight.

Through the glass the somewhat squat outlines of the *Pride of Bristol* could be seen a few miles upriver. All sails were set on its three masts and it was heeled over on the port tack with the wind behind it. In the powerful glass Maritza could easily see water foaming along the rail of the old brigantine and occasionally breaking over the full-breasted figurehead at the prow to flow into the scuppers and back into the bay from whence it had come.

"Lawdy me!" Tina exclaimed. "Ain't that something to see?"

All thoughts of Maritza's own discomfort from wind, sand, and the mosquitoes that had begun to drone around them were driven away by the beauty of the scene. As she watched the *Pride* plow southward toward the narrow channel and the open Gulf beyond, she could see Penn Darrow in his usual position. Clinging to the top of the mainmast with one leg wrapped around it and the wind tossing his dark hair, he was holding the eyepiece of a brass-barreled telescope pressed to one eye.

Roughly opposite where Maritza and Tina were standing, the ship changed course slightly and headed straight for a buoy marking the channel entrance. As it passed, Maritza saw Penn Darrow jerk loose the light kerchief he wore around his neck and wave it in acknowledgment that he had seen them.

Filled with a surge of happiness at the picture made by the ship and its master, Maritza, too, loosened the kerchief she had bound over her hair and waved it in return. With the wind molding the skirts of the riding habit around her superb limbs, she looked like some Viking goddess miraculously put down here on the shores of Mobile Bay in a place and a time far different from her usual milieu. And although the action itself was not deliberate, the picture was one she was quite willing for Darrow to carry with him.

Not until the *Pride of Bristol* had passed through the channel and was a mere dot on the southern horizon did Maritza slide the telescope into its case and start back down the dune to where the horses were tied.

"You just let a man leave who could have made you happy for the rest of your life," said Tina reproachfully as they prepared to mount for the ride back to the city. "Why did you do it?"

"I don't know, but I'm sure I'll see him again. Ever since Uncle John wrote me the South was going to secede and I should buy a shipload of weapons and ammunition before the price went up, I've had the strangest feeling that my destiny is here on this side of the Atlantic—but where, or with whom, I have no idea."

BOOK TWO

MONTGOMERY

I

As Maritza and Celestina were being driven from the boat landing at Montgomery, Alabama, to the Exchange Hotel, neither was impressed by the first capital of the infant nation bearing the imposing title of the Confederate States of America. Near the center of the state and more than a hundred miles by the winding course of the muddy Alabama River from the nearest large seaport on the Gulf of Mexico at Mobile, Montgomery was unsuited by location or inclination for the role thrust upon it almost entirely by geography alone. A somnolent Southern city of perhaps twenty thousand people, its selection because of its central location in the states that so far made up the Confederacy had made it almost overnight a center of interest for the entire world. Unprepared for such attention, however, the capital of Alabama had found few, except native Alabamians, to favor it for the new role.

To the leaders of the Confederacy, most of whom had served in the Congress of the United States before secession, Montgomery could not compare in any possible way to Washington. Dexter Avenue, main street of the rebel center, was paved with cobblestones, as was Pennsylvania Avenue in Washington. Both streets, too, were covered with uncounted layers of dust that rose in clouds—except in rainy seasons when it turned into mud—with the passage of any vehicle. There, however, all similarities ceased. Montgomery, still sleepy, Southern, and heavy with the traditions of the Old South, could boast almost none of the qualities fitting a new nation. Washington, on the other hand, was reported as having seethed with plots and counterplots since the election of Abraham Lincoln—damned by rebels as a Black Republican—in the fall of 1860.

Maritza held a handkerchief over her mouth and nose, the better to breathe as the rickety hack she had hired at the boat landing moved slowly uptown, drawn by a spavined horse driven by a gray-haired Negro wearing a high silk hat. As the old vehicle rattled over the cobblestones, she could almost wish she had remained in a civilized city, like Paris or London, after Étienne's death, rather than return to America. Only Jefferson Davis, however, could issue the letter of marque giving Penn Darrow the right to harry and entrap unprotected Union shipping, adding considerably to the future wealth of both Maritza and himself as well as the glory of the new nation. And however much discomfort her being here entailed, Maritza was where she should be until the letter could be procured.

Among the few things to recommend the Confederate capital, she was forced to admit as the hack slowly climbed from the riverbank, where river steamers were tied end to end loading cotton for transfer to the already jammed docks at Mobile, were the gardens. She'd last seen the city on a leisurely trip through the lower South four years before with Étienne, but the remembered fragrance of magnolia and wisteria from the verdant gardens surrounding the stately homes set back from the streets, and sometimes almost hidden by hedges of privet and boxwood, were still just as she remembered them. Splashes of color assaulted her eyes from flower beds lining the graveled driveways leading to the mansions, most of which were amazingly similar, as if cut from the same pattern.

Tall fluted columns of another architectural era characterized the houses of Montgomery's elite. Victorian, Gothic, and Romanesque façades ornamented even the office buildings, though the outer walls remained dingy from the constant pall of dust hanging over the city. In fact, everything about Montgomery gave it much the appearance of a museum whose founders had dropped everything into place willy-nilly, without bothering to pay attention to achieving a homogeneous whole.

"Ahead, ladies"—the hack driver's voice held a strong note of pride, however tortured the rhetoric—"you sees de state Capitol. I hears dat even in Washington, D.C., dey ain't got no dome on de Capitol like dis 'un. If you looks to one side, where dat little porch is, you can see where Mr. Davis was swore in to be President of the Confederacy."

"Don't you resent the South going to war to keep black people in slavery, driver?" Maritza asked.

"Not me, ma'am; I'se free like my father afore me. Got money in de bank, too, since Mr. Davis done brought so many people here to Montgomery." The driver touched his horse with his whip in a gentle reminder that the sooner they reached the hotel the quicker he could pick up another fare.

"Jes t'other side of de Capitol, ladies," he continued, "you can see where President Davis lives."

The two-story clapboard Executive Mansion was certainly not impressive compared to the White House in Washington, Maritza decided. But then she had heard that Jefferson Davis was known to disapprove of ostentation, even when he was Secretary of War in President Buchanan's Cabinet before the nomination and election of a Republican named Abraham Lincoln had suddenly torn the country asunder.

The hack stopped at the Exchange Hotel and the driver jumped down to unload the trunk and two portmanteaus containing Maritza's and Celestina's baggage. While a uniformed black doorman, his white gloves a dingy pink from the dust, opened the door and handed them down from the carriage to the sidewalk with a flourish, Celestina paid the driver, who looked with lofty disdain at the small tip which, with typical French frugality, she had given him.

"Thank you very much, driver," said Maritza as she started across the rutted sidewalk leading to the dingy hotel. "You were very helpful."

Mollified somewhat by her graciousness, he tipped his tall hat. Just then an imperious, middle-aged woman in a fussy cotton dress and an enormous plumed hat pushed her way through the crowd at the hotel doorway, almost knocking Maritza down in her eagerness to get to the carriage.

"Take me to Mr. Toombs's residence at once, driver," the woman ordered as she climbed into the hack, with some boosting by the doorman. "I'm already late for the reception."

Former United States Senator Robert Toombs—now Secretary of State for the Confederacy—was notable, Maritza remembered reading in the London *Times* before she left for America, for the way he had delivered a brief farewell address to the United States Senate two days after his state voted to secede from the Union.

"The Union, sirs, is dissolved!" Toombs had shouted, then added with the typical Southern bent for rhetoric: "You see the glittering bayonet and hear the tramp of armed men from yon Capitol to the Rio Grande."

Spouting fire and brimstone, it was also reported, Toombs had then stalked from the Senate chamber to the Treasury and there collected his salary, plus mileage back to Georgia.

"Lord, Miss Ritza, this place is a dump." Celestina's scathing comment brought Maritza's attention away from the imperious woman and back to the old hotel.

It was not, she conceded, an impressive structure, with its dusty façade, grimy windows, and crumbling brick corners. But from the steps of the old hotel on February 17, 1861—as reported in the London *Times*—a firebrand named William Lowndes Yancey, lately departed as the emissary of the Confederate States to the French government, had introduced a newly elected President, Jefferson Davis, to the enthusiastic crowds that had followed Davis from the station of the Montgomery and West Point Railroad, with the announcement: "The man and the hour have met."

Celestina, whose natural passion for cleanliness had been intensified by seven years of residence in France, took one look at the dingy small room to which she and her mistress were assigned and threw up her hands in a Gallic gesture of disdain.

"How can anybody even *live* in such a dump?" She turned savagely on the bellman who had carried up their baggage. "It's as filthy as a pigpen."

"All de rooms is like dis'un."

"Get me a bucket of water, some rags and soap," she ordered, adding as an afterthought, "and some carbolic acid, too."

"Dunno's I can, ma'am." The man was obviously uncertain about the status of the beautiful young woman. Her olive skin suggested that she might have just a touch of Negro blood, although she dressed, talked, and acted like a white woman of quality. Moreover, she was obviously accepted as such by the other one, whom the clerk downstairs had called "Countess."

"Would this help you to find out?" Removing a small purse from her reticule, Maritza held up a five-dollar gold piece.

"Yassum! It sho 'nuff would." The man took the coin and started through the door. "Right away, ma'am."

"The first thing I want is a bath," Maritza announced when the bellman had departed. "Half the dust in Alabama must be caked on my skin."

"Do you think I'm going to let you bathe in that dirty tub I saw in the bathroom down the hall before I scrub it?" Celestina demanded. "That bed looks like the sheets were last washed in a mud puddle, too—if they've been washed at all."

"We won't be staying here long," Maritza soothed her indignant slave. "As soon as Mr. Davis issues the letter of marque we'll take the train to Charleston and put it on a ship bound for England, addressed to Captain Darrow."

"And after that?"

"If the government is moved to Richmond, we'll be going with it. First, though, I must write an account for *Le Pays* of what's going on in the top levels of the Confederate government here in Montgomery."

"Who's gonna tell you all that?"

"The first handsome young government official I can get Uncle John Slidell to introduce me to," said Maritza. "When I registered downstairs I added the title, 'Correspondent for *Le Pays,* Paris, France.' You can bet that news will be all over Montgomery before morning and people will want me to be mentioning their names."

There was a knock on the door and Celestina opened it to find the bellman outside with a bucket, a mop, and, wonder of wonders, a bottle of carbolic acid.

"That's more like it," she said. "You want your bath before you go down to dinner, Miss Ritza?"

"I certainly do."

"Tell the maître d'hôtel that the Countess will want a table

reserved in the dining room at seven o'clock," Celestina told
the bellman loftily.

"Who dat you say?"

"We're in America now, Tina, not Paris." Maritza laughed
as she turned to the bellman. "She means the headwaiter, but
you'd better tell him to make it around seven-fifteen or, better
still, seven-thirty."

"Yassum, I'll tell him." The bellman departed, bowing and
obviously happy to be serving such a generous guest.

While Maritza undressed and put on a wrapper, Celestina
scrubbed the metal tub in the bathroom down the hall. Afterward, while Maritza dressed herself, Celestina also bathed and
dressed. But when the time came to go down to dinner—called
"supper" in the Southern city—Tina demurred.

"I'd rather eat with the help," she said. "I can learn more
down there about what's happening in Montgomery—stuff you
can use in your article for the newspaper—than I could with a
lot of people looking down their noses at me in the dining
room."

"And probably more than I'll learn eating with the upper
crust," Maritza agreed. "Don't ask too many questions, though,
or somebody will think you're a Northern spy."

II

The main dining room of the Exchange Hotel occupied more
than half the lower floor. The rest was taken up by the lobby,
where guests were milling about, and by the bar, at which a line
of men were bellied up elbow to elbow. At the door to the dining room, Maritza paused until the headwaiter, a suave, handsome black in evening clothes, hurried over to her.

"I am Countess Maritza LeClerc," she announced in a voice
loud enough to be heard by those at the tables near the door.
"You have a reservation for me, I believe."

"Of course, *Madame la Comtesse*. I am André—*à votre
service.*"

"You speak French?"

"*Mais oui*." The headwaiter seated her with a flourish. "I come from Martinique in the Caribbean." He produced the menu. "May I recommend *paella valenciana* for an entree, with perhaps a *vin rouge* from the South of France?"

"I had *paella valenciana* once in Havana and remember it well." Maritza's mouth had already begun to water at the thought of the delicious rice dish loaded with seafood and chicken. "I prefer Cuban black bean soup, however, as an appetizer, and a glass of sherry."

"As Madame wishes."

"I will choose a dessert later and a liqueur," Maritza added.

"*Naturellement, madame*." André snapped his fingers to a hovering waiter and gave the order before moving to the door, where a plump man, his cheeks flushed with indignation at being kept waiting even a moment, stood with an equally plump and overdressed wife.

At the appearance of such a beautiful woman as Maritza in the dining room, conversation had suddenly ceased and all eyes were turned upon her while she conversed fluently in French with the headwaiter. Heads were turned rapidly away when Maritza's cool gaze swept the room, but conversation was renewed when one awed Texan voice was heard to say above the others: "By God! There's one of the finest-looking fillies I ever laid eyes on."

During the meal Maritza was conscious of the admiring gaze of many men in the room, particularly those without female companions. She was having a delicious chocolate mousse for dessert, when a faintly familiar voice, coming from just behind her, said, "Countess LeClerc! You didn't lose any time getting here," and she looked up to see Colonel Richard Mann towering over her, smiling warmly.

"Good evening, Colonel," she said as he lifted her hand and touched his lips to her fingers.

"I judge by your being here that your ship was able to sail from Mobile with a load of cotton," he said.

"Captain Darrow left four days ago. No attempt was made to stop him."

"Secretary Seward and the U. S. Navy would know better than to stop a British vessel carrying only cotton," Mann assured her. "Will you do me the honor of having a liqueur with me?"

"I was about to order one myself."

"What do you prefer?"

"Cognac, if you please."

He smiled. "Naturally, after living in France." A waiter had appeared and he gave the order before turning back to pull out a chair at her table and seat himself. "Tom Anderson writes that, when he notified Moses and the other slaves on your plantation that you're not selling it, there was general rejoicing."

"I've always treated my slaves well. So do you, according to Moses."

"I'm afraid some owners are not held in such high regard by their slaves," said Mann. "Since secession, many have gone North. If Mr. Lincoln signs an act of emancipation soon, as many of his Abolitionist advisers want him to do, there may be a general exodus from the South."

"I thought Lincoln promised to free the slaves before he was elected."

"He's smarter than most Southerners give him credit for being and actually ran for President on a platform expressly allowing slavery to remain unchanged in states where it was already legal. It would be forbidden in any new states created from the territories, but only if the people decided against it."

"Then why are we at war?"

"Ask that question of a hundred Southerners and you'll get a hundred answers. The real truth is that it's a political war, designed to destroy the South, as the strongest political enclave in the nation, by presenting them with a challenge they could hardly fail to accept."

Their brandy had come and the handsome colonel lifted his glass to touch Maritza's. "To our continued friendship."

They drank and when he put down the glass his tone changed to a brisk note. "Would it be impertinent of me to ask your own plans for the future?"

"Not at all. I'm a native and a rebel; else why would I leave France?"

"Why else indeed? May I also ask just how you plan to help our Cause?"

"I've already helped it," Maritza said, somewhat piqued by his pointed question. "Surely you remember that I brought a shipload of Enfield rifles from the Royal Small Arms Factory and sold them to you as purchasing agent for the Confederate Army."

"You were a real help, too. Are you planning any more such ventures?"

It was Maritza's turn to be startled. "No, why do you ask?"

"Helping find weapons for the Confederacy is part of my assignment as an aide to the Secretary of War. I graduated from West Point about ten years ago but soon got tired of watching Indians from the walls of Fort Apache. After a few years I resigned my commission and returned to Mobile to start a cotton-growing and -shipping business but, when it became evident that war with the North was inevitable, I asked for a commission, which was promptly granted."

"As a colonel?"

"My initial rank was that of major but I've been promoted since."

"Which means you're either very, very good at your job," she observed, "or that you have powerful political connections."

She wasn't surprised to see a sudden flash of anger in his eyes but it lasted only a moment.

"I assure you that I have no political influence whatsoever," he said somewhat stiffly. "I am a graduate of the United States Military Academy, however, and I served for nearly ten years as an officer in the regular U. S. Army."

She put her hand over his in a gesture of apology. "Forgive me, I can be a witch, though not very often, I'm happy to say."

"There's no need to apologize; your observation about political influence is characteristic of the Confederate Army, I'm afraid. We've far too many chiefs and far too few braves."

"In answer to your question about my intentions, Colonel.

They're to undertake a venture in partnership privateering with Captain Darrow, if we're able to get a letter of marque. I also plan to continue writing for *Le Pays* in any event." She took a sip from her glass and put it down. "Which reminds me, is the capital really going to be moved to Richmond?"

"Yes, but don't quote me. I understand that the President will make the announcement in a few days."

"Does that mean an early attack on Washington?"

"I hope so. Many fine officers of the old U. S. Army I knew, men like General Robert E. Lee, General Joseph E. Johnston, and others, have resigned their commissions to join the Confederacy, weakening an already under-strength Army. In a memorandum to the Secretary, it was suggested that a direct attack on Washington be made by all the well-trained militia available—"

"Such as the Louisiana Zouaves, I hope?"

"Particularly the Zouaves, actually one of the best-trained militia units in the entire country. They are led by Colonel Richard Taylor, son of the former President."

"Those uniforms would be quite a sight in a parade marching down Pennsylvania Avenue."

"I would give a lot to be marching with them," Mann confessed, "but the President agrees with Mr. Walker that I can be of more use to the new nation as a procurer of armament and munitions. So here I find myself with a desk job which, until now, has been marked by considerable boredom."

"Why now, Colonel?"

"Because the level of feminine beauty and charm in a sleepy capital was suddenly raised sharply today by your arrival."

"Don't try to cozen me with compliments, Colonel; after living seven years in France, I know how little they're worth." Maritza shook a reproving finger at him. "For your information, I can shoot, ride, and handle business as well as any man. In fact, I wish there was some way I could serve as a soldier."

"I'm happy you cannot," he assured her. "Beauty such as yours should be reserved to the task of firing men with the fervor to fight, not firing rifles."

"You should have been a Frenchman, Colonel." Maritza

laughed. "Monsieur Claudet, editor of *Le Pays,* thinks the politicians—who seem to be running the Confederacy right now—
might be induced to confide in a woman. He offered me the role
of correspondent and tomorrow I plan to present my credentials to the Secretary of State."

"I know Mr. Toombs well. If I can help, please don't hesitate to call upon me."

"Thank you, Colonel. Senator John Slidell was my guardian
when I was very young; I'm sure he'll help me now."

"Slidell is a very able man. Actually, he should be in Europe
right now instead of Mr. Yancey, negotiating for recognition of
the Confederacy by France."

"Is Uncle John in Montgomery?"

"Yes—and very close to President Davis. You should encounter no difficulty in having your credentials as a correspondent recognized with both him and myself as sponsors. As
to obtaining a letter of marque, that may be more difficult."

"Why?"

"For one thing, the President hasn't signed any as yet, although I have it on good authority that he *does* plan to issue
some letters soon. With no navy of its own, the Confederacy is
going to have to depend upon privateers while one is being
built—if we're to stop much Northern shipping."

"Captain Darrow feels the same way. Which makes it all the
more important that I petition the President as soon as possible."

"You're lucky in that respect," Mann assured her. "Sometimes it takes days to make an appointment to see President
Davis but, as it happens, tomorrow evening he and Mrs. Davis
are giving a levee at home."

Maritza's eyes twinkled. "Which I may attend, accompanied
by a very handsome—and certain of himself—colonel in the
Confederate Army?"

"I'd be honored to escort you. Shall I pick you up here at
the hotel at seven?"

"I accept." Maritza rose and took the arm Colonel Mann extended. "I might add that I'd feel a lot better about winning this

war if you were commanding the troops of the Alexandria Line in Virginia, instead of Cousin Pierre Beauregard."

III

Maritza was awakened by Celestina bustling around the room.

"What time is it?" she asked sleepily.

"Nine o'clock. Time to be up and about if you're going to get that letter thing off to Cap'n Darrow like you promised."

"What time did you come to bed?"

Celestina rolled her eyes and chuckled. "Depends on what room you're talking about—André's or yours."

"So that's who you slept with?"

Celestina laughed. "That André! *Quel homme!*"

"What am I going to do with you, Tina?" Maritza pretended anger. "The minute I take my eyes off you, you're out rutting around like a bitch in heat."

"I was surprised not to find the beautiful Colonel Mann in *your* bed, *ma petite,*" Tina retorted. "What's the matter? Losing your touch?"

"He's handsome and he can help me a lot. In fact, he's taking me to a reception at the President's house tonight."

"André told me."

"How did he know?"

"His brother François brought you and the handsome colonel the cognac you drank after dinner last night and naturally listened to what was being said. What are you going to wear this morning?"

"Something simple—but obviously Parisienne. I don't want to make the Cabinet wives look dowdy and complain to their husbands so they'll avoid me when I come to interview them for *Le Pays.*" Swinging her legs off the bed and sliding her feet to the floor, Maritza pulled the nightgown over her head and tossed it on the bed. "I don't think I'll go through the ordeal of bathing in that tub down the hall this morning either, since I'd have to do it again tonight before the levee."

"The water for your partial bath is already in the basin." Celestina was making up the bed. "You'll have to do with towels that look like they've been washed in the Alabama River, though. Where do we go this morning?"

"Shopping first, then lunch where everybody can see us and start talking."

"They're already doing that. André says every unattached woman in Montgomery, and half of those with husbands, were after Colonel Mann before we came. Then you appear in the dining room the first night we're here and he comes to you like a mosquito to a bald head."

Maritza had finished her ablutions and was putting on her underclothing, fine garments of silk from the French colonies in Cochinchine. "Right now, the colonel can give me an entree into the offices of the most important politicians in the Confederacy." Picking up a silken shift with the initials MLC embroidered in exquisite script, she dropped it over her head before turning to look in the mirror. "The sun didn't do my skin any good when we stayed on the deck of that river boat because it was so hot in our cabin. I could pass for a quadroon these days."

"Might do you good to try," Tina said. "Then you'd get some idea what it's like to be black."

"Something you've never really known, my dear. Do I get my breakfast brought up or must I forage for it in the kitchen?"

"I ordered a tray for nine-thirty. It ought to be here about now."

There was a knock on the door and she opened it to see a beaming waiter with a loaded tray. "Nine-thirty on the dot, Mademoiselle Celestina," he said. *"Bon jour, Madame la Comtesse.* Shall I serve the meal?"

"I'll do that, François." Celestina's voice was warm. "François is a younger brother of André, madame. He is learning to be a maître d'hôtel."

"And doing very well at it. Thank you, François. Celestina and I can manage."

"À votre service, Madame la Comtesse." François departed, still beaming.

"Paris on the Alabama," said Maritza, sitting down to the small table where Celestina had deposited the tray.

"Yes, but don't forget, it took a war to bring it here."

"What did you learn during the night?" Maritza asked. "About politics, I mean?"

"The government will soon move to Virginia—to Richmond. President Davis has a nervous dyspepsia and almost everything he eats sours on his stomach. Senator Toombs won't last very long as Secretary of State; he tries to do everything himself and his health doesn't allow it."

"Sounds like the Confederacy is governed by a bunch of invalids."

"Invalids—or hotheads. Mr. Yancey had to be sent to France as Commissioner to keep him quiet, but he doesn't even speak French, so what good can he do there? The Emperor would make an ass of him—except that he's already one."

"Louis Napoleon is not to be fooled easily," Maritza agreed. "If the Cabinet is full of incompetents, how can the Confederacy expect to win?"

"André has the greatest respect for Mr. Benjamin, perhaps because he was born in the British West Indies, while André himself is from Martinique. He says Mr. Benjamin has more brains than the rest of the government put together. Then, of course, there's Colonel Richard Mann, your conquest."

"What about him?"

"Well, he's handsome, rich, not married—"

"And still only an aide to the Quartermaster General, with the task of procuring arms," Maritza said thoughtfully. "I wonder why he doesn't have a higher position?"

"André thinks Colonel Mann's assignment to the Quartermaster Department is only a front. He's probably the one Mr. Benjamin depends upon most."

"But Benjamin is only the Attorney General—practically a nobody."

"Not for long, they say downstairs. If he wasn't a Jew, he could one day be elected President of the Confederacy. As it is, he's already pulling most of the strings that make President Davis move."

Having been mistress of a large contingent of servants at Château LeClerc, near enough to Paris that Parisian gossip came there almost every time the head cook went shopping for food, Maritza knew very well that gossip in the servants' quarters was frequently more factual than what finally appeared in the newspapers. While Celestina was placing the tray of empty dishes outside the door, she considered what the two of them had learned and decided that she'd already achieved a major victory in her own campaign through the liaison—if properly followed up—with Colonel Mann. And having done so well in so short a time, she didn't propose to give up any of the advantage she had gained, however inadvertently.

"I've changed my mind," she announced. "Get dressed, Tina, we're going to see Uncle John Slidell."

"What do you need me for? I could use some sleep while you're out struttin'."

"I need you to hold a parasol over my head to protect my skin from the sun, like any other proper Southern lady of quality. If you insist on staying a slave, you'll at least be the only lady's maid in Montgomery wearing a Paris frock."

"That sure ain't sayin' much," said Tina, but began to dress obediently.

IV

John Slidell's secretary was Preston Harkness. A distant cousin of Maritza's, he greeted them warmly before ushering them into the office of the former senator, a suite that also housed the Department of State of the Confederate States of America.

"Maritza!" John Slidell embraced his ward fondly. "When I heard this morning that you had arrived in Montgomery, I could hardly believe my ears. And Celestina!" He turned to the octoroon and the glow in his eyes was now of an entirely different origin from the warm smile with which he had greeted Maritza. "Still as beautiful as ever, I see. I'll bet those Frenchmen really appreciated *you*."

"I was very happy in France, sir," said Tina demurely, well aware of the reason for the sudden change in John Slidell's manner.

"Why did you think I wouldn't come home, after Étienne died, Uncle John?" Maritza asked.

"Well, after being a countess—"

"I turned over the château to Philippe LeClerc but kept the title. Being a countess means a lot more socially here in America than in France."

"By God, you're right!" he conceded. "I'm glad to see you're still loyal to the South—"

"Loyal enough to become a rebel, Uncle John. That should be proof enough for anyone."

"Well put, my dear." He waved them to seats on the divan at the other side of the office. "Still, the South could have used your beauty and brains in France in the diplomatic area to even more avail than in America."

"I realize that now, although I didn't when I left France," Maritza admitted. "Still, with the South fighting against oppression by the Yankees under Abraham Lincoln, I would naturally want to be here to do my part."

"Are you planning to stay in Montgomery long?" Slidell asked on a casual note, the reason for which Maritza quite understood—knowing the rest of his family very well.

"Until the capital moves to Richmond. I'm sure I can find something to do there, too—perhaps as a translator in the State Department, in addition to my duties as a war correspondent."

"War correspondent!" He gave her a startled look.

"I'm going to be writing for *Le Pays*."

"The journal? I knew your husband owned it once, but I didn't know you wrote for it."

"During the months that Étienne was ill, I often supervised publication. Occasionally, when Monsieur Claudet was ill, I even edited the journal."

"You *did* sell it, didn't you?"

"Yes—to Monsieur Claudet, who had been the editor-in-chief for many years. He asked me to serve as correspondent here in America."

"Then you can help the Cause"—Southerners, Maritza had

learned, always referred to the affairs of the Confederacy as "the Cause"—"by writing favorably about it."

"The first duty of a correspondent is to write what he or she sees or knows to be true, Uncle John," she reminded him. "From what I've learned so far, the Confederacy seems to be governed by old men who are almost invalids."

"Who have you been talking to?" he demanded suspiciously.

"Just gossip around the hotel."

"Are you sure it wasn't Colonel Mann? He's known to be a climber—and close to those who would usurp the position of Secretary Toombs."

"Who is also ailing, I understand."

"A false canard, created by Toombs's enemies," Slidell snapped, then recovered his aplomb quickly, realizing how much he had revealed to someone as intelligent as he already knew Maritza to be. "Why should you write about politics when your cousin, General Beauregard, has won such a glorious victory at Charleston and is even now preparing to attack Washington?"

"With guns I bought in England and sold to our Army in Mobile."

"So you're the mysterious woman who was selling rifles in Mobile! I'm glad to hear that you followed my suggestion about buying the arms. Did you make a large profit?"

"I had a good teacher in you, when I was a girl, Uncle John. You can be sure I did all right for myself." Maritza changed the subject, having learned that the Confederate government was as riddled with political rivalries and infighting as Tina's informants among the kitchen staff of the Exchange Hotel had told her it was. "I hope Aunt Mathilde is well."

"She's doing poorly, I'm sorry to say," said Slidell. "The war has made her more nervous than before."

"Please give her my love. When she feels better, I would like to call on her."

"I know she will be happy to hear that you're home again— to stay," Slidell assured her.

"Well, we'd better be going, Tina." Maritza rose. "I want to rest before the reception tonight—"

"Mrs. Davis' levee? Are you invited to that?" Slidell's astonishment made his face seem even narrower. "I was told that you only arrived in Montgomery yesterday."

"Colonel Mann was kind enough to invite me," Maritza explained. "I'm looking forward to meeting the President, and Mrs. Davis too. All of Paris is eager to learn what they're like and particularly what the French government can expect from him."

"Nothing but friendship," John Slidell hastened to assure her. "France needs Southern cotton and we can use the products of French armament makers, so we have several areas of common interest."

"You can be sure my dispatches to Paris will be very complimentary to the South, Uncle John," said Maritza in parting. "After all, how could they be otherwise when we're fighting to preserve our sacred honor?"

"Well put, my dear," said Slidell as he ushered them to the door. "Well put, indeed."

"Everyone says Mrs. Davis is much more charming than that woman in the White House in Washington. Let me know when Aunt Mathilde feels like receiving me. I haven't seen her in so long."

"What did I tell you?" Celestina demanded when they were back on the street. "What they call the Confederacy is nothing but a lot of old men fightin' among themselves to keep the power they've got over black people—women in particular. Did you see the way he looked at me? If you hadn't been there, he'd have had me sprawled out on that couch before he finished saying hello."

Maritza burst out laughing. "With that white hair? Don't be foolish."

"Don't tell me I don't recognize the light that comes into even old men's eyes when they see somebody like me—and like you too, *ma petite*."

The White House of the Confederacy, though smaller and almost rustic compared to many other homes in Montgomery,
was ablaze with light. Richard Mann, resplendent in dress uniform, handed Maritza down from the buggy in which they had
waited about half an hour. As one of a long line of black servants drove the buggy away to the stables, the line of similar
vehicles moved, one by one, into place before the portico and
disgorged its richly dressed or uniformed occupants.

Maritza took the arm Mann offered her and they moved
slowly toward the old house through a gate in a black iron
fence. The Confederate flag was draped above the portico, even
though it was after sundown, indicating that the President was
in residence.

While Richard Mann signed their names in a book presided
over by one of the younger Davis children, Maritza looked
about her but was not impressed. Compared with the resi-
dences of other heads of government she had visited, the White
House of the Confederacy was shabby in appearance and very
small.

The reception hall separated two rooms, in the first of which
the Davises were receiving guests. Standing stiffly erect—apparently in pain, although he was gracious to all who came to
pay their respects—Jefferson Davis was every inch a Southern
aristocrat as well as a President. Mann whispered in Maritza's
ear that, because of his pain, Davis rarely did more than put in
an appearance at such functions and smile as the guests filed
by, retreating then to his study or, if he felt very badly indeed,
to his bed.

Beside her husband, Varina Howell Davis was the epitome
of gracious hospitality. Though not exactly beautiful, she was
obviously intelligent. "Clever" was the word Maritza had heard
several times used by other women to describe her, a word that
could mean various things, depending upon the intonation of
the speaker. She'd have no chance to approach Davis about a

letter of marque tonight, Maritza decided as she curtsied before her host and hostess—and resolutely hid her disappointment.

"May I present Countess Maritza LeClerc," Mann was saying. "A fellow Alabamian, returned home to help support the Cause."

"Countess." Davis' words were clipped. "You honor us by your presence."

"How lovely you are, my dear." Varina Howell Davis pressed Maritza's hand with a smile of welcome that was obviously sincere. "That gown has Paris written all over it. Why can't our Southern seamstresses learn to make anything like that?"

"Please don't think of me as still a Parisian, when the South is fighting for survival," said Maritza. "I'm much more proud of being a Southerner and, naturally, an Alabamian."

As others in the receiving line pressed forward, Mann steered Maritza into another room where punch and cakes were being served. A small man with decidedly Hebraic features and a black beard was standing almost alone in the corner with a half-filled cup of punch in his hand. As they approached, he turned and somewhat surreptitiously lifted a small silver flask, splashing perhaps an ounce of its contents into the cup. "I want you to meet Attorney General Benjamin, Maritza," said Mann.

The man in the corner turned, grinning like a small boy caught with his hand in the cookie jar, and dropped the flask into his pocket. "Ah, Dick!" he said with a twinkle in his eye that made Maritza like him immediately. "I see that, as usual, you've captured the reigning beauty of the occasion."

"Don't give me away, sir," said Mann. "Countess LeClerc, may I present Attorney General Judah P. Benjamin."

"Charmed, my dear Countess." Benjamin lifted her hand to touch his lips to it with a gesture of Old World courtliness. "You have added a rare beauty, all too often lacking on fussy occasions like this."

"To tell the truth, sir," said Maritza, "I'd rather be having a nip out of that flask of yours."

"Bring her some punch by all means, Dick, and some for

yourself," Benjamin ordered. "There're at least two more drinks left in the flask and we'll share it together."

Of all the people in the room, less attention seemed to be paid to the rather stocky Jew—whose influence on Jefferson Davis was said to be very great—than to any other of the half dozen cabinet members present. Each of these was surrounded by a group listening avidly to what he said and nodding agreement every now and then, as if hearing the Delphic oracle utter great truths. Watching the way Benjamin seemed to be somewhat isolated from the others, Maritza couldn't help wondering whether much of what she'd heard about the small, plump Jew with the black beard was to be believed.

"You are correct, my dear." Benjamin's voice intruded upon Maritza's thoughts, startling her, for it seemed that he had been reading her mind. "The Attorney General *is* least in importance among the posts in the Cabinet."

"Why did you accept it, sir?" Maritza asked. "I remember now hearing my husband say you were the smartest lawyer in Louisiana."

Benjamin smiled, albeit somewhat wryly. "Depending upon the inflection you give those words, my dear Countess, that could either be a compliment or a slur—particularly to a Jew."

"It was a compliment, sir, believe me. Your being a Jew would mean nothing to a Frenchman, when the finances of France—and even England—are controlled largely by men of the Jewish faith."

"You pay me too much credit by speaking my name in the same breath as a Rothschild or a Disraeli."

"Nonetheless, I'm reliably informed that you have the confidence and complete trust of President Davis."

Benjamin looked surprised. "Where did you get this information?"

"From my personal maid. She's made a conquest of André—"

"The maître d'hôtel at the Exchange?" Benjamin's laugh boomed out, louder and somewhat more boisterous than would have been expected from so short a man. "Then it's about as accurate as any other of the thousand or so rumors flying about the city."

Feeling a strange instinct that the man she was talking to was quite dependable, Maritza decided to take a giant step. "I hope you won't mind giving me some help, sir."

The merriment suddenly went out of Benjamin's face. "Concerning this project of yours to obtain a letter of marque?"

"Why, yes. How did you know?"

"Dick Mann told me after he came back from Mobile, where he bought the munitions you risked your life to bring us."

"And sold at a profit," she reminded him.

"Naturally. I never discuss politics or business at social gatherings, Countess. Too many ears are attuned to even a casual remark."

"Obviously, I shan't get another chance to speak with President Davis."

"He wouldn't approve without asking me anyway," Benjamin told her.

"There! Celestina was right after all."

Benjamin frowned. "That's a lovely name—"

"She's my maid—an octoroon and very beautiful."

"Which means she would be admitted to the bedrooms of as many whites as blacks and could be a great help to you in gathering information."

"Will you help me?"

"Only on one condition." Benjamin glanced across the room, where Mann was bearing down upon them holding two cups of punch. "Say nothing of this to anyone else for the moment and visit my office tomorrow morning at eleven. It's in the same building as that of Mr. Slidell but on the floor above."

Briefly Maritza wondered how Judah P. Benjamin already knew of her visit to Uncle John that morning and Slidell's warning to her against the very man she was talking to. Then Richard Mann, perspiring from the effort of pushing his way through the now jammed room in the cloying heat, arrived with the punch intact. Emptying the remainder of the potent rum from his flask into their cups in equal portions, Judah Benjamin lifted his own in a toast:

"To our passionate rebel, Countess Maritza LeClerc! And to the triumph of our arms!"

VI

Colonel Richard Mann was already at breakfast when Maritza came into the hotel dining room the morning after the levee. He rose immediately and hurried across the room, leaving alone at the table a tall man with whom he had been eating.

"Good morning!" he said with a welcoming smile. "How you manage to look so beautiful at this time of the morning is a mystery to me. Will you join us at my table?"

"You already have company."

"Only one of your fellow newsmen, Mr. William Russell of the London *Times*."

"The one who writes such witty accounts of life in the South? I used to read his reports when I was in England."

"The same—and all the more reason why you will enjoy meeting him."

As they approached the table the English correspondent put down his napkin and pushed back his chair to rise.

"Countess LeClerc, may I present Mr. William H. Russell, correspondent for the London *Times?*" said Mann.

"Mr. Russell. This is an honor indeed." Maritza acknowledged the introduction as Russell bent over her hand. "I remember reading your accounts from Sebastopol."

"You flatter me, Countess." Russell was obviously pleased at her remembering his writings, which had made him one of the most famous of the British correspondents. "May I say that I have at last seen a flower of Southern womanhood in full bloom?"

"Only because I'm back home where I belong."

"I'm told that you recently spent some time in France?" said Russell.

"Seven years, from my marriage to Étienne—the late Count LeClerc—until his death."

"I met the count once in the Crimea," said Russell, after Maritza had given her order. "He wrote for *Le Pays*, didn't he?"

"Étienne owned *Le Pays* and I occasionally wrote an article for it," she explained. "After his death the journal was sold to the former editor-in-chief, Monsieur Claudet. He has honored me by asking me to represent *Le Pays* here in America."

"I know Claudet well," said Russell. "You must be more than just a casual writer of trivia for him to give you such a responsibility."

"I was honored when Monsieur Claudet asked me." Maritza stirred sugar into the coffee the waiter had set before her. "I'm a Southerner by birth and feeling, but I must be impartial in what I write."

"Frankly," said Mr. Russell, "you'd be of much more value to the Confederacy as its representative to France than the fiery Mr. Yancey now in Paris."

"Few would dispute you there," said Mann. "The President could hardly have made a worse choice than sending a strong proponent of slavery to a country where it was outlawed years ago."

"The rumor in Montgomery is that Yancey is about to be recalled, Countess," said Russell. "I'm wondering if your presence here at this moment could have any particular significance in that connection. After all, Napoleon III is known to have a weakness for beautiful women."

"I've had no experience as a diplomat, Mr. Russell," said Maritza sweetly. Then her voice sharpened: "But the demands of loyalty to the homeland would hardly include a visit to the royal bedchamber."

"Well spoken, Countess," Mann exclaimed heartily. "I guess you'll admit now that Southern women can be something more than simpering idiots as you've been picturing them in the London *Times*, Russell."

"*Touché, Madame la Comtesse,*" Russell conceded. "You have no idea how much secret information is often revealed by such a direct frontal approach."

"I recognize the technique, sir." Maritza was eating bacon and eggs with a hearty appetite. "Parisian newspaper correspondents often use the same methods."

"I hear that Virginia will soon vote to secede," said Maritza.

"Will that mean Her Majesty's Government might recognize the South as an independent nation, Mr. Russell?"

"I doubt it," said the London correspondent. "On my way South when the government of President Davis was first set up here, I traveled through Virginia. There is little sympathy for slavery west of the Blue Ridge Mountains and none at all beyond the Alleghenies. If Mr. Lincoln is as smart as I think he is, he'll soon send an army eastward from the Ohio River area and create another state for the Union out of what is now the western part of Virginia. With a loyal state on their western border, Virginians may have little chance to press against Washington."

"Just which side do you favor in this war, Mr. Russell?" Maritza asked.

"I favor neither, Countess; as you said just now, a correspondent needs to be neutral if he is going to write the truth. Besides, I saw enough of war at Sebastopol and Balaklava not to wish it on any country. My personal belief is that Abraham Lincoln is not so black as he is painted here in the South, and that hotheads like Mr. Yancey and Secretary Toombs should have been muzzled years ago."

"One thing is certain," said Mann. "When Virginia is no longer officially in the Union, the government will be moved to Richmond."

"Will you be going there, Mr. Russell?" Maritza asked.

"I'm taking the train north tomorrow. What about you?"

"I'll go where I'm needed most."

"That's sure to be in a military hospital," said the correspondent. "As you may know, I had the good fortune to write the story of Florence Nightingale in the Crimea."

"For which you will always be remembered," Maritza assured him.

"A lot of Southern politicians would like to see Russell muzzled," said Mann after Russell had left the dining room.

"Why?"

"Because he writes the truth about them and that can often be painful."

"Do you know why Mr. Benjamin wants to see me this morning?" she asked.

"I'm as much in the dark there as you are, but one thing I can assure you. Whatever Benjamin does have in mind is for what he considers the good of the Confederacy and has no relationship to his own interests."

"Then I can trust him?"

"With your life."

Looking back on the conversation a few months later, Maritza was certain neither of them had dreamed that morning just how true Mann's assurance would be. Nor could they have had any inkling of how both their lives would be intertwined with that of the plump little Jew who, though not even born in America, was yet fired by a zeal and a loyalty for the Southern Cause none of the firebrands now shouting for victory could even begin to equal.

VII

Celestina did not accompany Maritza to the meeting with Attorney General Benjamin. She had found a woman whose pots and irons she could use to launder some of their soiled clothing, since she wouldn't dare trust a black native of Montgomery to touch the delicate underthings the two women, mistress and slave alike, had brought from Paris.

Maritza was ushered into the Attorney General's office as soon as she arrived, although several people were waiting in the anteroom outside. Unlike John Slidell's office, that of the Attorney General was sparsely furnished.

"Am I to get the letter of marque?" she asked when the greetings were over.

Benjamin had not gone back to his desk after greeting her but stood in front of one of the open windows with his hands behind him, a position she was to see many, many times in the future.

"I'm afraid not," he said.

"What possible reason could the President have for not issuing it? After all, we didn't ask for any special consideration."

"I know, Countess, but a great deal is involved."

"Is it because he doesn't think Captain Darrow could handle a ship of war?"

"On the contrary; both President Davis and I have the very highest respect for him. We were in the Senate when Darrow's difficulties at the Naval Academy arose."

"Then you must have known he was no more guilty than a half dozen others at least."

"Less guilty, if anything," said Benjamin dryly. "The ones who brought the whor—the young lady—into the barracks were not punished, largely because their fathers were high up in government or had friends in high positions. Ensign Darrow's family, on the other hand, had always stayed out of politics and were therefore not well known."

"Which made him the logical scapegoat."

"True. Darrow joined the British merchant marine immediately after his dismissal, however, and got his own ship long before most of his classmates did. In fact, many of them still have no command, so he really came out ahead."

Penn Darrow, Maritza remembered, had once voiced much the same thought.

"President Davis and I believe both you and Captain Darrow can serve the South much more effectively in other ways," Benjamin continued.

"How?"

"First, let me point out a few facts which, with your intelligence, you have probably thought of already. England's economy depends upon manufacturing, largely the spinning and weaving of cotton it buys from the South, but it also needs to sell machinery and many other things to the North as well in order to prosper. As Prime Minister, Lord Palmerston is really the British government, Queen Victoria being little more than a figurehead. He knows all this and is carefully balancing one against the other."

"For his own benefit," said Maritza.

"That is only one of the many facts of international trade

and relations in which the South is involved," Benjamin agreed dryly. "It also explains why England is not going to recognize the Confederacy as a nation unless we first win our own independence from the North."

"Surely you aren't saying we in the South don't want to conquer the North?" Maritza asked incredulously.

"The Confederate States of America desire nothing but the status of an independent nation, Countess, something we already are by heritage, political convictions, geography, and cultural backgrounds. President Davis made all these things quite clear from the start in his public addresses."

"But if we conquered the North . . . ?"

"Even if by some miracle we did, the South couldn't hold a population four or five times our own in thrall while adhering to the principles of democracy both North and South have upheld from the very beginning of our country. Our own strategy can only be to hold what we have while wearing the North down until they lose what little enthusiasm they have for the war."

"Why shouldn't their enthusiasm be as great as ours?"

"The South has a rather homogeneous population—if you leave out the slaves—while the North is a hodgepodge of varied ethnic groups." He smiled wryly. "Actually, we Jews are a religious community, not a separate people, yet we are hated because we have always managed to direct our efforts toward—and sometimes control—banking and other business. How could you expect a mélange—to use a French term with which I'm sure you're quite familiar—of people from many and varied origins to ever develop a cohesive pride in themselves as a nation?"

"Just how does this concern me and Captain Pennington Darrow, with regard to our obtaining a letter of marque, Mr. Benjamin?"

"It puts you in a very favorable position, if *you* agree to accept two roles President Davis and I would like you to play. One of them concerns both you and Captain Darrow, the other yourself alone."

"Surely you don't think I'm such a fool as to agree with all this sight unseen?" Maritza asked somewhat tartly.

Benjamin smiled. "I bet Dick Mann a bottle of brandy last night that you'd use those words. After I finish telling you what I have in mind, I hope you'll broach the bottle with us."

Maritza settled back in her chair. "Go on, please. Since it appears that I'm to be auctioned off—like a cow for sale at the county fair—I might as well listen to the auctioneer's spiel."

"I'll be brief, Countess, now that you're familiar with the questions involved. To fight this war, the South must buy munitions. You and Captain Darrow had tangible proof of this when you sold ten thousand Enfield rifles with ammunition and other necessities to Colonel Mann as purchasing agent for the Quartermaster Department."

"The acclaim is due Captain Darrow for refusing to heave to."

"Exactly. But if the *Pride of Bristol* had been overtaken by the U. S. S. *Montgomery* at sea while carrying a load of munitions, those Enfields would never have gotten to the South. Even with a letter of marque and a fair sloop, however, Captain Darrow might not be so lucky again. If his ship once came within range of the eleven-inch guns on a Union battleship, the career of your partnership could end abruptly. You would not only lose everything you'd put into the vessels but Darrow could be killed. Have you thought of that?"

"Mostly we've been counting the money we'd make when our prizes were sold in Brazil," Maritza admitted.

"Your prospects were good a month ago. When Fort Sumter was seized, most Union warships were in foreign ports but now they're steaming home as fast as they can to take up blockade duty. Those not coming home are cruising off ports on the British and Scottish coasts, ready to catch any vessel from the South that tries to make port with a load of cotton."

"Isn't the Union still shipping goods to England and France on unarmed vessels?"

"They are and your privateer might even take a few prizes before the Union Navy becomes formidable enough to drive you from the seas. Take my word for it, Countess, just that is bound to happen eventually, if you and Captain Darrow carry out your plan."

Maritza shook her head slowly. "You're the most discouraging man I've talked to since I returned home—"

"I'm only a realist but, nine times out of ten, the realists come out ahead of the romantics in this world—which may be why it's in the mess it's in. Don't forget two things, however: England and France have ships of their own and they need cotton from the Southern states. If they were willing to take the risk of starting a war, nothing could prevent their sailing empty hulls right into the harbors of Charleston, Wilmington, or New Orleans, loading the cotton they need, and sailing out again. Since they'd be carrying cargoes with no military value, nothing in international law at this moment would forbid them."

"Aren't they liable to do it?"

"I'm betting they won't."

"Why?"

"Sailing an empty ship across the ocean wouldn't be profitable and English merchants always have a weather eye open for a profit. Too, England fought a brutal war a long way from home in the Crimea less than ten years ago. They got nothing for it except a lot of lives lost, so they're not liable to risk undertaking a similar operation on this side of the Atlantic."

"What about France?"

"Napoleon III wants badly to expand to the American continent by seizing Mexico, which is simmering in a state of near explosion with Juárez, Díaz, and others fighting among themselves. No faction in Mexico is able to control the weak *imperialistas,* though, so Napoleon's strategy is to let the North and the South destroy themselves. After which, he can walk in and take Mexico almost without a shot, giving him the foothold he wants on the Western Hemisphere from which he could expand in either or both directions."

"So what's the answer?"

"England's got ships, plus nearby ports in Nassau, Bermuda, and Nova Scotia, while the South has thirty-five hundred miles of coastline with a number of ports. If British ships land munitions and supplies of war on English territory like Nassau, fast

Confederate blockade runners can pick them up by day and slip into a half dozen Southern ports by night to unload their cargoes. Then they load their hulls and decks with cotton and slip out again for Bermuda or Nassau a few nights later. That way, only we take the risk and England's problem is solved without the British Navy taking the chance of boarding a neutral ship not carrying munitions and creating an international incident."

"It does sound feasible," Maritza admitted.

"It *is* feasible." Benjamin crossed to his desk and perched on the corner. "Actually, we're already engaged in blockade running on a small scale, but we need more and larger vessels. That's where you and Captain Darrow can help us tremendously."

"How?"

"English shipyards are having trouble getting permission from the British Foreign Secretary, Lord Russell, to sell ships to the Confederate States of America, because Russell doesn't want to offend the Union government. On the other hand, you and Captain Darrow are already in the shipping business, so there's nothing to prevent an English shipyard from selling you a vessel."

"I follow you so far," said Maritza. "Please go on."

"In Scotland, the shipyards along the River Clyde are clogged with vessels. Most of them are slender, low in profile, and side-wheeled—a screw-driven vessel needs more draft and the channels these blockade runners must scoot through are often relatively shallow."

"Can you be more specific?"

"Gladly. The ideal ship for our purposes should be about five hundred tons and, roughly, nine times as long as it's wide. The hull must be painted gray so it won't be easily seen at night and the fireboxes need to burn anthracite because it gives off little smoke."

"Sounds as if you know exactly what you need."

"Captain Darrow would tell you the same thing if he were here. We have just sent Captain J. D. Bulloch to Scotland as our representative to negotiate for building several vessels like one recently launched into the Clyde. It was about to sail but

Lord Russell won't let the Confederate government buy it openly. As a French subject, however, you could easily have your London agents negotiate for the purchase of the vessel and place Darrow in command."

"I don't have that much money, Mr. Benjamin—and Captain Darrow has less."

"The Confederate government is ready to advance three fourths of the cost of the ship, with only a mortgage on it as security."

"Which you would lose if it's sunk by a Union warship?"

Benjamin shrugged. "The munitions your vessel could bring from Nassau or some other English port on the west side of the Atlantic would be invaluable to us. Moreover, since such a blockade runner would draw little water, it could make port at Charleston, Savannah, or even at the mouth of some Southern river. The Cape Fear on the North Carolina coast near Wilmington is ideal for our purposes."

"With what profit to the owners besides the patriotic satisfaction of getting munitions to the South?" Maritza asked shrewdly.

"You sell us materials of war at the same price you pay for them on the docks at Nassau or Bermuda," he told her. "Then you sell the cotton Captain Darrow carries to a British port afterward for whatever profit you can make."

"Let's see," said Maritza thoughtfully. "When I left England, cotton was selling at about thirty-five cents a pound—"

"You can load all you want at Wilmington, Charleston, or even at Matamoros, in Mexico, for five to ten cents a pound. Those ports are glutted now because of the Union blockade. That way, you and the captain would be fighting for the Confederacy even more effectively than if you were sighting down the barrel of an Enfield rifle this morning in General Beauregard's Alexandria Line, waiting to drive Abraham Lincoln out of Washington."

"You've sold me," said Maritza promptly. "I'll write to Captain Darrow today explaining why we need a blockade runner instead of a privateer. He can get in touch with your Captain Bulloch in London."

"I'll send your letter in a diplomatic pouch with some correspondence leaving Charleston the day after tomorrow on a British vessel," Benjamin promised. "Our agents in Scotland will also be instructed to draw up the necessary mortgage and pay the shipbuilders. The vessel itself will be handed over to Captain Darrow as soon as she's ready to sail for Nassau." He struck a small bell on his desk and a clerk appeared. "Ask Colonel Mann to come in, please, and bring that bottle of brandy I put in the wall closet this morning with three glasses.

"Countess, we're in business." Benjamin turned back to Maritza as the clerk hurried away. "Before this war's over you'll not only be a rich woman but a heroine of the Cause into the bargain."

"Neither the money nor the acclaim really counts; it's what I can do of importance to help the South. I believe you spoke of something else—"

Benjamin reached into a drawer and, taking out a sheet of newsprint, handed it to her. "I think you'll find satisfaction in doing something about *this,* too, by seeing that the truth is told in France."

The sheet was in French, from a French newspaper about a month old. A poorly drawn caricature showed a bloated man in planter's clothing, with a napkin tucked under his chin. He was obviously ready to eat, with knife and fork poised over the body of a small, and black, infant. The latter rested on a large platter and was garnished with sweet potatoes, baked apples, and an ear of corn. SOUTHERN BIGOT DINES ON NEWBORN BLACK INFANT was the caption, and reading the lurid description of the alleged cannibalistic practice of slaveholding Southerners in eating the tender bodies of black newborns, Maritza could hardly keep from vomiting.

"I can't imagine that being printed in France," she protested.

"Nevertheless it was—in *Le Temps.* The story was actually written for a fee by a French correspondent for the paper in Washington. The drawing was furnished to him by a propaganda agent employed by the Union government."

"Surely no intelligent—"

"You're right; no intelligent Frenchman would believe such

accounts. Nevertheless, it would appeal to the masses, who regard all Southerners as aristocrats. And I don't need to tell you that your lower-class Frenchman has an instinctive distrust of an aristocrat."

"What can I do?" Maritza asked. "The story and the drawing are already in print."

"More like it are being printed every day," said Benjamin. "If you were writing from Washington as correspondent for *Le Pays* and told the real truth, however, much of that propaganda would be counteracted."

"You're asking me to go to Washington?" she demanded incredulously.

"If you're prepared to take the slight risk involved."

"I'd do anything to stop such canards from being printed about the land I love. Only tell me how."

VIII

"Good morning, Richard," said Benjamin when Colonel Mann came in and took a chair. "Aren't you going to say good morning to the countess?"

"We had breakfast together," said Mann; then, as Benjamin's eyebrows rose, he added: "In the dining room; I was telling William Russell good-by when the Countess came in."

"I'm sorry to see Russell go," said the Attorney General. "We've had some interesting discussions of world affairs and, on the whole, I think he's told enough of the truth in the London *Times* to give England a fair picture of our Cause."

"You'd find many in the Cabinet who wouldn't agree with that evaluation, sir," said Mann.

"And also in Montgomery."

"Perhaps you can continue your discussions with Russell later in Richmond," Mann suggested.

"He's not going there. Just this morning, President Davis signed a passport for him to cross the lines into Washington."

"Washington!" Maritza exclaimed. "Why would he go there instead of reporting from the South?"

"As correspondent for the London *Times*, Mr. Russell has to be neutral, but once Virginia makes her decision in our favor, Washington may well become a battlefield in less than a month. Naturally a war correspondent wants to be where the fighting is liable to start."

The last sentence was spoken casually, but Mann caught Benjamin's meaning.

"No!" he protested. "That's too dangerous."

"Everything about war is dangerous, Dick," the small man with the black beard said imperturbably. "Each of us has to decide for himself whether to face it or evade it."

"Or *herself*," said Maritza. "Sit down, Colonel. I want to hear what the Attorney General has to suggest."

"But—"

"I'm not going to ask the countess to do anything she isn't willing to do of her own volition, Dick," Benjamin said mildly. "But she *is* a French citizen."

"And also an American."

"Exactly," said the Attorney General. "In fact, Countess, you're the answer to one of our prayers."

"I'm glad of that," said Maritza.

"Wait until you hear what he has in mind," said Mann grimly.

"She already knows some of it." Benjamin turned back to Maritza. "As a French citizen visiting in the United States, you can go anywhere you wish, Countess—Washington, Richmond, Nassau, even to Mexico or Paris if it becomes necessary to negotiate sub rosa, so to speak, with other governments. Being a born Southerner, too, your loyalty to the Cause is assured, even though you may safely appear to be neutral. By the way, do you know Henri Mercier, the new French minister from Paris to Washington?"

"He has been a guest at Château LeClerc. Why?"

"Mercier is sympathetic to our Cause. You might persuade him to remain so."

"What is it you want me to do, sir?"

"Your credentials as correspondent for *Le Pays;* how do they read?"

" 'To whom it may concern—' "

"Enough. Secretary Seward of the Union State Department can have no hesitancy in accepting you as a bona fide representative of your journal. After all, he doesn't want to do anything to anger the French or influence them to favor the Confederacy. Besides, the fact that Mr. Russell of the London *Times* has been in the South for some months reporting from here, but is now going to Washington, establishes a precedent any other correspondent can follow."

"You're asking her to risk her life, sir," Mann protested. "If the deception is realized in Washington, she could be treated as a spy—perhaps even shot."

"Hardly that, Dick," said Benjamin. "President Davis' announced willingness to issue passports to anyone wishing to leave the Confederacy and take up residence in Union territory gives us the very tool we need to get Countess LeClerc in the midst of where the action is bound to start soon."

Maritza's pulse was beginning to quicken at the thought of playing a far more important role in the coming conflict than she'd ever hoped—plus the excitement of acting the double parts of spy and correspondent.

"What about my dispatches to *Le Pays?*" she asked. "Do you expect me to emphasize the justness of our Cause—"

"You will function like any other correspondent, writing happenings as they appear to you," said Benjamin. "With Virginia in the conflict, General Robert E. Lee will no doubt command the Virginia troops and before long, hopefully, the entire Confederate Army. He refused command of the Union forces because of loyalty to his native Virginia, so he can hardly be offered a lesser post by our side. Therefore, we can logically expect a forthright attack against Washington soon, certainly as forthright as the one the Virginians made in capturing Harpers Ferry and the munitions works there."

"Putting Maritza—the countess—in the midst of danger, if Washington is shelled by our artillery," said Mann pointedly.

"*When* Washington is shelled by Confederate artillery, not *if,*

Dick," said Benjamin bluntly. "Our only hope of bringing this war to an end is quick action; if it drags on, we are lost." The Attorney General smiled briefly, but without humor. "Even if the countess and Captain Darrow do become rich from blockade running."

Before Mann could speak, Maritza asked: "Besides writing dispatches to *Le Pays* describing the actual war, what will I be expected to do, Mr. Benjamin?"

"Very little, ma'am—certainly not anything that would pose a risk to your safety or compromise you in any way. If the South is victorious in an attack already being planned, you can help immensely by sending information on the victory to France. Naturally, the Union censors will probably try to keep the truth from reaching French newspapers, especially if it is not favorable to the Union, but I believe we've figured out a way to take care of that."

"Suppose I should learn of some impending Union action—what then?"

"No!" Richard Mann exclaimed heatedly. "If you accept this assignment—and I recommend against it—you're to stay away from spying."

Maritza gave the handsome officer a quick, probing glance. "Just where do you come in as far as this assignment is concerned, Colonel?"

"You will be under Colonel Mann's orders, Countess," Judah Benjamin answered instead of Mann. "For your information—information which must not go any farther than this room—he commands a very elite group."

"Of spies?"

"Secret agents," said Mann. "And right now I—"

"You have no responsibility for the countess' decision, Dick," said Benjamin firmly. "If she accepts, she will report to you, or to me, like anyone else. If not, this conversation never happened," he added pointedly to Maritza as he rose to his feet, terminating the conference. "Don't make your decision now, Countess. Think about it for a day or two and let me know."

"We need to talk this over, Maritza," Richard Mann said urgently as they walked through the corridor outside Benjamin's office. "I have an appointment for dinner this evening with a German arms agent but I can make it early. There's a magician on the program at the Bijou Theater who is said to be very good. If you're free around eight o'clock, I'll arrange for a box and we can have supper together after the performance."

IX

Celestina received the news that they would be going to Washington with consternation. "Now I know you've gone crazy," she assured her mistress. "You know what they do with spies?"

"Certainly. But whoever heard of shooting a woman spy?"

"There has to be a first time for everything. We'd have been better off if we'd gone with Captain Darrow back to England."

"Then you would have missed knowing André."

The reminder stopped the flow of protest and, her pique forgotten, Tina even smiled. *"Ma fois! Quel homme!"* she exclaimed. "Wants to make love all the time." Then she remembered the subject they were discussing and started wailing again. "But if we go to Washington, I'll never see André again."

"He's planning to go to Richmond to work when the government moves there," Maritza reminded her. "You told me yourself he's been invited to be maître d'hôtel at the Hotel Spotswood."

"François is going too." Celestina brightened again. "Both of them were born free in Martinique so they can go wherever they want to." Then her face fell. "But we'll still be a hundred miles away."

"Unless I miss my guess, we can figure some way to get to Richmond a few times before the war's over," Maritza promised.

"So you can play footsie with the handsome colonel?" Tina's good humor was restored. "And I can be with André?"

"Any time you want to marry André, I'll set you free," Maritza assured her.

"Marriage!" Celestina was serving Maritza her dinner on a tray, since she had decided against going down to the dining room because she would be going to the theater later with Colonel Mann. *"Pouf!* Who wants it? If we were married, any time André wanted me and I didn't want him, he could come at me and not even the gendarmes, the police, could stop him. Now when I want him, all I have to do is give him the eye. But what about you, *ma petite?"*

"What do you mean?"

"You know perfectly well what I mean. Two handsome men want you very much, even enough to marry you is my guess. Who will it be?"

"Neither, at the moment," said Maritza. "Starting tomorrow, I've got one of the most fascinating jobs any woman could want. As for men, they can wait."

"How long before we're going to Washington?" Taking away the tray, Celestina poured Maritza a small glass of cordial to go with her dessert—a blueberry tart with a glaze of damson plum jam covering it and a small mound of whipped cream in the center.

"In a few weeks; once Virginia secedes and the government moves to Richmond. As correspondent for *Le Pays,* I'll be writing about what's happening in Washington and if it turns out to be of value to Mr. Benjamin and the Confederacy, so much the better."

"How will you get what you write to the colonel?"

"Maybe I'll use you as a courier."

"Over my dead body! The Yankees may not shoot white women spies, but nobody says they wouldn't shoot a *black* one. What are you going to wear to the theater?"

"The pale blue, I think. What are your plans?"

"André's takin' me to a fish fry and a hay ride." Tina rolled her eyes expressively. "Till you've had fried catfish, plenty of corn likker, and ended up on a hay ride, you don't have any idea what heaven's going to be like—even if you do spend the next day pickin' wheat straw out of your tail."

"Don't come home early, then," said Maritza, rising and dropping the silken peignoir that was her only garment in the heat of the late spring evening. "I'd better start dressing; the colonel is coming for me at a quarter to eight."

X

The theater program proved to be quite mediocre, compared to what Maritza was familiar with in Europe. Richard Mann's fervent admiration was enough to stimulate any woman, however, and she wasn't bored for a minute. The climax to the performance was the magician, who was surprisingly good. After performing all the usual illusions, such as pulling cards from the air, rabbits from a hat, and making various objects disappear, he announced that he would perform a new illusion, that of making water turn into flame.

"Don't be deceived by this trick," Mann warned. "We studied it at West Point."

"Why?"

"Setting something afire, even with matches, is always pretty difficult under wet conditions, so it's a good idea to know all the possible ways. Watch now; I'll tell you at supper how it's done."

A shapely assistant in tights had brought on a shallow bowl of water, placing it on a small table before which the magician was standing.

"What you see here is a bowl of water from the tap," he told the audience. "Watch very closely now, for I am going to set this water afire before your very eyes, breaking all the laws of both physics and logic."

The theater was silent as the performer passed his hands swiftly across the surface of the bowl and back. Through her opera glasses, however, Maritza saw him sift a yellow powder—largely invisible to most of the audience, who didn't have opera glasses—upon the surface of the water. With a second pass, he spread a white powder on the surface.

"Here comes the climax," said Richard Mann. "Keep your glasses focused on his hands."

As Mann was speaking, Maritza saw in the opera glasses that, probably from reservoirs inside his flowing sleeves, the magician was spreading a layer of some other substance, yellowish white in color, upon the surface of the water. Wherever the whitish powder fell the water started to boil and, an instant later, burst into flame.

"*Voilà!*" the magician shouted triumphantly, as flames covered the shallow dish of water and rose about a foot above the surface, accompanied by the faint aroma of brimstone. "The legendary Greek fire! Created for you once again from an ancient time."

The curtains swept together, shutting away the stage, as a thunder of applause shook the theater, preventing the audience, Maritza suspected, from seeing the quick subsidence of the "Greek fire."

"That's the end," said Richard Mann, rising to drape the light wrap Maritza had worn about her shoulders with hands that lingered upon the satiny surface of her skin until she moved, breaking the contact.

"How did he do it?" she asked as they moved from the box.

"I promised to tell you at supper. The hotel dining room stays open till midnight."

The dining room wasn't crowded and they were escorted to a secluded table by a beaming François, who waited to take their orders.

"I can recommend the omelet," said Mann. "It's light and very fluffy, mainly air."

"I don't need anything heavier," said Maritza. "I've already gained three pounds since I came back home."

"They're well placed and that's what counts. Some wine? André has the importing concession here and brings in excellent French vintages."

"Would you think me bold if I ordered brandy and soda? I acquired a liking for it while I was in England."

"I can't imagine a better choice for a nightcap," said Richard Mann. "That about covers the order, François—unless the countess would like something else."

The omelet was delicious, and as light as Richard Mann had

promised. The brandy was French, which was all that need be said. Maritza found that she was both hungry and thirsty, so both disappeared with considerable rapidity. Finally she pushed her plate aside and François refilled her empty glass before removing it and the cutlery.

"You promised to explain the Greek fire to me," she reminded her companion, who had spent more time admiring her than he had eating.

"The first ingredient was sulphur. You smelled the aroma of brimstone before they closed the curtain, didn't you?"

"That was quite apparent, but how did he ignite it?"

"Several methods are used. One is metallic sodium, but that's hard to handle since it has to be kept immersed in some non-combustible liquid. In this case, I'm pretty sure he used powdered lime. Mixed with water, it reacts immediately and produces enough heat to ignite any highly combustible material."

"What was the second ingredient?"

"Probably naphtha. A small amount, concealed in a flask or bottle by those flowing sleeves, would quickly spread over the surface of the water. When lime was added, the heat formed in the chemical reaction could easily set the naphtha afire. I haven't seen a demonstration of it in years, but we were told at West Point that it was widely used in ancient times to produce fire." He smiled and reached for her hand on the table, covering it with his own. "Any more questions?"

"Not about the Greek fire, but I do have some others. How did you become associated with Mr. Benjamin?"

"I have a plantation in Louisiana that adjoins his, and visited him there occasionally when the Senate was in recess. We often indulged in religious and philosophical arguments over a bottle or two."

"But how did you become associated in the war effort?"

"I had already joined the Army when he asked me to assist him in his work but, being a soldier, I couldn't legally be assigned to his staff. He therefore asked me to function sub rosa, so to speak."

"An ideal arrangement for a secret agent, but what is his

connection with the government and the war? In general, Jews aren't that highly regarded in the South."

"Benjamin is. The people of Louisiana sent him to the United States Senate."

"I'd forgotten that," she admitted.

"Does he arouse any prejudices in you?"

"If I had any, which I don't think I do, I lost them when I went to Paris."

"Before this war is over, you're liable to see Judah P. Benjamin play a very important part indeed in the Confederacy." Mann was entirely serious now. "Look how easily he talked you into becoming a secret agent."

"Of which you don't approve. Will you tell me why?"

"Spying is better left to people like our top agent in Washington, Mrs. Rose O'Neal Greenhow. She moves in some of the highest social circles there and specializes in extracting information from Union officers, either out of bed or in."

"She sounds like a very effective agent." Maritza's eyes twinkled. "Why should you be so concerned with her morals?"

"I'm not. She can sleep with whomever and wherever she wishes, but I don't want her name linked with yours when you get to Washington, so steer clear of her."

"Don't you want me to be an effective spy?" Maritza teased but he was not amused.

"I want you to stay alive so we can be married when all this is over."

Maritza drank deeply from her glass before answering, and felt a sudden warmth in her body, both from the alcohol and from the unexpected proposal by the handsome man sitting across from her and still holding her hand. In no more than ten days she remembered suddenly, two of the most attractive men she'd ever known had asked her to marry them. Moreover, she'd taken one of them into her bed and, she was sure, would find Richard Mann quite as effective a lover as Penn Darrow had been. But it had been duty, not the need for husband, lover, or both that had brought her back to the South. And, as she'd told Celestina, she was convinced that her own role, for the moment at least, lay in another direction.

"You're handsome enough to turn any girl's head but I have a job to do, as you do," she told her companion. "Until that is finished we can hardly think of marriage."

"Of love then?"

"Loving you would be easy, Richard." Her fingers closed upon his in a warm gesture of affection. "In fact, it will be hard to resist falling in love with you. But we can't work together very effectively, as we're obviously going to have to do part of the time, if we let emotions interfere with our relationship."

"Interfere?" His voice was harsh. "I'm not made of stone, Maritza."

"Nor I," she admitted. "In fact, I've already had too much brandy to be able to think intelligently. You'd better take me to my room before I do something very unladylike, such as revealing that I'm half drunk."

"We'll go in a moment," he told her, "as soon as I've given you the instructions Mr. Benjamin wants you to have."

"Then I won't be seeing him again?"

"Perhaps, but I shall be away for the next several weeks. Now listen carefully; I'd write them down but I'd rather not put anything on paper that might be found on your person when you cross the border at Alexandria. When arrangements are completed, probably in a couple of weeks, you will board a train going north on the Atlanta & West Point Railroad. You and Celestina will occupy a drawing room, coming out as little as possible. She can bring your food from the dining car, if you're lucky enough to find one attached to the train. If not, she can get off to purchase food at station restaurants."

"It sounds exciting." Maritza's eyes had begun to sparkle.

"Believe me, it won't be. The tracks are poor, the connections bad, and the train will be very crowded. You're to keep out of sight as much as possible, too, until you reach Manassas Junction."

"Why not Richmond? I've been to Manassas and it's a horrible place."

"Mr. Benjamin doesn't want you seen in Richmond. Officially, you will be the French correspondent for *Le Pays* on your way to an assignment in Washington. The brief trip you've just made through Confederate territory was solely to enable you to write a report to your editor on both the Northern and Southern capitals and their governments."

"I've already started doing that."

"Good. We'll include your dispatches in the diplomatic pouches for Paris being sent to Charleston."

"What will I do in Washington?"

"Assume the duties of a foreign correspondent. Find a place to live, present your credentials to Mr. Seward, Secretary of State, and to the French minister, Henri Mercier, whom Benjamin tells me you already know. Write as much as you can about what is happening to Washington, just the way an intelligent and perceptive woman would see it, but be very careful not to give the impression that you're spying, or even that you are a fervent sympathizer with the South."

"Suppose the Union censors won't let my writings go to Monsieur Claudet in Paris? They're not likely to, you know, if I criticize the Union."

"Censorship in Washington is widespread, so your reports are certain to be read. Anything derogatory to the Union will be removed, so you will make two copies exactly alike. One goes to the censors, where, if you're as frank as we hope you will be, it will be cut to pieces. The other, intact, you will mail to a Georgetown address, from which it will find its way to us in Richmond, giving us a true picture of what's happening in Washington. The uncensored copy will be sent to your editor in Paris, who will recognize its truth. By all means, name names, dates, and places. I'm sure I don't have to tell you how to worm that information out of Union officials and officers."

Maritza pretended to be serious. "If I have any trouble, I can always use the same method your Mrs. Greenhow uses—"

"Like hell you will!" he exploded, then, seeing her smile, realized he was being teased. "You don't even have to know the real identity of the person you will mail copies of your dispatches to. That way you can't be connected with any Confederate agents."

"Is that all I have to do? It sounds boring."

"I imagine listening to most men talk is boring to any intelligent woman, but you'll be our sharp ears and keen eyes in Washington. That's something we need badly, so leave the cloak and dagger work to Mrs. Greenhow and her helpers. One other thing, protest sharply every now and then to Mr. Seward about the way his censors are cutting the heart out of what you're writing. We want you to be genuinely what you make yourself out to be, an American-born French subject, living in Washington with her faithful maidservant, a former slave she freed long ago."

"How long ago?"

"Shortly after you went to France as a bride—for the record. The manumission papers will be given to you for Celestina tomorrow, as soon as they can be treated so as to appear about five years old."

"You think of everything, don't you?" Maritza asked on a genuine note of admiration, but Richard Mann shook his head.

"I wish I could claim that responsibility; it might give me more stature in your eyes. The truth is, Mr. Benjamin worked this plan out and I've been opposed to it all along."

"Why?"

"I told you why just now," he said almost angrily. "Because I love you and want to marry you *if*—no, *when*—this is over. Now I'd better take you upstairs to your room before love gets the best of my patriotism and I tell Judah P. Benjamin to go to hell."

XI

Virginia seceded from the Union on May 23, 1861. On the twenty-seventh Maritza boarded a train for Manassas Junction, Virginia, with her baggage, plus a passport signed by Jefferson Davis, who traveled on the same train. The passport permitted her to leave the territory of the Confederate States of America at her own request as a neutral correspondent for the French journal, *Le Pays*. Celestina needed no such passport; the certificate of manumission she carried insured her undisputed right to cross the lines as a free slave.

BOOK THREE

WASHINGTON

I

"Countess LeClerc! What an unexpected pleasure!" Maritza looked up from the breakfast table in the dining room of the Willard Hotel in Washington to see the tall form of William H. Russell standing beside her table, smiling warmly.

"Mr. Russell, how nice to see you again. Won't you join me?"

Maritza had given the invitation, shrewdly realizing that she could probably get a lot of information about Washington from the highly observant British correspondent. He had been there much of the time since Lincoln's election, she knew, along with trips to Montgomery and elsewhere in the South to study the developing situation.

"I've already breakfasted," said Russell, "but I *would* enjoy another cup of coffee with you, if you don't mind the intrusion."

"Be my guest." A waiter had appeared at Maritza's elbow and she gave him the order. "Are you staying at Willard's too?"

"Heavens, no!" Russell repressed a faint shudder of distaste. "I've been entertaining one of Mr. Seward's secretaries at breakfast; that's the cheapest way these days to get an appointment with the Secretary of State. As unofficial dean of the newspaper correspondents covering this war, I was given the task of arranging a conference with the Secretary."

"Even as cold a man as I'm told Mr. Seward is could hardly turn down the London *Times*."

Russell shrugged deprecatingly. "I must say I'm surprised to find a discerning person like yourself at the Willard. Most of the politicians and war profiteers in Washington congregate here, but you certainly have no place among actresses and the like who always turn up at times like these."

"All the more reason why a female newspaper correspondent should be here," Maritza said, laughing. "They tell me more military and political activities are discussed at Willard's Bar than in the White House or the War Department. Actually, I'm only staying a few days, though, until rooms for me and my maid can be vacated at Monsieur Cruchet's establishment nearby."

"Cruchet's! I applied to him for accommodation as soon as I arrived in Washington but was told no rooms were available."

"My husband and I stayed there several years ago, when we toured much of the United States," Maritza explained. "Besides, these rooms were vacated rather suddenly, when a member of the Peace Commission from Virginia had to leave after his state voted to secede in the recent referendum."

"Your being a French countess no doubt influenced Monsieur Cruchet too." Russell shrugged. "Well, *c'est la guerre.*"

"Where are you staying?" Maritza was pouring coffee from a steaming fresh pot for the Englishman.

"I've taken rooms on what's called Newspaper Row, around the corner on Fourteenth Street. They're not elaborate but being there puts me near the newspaper offices and particularly the Willard Bar. As you said just now, that's where most of the war's been fought so far. How did you like Richmond?"

"I didn't stop there," said Maritza. "When I left Paris, Monsieur Claudet, my editor, instructed me to visit both capitals. Naturally, I came on to Washington as soon as I learned that the United States had invaded Virginia by seizing Alexandria and the heights at Arlington. Incidentally, too, Mr. Jefferson Davis was on the same train with my maid and myself as far as Lynchburg."

"Is it true that he rode in the coach, like a second-class passenger? I was told that but I could hardly believe it."

"I didn't see him myself, but enthusiastic crowds greeted Mr. Davis at every stop. I've rarely seen people worship a political leader the way those in the South worship him."

"Certainly he's getting a considerably warmer reception than the Union adherents give Mr. Lincoln," Russell observed. "When he came to Washington from Illinois to be inaugurated in March, Mr. Lincoln's cohorts persuaded him to sneak into Washington the back way. You should have seen what some newspaper cartoonists did with that."

"I saw a lot of military activity on the other side of the Potomac, when I crossed the lines at Alexandria a few days ago," said Maritza. "Is it true that General McDowell is preparing to invade Virginia and seize Richmond?"

"Seize Richmond?" Russell's laugh was sarcastic. "Nobody with any knowledge of military strategy can understand why the Virginians didn't seize Washington as they did Harpers Ferry less than a week after Fort Sumter surrendered. The whole city was defended then by less than a thousand regulars and militia, while the roads south were clogged for miles with people and their possessions fleeing into Virginia."

"Could the South still take Washington?"

"Possibly, now that General Beauregard is in command of what the Confederates call the Alexandria Line. The six weeks since Fort Sumter fell has made a lot of difference in military strength, though, and I don't believe even Beauregard is rash enough to risk defeat this early in the war."

Maritza had about decided she'd extracted as much information from the Englishman as she could attempt at one sitting, when a sudden inspiration struck her.

"I understand that newspaper correspondents from other countries are supposed to present their credentials to the Secretary of State," she said. "If it's as hard to get an appointment with Secretary Seward as you say—"

Russell rose to the bait. "I'd be honored to present you to the Secretary tomorrow morning, Countess."

"The honor would be mine, Mr. Russell. After all, you are without a doubt the most famous correspondent now in Washington."

"From a foreign country, probably yes," Russell conceded modestly. "Horace Greeley is here from New York but he is a fiery opponent of the South and sounds off at will. I understand Mr. Lincoln and Mr. Seward would be happy for him to remain

in New York and edit the *Tribune*." The Englishman rose.
"Thank you for the coffee and the company, Countess. Shall I
call for you here tomorrow at, say, ten o'clock?"

"I'll be ready," Maritza assured him. "When I'm settled in at
Monsieur Cruchet's, you must have dinner with me there."

"I should be honored." Mr. Russell bowed deeply. "When
you write Claudet again, by all means remember me to him."

"I'm going to dinner tonight at the home of the French minister, but I shall be writing Monsieur Claudet tomorrow."

"Don't expect what you write to pass the censors, if you say
anything good about Jefferson Davis," Russell warned. "I've
complained more than once about censorship here in Washington but it seems to grow worse rather than better."

"Perhaps I can write so Monsieur Claudet will read between
the lines. Many French words have several meanings and he is
experienced enough as an editor to recognize them."

"I may have to resort to asking you to translate my dispatches into French before they go to London then," Russell
said somewhat ruefully. "Not many Americans understand
French here in the North, so you might get what I'm trying to
say through without the censors realizing what is being said."

"French was my first language when I was growing up.
That's another reason why I'm looking forward to dining with
the Merciers tonight."

"The minister has a lovely new home in Georgetown; I've
been to dinner there once since I came to Washington. But
don't make the mistake of going unescorted, Washington after
dark is like a jungle. I'm almost afraid to walk late at night
from the Willard Bar to my rooms around the corner on Fourteenth Street."

"The minister is sending a carriage for me and several other
guests, so I'm sure we'll be safe. *Bon jour* until tomorrow, Mr.
Russell."

II

The carriage that was to take Maritza to the new home of Henri Mercier arrived at the Willard just as the nightly five o'clock exodus from the government offices to the bar was in full swing. It had rained that afternoon and the constant stream of conveyances of every kind—hansom cabs, buggies, surreys, hacks, and an occasional Army officer on horseback—had already churned Pennsylvania Avenue, which the hotel faced, into a sea of mud. The rain had accomplished one good effect, however. The so-called "city canal," a somnolent stream bordering the opposite side of the street and normally polluting the air with an effluvium of garbage, sewage, and all kinds of refuse, no longer gave the air a palpable stink.

Maritza's own passage across the lobby against the tide of men flowing toward the bar was accompanied by turning heads, soft whistles of appreciation, and a few ribald compliments. Outside at the mounting block, a coachman in livery handed her ceremoniously into a carriage. Closing the door, he climbed back to the box and the carriage rolled away, to jeering comments from the passengers of an omnibus disgorging its human contents in front of the hotel.

Crossing Rock Creek on a stone bridge into Georgetown, Maritza felt as if she was entering another world. Staid houses of red brick lined the streets, each with its border of beds in which snowdrops, hyacinths, lilacs, and other flowers were in full bloom. Even though darkness was falling, children were playing everywhere, something they wouldn't have dared to do, she was sure, in Washington itself.

The other occupants of the carriage were a secretary from the French Embassy and his wife, and a young newspaper cartoonist from New York named Thomas Nast, who had already achieved considerable fame with his caricatures. The New York *Herald,* Nast told Maritza with a sneer that seemed to be his perpetual expression, once characterized Georgetown as "the abode of a very slow and respectable people, who cool themselves during the hot weather by the delightful remembrance that they are of gentle blood." Most of them, he also said, were sympathetic to the South.

"I gather from your tone that you don't approve of such people, Mr. Nast," she said.

"I came here as an emigrant from Germany with my mother when I was six years old," he said. "Would you expect me to bow down and worship people who live on the labor of their slaves and give nothing in return?"

"I wonder if you include French aristocrats in that category, Mr. Nast?"

"If they deserve to be there," said the young artist loftily.

"Then you can count me out," she told him. "My ancestors came to Louisiana when it was a French colony. They came from Canada—Acadia, in fact—having left there because they refused to swear allegiance to England when the French lost Canada."

"But you do have a title."

"By marriage, to a French nobleman noted for his fairness to the tenants of his estate. When we visited New England several years later, I saw children of twelve and less laboring at looms and spinning jennies. You can take my word that they were treated far worse than workers on my husband's estate."

"Didn't you own slaves before your marriage?"

"Only one. She grew up as my companion, was educated at the same schools, and enjoyed the same privileges that I did. I gave her a certificate of manumission five years ago but she refused to leave me."

"That doesn't change the fact that she was a slave."

"No, but she remained so by her own choice. I imagine you studied American history when you were in school?"

"I did."

"Then you know that, even after the importation of slaves was forbidden in the United States in 1809, New England shipmasters, whom you appear to admire, continued to smuggle them in for many years afterward."

The coach stopped just then before a fine brick house in Georgetown and the coachman jumped down to open the car-

riage door for the visitors. Henri Mercier himself stood in the
open doorway to greet his guests. Young for such a high diplomatic position, he was tall and handsome, with flaring side
whiskers worn in the latest Washington custom and impeccable
manners.

"My dear Countess, you honor us with your presence," he
said, bowing over her hand. "I remember well the kindness of
yourself and your late husband when we were guests at Château
LeClerc several years ago."

Cécile Mercier echoed her husband's warm greetings. Slight
of stature, she was lovely and exquisitely French.

The house was furnished in exquisite taste, Maritza saw as
the other four guests were being introduced. A rather statu-
esque blond girl with a distinct German accent had obviously
been invited as a dinner companion for Thomas Nast, for she
already knew him and they started speaking German immediately. The military attaché from the British Embassy, a brigadier in the Royal Horse Artillery named Cecil Twombley, and
his wife were typically English with manners as impeccable as
their speech. The fourth guest was a United States Army officer
in uniform, Major Thaddeus Morton. Quite handsome, he appeared to be about forty-five, with a sprinkling of gray at his
temples giving him a very distinguished appearance, and the insignia of the 1st U. S. Cavalry at collar and shoulder.

"Major Morton is an aide-de-camp to Brigadier General
Irvin McDowell, commanding the troops defending Washing-
ton," Mercier explained as the major bowed and lifted
Maritza's hand to his lips.

"With such handsome officers to protect us, I am sure we are
in no danger of the invasion I've been hearing so much about
since I arrived." Maritza spoke graciously, realizing that, if she
could gain an admirer in such a high military position, she
might very well derive considerable help in carrying out the
purpose for which Judah P. Benjamin had persuaded her to
come to Washington.

"I am honored, Countess." Major Morton was obviously as
much at home in the parlor as he was in camp.

"The major is a widower," Cécile whispered to Maritza.

"Don't lose your heart to him. He's a connoisseur of women but drops his conquests once they make the mistake of succumbing to him."

"I'll remember that," Maritza promised. "We had many such in France."

When entertaining guests from Washington who must return that evening, residents of Georgetown served dinner early. Little time was wasted in small talk, therefore, and the group soon repaired to the dining room. Although the service—particularly the wine—was exquisitely French, the food itself was American. Somewhat to Maritza's surprise, it was also distinctly Southern, with terrapin à la Maryland as the main dish.

"You should have invited General Winfield Scott, Mr. Minister," Major Morton said with a smile when he saw the dish being brought to the table. "He maintains that 'tarrapin,' as he calls it, is the best food vouchsafed by Providence to man."

"The general is an epicure," Henri Mercier agreed. "I understand that he lives at Cruchet's solely because of the excellent table."

"I'm moving to Cruchet's in a few weeks," said Maritza.

"Then you're in for a series of gastronomic treats, Countess," said Morton. "Not even President Lincoln himself sets a better table than Monsieur Cruchet."

"Is it true that General Scott is almost an invalid?" Maritza asked. "He was a national hero when I was a girl in Mobile and New Orleans during the Mexican War."

"He still is, to the rank and file of people," Morton assured her, "but it was General McDowell who ordered the march across the river into Virginia that took Washington from under the mouths of rebel cannon—with no encouragement from the general-in-chief."

"I was reading in the New York *Times* a few days ago about the number of veteran young officers of the Mexican War, who are now playing a prominent part in this one," said Henri Mercier. "General Robert E. Lee was especially singled out."

"Is it true that Lee was offered the post of general-in-chief of the Union forces?" the British brigadier inquired.

"It's true all right," said Morton. "And there lies the tragedy —for both the North and the South."

"Why do you say that?" Maritza asked.

"As general-in-chief, Lee would have brought experience, intelligence, and a rare degree of military skill to our side. Now he will bring the same thing to the Confederacy—"

"Has he been made general-in-chief by the South?" the English diplomat asked.

"Not yet, but Jefferson Davis knows Lee's ability. They not only served together in the Army in Mexico, but Davis was Secretary of War during the Buchanan Administration before President Lincoln was inaugurated. Davis is certain to know Lee's qualifications even better than Governor Letcher of Virginia and the first thing Letcher did, when Lee resigned from our Army, was to put him in command of the Virginia military forces."

"Isn't General Lee a slaveholder?" Thomas Nast asked with the sneering note that always seemed to be in his voice whenever he spoke of a Southerner.

"Not at all," said Morton. "Lee is opposed to slavery and doesn't own any slaves himself. Like many in the South, though, he's a Virginian first and a United States citizen second, so when the Confederacy is defeated Lee will lose everything he owns. In fact he's already lost the beautiful home in Arlington that General McDowell is now using as headquarters. If it had happened to anyone else, we of the Union might be jubilant but those officers and men who served under Lee can only be sad."

"No matter who he is and how high his position"—the voice of Thomas Nast was hot with the indignation of youth—"Lee is a traitor and deserves what he receives. Where the Union made a mistake was in not arresting him the minute he refused to become general-in-chief, depriving the North of a traitor and the South of a leader in one fell swoop."

"I'm afraid you would have had to arrest nearly half the Senate and much of the population of Washington, if you'd touched Robert E. Lee, Mr. Nast." Morton's voice was sharp. "Those of us who know the Southern officers who chose secession as a matter of principle have no less respect for them than we had before they left the Army. Actually, many promising officers had already resigned their Army commissions for civil employment because for the past ten years nobody who was not a favorite of Scott's received a promotion. I could cite you men like McClellan, Sherman, Ulysses S. Grant, and others—to say nothing of an eccentric major named Thomas Jonathan Jackson, who distinguished himself in Mexico, yet resigned to become a teacher at the Virginia Military Academy."

"And almost put a noose around Washington by shutting down the Baltimore & Ohio Railroad at Harpers Ferry," the British attaché observed. "Do you know how long the Confederacy can hold Harpers Ferry and block the B. & O.?"

"They're not holding it," said Morton. "Jackson was recently replaced by General Joseph E. Johnston and on our side Major General Robert Patterson is already advancing into the Shenandoah Valley of Virginia from Pennsylvania. With McClellan moving east through the Alleghenies, Johnston and Jackson will soon be driven south down the valley. If Patterson and McClellan move fast enough, McDowell may not even have to carry out the attack on Manassas Junction President Lincoln is urging. A sweep eastward from the Shenandoah Valley through the mountain passes of the Blue Ridge could put strong Union forces on Beauregard's left flank and endanger Richmond, hopefully ending the war in the first battle."

"Is that what McDowell plans to do, Major?" Maritza pretended complete ignorance.

"The rebels have been massing troops and the matériel of war at Manassas in large quantities," said Morton. "Obviously, Beauregard feels that the large forces he's concentrating against Washington at Manassas Junction are the only barrier between McDowell and the capture of Richmond and Jefferson Davis by the Union."

"As I remember it, when my husband and I visited Washington several years ago, we couldn't even get a decent cup of coffee in the station restaurant at Manassas."

"You'll soon be hearing the name much more often," Morton promised, "but I can't say more."

"Everybody knows McDowell has set Manassas Junction as

his target for the first real battle of the war." The British diplomat was already mellow on French wines. "If he throws green
levies against natural fighters like the Southern militia companies that took Harpers Ferry almost without a shot, it could
be the biggest mistake of his career."

"May I remind you, sir, that the Federal garrison at Harpers
Ferry was very small and had already been ordered to evacuate
the place after destroying the munitions factories," said Morton, a little stiffly.

"What is the news from Paris?" Cécile Mercier asked
Maritza, breaking the momentary tension between the military
men.

"I'm afraid I know as little about that as you do," Maritza
confessed. "I was in England for several months after I gave up
the château to my husband's nephew, Philippe LeClerc. We
came to America directly from Liverpool."

"We?" Madame Mercier asked.

"I was accompanied by my companion, Celestina. She's been
with me since I was twelve."

"Getting back to the coming attack on Manassas, Major
Morton." The English brigadier was insistent on discussing the
war. "How long will it take Northern textile factories to run
out of cotton, with none coming from the South because of
your blockade?"

"The blockade is little more than a name," Maritza interposed. "The ship I was traveling on ran into a storm and was
driven quite far south. The captain chose to make Mobile, Alabama, his port of call, but we had very little trouble entering
the harbor."

"A lovely city, Mobile," said the brigadier's wife. "We were
there for a week when we first came to America and I could
have stayed a year."

"The docks of Mobile were crowded with cotton," Maritza
continued. "I was told that a great deal of it is already being
shipped to Nassau, Bermuda, and even to Halifax in Nova Scotia through the Union blockade."

"Where it is transferred to British ships for the spinning jennies and looms of Manchester," Major Morton said somewhat pointedly.

"All in accordance with international law, Major," said the English brigadier affably. "Let me remind you, too, that U.S. merchant vessels often load cotton in British territory, then haul it to Boston and even New York, where it is being turned into both gray and blue uniforms."

"I heard that rumor, too, but found it somewhat difficult to believe," said Maritza.

"It's true enough," Major Morton admitted. "Yankee manufacturers and merchants are not above selling gray uniforms to speculators who resell them to the Confederacy—and not just uniforms either."

"It seems that Yankee manufacturers are as shrewd as what I've heard called 'Philadelphia lawyers,'" Cécile Mercier remarked. "Won't this practice be stopped, once the United States builds up its Navy?"

"Slowed, madam, but not stopped," said Morton. "I was stationed for a while at Fort Fisher, one of the fortifications guarding the channels leading into the Cape Fear River and Wilmington, North Carolina. A swift Confederate blockade runner can easily sneak into the river under cover of darkness and be safe inside from even the largest Union battleship."

"What's the answer then?" Brigadier Twombley asked.

"Seize the coastal areas of Virginia and North Carolina," said Morton. "Norfolk is already in our hands and, if an expedition now fitting out against the North Carolina coast is successful, two major rebel ports will be closed with more to come later."

"Charleston?" Maritza asked with a smile.

"Charleston later, Countess."

"With Fort Sumter sitting squarely in the center of the channel and now in Confederate hands, that one won't be easy," said Brigadier Twombley.

"At West Point we studied the best ways to seize the most important ports along the Atlantic coast against just such a situation as has arisen," Morton continued. "Charleston was chosen because taking it would appear to be more difficult than any of the others."

"Surely the answer wasn't a frontal assault on a powerful fort," said Brigadier Twombley.

"No," said Morton. "We have other plans."

Maritza wanted desperately to ask the point on the coast selected for the land invasion but dared not do it for fear of revealing undue interest. Besides, she didn't want the talkative major to get the idea that she was as smart as she was beautiful and stop talking so freely about military secrets. Fortunately, Brigadier Twombley's curiosity had also been aroused.

"With Norfolk too far away and Wilmington probably still in Southern hands, Major, where would you find a port you could invade?"

"Port Royal, South Carolina."

"Never heard of it," said the Englishman.

"The town is of no consequence, but the sound lies about a third of the way from Savannah to Charleston," Morton explained. "It has the most capacious natural harbor along the southeastern Atlantic coast and could hold our entire Navy twice, with some to spare. With Port Royal as a major Union base, both Savannah and Charleston would be at our mercy. Then, whole fleets of blockade runners could be bottled up in port and destroyed, if they dared to make a run."

"Too bad your planning board didn't pay more attention to the defenses of Washington," said Twombley. "For a few days after the Southerners opened hostilities by firing on Fort Sumter, I could have seized your capital with a single regiment of British grenadiers."

"I don't doubt that, sir," said Morton. "But President Lincoln was still hoping to avert an actual war."

"Do you think the President will be as energetic in prosecuting the war as he was in working for peace?" Cécile Mercier asked.

"Absolutely," said Henri Mercier. "My personal preference would be to see the South allowed to go its way as a separate nation, with peace between the two halves. But with Jefferson

Davis insisting upon independence for the Confederacy as an absolute provision in any treaty—the way he has stated in the newspapers—I think you will find Lincoln fully as adamant in crushing the South."

"The main question," said the English officer's wife, "is can he do it?"

"He can, madam, take my word for it," said Morton. "The manufacturing capacity of the North exceeds that of the South at least ten to one, roughly the ratio of the population. When both are finally thrown against an essentially agricultural economy with few facilities for manufacturing military equipment and supplies, and a large part of the population composed of Negro slaves, there can be only one answer."

III

Celestina was asleep on a cot provided for her comfort by the hotel. She was wearing a flimsy cotton nightgown and nothing else, the early June night being hot and sultry. "You look like what you ate tonight gave you indigestion," she said, yawning as she helped Maritza undress. "What was wrong?"

"Nothing. The food was excellent and so was the wine and the company. I even met an aide-de-camp to General Irvin McDowell—a Major Morton."

"Married, fat, and bald?"

"Forty-five, handsome, and a widower."

"Then what are you doing here? They tell me Washington is full of small restaurants where a couple can go after the theater or a dinner party for supper and a *rendezvous à deux* in a small but very private dining room."

"I'm not interested in *rendezvous à deux*." Maritza slid a sheer nightgown over her head and let its folds drop to her ankles. "Don't forget why we're in Washington."

"*That* worries me. Everywhere I go people are saying the Yankees will whip Johnny Reb—as they call the Southerners—this summer and hang Jefferson Davis into the bargain. Where will we be if somebody blabs about your selling those rifles to the Confederate government in Mobile?"

"We may have to leave the country—at least I may—but you're free, so nobody will bother you. In fact, the smart thing for you would be to go to New York or Boston, pass as white, and maybe even marry yourself a rich husband."

"It wouldn't work," said Celestina.

"Why not?"

"Remember that monk named Mendel whose writings caused such a stir in Paris?"

"What does Mendel have to do with you?"

"I could pass for white; plenty of foreigners in America have skins darker than mine. But suppose I married that rich man you're talking about and had a baby that turned out to be coal black. It could, you know, if that monk's theories are fact."

"They're true enough. Étienne repeated some of Gregor Mendel's experiments in heredity with sweet peas in our garden, and everything turned out exactly according to the monk's theories. There's nothing to keep you from becoming the mistress of some rich white man, though. You certainly know how to keep from having babies, so nobody would ever suspect."

"That would mean losing André."

"Do you love him enough to be the wife of a chef all your life?"

"How do I know whether I love him or not? All I've done is go to bed with him a dozen times or so—"

"A dozen?" Maritza's eyebrows rose. "As I remember it, you were out with him only a few times."

"But what a *fréquentation* every one of them was." Celestina's eyes kindled with the memory. "I get all warm inside just thinking about them."

"Keep your memories warm then," said Maritza as she got into bed and pulled up the sheet. "What do you think about Washington?"

"*C'est une contrariété*—a slattern taking on airs."

"What makes you say that?"

"The Capitol has no dome. The main street is a mudhole

with an open sewer beside it. Tonight I went to a restaurant named Harvey's—"

"Not walking, I hope."

"I might as well have been. The iron tires of the omnibus jarred me so much going over the cobblestones on Pennsylvania Avenue, I thought my *derrière* would be black and blue by the time I got to the hotel." Celestina threw up her hands in a typically Gallic gesture. "And crowded! *Nom d'un nom!* I thought I would have to eat standing up until a gentleman shared his table with me—and propositioned me afterward."

"What else did you expect, a woman eating alone in one of Washington's most popular restaurants? At least it was a compliment."

"Compliment be damned! He offered me two dollars!" Celestina's indignation momentarily overcame her ability to speak. "Two dollars? What kind of a *prostituée* did he think I was?"

"I hear that Washington is full of whores. He was probably just offering you the going price."

"Well, *I* didn't go," Celestina spluttered. "In New Orleans—or Mobile—Southern gentlemen know how to appreciate women of color like myself."

"You're free here," Maritza reminded her. "You can go where you wish—and associate with whomever you wish."

"*Quelle tromperie*—what a fraud! The Yankees say they're fighting to free the Negroes, yet they treat us like dirt. There's even talk of conscripting black men and setting them to fight against the South."

"Where did you hear that?" If true, this information could be valuable to Richard Mann and Judah Benjamin.

"In the restaurant tonight. You can bet where the black troops will be put, too—at the very front of the battle when General McDowell leads the march on Manassas and Richmond."

"Did anyone say when the attack would be launched?"

"Not exactly—but a drunk corporal was offering to bet they'd take Richmond before the end of July."

"That could mean McDowell is almost ready to move."

Maritza sat up in bed. "I wonder how I could find out the exact date?"

"I can tell you how," said Celestina. "This major—what did you say his name is?"

"Morton."

"If he's an aide to McDowell, he must know what's in the general's mind. All you have to do is get him in bed and *voilà!*—he tells all."

"I'm not selling my favors—"

"It's still a lot better than giving them away," said Celestina practically. "This time you'd be serving your country—*une fréquentation patriotique,* so to speak."

"The answer's still no."

Celestina shrugged. "Everybody's talking about when the Army is going to invade Virginia anyway, so we'll probably hear some soldier blab out the time, like that corporal tonight."

An idea suddenly struck Maritza so forcibly that she wondered why she hadn't thought of it before. "This soldier you heard boasting, Tina," she said. "Did he say anything about which direction the Army was going to take in the attack against Richmond?"

"He kept talking about Manassas, but that place is a desolation. You must remember it from when we came through on the train less than three weeks ago."

"Say that again, please."

"What?"

"About Manassas being a desolation."

"You're bound to remember the place. Why the sudden interest?"

"Everybody's talking about it just as you said, so I wonder why?"

Celestina shrugged and lay back on her cot. "I guess because they've got to capture it before they go on to take Richmond. Besides, from what that corporal was saying, the South has a lot of troops there."

"When you find something bigger than you want to climb over ahead of you, the sensible way is to go around it," said Maritza, as if talking to herself.

"Any fool knows that. Good night."

It was a long time before Maritza was able to go to sleep. If General Irvin McDowell was as smart as Major Thaddeus Morton thought he was, he'd be clever enough to plant the idea in the minds of as many people as he could that he was going to launch a frontal attack on the South through the Manassas region. On the map, however, Maritza had noted that the rail junction itself lay almost directly west of Washington, so McDowell could actually be concocting a red herring to keep the Southern military commanders thinking his goal was Manassas. Meanwhile, he could be preparing a plan to drive directly south toward Richmond, ending the war suddenly by seizing the capital of the Confederacy with its leaders, leaving the major portion of the troops in eastern Virginia hanging on the vine.

That knowledge could be very important to Richard Mann and Judah P. Benjamin, she realized, too, but she had no way of getting the information to them. Richard Mann had cautioned her not to be seen in the neighborhood of Mrs. Rose Greenhow's home, much less communicate with her. He had also been equally emphatic in warning her to use the Georgetown address to a pseudonymous Jeremiah Smith only for mailing copies of her dispatches in French to *Le Pays,* after turning over the original to the Federal censors to be forwarded to Monsieur Claudet in Paris. Unable to arrive at any conclusion to the problem, she finally drifted off to sleep.

IV

Maritza had suggested to William H. Russell that they meet for breakfast in the main dining room of the Willard before going to the State Department. She was just being seated by the headwaiter when the British journalist arrived.

"A thousand pardons, Countess." Seating himself, he tucked a spotless napkin under his chin. "Have you ordered?"

"Not yet. I just arrived."

"Then allow me to recommend the Virginia ham and eggs. The chef here has many deficiencies but that isn't one of them."

"I'll take your recommendation," said Maritza. "With coffee, of course."

"Coffee, by all means, but I don't know what I'm going to do when I go back to England," said Russell. "I've been away so long that tea doesn't even taste right any more. By the way, I just finished a story that will interest you. It's about a shy little lady of around forty, a Miss Clara Barton. She has become the apotheosis of Florence Nightingale in caring for the needs of the troops." William Russell snorted indignantly. "Can you imagine? The U. S. Army medical service is called the Sanitary Commission and their male nurses are often too drunk even to watch over patients."

"Is Miss Barton going to take over?" Maritza asked.

"Hardly that; a Miss Dorothea Dix seems to be in charge. Miss Barton did meet the train from Baltimore bringing the troops of the 6th Massachusetts Regiment to Washington in April, though. They were badly mauled in Baltimore by an enraged populace, when they had to cross the city from one station to another, but you can be certain there'll be no repetition of that. Not with General Ben Butler in command; they're already starting to call him 'Bloody Ben.' "

"You were speaking of Miss Barton," Maritza reminded him.

"Oh yes. Since then she's been a thorn in the side of both the Quartermaster Department and the Sanitary Commission, badgering them to provide better facilities for treating the sick and administering to them herself. When my story is printed in the London *Times,* Miss Clara Barton will be a heroine everywhere."

Their food came and Mr. Russell devoted himself to demolishing it—with perfect manners but a speed of action that left Maritza, no mean trencherman herself, at the post.

"Perhaps I should bring you up to date on Secretary Seward before we go to the conference," the newspaperman said when he had pushed back his empty plate and wiped his mouth with the napkin.

"Please do."

"Seward is a consummate politician. Before the war he was a senator from New York and actually ran against Lincoln for President in the Republican primaries last year."

"If Mr. Lincoln still invited Mr. Seward to be Secretary of State in his Cabinet, doesn't that mean he has a lot of respect for him?"

"That or else the President wants to keep Seward where he can watch him closely; the Rail Splitter is an experienced politician himself. Seward worked hard to keep the Union from being broken, even proposing an amendment to the Constitution, after South Carolina seceded, forbidding Congress from interfering with slavery in the states. When it became evident that war was inevitable, though, he gave up the attempt to bring the two irreconcilables together. Make no mistake about it, Countess, William H. Seward is the cleverest man in the Lincoln Administration and also the most powerful." Russell rose to his feet and moved around the table to pull back her chair. "Shall we go? Mr. Seward demands punctuality in those to whom he grants the privilege of questioning him."

As they went down the steps leading to Pennsylvania Avenue a short man with a face like a weasel lifted his bowler hat politely and continued on into the hotel—but not before his somewhat beady eyes had swept Maritza from her stylish Parisian hat to her equally stylish high-top shoes. She was accustomed to such surveys from strange men but this one was different, almost sinister in the way he scrutinized her.

"That's Allan Pinkerton, head of the Union Secret Service," said Russell. "His agents are mostly plug-uglies recruited from the ranks of barroom bouncers. They're not above picking the pockets of those they have an excuse to bludgeon in times of riot either."

"He looked harmless enough," said Maritza as Russell handed her into the hack he managed to commandeer when it discharged two men in front of the hotel.

"So does a snake asleep in the sun. Steer clear of Mr. Pinkerton—or E. J. Allen as he sometimes calls himself—my dear.

The mere fact that you write for a newspaper makes you suspect in his small mind."

"Why?"

"Honest newspaper reporters have a habit of describing things the way they actually happen, not the way some politician wants them to appear. To understand politics here in the United States, you must remember that really die-hard Republicans don't trust even Abraham Lincoln because they think he's too soft on the South. Pinkerton was in their pay back in Illinois before Lincoln came to Washington, and probably still is. I can't prove it, but I'd bet five pounds that he's responsible for the censorship we have to put up with."

"Can't you protest? The First Amendment to the United States Constitution does guarantee freedom of speech."

"This is war and President Lincoln can suspend any provision of the Constitution he doesn't like. Mark my words! When the going gets rough—and it will be with men like General Robert E. Lee leading the Southern forces—Lincoln will trample on your so-called constitutional rights with no more compunction than he would stamp on a snake."

The small red brick building housing the U. S. Department of State occupied part of the northern end of the President's Park, an unkempt open space devoted, apparently, to the deposit of refuse and growing a fine crop of weeds. In structure, the State Department was hardly distinguishable from the Treasury Building and not much different from the War and Navy Departments across from it, with the White House in between.

As the hack deposited them in front of their destination, the driver grumbling at the shortness of the ride through the mud of Fifteenth Street and the small size of the tip Russell gave him, Maritza studied the home of America's presidents. In size and appearance, it was not much more prepossessing than an ordinary country house and far less splendid than Château LeClerc. A rocking chair occupied the front portico and a tall man, whom she recognized instantly even at the distance of several hundred feet as Abraham Lincoln, was rocking gently while reading the newspaper.

"Most Washingtonians are afraid of the miasma from the swamp at the south end of the President's Park," Russell told her as he took her arm to guide her up the stairway leading to the State Department. "They think it causes the chills and fever that are prevalent here in the summer. Lincoln doesn't seem to mind, though. You can often see him sitting in that rocker just as he is now. Claims he does his best thinking there."

Inside the building they were conducted to a conference room where perhaps a dozen correspondents from leading newspapers of the world were already seated. There was a stir of interest at Maritza's appearance but she ignored it, having long since become accustomed to the effect of her startling beauty on men. A few chairs were vacant near the front, where a clerk sat before a table with a pile of notes before him. Russell pre-empted two of them.

"Your commission from Monsieur Claudet? Is it in French?" he asked Maritza.

"No. I translated it for him as he dictated it to me before signing."

"Good! The Secretary spent some time in France but his French might be less than fluent and we don't want to embarrass him."

A door opened at the back of the room and a slender man entered. His hair was gray and he looked somewhat older than his sixty years. Although dressed in what appeared to be the uniform of the Washington political corps—a gray frock coat, dark trousers, and a large cravat encircling the high, stiff collar and tied in a prodigal bow—he wasn't quite what Maritza had expected. Accustomed to the suave manner and savoir-faire of European diplomats, she recognized Seward at once as an outlander.

"Mr. Secretary." William Russell had remained standing when the others took their seats after Seward entered.

"Yes, Mr. Russell?" Seward's voice was a little hoarse, but his smile was warm. "Glad to have you back in Washington after your trip through rebel country."

"Thank you, Mr. Secretary," said Russell. "I have the honor

to present to you a new correspondent, Countess Maritza Le-Clerc of the Paris journal *Le Pays.*"

"Welcome to Washington, Countess." Maritza had risen at the sound of her name but was surprised when Seward came forward and lifted her hand, touching the glove that covered it to his lips. "I am familiar with *Le Pays* and had the pleasure of meeting the editor, Monsieur Claudet, when I was in Paris two years ago. I hope he is well."

"He is in excellent health, Mr. Secretary." Maritza handed her commission to Seward, who gave it to the clerk without reading it, as he moved back to take a position behind the table.

"My late husband owned *Le Pays,* but after his death I sold it to Monsieur Claudet." She added, "Since I was coming to America, he asked me to report on activities here from time to time, if I have your permission."

"By all means," said Seward. "Within the next few days you will be issued the credentials needed to pass through any part of the country." He smiled. "I hope you won't take up Mr. Russell's habit of crossing the lines at will, though. Our soldiers aren't accustomed to seeing Paris frocks and a colorful one such as you're wearing might be an irresistible target for a minié ball."

"I'll try to keep my place, sir," said Maritza. "My task is only to report the news to the people of France. Having so recently undergone a turbulent political crisis themselves, they can appreciate all the more what is happening on this side of the Atlantic."

"Can you tell us when actual fighting will begin, Mr. Secretary?" another of the reporters asked.

"I'm afraid you'll have to ask Mr. Cameron that." Simon Cameron, Maritza had learned since her arrival, was said to possess no other qualifications for becoming Secretary of War than having delivered the Pennsylvania delegation to Lincoln at the Republican convention.

"I can, however, tell you this much," Seward continued. "Our motto of 'Forward to Richmond' will become reality before much longer."

"Do you know of another war, Mr. Secretary, that has been fought with the capitals of the nations involved only a hundred miles apart?" another correspondent asked.

"You're using the wrong terms, sir." Seward's tone was like a whiplash. "The Confederacy is not a nation, only a group of rebel states. No country in the world has yet dignified it with the word 'nation.'"

"The capitals are still only a hundred miles apart," the questioner insisted.

"Granted, sir, which gives us the advantage of having to go only a hundred miles to show our Southern brethren the error of their ways."

"And vice versa?"

"Again, I must disagree," said the Secretary. "There was a time when the rebels could have had Washington for the taking; nobody who knows the facts denies that. The situation has changed recently, however, and even if Washington were taken, something not likely to happen, I assure you, we could retreat to Philadelphia—"

"Or Baltimore?" There was a flurry of laughter, for Baltimore had been riot-torn since the very beginning of the war and was still held in check only by Union troops under General "Bloody Ben" Butler.

"Baltimore might not be suitable." Seward's good humor was restored. "Don't forget that, even when defeat seemed inevitable with the British holding New York and Philadelphia, General Washington retreated to Valley Forge. From there, he launched the attack on Trenton that brought about a sudden change for the worse in the fortunes of war for Mr. Russell's ancestors."

Here was no fool, Maritza decided, as laughter swept the room, but a facile mind and, she suspected, no scruples when it came to accomplishing his country's ends. She decided to be very careful what she said and did where William H. Seward was concerned.

"With the rebels massing at Manassas Junction, Mr. Secretary," a Dutch reporter was speaking, "aren't they still uncomfortably close to Washington?"

"Uncomfortable for them, I'm sure, since they can never be certain just when General McDowell will descend upon them. Best for us, however, because, when the attack is launched soon, our brave soldiers will not have to tire themselves out marching before they go into battle."

"Then Manassas is going to be the first target?" Russell asked.

"You've been there recently, Mr. Russell, and you've had considerable experience with battle in the Near East. Wouldn't you destroy a strong point rather than leave it in the rear?"

"Not if I could capture the enemy capital and its leaders first by a flanking movement, before turning back to deliver the coup de grâce to the remaining enemy troops."

Seward smiled. "When it comes to such things as the coup de grâce you mentioned, Mr. Russell, I must refer you to Countess LeClerc, who is more familiar with French than I."

"It is not a term I ordinarily use, Mr. Secretary." Maritza pretended ignorance. "One thing does disturb me, however." From her reticule she took the sheet of newsprint containing the cartoon Judah P. Benjamin had given her and held it up for the Secretary and the rest of those in the room to see. "I believe Mr. Lincoln said of the South in his inaugural address, 'We are not enemies but friends.' I can't help wondering if this is what he wants the world to believe about those in the South he calls his friends?"

Secretary Seward had stiffened at the sight of the caricature of a bloated Southern planter dining on a black infant. For a moment he didn't speak, then he said softly, "Would you mind telling me where you got this abominable caricature, Countess?"

"It came from France, where I believe it appeared in a French newspaper." Maritza didn't hesitate to stretch the truth a little. "If you look carefully, you'll see the name of the artist scrawled in the corner. I have difficulty making out the name, but it looks like 'Nast.'"

"It's Nast's style all right," said one of the reporters. "I told him he was going too far but he hates the South—"

"We owe you a debt for bringing this kind of thing to our attention, Countess," said Seward. There's no place for it in war or in peace." Turning then to address the small audience, he added, "I charge you, gentlemen, and lady, to make clear to the readers in your respective countries that the United States does not fight with such weapons." Turning, he left the room, the clerk following.

"You certainly exploded a bombshell that time, Countess," said Russell as they were leaving. "I've attended a dozen or more of these conferences since March 4, when the Lincoln Administration took over the government, but I've never seen Seward show that much emotion."

"Perhaps he's a better man inside than you thought. From what I read, he did try to keep the country from breaking apart."

Outside the State Department building, Maritza put her hand on Russell's arm in a restraining gesture when he started to hail a passing hack.

"Would you mind if I walked back to the hotel?" she asked. "It's only a few blocks and the sun has already dried the streets considerably."

"Certainly, if that's your wish," said the Englishman. "Don't wander into the southern part of that cesspool they call the President's Park, though. Every few days the police find a body in there and more often than not it's a woman."

"I can look after myself." She opened her reticule to take out the small pistol which she was rarely without.

"But that's a mere toy."

Maritza laughed. "If it wasn't for perhaps starting a small riot here so close to the White House, I'd prove to you that it is not, sir. This pistol was made for me by Mr. Derringer himself, when my husband and I visited the United States a few years ago. At the range I would be using it, if someone tried to attack me, it can blow a hole in a man large enough to shove a ramrod through." She lifted the hammer gently to show him the fulminate cap on its small tube leading to the powder and ball inside the barrel, then lowered the hammer carefully.

"Put that thing away, please, Countess." Russell was visibly shaken. "I have a horror of firearms. Good day."

"Good day, Mr. Russell. Thank you for sponsoring me this morning. I will mention your kindness in my next dispatch to Monsieur Claudet."

V

It was a beautiful late June day and the fragrance from the flowers growing in the upper part of the President's Park, as well as along the edge of the sidewalk on Fifteenth Street, almost overcame the noxious miasma from what had until recently been a sewage overflow area for the City Canal. South of Pennsylvania Avenue, beyond a swampy area she had heard called the Potomac Flats, Maritza could see what was called the Long Bridge, one of three leading to Alexandria across the Potomac River. In the nearer foreground, the truncated column of the Washington Monument, only 154 feet high and far from finished, was a forlorn sacrifice to the god of war.

At the corner of Pennsylvania Avenue and Fourteenth Street, almost on the steps of the Willard Hotel, Maritza paused amidst the crowd to watch a detachment of the famed Garibaldi Guards from New York go marching by. A mélange of Germans, Croats, Hungarians, Spanish, Swiss, and a half dozen other nationalities, the Guards had been recruited and trained in New York. Commanded by Colonel d'Utassy, a former dancing master, they swaggered by in red blouses and bersaglieri hats with drooping plumes. Though a picturesque group of scoundrels, they were no more so than their own particular group of *vivandières*—loosely translated as "camp followers"— marching beside them in feathered hats, blue gowns, and red jackets.

The Garibaldi Guards were a sight to stop traffic and did, even drawing attention away from a company of the 79th New York, picturesquely attired in kilts and preceded by a file of pipers to set the rhythm. The marching troops finally passed but the row of buildings of all kinds lining Pennsylvania Avenue on the other side held no temptation to Maritza to cross over. For the most part, they made up what was called the "City Market," its booths interspersed with shacks, gambling establishments, and even a couple of brothels. The occupants of the latter brazenly perched on window sills and porch railings, calling out invitations to the soldiers marching by.

The whole outlook was infinitely depressing to Maritza, as she surveyed the mall leading to the Capitol, itself truncated by a half dome and the partially finished wings on either side where the Houses of Congress met. With the delicate beauty of spring in Paris and the Tuileries Gardens, there was no comparison between the United States capital and that of France. Instead of a city of style, beauty, and tradition like Paris, Washington was the brawling capital of a nation girding itself for war against an opponent it outnumbered more than ten to one.

She couldn't help remembering, too, the grace and charm of Richmond, Charleston, Savannah, or even Montgomery, with its faded elegance. Or wondering how those lovely cities would look and what would be left of the flower of America's young civilization after Union cannon had finished hurling the missiles of war against them and a rabble like the Garibaldi Guards and the Chicago Zouaves had torn the Southern capitals asunder.

From the window of her room at the Willard Hotel, Maritza had watched trains clogging the yards north of the capital, their cars disgorging weapons and ammunition to be hauled across the river to the battle lines on the south bank. There recently had stood the gracious mansions of Alexandria and Arlington but, set against the brawling strength of the North, the charm and elegance of the South, however admirable, betrayed an inner weakness that could be fatal, she decided. Its essence—a devotion to the past—its memories, seemed a poor defense indeed against the purely animal vigor and brashness of a country —or part of it—that could produce the Garibaldi Guards and the Chicago Zouaves, for all their lack of polish and manners. Thoroughly depressed, Maritza was turning into the lobby of the Willard when a carriage drew to a stop at the mounting block. She recognized the Mercier coachman even before Cécile called to her.

"Maritza! Wait!" Cécile opened the carriage door herself and stepped down to the block, thence to the street. With the typical hauteur of a French aristocrat, she ignored a knot of passers-by who had stopped to ogle the diplomat's coat of arms on the door of the coach or the striking pair of bays that drew it. "I've something to tell you."

"There's a tearoom around the corner." Maritza hastened to meet her distinguished visitor. "I could use a little refreshment myself."

"By all means let us go there." Cécile's English was not yet quite so fluent as her husband's. *"Je meurs de faim."* She turned back to the coachman. *"Attendez-moi, Pierre."*

The coach followed as they turned the corner and found a table in the small tearoom. Madame Mercier was fairly bubbling over with excitement.

"Prince Napoleon is coming to America in late July or August," she confided. "As yet, it is not official; Henri only received notice this morning of the visit."

Maritza didn't need further identification of the expected visitor. Something of a playboy, with an eager eye for the charms of women in the French court, the prince was a cousin of Napoleon III. Although he had no official duties connecting him with the affairs of the Quai d'Orsay, Prince Napoleon loved to travel and often served as a good-will ambassador for France's ruler. Moreover, he faithfully reported on conditions in the countries he visited, as they might affect the fortunes of France, a subject of considerable interest to so ambitious a man as the ruling member of the Napoleon family.

"Is this a diplomatic visit?" Maritza asked while they were being served.

"Oh no!" Cécile nibbled at a cruller and sipped from a cup of tea. "It's only a social visit; he has never seen America."

"Then he'll probably not go anywhere except New York and Washington."

Cécile Mercier shrugged. "You must know Prince Napoleon better than I do, Maritza. After all, you did move in the highest circles in Paris."

Maritza laughed. "If you mean I received more than one invitation to repose in the princely bed, yes, but that's hardly a distinction in Paris; the prince is noted for his democratic approach to *affaires d'amour*. Still, there's certain to be another reason for his coming here just now at the very beginning of the war."

"That's what Henri thinks, although he's had no official instructions yet from the Quai d'Orsay. He asked me to drop by the hotel here and tell you that, when the prince lands in New York, he would like you to be there with us to greet him. After all, I'm sure he would rather see a correspondent for one of our French newspapers—particularly one so lovely as you—than a lot of men in tail coats and top hats."

"I'll be happy to join the welcoming party," said Maritza. "But you'll have to give me a few days' notice."

"We should know several weeks ahead. I'm glad you're going to be with us."

VI

Celestina was washing some fine silk lingerie in their room on the top floor of the Willard when Maritza ascended in the hotel's wheezing elevator. She had just finished hanging the garments on a line she had improvised across the room where the warm breeze would quickly dry them.

"I'm going to find a laundress for our dresses and other things," she told her mistress. "One of the chambermaids gave me the address of a woman who might do them decently."

"Did you get some breakfast?"

"Ham and eggs, just like you had with Mr. Russell."

"In the dining room, I hope."

"And set all of Washington talking?" Celestina cackled derisively. "Lincoln may free the Negroes but you won't find him—or any other of the whites in Washington for that matter—sitting down to dinner with us. Speaking of *snobisme*—" She came to a spluttering halt in the midst of a stream of profanity.

"What got your dander up?" Maritza inquired and Celestina took a long breath before answering.

"One of the Garibaldi Guards, an officer no less. The door to a room on this floor was open and, thinking the chambermaid was cleaning it, I went in to ask her about a laundress. The *bâtard* slammed the door and tried to rape me, but I gave him a *coup de pied* in the crotch that will keep him from trying to rape innocent women for a week. By the way, take a look out the front window."

Maritza obeyed but could see nothing on the street except the stream of carriages, horses, and a couple of omnibuses stirring up the usual cloud of dust. Fortunately, only a small part of it rose as high as their windows along with a faint whiff of the miasma from the canal across the street.

"Not on the street; we know what's down there," said Tina. "Up in the air, across the river."

Maritza could see what Tina was referring to now. The globular object floating high above the military lines just south of the Potomac could be nothing except one of the balloons that had been popular for thrill rides when she left Paris.

"The morning paper says a Professor Lowe is trying to sell those things to the Army," said Celestina. "Claims he can float over enemy lines and report everything happening below."

"He's still got to get the messages to the troops on the ground—and that takes time."

"This professor has solved that problem, too, they say." Celestina was pouring the water she had used for washing lingerie into a slop jar and putting fresh water from the large pitcher into the washbowl for rinsing the filmy silk. "He drops a telegraph wire from the balloon to the men on the ground and reports what he sees. It's all in the paper I bought downstairs this morning."

"I haven't got time to read it now," said Maritza. "Hurry with your laundry so I can wash off some of the perspiration from the heat outside and change into a wrapper before I start writing my dispatch to *Le Pays*. By the way, Prince Napoleon is coming to America in about a month."

"I know."

"But Madame Mercier just told me!"

"I saw a piece about it in a Richmond paper this morning. They're on sale only a day late on all the Washington newsstands."

"Your buying one could throw suspicion on us," Maritza protested.

"I'm black, remember? I was once a slave, too, so I'm very much interested in how the war's going. Naturally I would buy a rebel paper in order to find out."

"I still—"

"Don't worry. The man I bought it from is an escaped slave and understood exactly what I meant. It will be helpful to see what's happening in Richmond occasionally; the paper even lists the arrival of ships loaded with cotton from the South at English and French seaports."

Maritza had been undressing but stopped suddenly. "Was the *Pride of Bristol* mentioned?"

"No, it's hardly had time to slip the blockade, get to England, and be listed in the maritime news that would come back to the South. But it will; I'd bet on Captain Darrow any day."

Maritza had to be content with that but she was heartened by the knowledge that, since Confederate and Yankee newspapers seemed to travel the hundred miles between Richmond and Washington relatively unimpeded, she would be able to follow Penn Darrow's progress through newspaper reports.

"Why do you suppose the Emperor is sending Prince Napoleon to America?" Celestina asked as she took from a closet a wrapper for Maritza to wear.

"To find out where he can gain the most: either by trying to stop the war before it really cuts down the supply of cotton shipped to France, or letting it go on until America wears itself out. Then he can do anything he wants to do in the Western Hemisphere without getting involved in a war that would probably bring England in on the other side."

"The prince's visit will be something to watch; you can bet on that." Tina stopped suddenly. "Oh, by the way. A note came for you this morning by military courier."

Maritza took the stiff envelope with her name printed across the front and opened it. Inside was a formal invitation which read:

> Brig. Gen. Irvin McDowell and his staff request the pleasure of your company at a military review and reception, July 4, 1861.
>
> > Headquarters,
> > Department of Northeastern
> > Virginia, Arlington Heights, Va.

At the bottom of the invitation was scrawled:

> Please say you'll come, I will send an escort to bring you.
> > Thaddeus Morton, Major, U.S.A.

VII

Like many other things about the Union war effort, the strategy for defending Washington itself had been based more on political expediency than on military wisdom. Immediately after the fall of Fort Sumter an old New York lawyer, Charles W. Sandford, had been put in command of the troops in the capital. For many years head of the militia in New York, Sandford had kept his militia rank of major general when he came to Washington. Brigadier General Irvin McDowell, on the other hand, though assigned the important job of attacking and capturing Richmond, had refused to take a higher rank—when promoted from that of major on May 14—lest he cause envy among fellow officers moving from the old Regular Army into the new one.

Although the command in Virginia across the Potomac was far more important and involved many more troops than the defenses of Washington itself, the disparity in rank between the two generals caused endless friction. Moreover, the troops in Washington were considerably more noted for their colorful uniforms and fancy drills than for any actual military experience. As a result, two Independence Day celebrations occurred. One in Washington in the morning was largely confined to the populace and the New York militia regiments. The other, held in the afternoon at McDowell's camp across the Potomac in Alexandria, consisted of a mass review of the troops preparing to carry out the Union motto of "Forward to Richmond." Congress, too, had been called into session on July 4 to be presented the next day with a stunning demand from Abraham Lincoln for the raising of four hundred thousand troops and the appropriation of monies to organize, equip, and supply them.

Eager for the opportunity of gaining a firsthand glimpse of the Union Army being massed on the extreme northern border of Virginia, Maritza immediately sent a note to Major Thaddeus Morton, accepting the invitation to the military review and reception. Promptly at noon on July 4 an apple-cheeked and loquacious lieutenant named Jed Smith arrived with a buggy drawn by a spirited roan mare.

As they were crossing the Long Bridge from the District of Columbia into Virginia, several regiments that had responded to Lincoln's first call for volunteers by enlisting for the specified three months' period were marching through the city on their way to the depot. The 7th New York, in particular, were notable for their small brass howitzers and the rest of their equipment—some of the best in the Federal forces—which they were taking home with them. The soldiers made no bones about their happiness at the idea of getting out of the Army after a three months' lark which had consisted mainly of parades and hell raising in general.

Across the Potomac that afternoon the situation was considerably different, as Maritza saw immediately when the buggy left the planking of the bridge that had replaced the rails formerly traversing it. Confederate troops of the Alexandria Line had thrown up extensive breastworks when they first went into position across the river from Washington shortly after Fort Sumter. Later, however, they had withdrawn to the vicinity of Fairfax Courthouse and Centreville, in order to protect the vast quantities of military supplies being accumulated where the Manassas Gap Railroad from the Shenandoah Valley west of the Blue Ridge Mountains joined the Orange & Alexandria at Manassas Junction. South of the Potomac, Federal forces had not only occupied the breastworks already thrown up there by the Virginia troops but had also extended them considerably and built them up as a more solid protection for Washington.

Drawn by the festive afternoon review, much of the population had forsaken the city. Accustomed to the antics of the Fire Zouaves and others of the New York regiments parading through Washington almost every day, the populace was eager to see the considerably more important group of soldiers who would carry out the march toward Richmond shortly expected to begin.

"You were smart to wear a summer frock, Countess." Lieutenant Smith was a short, sandy-haired young man who was obviously not yet a professional soldier but very much impressed with his assignment for the afternoon and his beautiful companion.

"Have you been with Major Morton long, Lieutenant?" she asked.

"Only since General McDowell took possession of the Virginia side of the river, ma'am. I was scheduled to enter West Point in the fall but gave up the chance."

"Why would you do that?"

"The war will be over before I could graduate. This way I got a commission from the very start, elected by my company of the 1st Ohio."

"How did you happen to be attached to Major Morton's command of a cavalry brigade then?" Maritza asked.

"The major is from Ohio and knew my father at West Point some years ago. Out where I come from, we're all excellent riders and, as an aide-de-camp to General McDowell for cavalry, the major needed someone familiar with this area."

"Are you also a Virginian?" Maritza asked.

"I wasn't born here, ma'am, but I have relatives on the Southern side and used to visit them near Culpeper. Would you believe General McDowell hasn't yet been able to get a decent map of Virginia?"

"In Washington I could—everything seems to be confusion there. But here on the Virginia side, the situation seems to be much more under control."

"Major Morton doesn't think so and neither does General

McDowell, ma'am. They say we need another two months to train the troops, but by that time most of their enlistments will expire and they'll be going home like the New York troops we saw today marching to the depot."

"I take it that General McDowell doesn't approve of three-month enlistments?"

"Approve? You ought to hear him cussing the politicians in Congress who are demanding that we attack the enemy right away."

As their buggy rolled off the Long Bridge, a sharp command came from the guard stationed there: "Halt, and give the countersign."

Lieutenant Smith stopped the buggy and spoke briefly to the sentry. The soldier, Maritza noted, carried an almost antique Springfield smoothbore rifle, a far less effective weapon than the Enfields she had sold to Richard Mann in Mobile for the Confederate Department of War.

No one else stopped them as they drove on to the eminence on which stood what had been the lovely home of Colonel Robert E. Lee, when he commanded the 1st U. S. Cavalry stationed in Washington. Little damage had been done to the house by the Union occupation, a tribute to the affection for its former owner shared by much of the country. Chairs had been placed on the portico, with its tall white columns two stories high, and tables erected on trestles for the reception that would take place after the military review.

Maritza's escort found seats for them in the shade near the reviewing stand erected at one side of the lush green lawn. At his signal, an orderly appeared to serve them glasses of lemonade. Looking back the way they had come from the heights on which the onetime Lee mansion stood, Maritza could see the central part of Washington spread out in plain view. She could even make out a colorful line moving along Pennsylvania Avenue that could hardly be anything except one of the Zouave regiments on the way to the depot to start home at the end of its three months' tour of active duty.

On this side of the Potomac, most of the color was provided by the flower beds around the mansion and the waving of regimental and company guidons as the Army, said to number thirty thousand men, were now beginning to mass on the field preparing to pass in review before their harried commander-in-chief.

A feminine voice almost at Maritza's elbow startled her and she turned to see a richly dressed and very handsome woman passing by on the arm of a rather corpulent and distinguished-looking civilian, considerably older than herself. To Maritza's expert eye, the woman appeared to be in her early forties. Possessing olive skin and extraordinarily brilliant eyes, her hair was drawn back from a strong face and she carried herself with complete self-confidence. Her male companion, on the other hand, appeared to be scowling most of the time, although his striking-looking companion was talking to him animatedly.

"That's the famous Mrs. Rose Greenhow," Lieutenant Smith confided. "She makes no bones about having strong Southern sympathies and some even say she's the kingpin of a rebel spy ring in Washington."

"If that's true, why is she allowed to go on with her spying?"

The young lieutenant shrugged. "If you have friends high enough in Washington circles, you can get away with almost anything. There's talk that before Mr. Lincoln was inaugurated President Buchanan's carriage was seen at Mrs. Greenhow's house often—and very late at night."

"Who is the gentleman with her?"

"Senator Henry Wilson from Massachusetts."

"The chairman of the Military Affairs Committee?" Maritza asked, startled by the information.

"The same. General McDowell and Secretary of State Seward sometimes attend the receptions she holds at her house on Sixteenth and I streets, too."

Somewhere in the cloud of dust that almost hid the troops massed on the field before the reviewing stand, a bugle sounded smartly. As the last notes died away, a robustly built man in a uniform bearing the stars of a brigadier general took the central place on the reviewing platform. He was flanked by other high-ranking officers and important-looking civilians, including

Major Thaddeus Morton, straight and handsome in the uniform of the United States Cavalry.

When the strains of the national anthem died away the band switched to a marching air and the first of the massed ranks of troops began to pass in review. Colors of every hue marked the insignia of the various organizations fluttering in the afternoon breeze, as the honor guard led the column past the stand where General McDowell stood, stiffly erect, to receive the salutes of the troops.

"I never saw so many soldiers at once," Maritza confessed.

"Thirty-five thousand of 'em," Lieutenant Smith said proudly. "Another eighteen thousand or so are located in the Shenandoah Valley south of Harpers Ferry under General Patterson."

"The Union forces must outnumber the Southerners two to one."

"Not quite, ma'am. They say Beauregard has twenty-two thousand defending Manassas Junction and General Joseph E. Johnston has around twelve thousand in the Shenandoah Valley. The Blue Ridge Mountains lie between Johnston's troops and Manassas, though. And with Patterson holding the Confederate forces on the other side of the mountains, they're not likely to be of much help to Beauregard."

"I judge that you think defeating the Southerners will be an easy task then?"

"Easy as falling off a log, ma'am. When I lived in Virginia, I always heard people tell what a fine place the Spotswood Hotel in Richmond is. A couple of weeks or so from now, after we've taken Richmond and hung Jeff Davis with some others, I'm going to walk into that hotel and order me the biggest steak you ever saw."

Watching the seemingly endless columns of troops go by, many of them carrying the deadly Enfield rifle, Maritza could find no reason to doubt the young lieutenant's optimism about the outcome of the approaching battle.

"If General Robert E. Lee was respected enough as an officer for General Scott and President Lincoln to offer him the command of the Union Army, maybe he'll have some tricks up his sleeve," she suggested.

"He might if he were in command, according to Major Morton, but the Richmond papers say Lee won't even be in on the fighting. He's only acting as a military adviser to Jefferson Davis and, from what I hear, Davis already has so many advisers another one is not going to make much difference."

VIII

By six o'clock the afternoon review was over and the impressive ceremony of Retreat ended with the lowering of the flag on its tall pole in front of the former Lee mansion. The watchers and many of the officers who had been leading the regiments and divisions now repaired to the mansion for the reception. Major Thaddeus Morton met Maritza at the door and thanked Lieutenant Smith, as did she, for taking care of her. Taking Maritza's arm, Morton guided her through the crowd to a front parlor of the Lee mansion where a receiving line had been set up.

"You're even more beautiful by daylight than you were by candlelight at Mercier's the other night." Morton was looking down at her admiringly as they made their way slowly toward where General McDowell was holding court for the invited guests. "Did you enjoy the review?"

"I never saw such a large one before."

"It's the last before we move against the rebel Army in a couple of weeks. General McDowell still claims the troops aren't half trained but I thought we put on a rather good show this afternoon. Better, I'm sure, than that gang of ruffians from New York who were parading down Pennsylvania Avenue this morning for President Lincoln."

"Several New York regiments were marching to the depot as our buggy crossed Pennsylvania Avenue on the way to Maryland Avenue and the Long Bridge."

"Sandford lets them get away with murder." Morton's tone

was angry. "Can you imagine what would have happened if he'd been allowed to assert his rank, the way he tried to do, and take command on this side of the Potomac?"

"Obviously there's a considerable difference between the discipline here and what passes for it north of the river."

"You'll see more, as the training steps up in the next few weeks. I'm going to be reassigned to a new cavalry brigade that's being organized. Which means I'll be busy finding horses, equipping my men, and making sure they can ride without falling off of a horse."

They had come to the receiving line and Morton took Maritza's hand to guide her into a position before McDowell.

"General, sir," he said, "it is a distinct honor for me to present Countess Maritza LeClerc, representing the French journal *Le Pays*."

"You're most welcome, Countess," said McDowell as Maritza curtsied politely. "When I was studying in Paris long ago, I used to read *Le Pays* regularly."

"My late husband owned the journal," Maritza explained. "After his death I sold it to Monsieur Claudet, who had been editing it for us."

"I'm afraid Washington must be a disappointment to you after living in Paris, Countess. You probably know that one of your countrymen, Pierre L'Enfant, designed it in 1792, but I'm afraid L'Enfant's plans haven't been carried out very well."

"I was born in America, General, but married a Frenchman."

"Do you intend to remain here after the war is over?"

"My roots go as deep in American soil, sir, as the Acadians of Louisiana and the Spanish settlers of Mobile. When this unfortunate conflict is finished, I shall stay here where my people have been for over a hundred years."

"Speak well of us in your writings, please," he said graciously. "Our greatest hope is that our friends in England and France will understand the travail we are going through on this side of the Atlantic."

Maritza and Morton moved on into another room, where punch was being served. "Sorry we can't offer you a really fine wine," he apologized. "The general is a teetotaler and we have to be careful what we serve, even in the officers' club bar." He lifted two glasses of champagne from a passing waiter's tray. "It certainly can't compare with what you were accustomed to in Paris."

Maritza sipped the champagne. "It's good enough. I shall assure my compatriots in France that America is trying to live up to the hopes of Pierre L'Enfant, even though William Russell has had little good to say about either the city or the Army."

"The trouble is that Russell's usually right," Morton confessed. "The Army lost the cream of its officer corps to the South, when Beauregard opened fire by taking Fort Sumter. So far, our leadership has been largely confined to former militia officers but they're not in the same league with men like Lee, Johnston, Longstreet, Ewell, and—"

"Beauregard?"

Morton shrugged. "To my way of thinking, the elevation of Beauregard to command of an important Confederate army was the best thing that could have happened for our side." He brightened suddenly. "Mrs. Rose Greenhow seems to be holding court in the corner. Do you know her?"

"No, but Lieutenant Smith pointed her out to me earlier. He says she's supposed to be a spy."

"She probably is, but most women in Washington still envy her because she's on friendly terms with so many men who occupy very high places in the government."

"Why would the government tolerate her in Washington where she can learn so much about Union plans, if they think she's a spy?"

"I suspect because Seward and Lincoln are smart enough to know how valuable a pipeline into the enemy camp can be. This way they can supply her with misinformation the Confederate leaders will accept as being true."

"You mean deliberately lead them on?"

"Deceiving the enemy is an old military principle and nobody in Washington could be better suited for the job."

Morton had been guiding Maritza through the crowd while

he was talking. They finally penetrated the circle of men around Mrs. Greenhow and gained her attention.

"I want you to meet Countess Maritza LeClerc, a newspaper correspondent from Paris, Rose." Obviously Morton was on very friendly terms with the tall, dark-haired woman with the olive skin.

"I can't imagine all that beauty being wasted on a newspaper correspondent, my dear." Mrs. Greenhow's tone was patronizing. "But then, you're the first such I've ever known."

"I don't know of any others myself," Maritza confessed.

"All of Washington is talking of the way you exposed that horrible Thomas Nast to Secretary Seward," Mrs. Greenhow informed her. "Imagine picturing a planter eating a black infant for breakfast."

"I'm not sure Mr. Nast drew the particular cartoon."

"Has he denied it?"

"Not that I know of."

"Then he probably did. Only an abominable cad like Nast would dare to malign a people whose representatives played such an important part in governing the country before this unfortunate war broke out." She touched Major Morton on the shoulder. "I suppose you know you've captured the handsomest and most eligible officer in Washington in Thad Morton, Countess." The words now had a cutting quality that Maritza didn't miss. "But then youth must be served."

"I'm indebted to Major Morton for inviting me to the review and reception," said Maritza sweetly. "With only a few friends in Washington, I'm afraid I would never have been invited."

"You'll soon be receiving more social invitations than you can possibly fill," Rose Greenhow assured her. "Not every man can enjoy the company of a beautiful young woman with the full knowledge that his name will be mentioned favorably later in an influential foreign journal."

"When it comes to newspaper writing, I follow the dictum of my friend, Mr. William H. Russell of the London *Times,* and report only the news," Maritza assured the older woman. "It was a pleasure meeting you, Mrs. Greenhow. I hope we shall meet again."

"We shall, my dear—if for no other reason than because I can't afford to have you stealing away close friends like Thad Morton here."

"That conversation had all the subtlety of a *pas d'armes*," Morton observed as they moved into another room. "Mind telling me what it was all about?"

"She's jealous—of your attention to me."

"But we're only friends; she must be ten years older than I am."

"The Rose Greenhows of the world don't give up their admirers easily, especially handsome men destined to occupy positions of importance."

"But—"

"You're already a trusted aide to the most important general in the United States Army," Maritza reminded him. "There's only one way for you to go—up."

"I hope you're right," he said. "I'm scheduled to be breveted tomorrow to the rank of colonel, when I'm placed in command of a new cavalry brigade."

"That will be just the start. Congratulations."

He slid his hand down her arm to press his fingers around hers. "I trust you won't forget a mere colonel, once you're busy writing about politicians and generals in high places in Washington."

"I never desert my friends," she assured him lightly, giving his hand a squeeze. "Do you suppose we can find some more champagne and some food? I'm starved."

"Certainly." As they started through the door into an adjoining parlor, they almost collided with Secretary Seward, who was going in the other direction.

"Countess LeClerc!" He bowed low. "I see that you're getting around."

"As a good correspondent should, Mr. Secretary," said Maritza. "Do you know Major Thaddeus Morton, General McDowell's aide-de-camp?"

"Of course." The two men shook hands. "I hope you're going to write something good for your French readers about the review you've just witnessed, Countess."

"It was most impressive," Maritza assured him.

"How about Mr. Lincoln's request to Congress tomorrow for more men, Mr. Secretary?" Morton asked. "Is there any hope of legislation to that effect?"

"Eventually, perhaps, Major," said Seward. "At the moment Congress seems to feel that, since General McDowell hasn't been able to march on Richmond by now with thirty-five thousand, giving him hundreds of thousands more isn't going to help the situation."

"They don't understand that you can't make a soldier out of a civilian overnight, just by putting him in uniform, sir."

"I quite agree, Major. Fortunately, my task is maintaining the best possible relations with other countries, particularly England and France. I must leave the task of turning civilians into soldiers in hands far more skilled than mine. Good day, Countess—and Major."

The dancing started at eight, but after about a half an hour dancing with Major Morton and other officers who insisted upon being introduced, Maritza pleaded weariness and Morton immediately sent for a carriage to take them back to Washington. To Maritza's surprise, the carriage carried the insignia of the commanding general of the Army of the Potomac on the door.

"My, oh, my!" she exclaimed when Morton handed her into it with a flourish. "I'll wager not even Mrs. Greenhow has a conveyance at her call like this one."

"She'll no doubt be using Senator Wilson's carriage," said Morton. "I must confess that ordinarily I wouldn't have this one, if the general were going into the city tonight. Fortunately for me, he's staying in camp and was kind enough to place it at my disposal."

In the carriage Morton managed to capture Maritza's hand again and she did not resist, although discouraging further intimacies. She was attracted to the handsome widower, more attracted than she cared to admit, even to herself, and he'd already given her important information by revealing that McDowell would probably move against Manassas Junction and Richmond in about two weeks. That placed the attack date around July 19 and she wondered if she should try to convey the information to Beauregard's headquarters at Fairfax Courthouse, barely fifteen miles from the Union camp on the south bank of the Potomac.

"Why so thoughtful?" Morton asked as the carriage rolled off the planked surface of the Long Bridge onto the rough track of Maryland Avenue.

"I hate the thought of war actually beginning and so many people losing their lives, just to preserve something as outmoded as slavery," she confessed.

"Slavery may be the least important issue, as far as many of my former fellow officers fighting on the Southern side are concerned."

"What else, then?" She saw in the dim light of the street lamps along Maryland Avenue that he was more concerned than he had been at any time since she'd met him.

"The real issue goes back to the deliberations of the Continental Congress after the Revolution, and the question of states' rights under it. The Founding Fathers, especially those in Virginia and farther south—but many in the North as well—wanted a government made up of a loose federation of states. Fortunately Thomas Jefferson and a few others had the good sense to see that anything so easy to break up would never create a nation that could defend itself, as America had to do twice before the War of 1812 ended."

"Perhaps I've been in France too long to remember as much United States history as I should," she confessed. "I always thought states' rights was only a motto for preserving slavery."

"To many it was—but thoughtful men like Abraham Lincoln feel we must be one nation with equal rights for all. The cotton growers of the South cannot survive without the spinning jennies and looms of the North to turn their raw materials into finished goods. By the same token, the anthracite needed in smelting steel for railroads and great buildings—as well as for cannon and other military equipment—can only come from western Virginia and Pennsylvania, neither of which lies in a Southern state."

"Virginia is in the South."

"Not the western half. General McClellan already holds much of that for the Union and, when the proper time comes, Lincoln is sure to turn it into a separate state on the Union side."

"You talk as though war wasn't really inevitable, as so many Southerners believe."

"It wasn't; all our difficulties could have been settled by men of good will if a few hotheads, like Beauregard, could have been held in check. A Virginia convention was negotiating in Washington right up to the day the state referendum went for secession in the eastern section, and North Carolina was holding out, too, hoping for a peaceful settlement. Growing cotton economically with slave labor became impossible after Eli Whitney invented the cotton gin over sixty years ago."

"I've heard it argued that the dominance of Southern representatives in Congress over Yankees was also a contributing factor."

"Only where the hotheads who coveted political power and saw it slipping from their grasp were concerned."

"Why did they lose it?"

"The population of the North began to outstrip that of the South by a wide margin when immigration laws were relaxed to provide cheap labor for Northern mills and factories."

"Maybe, with so many factors involved, war was really inevitable anyway," Maritza commented.

"Not where really civilized men are concerned," said Morton. "When I was a student at Harvard we argued such questions endlessly but, outside of wars for territorial expansion alone, we could find no reason for them. The Mexican War in 1845 ended all needs of the United States for expansion."

"It was no secret before I left Paris that Napoleon III had his eye on gaining a foothold in the New World—"

"Where?"

"Mexico. With the United States divided in two halves, each busy killing the other off, what better time for him to move in than now?"

"Did you see any signs of preparation for annexing Mexico by France before you left Paris?"

"Nothing definite, but I was in England for several months before coming to America, so I can't speak with authority where Napoleon III is concerned."

"Maybe he's given up the idea."

"That's not very likely. In fact, he's probably more intrigued with the possibility of annexing Mexico now than he was before."

"Why do you say that?"

"Henri Mercier has just learned that Prince Bonaparte will be visiting the United States late this summer. He acts the playboy and pretends to know nothing of politics, but he's shrewder than most people give him credit for."

"Do you think he's looking over the ground for Napoleon III with a view to moving into Mexico when neither the Union nor the Confederacy could stop him?"

"I'd bet on it."

"You may be right," Morton said thoughtfully.

"My late husband knew Napoleon very well—and disliked him intensely."

"Because of his morals?"

"Those, too, but mainly because of his obvious plans for expansion in Cochin China and the Crimea. To say nothing of his interference in the affairs of Italy, a peaceful nation with which the French had no quarrel."

"You seem to know a lot more about politics than the average woman," Morton commented.

"That's because I'm not an average woman," she assured him. "In the seven years I was married to Étienne LeClerc, I was given an education in world affairs few women are ever privileged to have."

"No wonder your editor selected you to report on what's happening over here. The government ought to employ you as an adviser in the State Department."

Maritza laughed. "Can you see Secretary Seward listening to advice from a woman?"

"From a woman as beautiful as you are, yes. Seward's been a close friend of Rose Greenhow for many years and she can't even hold a candle to you."

"She's been a close friend to a lot of other men in high positions, from what Lieutenant Smith said. How does she do it?"

"For one thing, until Lincoln came to Washington and brought a lot of rough Middle Western Republicans with him, she was the most influential hostess here."

"Is it true that she was President Buchanan's mistress?"

Morton shrugged. "He was a bachelor and fond of feminine company, so she may have been. I remember seeing his carriage at Sixteenth and I streets many a night late when I was coming home."

Maritza squeezed his hand. "From an assignation of your own, no doubt. You're a very handsome man, Thad, but Cécile Mercier warned me that you drop your conquests as soon as they yield to you."

"Cécile's exaggerating," he protested. "There's no denying that being a bachelor officer in Washington is the next thing to hog heaven." His tone was suddenly serious. "This time, I'm afraid, I've been shot down on the battlefield of *l'amour,* Maritza. You took my heart prisoner without firing a shot."

"I'm very fond of you, Thad—"

"Enough to marry me?"

She leaned over to kiss him as the carriage drew to a stop before the mounting block at Willard's. "In the past few days you've become very dear to me—as a friend."

"But not as a potential husband?"

"It's much too early to tell," she protested. "Besides, when I was only eighteen I missed my girlhood, so I'm entitled to a few years of freedom at least, before settling down with a husband and starting the family I want. After all, what woman of twenty-five could want a more glamorous and satisfying occupation than that of a newspaper correspondent in a nation at war?"

"Is there anyone else?" he demanded and Maritza laughed.

"Spoken just like a man who'll soon be assuming the responsibility of leading a cavalry brigade. I've had marriage offers from several men—but I've refused to consider them, as I'm refusing to consider yours, Thad. Let's finish this war and bring things back to normal before we consider what any of us is going to do afterward."

"The day a peace treaty is signed, I'll be camping on your doorstep demanding an answer," he warned.

"And I'll be happy to see you, whether as potential husband or friend," she promised. "Shall I see you again before . . . ?"

"Before we go into battle? I'm afraid not. Beauregard is already drawing back to previously established lines along a creek called Bull Run before Manassas Junction. According to the plan of battle, my job is to use my cavalry and probe across the creek at a place called Blackburn's Ford to sound out rebel strength there. One of our intelligence agents thinks Beauregard intends a major attack through that area but I doubt it. We'll probably chase a few rebels away who've been guarding the ford and then go back to Centreville. Meanwhile, McDowell will strike directly through the center and take Manassas Junction, rolling up the rebel left in the process."

Maritza concealed her surprise at having the Union battle plan practically outlined for her. "I'm ignorant about military matters," she confessed. "Wouldn't that be taking quite a risk?"

"A large one," said Morton. "If the enemy turns out to be in force at that point when the attack begins, it would mean that he plans to turn our left flank, information McDowell would need badly."

"Obviously he has a lot of confidence in you to give you the job of getting it for him." Maritza took his hand and stepped down from the carriage. "Good night, Thad."

Maritza stood on the steps leading up to the lobby of the big hotel until the somewhat ornate carriage had disappeared into the darkness. Then, turning, she walked across the lobby to the steam-driven elevator in deep thought, ignoring the usual expressions of admiration and invitations for supper—and other things—that floated her way. Perturbed as she was, she didn't notice the small man with the round face, shoe-button eyes, and bowler hat she'd seen at Secretary Seward's office the day she presented her credentials. Or note the suspicious way he'd watched her being handed down from the carriage which bore

the crest of the commanding general of the Army of the Potomac.

IX

Maritza had shrewdly decided that her first several reports to
Monsieur Claudet in Paris should contain only ordinary news,
such as any other correspondent would write. In that way, she
hoped to convince the censors, against whom she'd been
warned by William Howard Russell, that she was in actual fact
just what she appeared to be. Once convinced, they might be
inclined to give what she wrote no more than a casual examination and, thus, fail to read between the lines—so to speak—
where the real truth lay.

Unable to sleep after leaving Morton, she took paper, pen,
and ink and, writing steadily, described in detail the July 4 fes-
tival in Washington itself, plus the military review at Arlington
Heights, with the tremendous strength it had revealed. She had
almost finished the report to Paris when the sound of a key in
the lock distracted her. It was Celestina, somewhat the worse
for wear but half drunk and still very beautiful.

"Where in the world have you been?" Maritza demanded,
though not in a tone of reproof, because she'd given her companion the afternoon and evening off to do as she pleased.

"To President Lincoln's soiree, no less," said Tina proudly,
only to have the whole effect disturbed by a loud hiccup.

"You're drunk! I'll help you get your clothes off before you
tear that expensive Paris dress."

"Unhand me, woman! I'm a free citizen of the United States,
not a slave any more."

"So you're free—*and* drunk. Where did you really go?"

"As I told you—to the President's soiree."

"Get your clothes off and go to bed. Obviously you're talking nonsense."

Celestina drew herself up proudly—and almost fell over.

"Guess I did have what the English call 'one over the

eight,'" she admitted. "But it was in a good cause, helping my mistress."

"I told you I'm not your mistress any more," said Maritza. "You're free and only one eighth, or maybe even as small as a sixteenth, black. You can go wherever you want to or associate with whomever you wish."

"I associated with a lot of people tonight." Celestina was peeling off the lingerie from her somewhat sweaty body. "High muck-a-mucks, too—'most as high as a countess." She giggled. "Though I'm sure anybody that knows you was surprised to see me there."

"They'd have been a lot more surprised if they'd known you've got black blood. These Yankees are pretty race-conscious, even if they're trying to set the Negroes free."

"You can say that again," said Tina. "The way it all happened was I attracted the interest of a colonel from Pennsylvania, Secretary Cameron's state." She shrugged, an action that dropped the rest of her lingerie at her feet, leaving her a nude statue of startling beauty. "We had a few drinks and then he suggested going to the President's Fourth of July reception."

"Naturally, you jumped at the chance."

"Of course." Tina was properly indignant. "How many times in my life could I expect to meet a President and his wife?"

"I'm not criticizing you, just trying to learn what happened."

"We went to the White House and you'll be proud to know I was the best-dressed woman at the affair."

"Why not? Alphonse makes the most fashionable clothes in Paris—or America."

"You'd have been proud of me," Tina assured her. "The place was lousy with people but this Colonel Cameron must have some influence—"

"His brother is Secretary of War."

"Anyway, we went in like we owned the place and marched right through the receiving line. I'm telling you, that Mrs. Lincoln is the dowdiest woman I ever saw."

"What about the President?"

"He's tall and looks like one of the black cranes you see stalking around here on the Potomac Flats, but he was polite. I was using my best French accent, so I think I fooled the whole crowd into believing I'm really who I said I was, Mademoiselle Toutant."

"I've been thinking about what sort of position you really ought to have here, now that we're in the North," said Maritza. "How would you like to be employed as my secretary-companion and continue using a family name—Toutant?"

"Not be your maid any more?"

"You're free; I gave you the papers. You don't have to be a maid unless you want to."

"As far as I'm concerned, I'm still your slave," said Tina. "You can call me whatever you wish."

"From now on you're officially Miss Celestina Toutant, my secretary and traveling companion. Your handwriting's as good as mine and I've got to have several copies made of everything I write to preserve for my own protection. Carbon paper makes poor copies, so you can be a lot of help to me. Now go to bed and tell me in the morning some more about what happened at the reception."

"You can be sure of one thing," said Tina as she lay down on the cot where she slept. "I was the belle of the—" A soft snore punctuated the sentence.

Maritza was sitting at a table by the window the next morning, writing her dispatch to Paris describing the military review and reception the day before, when Tina groaned and rolled over about nine o'clock. Swinging her legs off the cot, she yawned and stretched her back.

"How long've you been up?" she asked.

"Since dawn. The stench from the City Canal, plus the mosquitoes, wouldn't let me sleep."

"You should've gotten drunk like I did. Drunk, you can't even smell something as foul as that cesspool and you don't feel the mosquitoes bite either. Have you had breakfast?"

"No. I was waiting to order some after you woke up."

"Give me five minutes to dress and I'll go down for it myself. You'd think the chef of the biggest hotel in Washington would know how to cook eggs decently. I'll be glad when we can move to Monsieur Cruchet's where there's a French chef."

"Our rooms are supposed to be ready in about two weeks. Did you learn anything yesterday that should go into this dispatch to *Le Pays?*"

"Only that the President of the United States chews tobacco and sprays the juice all over the spittoon. His wife's about to bankrupt him, too, buying the dowdiest-looking clothes you ever saw. A Parisian whore wouldn't be seen in them."

"That's not much help."

"Oh yes, the girls in the local brothels are mad at the Garibaldi Guard for bringing their own women from New York."

"Still no information I can use about the war."

"Everybody's saying General Winfield Scott would like to see General McDowell replaced by somebody named McClellan who's in command out in western Virginia. He's been doing more fightin' and winnin' out there than anybody else in the Army. They say if General McDowell doesn't get moving and take Richmond soon, Congress will insist on handing the job to this McClellan."

X

Celestina returned in less than half an hour, with a bellman pushing a cart on which was a large tray covered with a napkin, a steaming pot of coffee, and two newspapers.

"They had copies of both the Richmond and New York papers at the newsstand in the lobby," she said after the bellman departed. "The Richmond paper is yesterday's issue."

While Tina set up their breakfast on a table and prepared to cook the eggs in a chafing dish, Maritza glanced at the Richmond paper.

"At Manassas," the Richmond *Examiner* stated, "General P. G. T. Beauregard issued a proclamation yesterday to the people of northern Virginia upon the occupation by the Union States of the south bank of the Potomac, including Alexandria and Arlington Heights. In it he said: 'A reckless and unprincipled tyrant has invaded your soil. Abraham Lincoln, regardless of all moral, legal and constitutional restraints, has thrown his abolitionist hosts among you, who are murdering and imprisoning your citizens, confiscating and destroying your property, and committing other acts of violence and outrage too shocking and revolting to humanity to be enumerated.' "

"Your cousin Pierre doesn't seem to have lost much of his oratorical steam," Celestina commented.

"He isn't through yet. In the next sentence he avows that the Northern war cry is 'Beauty and booty.' "

"I thought it was 'Forward to Richmond.' At least that's the headline on Mr. Horace Greeley's New York *Tribune* this morning."

"So far this seems to be a war by slogan," Maritza observed, then gave a quick cry of pleasure. "Listen to this."

" 'The brigantine *Pride of Bristol* arrived at Liverpool, loaded with cotton from Mobile. Captain Pennington Darrow is in command.' "

"Our ship got through!" Jumping up, Maritza seized the startled Tina around the waist and started dancing her across the room. "The old *Pride* docked safely in England."

"We'll soon need the money, the way these patriotic Yankees jacked up the price on everything the moment war was declared." Tina stopped in the middle of warming Maritza's eggs. "The paper also says a Confederate gunboat, the *Sumter,* landed seven prizes taken from the Yankees yesterday at Havana. Maybe you and Captain Darrow would have been better off buying a privateer in England instead of that blockade runner he's probably dickering for right now."

"We're not buying the blockade runner," Maritza reminded her. "The Confederate government's buying it for us. We're only a front."

"But a front that'll make most of the profits, and that's the best arrangement anybody could make. How soon do you suppose Cap'n Darrow will get back with a load of munitions to run the blockade?"

"I guess we won't know that until we read about it in the Richmond papers." Maritza seated herself at the small table and Tina served her a plate of scrambled eggs and crisp bacon with buttered toast on the side.

"Too bad you can't get hominy grits up here in the North," Tina observed as she poured the coffee. "Or even coffee with chicory. Somehow breakfast doesn't taste right without 'em."

"Or croissants; maybe Monsieur Cruchet will have them. Fill your own plate, Tina, and sit down. You're no servant any more, not that you ever really were."

"You ought to see the way the Yankees treat their white help." Tina's tone was indignant as she took her place at the table. "I heard the housekeeper at the reception the President gave yesterday afternoon cussing an Irish girl who was helping serve the tables. The language she used would have put a fishwife to shame." Tina took a forkful of the eggs and washed them down with coffee. "Speaking of liking—did you enjoy your afternoon and evening with Major Morton?"

"Very much. He's being breveted—"

"I keep hearing that word. What is it?"

"A temporary promotion usually for the duration of the war. He will command a brigade of cavalry that's supposed to probe the Confederate right flank in the neighborhood of Blackburn's Ford on a creek called Bull Run."

Celestina's eyes opened wide. "You discovered all that in one afternoon?"

"And a lot more. The Federal troops before Washington are reported as numbering thirty-five thousand against the Confederate's twenty-two thousand, but a lot of Union regiments have finished their three months' enlistments and gone home."

"The streets were full of 'em staggering to the depot yesterday afternoon—at least half of 'em as drunk as owls."

"Colonel Morton says Cousin Pierre Beauregard is counting on around twelve thousand Confederate troops from beyond the Blue Ridge in the Shenandoah Valley to help him, once the battle begins. That's why the Manassas Gap Railroad from the West is so important, and the junction with the Orange & Alexandria at Manassas Junction. A Major General Patterson has been given the job of holding General Johnston and the Confederate Army in the valley."

"With one Southern soldier worth two Yankees, that still leaves the odds in our favor," Tina insisted. "How are you going to get the information about the Federal plan of attack to General Beauregard?"

"I'm not; Mrs. Greenhow is supposed to take care of that part. From the way she was hanging onto the chairman of the Military Affairs Committee of the Senate yesterday, I suspect she already knows more about Yankee war plans than the Secretary of War."

Tina poured a second cup of coffee for them both. "The next question is, what's between you and Major—no—Colonel Morton, that he would trust you with all that information? Especially when I found no sign this morning that a man had been in your bed."

"I came home early and didn't even give him so much as a good night kiss," said Maritza. "Even though he wants me to wait for him until this war is finished."

"Are you going to do it?"

"Of course. I don't intend to marry anybody until it's all over and I have a chance to make up my mind."

"If you ask me, my mind would have been made up when I got a glimpse one morning of a naked Captain Penn Darrow in your berth on the old *Pride of Bristol*."

"You can forget about that too," said Maritza firmly. "Colonel Morton is very handsome and a fine gentleman—"

"He's also a Yankee and an enemy."

"Four men in my life have met fully the standards I set up long ago in a husband, Tina. One I married and found him to be a perfect lover."

"The second you found to be the perfect lover, too, without having to marry him," Tina reminded her.

"Admitted. The third I think could be both."

"Colonel Mann?"

"Yes."

"Which leaves only this Colonel Morton. How about him?"

"He's handsome, obviously an aristocrat, well educated, and a gentleman as well. Just the sort of man I should settle down with once this war is over."

"Except that he's an enemy whose oath of allegiance would force him to turn you over to be shot, if he had any idea just why you're in Washington."

"I can't hold that against him. He's only doing what he considers to be his duty just as I am," said Maritza. "What am I going to do, Tina, if all of us come through this war and I'm forced to make a choice?"

Celestina shrugged. "The French have the right idea. No matter how wonderful you think a man is, never marry him until you've slept with him, preferably quite a number of times. So far, you're fifty-fifty, in spite of all the opportunities I've given you—like staying out practically all night last night."

"You were whooping it up on your own. By the way, what would André think of that?"

"What André doesn't know won't hurt him. Besides, how am I ever going to see him again, unless these Yankees take Richmond in the next few weeks like Mr. Horace Greeley says they will?" She unfolded a copy of the New York *Tribune* and handed it to Maritza. Across the top of the front page was a motto in heavy black type: FORWARD TO RICHMOND.

"The Yankee cartoonists are up to their old tricks again, too," Tina added. "There's one inside of Jefferson Davis dining in state in Richmond with a dozen slaves crawling on their knees to serve him and an overseer standing over them with a whip." She laughed suddenly. "At least we Southerners got back at them, though. A cartoon on the front page of the Richmond *Examiner* shows a tree full of monkeys with the faces of Yankee senators and congressmen—plus Abraham Lincoln at the top as the biggest monkey of them all. Whoever drew that cartoon isn't quite as good as your friend Mr. Nast, but the President is easy to draw as a monkey—which a lot of people in Washington seem to think he is."

"I'm not sure at all that Lincoln's quite the oaf his political opponents insist on making him out to be," said Maritza. "At least he's willing to face the fact that this isn't going to be an easy war, which is more than half the inhabitants of Washington and a lot of the soldiers do. Colonel Morton said he's going to ask Congress for four hundred thousand men and four hundred million dollars. That doesn't sound like a short war."

"Think he'll get it?"

"My guess is that Lincoln is a smart enough politician to ask for twice what he expects to get. Then he can say, 'I told you so,' if the Union should lose."

"One thing you can bet on," said Tina as she put the breakfast dishes and tray on the cart and pushed it outside the door. "The Confederate government in Richmond doesn't have any doubts about winning the war. Everything except the front pages of the paper is taken up with balls and other social affairs. Your cousin Pierre is hogging the spotlight, too, by announcing that he'll destroy McDowell and his army or drive them into the Potomac River by the first of August."

The three copies of the dispatch were finished before noon. The second copy Maritza sealed in an envelope to be turned in at the State Department for transmission to Paris. The original she placed in a second envelope and addressed to a Jeremiah Smith in Georgetown as she'd been instructed in Montgomery. The third was filed for her records.

"You can mail the copy to Georgetown," she told Celestina. "I'll deliver the one for Monsieur Claudet to the censors at the State Department. From what Mr. Russell tells me, they'll cut it to pieces before sending it on to Paris. Meanwhile, Monsieur Claudet will get the top one by way of Richmond in the next blockade runner."

"How soon do you think it will be until Captain Darrow comes sailing through that blockade?"

"Several months, I imagine. He has to move cautiously to keep the British from having to admit publicly that they're supplying ships for carrying munitions and supplies to the South, and cotton back to pay for it."

XI

As it happened, General Pierre Gustav Toutant Beauregard didn't get the chance to push his Yankee opponents into the Potomac River after all, although he did come closer to it perhaps than even he expected. At three o'clock on the afternoon of July 16 the Union Army started moving southward and westward from its bivouacs in Arlington and Alexandria toward the hamlets of Annandale and Fairfax Courthouse. No attempts were made at secrecy since the objective would have been evident to a West Point plebe. By moving westward, not directly south toward Richmond, McDowell practically announced his plan to seize Manassas.

It was a logical move for success in that the endeavor would break the somewhat tenuous line of iron rails snaking westward through the Blue Ridge foothills to the village of Piedmont on the east side. From there a low mountain pass through the lower peaks of the Blue Ridge carried the rails to Strasburg in the Shenandoah Valley. By breaking the only railroad that linked Beauregard's army at Manassas Junction with the Confederate force of twelve thousand under General Joseph E. Johnston—now engaged in holding back Union General Patterson's much larger force at Bunker Hill, a few miles from Winchester in the Shenandoah Valley—McDowell obviously intended to strike a crippling blow against the Confederate forces protecting Richmond.

By the night of July 16 most of the troops, except those still bivouacked in Washington itself, had reached Annandale, roughly ten miles west of Washington. To a skilled military observer like William H. Russell, that in itself was not a very impressive accomplishment for a first day's march. Maritza was having dinner with Russell and several other foreign newspapermen at the Willard about nine o'clock, within listening distance of the Washington newspaper presses roaring out special editions around the corner as couriers brought back information from across the river.

"After the Crimea and Balaklava, I'm surprised you're not at the front, Mr. Russell," she said over smoked ham, biscuits, and candied yams.

"Front!" Russell snorted. "There won't be any front before the day after tomorrow, if then, my dear. I had some advance knowledge of today's movement and rode across the Long Bridge about five o'clock to see for myself. Those green troops from the Middle West were marching as though dead lice were falling off them."

"In this heat, I expect they were." A young German correspondent named Karl Wertheim was dining with them. "Soldiers and lice are always close companions in wartime, you know, Countess."

"This is my first war," said Maritza.

"Take my advice and make it your last," said Russell. "Women aren't cut out for this sort of business."

Maritza didn't argue the matter, since her own reasons for being there did not fit the traditional role of a foreign correspondent.

"Do either of you have any knowledge of what the Northern strategy will be?" she asked.

A newsboy burst in just then shouting, "EXTRA! UNION STRATEGY REVEALED!"

"There's your answer, Countess." Russell stopped the boy and bought a paper, spreading the front page, upon which a large map was printed, on the table. "Here are the important railroad lines. One runs from the Shenandoah Valley to Manassas, the other from Lynchburg to Alexandria with a connection just north of Charlottesville to the Virginia Central & Richmond. If Beauregard can get those troops from the Shenandoah Valley across the Blue Ridge to Manassas on that dinky little railroad from Strasburg before McDowell cuts it, he'll be about as strong as McDowell."

The tall Englishman stood up. "I'd better be getting to bed, my friends. If the Union forces really start moving, I'll be putting your suggestion into action about going closer to the fighting, Countess. Good night."

"Good night, Mr. Russell." Maritza turned to the young

German. "How do you think this is all going to turn out, Mr. Wertheim?"

"The only way it can, with the South having maybe a tenth as much manpower as the North and no manufacturing capacity to speak of. If you're going to the front, Countess, I'd advise hiring a horse and buggy early tomorrow morning. They're already getting short and prices have gone high."

"I hired mounts for myself and my companion when I learned McDowell had decided to move," she told him. "I've got a feeling that watching a battle is going to be like fox hunting and it's better to be as mobile as possible."

"They're taking bets down in the bar that McDowell will capture Richmond by August 1," said Tina when she brought up their breakfast in the morning.

"I'd like to take some of that money but I'm afraid it might make the authorities suspect I'm a Southern sympathizer."

"That's no crime in Washington, judging by the way Union money was being snapped up as fast as it was offered."

"What were the odds?"

"Three to two on the Union, sometimes two to one. The way the Yankees moved yesterday, it'll take them a week to get to Manassas Junction. Anyway, we won't be there."

"We will, if there's likely to be any fighting."

"*Nom d'un nom!*" Tina threw up her hands in a typically Gallic gesture. "Do you want to get yourself—and me too—killed?"

"You don't have to go—"

"Do you think I would stay here while you're out being captured and probably raped?"

Maritza laughed. "The South's on our side, remember? Actually, we're not liable to get that close to the fighting. I understand that much of Washington society is going out to see the rebels—as they call them—driven back to Richmond. We'd just be going along with the crowd."

Tina shook her head lugubriously. "If I know you, we'll be riding right into the middle of the fighting."

"At least Monsieur Claudet will know I was filling the role of a foreign correspondent the way the professionals do."

"A female Mr. Russell? Is that what you want to be?"

"It's what I'm here to do. Don't forget that."

Breakfast finished, Maritza studied a copy of the *National Republican*. As would be expected, the newspaper of the reigning party had put as bright a face as possible on the slow progress made so far toward carrying out the Yankee motto of "Forward to Richmond."

"Federal troops," the paper reported, "are pushing on to Fairfax Courthouse today, another ten miles, and are said to be finding no resistance. The Confederates, in fact, have retreated steadily in the face of overwhelming Union strength, leaving behind vast amounts of booty."

Later papers carried the statement that Federal troops had paraded through the town of Fairfax Courthouse in a column of fours with bands playing and battle flags waving in the breeze, while Beauregard's forces had withdrawn to a creek called Bull Run, a natural barrier. It even listed the crossings of Bull Run that would be available to the invading Federal force in pushing the Confederate Army toward Richmond and certain defeat. One of these spots, Maritza was startled to see, was Blackburn's Ford, plainly indicated on the map that occupied half of the front page of the paper. That ford, she remembered, was the same one Colonel Thaddeus Morton had mentioned as the spot where he was supposed to probe the Confederate defenses with his cavalry brigade.

"You'd better lay out our riding habits tonight so we can dress early in the morning in case General McDowell starts to make his big move," Maritza instructed Tina and felt her pulse stir with anticipation at the thought of watching the first of the fighting and reporting on it even before William Russell.

BOOK FOUR

MANASSAS

I

Just after dawn on the morning of July 20, Maritza was awakened by the steady tramp of marching men. Looking out the window, she was surprised to see a regiment of New York Zouaves, the rays of the early morning sun setting off the bright colors of their uniforms and being reflected from the metal fastenings of their gaiters and the barrels of their rifles.

The Zouaves had been stationed in Washington for so long, they'd practically become a part—though a considerably rowdy one—of the police force. It was generally accepted that they had not joined McDowell's more battle-ready troops across the river because of strong opposition from their commander, General Sandford, to depleting the forces guarding Washington itself. That being true, their movement toward the Long Bridge in Virginia at this hour of the morning could mean only one thing, the beginning of the real campaign for northern Virginia.

"Tina! Wake up!" Maritza shook her companion into wakefulness. "We'll ride as soon as we can get some breakfast and the horses. And pack us a hamper of food and a bottle of wine too, with a couple of blanket rolls. We may be away overnight."

Tina didn't waste time arguing. The two women dressed in a hurry in stylish riding habits Maritza had bought in Paris before coming to America. Less than an hour later they were waiting at the nearby livery stable for a sleepy hostler to saddle their horses.

At the Washington end of the Long Bridge, they could see equipages of all sorts moving from various parts of the city toward Virginia. Many private carriages were among them, the women dressed as if for an afternoon reception, indicating that

Washington society expected a short battle and intended to make a picnic of the whole affair.

Maritza had only the map published in the newspaper the day before, showing the likely battlegrounds to guide them, but that was ample. According to the map Blackburn's Ford, where Morton had told her his cavalry would open the battle with a sortie in force to test the strength of the Confederate right, lay some distance south and west of Centreville. Toward the latter village, spectators and wagon trains of supplies and the matériel of war were moving, clogging the main road until progress was almost impossible. Pulling off the road to Centreville just north of where it would cross the Warrenton Turnpike and become presumably even more impassable, Maritza drew rein.

"We'll never get through this mess to Blackburn's Ford if we follow the main road," she told Celestina.

"I'll be glad to get off of it, preferably headed back to Washington; this dust is choking me to death."

"We can swing around Centreville to the east and cross the Warrenton Turnpike, though." Maritza was studying the map. "That way we can follow a branch called Little Rocky Run that will take us to Blackburn's Ford. If I get within watching distance of it I'll be the first correspondent to report on the actual fighting."

"You could be the first woman correspondent to be shot, too —and her maid with her."

It was midafternoon before they came into a heavily wooded section that, according to the map, appeared to lie between the stream they were following and a narrow road leading southward across Bull Run, of which Little Rocky Run was a tributary. While Maritza was studying the map from the newspaper, the sudden rattle of gunfire and the louder boom of a cannon sounded not far ahead.

"The fighting's already started," she told her companion. "We got here just in time."

"In time to turn around and go back." Celestina was having some trouble with a gun-shy horse. "Even this nag knows we've got no business here."

"Let's get off this road." Pulling her horse away from the

path, Maritza guided it through the woods toward a low hill, from the top of which she was able to look down at the ford.

A sharp engagement seemed to be going on with most of the firing coming from Confederate troops defending the shallow crossing. The Union troops seeking to cross the run had brought up several small cannon, and their roar, as they hurled shells across the narrow, steep-sided creek into the woods beyond, was almost deafening.

While Maritza watched, the Union forces testing Confederate strength on the southern flank grew bolder and the firing became even hotter. The Confederates as yet were only answering gun for gun and finally the Union commander ordered his troops to cross the ford.

The Federal detachment, Maritza saw, wasn't large—one cannon and its handlers, some forty infantry and a squadron of cavalry. When she focused her powerful binoculars on its leader, she wasn't surprised to recognize Colonel Thaddeus Morton, the promotion he had so recently received indicated by the silver insignia on his shoulders and the collar of his uniform tunic.

The small Union force made a brave show, storming across the ford dragging a battery of artillery with them. One moment only the hoofbeats of the horses splashing through the shallow stream could be heard above the occasional crack of an Enfield —plus the grunts and curses of the gun crew maneuvering the heavy weapons through the soft earth of the ford. Then, as the infantry ran on ahead and the cavalry squadron followed, all hell broke loose on the south bank of Bull Run.

Maritza sensed at once the strategy of the Southern commander. Correctly assuming that the sortie against Blackburn's Ford was being undertaken to gain information about the strength of the Confederate's right flank, the Southern troops had been ordered to hold their fire to little more than the appearance of a small group protecting a relatively unimportant ford. Now they attacked in force.

Before the Yankee cannon could be brought into place, a hidden Confederate battery went into action, spraying grapeshot and shrapnel into the very faces of the advancing Yankee troops. At the same moment a hail of fire—minié balls and round bullets from muzzle-loading Springfields, mixed with pistol balls from the side arms of the officers—struck the ranks of the advancing blue-clad men.

One minute the Union forces were moving confidently, the next their ranks wilted and the men began to turn back, while the famous rebel yell echoed and re-echoed from the south bank of the ford. Through the powerful glasses, Maritza saw Thad Morton maneuver his plunging mount into the very face of the retreating Yankee infantry, trying to drive them back into battle by slashing at them with the flat of his sword. Against the hail of shot and flame belching from the Confederate cannon, however, even his daring attempt was doomed to failure. Hopelessly disorganized, the New York infantry regiment that had waded Blackburn's Ford so confidently moments before stumbled back, more than half of them cut down in the first hail of lead.

The intensive firing lasted only a few moments. Then Maritza cried out in horror as a minié ball, fired at close range, struck Morton in the right shoulder, exploding flesh and bone when it emerged and leaving a gaping hole from which blood gushed. His sword clattered to the rocky ground as it fell from a nerveless hand and his body slumped across the horse, the mark of death obvious in the gushing torrent of blood from the massive shoulder wound.

With its master's control on the reins released, Morton's mount turned too. In one mighty plunge, it cleared the high bank of the ford to the Union side, continuing up along the bank in great leaps of pure terror. It passed the stream of men in blue now splashing back through the ford in a frantic attempt to escape, many of them throwing down weapons and haversacks as they ran.

Instinctively, Morton's horse headed toward the spot where Maritza and Celestina were struggling with their mounts several hundred feet away, fighting to control them in the face of the thunder of rifle and cannon fire. Just before the terror-stricken animal reached Maritza, a low-lying limb jerked its dying master from its back and Thaddeus Morton fell almost at her feet. Forgetting the danger to herself from the now waning fire, she swiftly dismounted and handed the reins of her mount to Celestina, who was staring down at the body of the Union officer, her mouth agape with horror. As Maritza knelt beside him, Morton's eyes opened and the glaze of death upon them momentarily cleared enough for him to recognize her.

"Maritza!" The words were barely more than a whisper. "The breast . . . pocket . . . tunic . . . letter." He managed a gasping intake of air, enough to finish the sentence. "Letter to . . . Mother . . . please mail." Then the words died on his lips as he gave one shuddering gasp and was suddenly limp.

"Miss Ritza!" Tina's voice was suddenly urgent with fear. "We gotta get out of here. We gotta save ourselves. They're fightin' all around us."

"One moment."

Conquering her natural aversion with a powerful effort, she slipped her right hand into the inner breast pocket of the dead man's tunic. Her fingers found two folded papers inside. One, she saw, was an envelope addressed to Mrs. Thaddeus Morton, Sr. The other appeared to be wrapped in isinglass, as was sometimes done with maps to protect them from the rain.

She opened it instinctively and a single first glance told her she had found a detailed map of the Union battle plan for the attack upon Manassas Junction, even to the locations and names of the organizations that would take part in it and exactly where they would be located. She was still staring at it when a harsh male voice said from only a few feet away: "I knew the Yankees were losing their three-month enlistees by the thousands, but I hardly expected them to be putting women into the front lines."

II

Maritza stood up quickly, the map and letter still in her hand, to find herself facing a Confederate officer on horseback. The insignia of a captain was on his uniform and a scowling expression on his somewhat craggy features.

"If you have finished corpse robbing, madam," he said,

"may I inquire who you are and what the hell you're doing here?"

"Countess Maritza LeClerc," Maritza snapped, angered by the accusation of corpse robbing, a not unusual occurrence, she had heard, on the field of battle. "I'm correspondent for *Le Pays,* a Paris newspaper of which *you* have probably never heard, Captain—"

"Stewart, Abner Stewart. Second Alabama, General Barnard Bee commanding. I still want to know what you're doing here at a scene of action, Countess?"

"I just told you I'm a newspaper correspondent, Captain. When I learned that the first action of the war would probably take place here at Blackburn's Ford, I came here with my companion, Mademoiselle Toutant, hoping to report on it. Instead, we found ourselves in the middle of heavy fighting."

"Where neither of you has any business being, either as women or newspaper reporters," he retorted. "Would you mind telling me just how you learned that an early action would take place at this ford?"

Maritza hesitated, then decided to tell the truth—especially with Captain Stewart showing evidence of suspicion that she was something besides what she claimed to be.

"I was the guest of Colonel Thaddeus Morton at Union Army Headquarters on the Fourth of July and attended a military review and reception at General McDowell's headquarters that same day, Captain. Colonel Morton mentioned Blackburn's Ford as his assignment."

"Is he Colonel Morton?" Stewart pointed at the dead body with the tip of his saber.

"Yes." Maritza kept her voice from breaking with difficulty.

"Was he perhaps your fiancé, Countess?" Stewart's tone had lost some of its harshness.

"A friend—nothing more."

"I'm afraid you used his friendship rather badly to gain information that would promote your own ends as a correspondent."

It was a charge Maritza could not deny any more than she could deny the heartsick feeling that had gripped her as she knelt beside the dying Union officer. Or at obeying his request to extract the letter from the pocket of his tunic, a request which had also revealed the battle map.

"Catch Colonel Morton's horse and strap his body across the saddle," Stewart called to several soldiers who had crossed the creek and now stood just behind him. "Then send the horse to follow the enemy troops that ran away."

Maritza couldn't have told why she moved her own horse closer. Or just why, in spite of her reluctance to touch the body, she reached over to tuck one of her gloves under Morton's sword belt in a final gesture of farewell to a brave man, who was also an aristocrat and a gentleman. As she moved her horse away, one of the soldiers gave Morton's mount a slap on the rump and it started back toward Centreville, over the same road along which the New York troops, who had stormed so confidently across the stream only a short time before, had fled in disorder.

"See to your own wounded," Captain Stewart ordered the few soldiers who had crossed it. "Then form on the south side of the run."

"Aren't you going to follow up what was obviously a rout?" Maritza asked incredulously.

"Our orders are not to be drawn across the ford but to defend it," he said shortly. "May I see those papers you are holding?"

"One is personal, a letter Colonel Morton asked me just before he died to mail to his mother. The other appears to be a map of the battlefield area."

Spurring his horse up beside her, Stewart took both from her hand. Glancing at the letter, he handed it back to her. The map he opened wide on the saddle in front of him while Maritza remounted and moved closer so she could see.

"It's the Union battle plan, isn't it?" she asked.

"What *looks* like the Union battle plan," he corrected her. "It could also be a decoy."

"Why a decoy?"

"Did you ever hunt ducks, Countess?"

"Yes. At our château in France."

"Then you know decoys carved from wood and painted to look like real birds are often floated on the surface of a pond or lake by hunters. When the wild ones see the decoys, they fly down and are shot by the hunters."

"Surely you don't—"

"Suspect you and your elaborately drawn map of being a decoy designed to mislead us? The idea had occurred to me—yes."

"And you think I could help set such a trap?"

"Look at the evidence, Countess—if that's what you really are. You claim to be a neutral, yet I find you in a battle area."

"How could I know this was going to be a real battle? Colonel Morton was only leading a sortie to feel out the Southern strength. If anybody set a trap here, Captain Stewart, it was you."

"If you saw the whole engagement, you no doubt realize that your friend lost his life trying to make his own men fight."

"If you hope to convince me all Yankees are cowards, the way a lot of people believe, you're wasting your time."

"I have no such intention, believe me," he assured her. "I graduated from West Point myself and have many friends fighting on the Union side. They are brave men but I shall undoubtedly have to kill some of them or they will kill me. I can take no pleasure in this war, Countess, even though I am a professional soldier."

"May I use that quotation in my dispatch to Paris describing this as a typical example of what the fighting will be like—brother against brother?"

"If you really are a newspaper correspondent, why not?"

"Here's the proof." From a pocket in her jacket Maritza produced a copy of her commission from Monsieur Claudet and handed it to the Confederate officer. "You can see for yourself."

He glanced at the commission and handed it back to her. "This still doesn't alter the fact that you undoubtedly know a lot about the enemy. For the time being, therefore, Countess, you and your companion are prisoners of war."

Maritza started to object, then changed her mind when a

possible headline in *Le Pays* flashed across her mind: I WAS A PRISONER OF THE AMERICAN REBELS.

"Very well, Captain," she said. "But since we are neutrals, neither Mademoiselle Toutant nor I can be made to give you any information we think you shouldn't have."

"Suppose we leave that question to General Beauregard, Countess? Follow me, please." He turned his horse and started back across the creek.

"Where are you taking us?" Maritza asked as she followed with Celestina close behind.

"To Army Headquarters at McLean House near Manassas."

III

General Pierre G. T. Beauregard was sitting behind a desk in the parlor of McLean House, a two-storied structure of red brick with a white trim, standing at the end of a short avenue of poplars and oaks just outside Manassas. Beauregard was busy signing papers when Maritza and Celestina were ushered into the parlor and did not look up immediately. When he did, the expression on his dark-skinned, heavily mustachioed countenance was so comical that Maritza couldn't help laughing.

"Good afternoon, Cousin Pierre," she said impishly.

"My God, Maritza!" Beauregard came around the desk to give her a bear hug and a kiss on the cheek. "Where the hell did you and Celestina come from?"

"I'm a prisoner of war. Captain Stewart here captured me in the middle of a battle at Blackburn's Ford."

"In the middle of a battle?" The swarthy leader of the Army of Northeastern Virginia chortled. "Which side were you fighting on?"

"Neither. Celestina and I are neutrals."

"Like hell you are; some of the finest blood in the South flows in your veins." Then he wheeled to face the now slack-jawed Stewart. "What is this all about, Stewart?"

"Don't blame the captain," said Maritza. "I really am a neutral acting as correspondent for *Le Pays* in Paris. He didn't know what to do with me when he found me at Blackburn's Ford, so he brought me here."

"General Longstreet sent me a report on that action, Stewart; it arrived a few minutes ago by courier," Beauregard told the Confederate officer. "He said you handled it very well indeed, but he didn't mention any prisoners."

"I sent a report to the general, sir, but considering that Countess LeClerc was carrying a set of what purports to be Union Army battle plans, I thought I should bring her directly to headquarters. Incidentally, we routed the enemy at Blackburn's Ford but went no farther, as you ordered."

"Good! Good!" said Beauregard. "When you failed to pursue the Yankees, I'm sure they figured we weren't there in strength, just as we wanted them to think. They'll get quite another surprise when Longstreet leads the attack on Centreville by that route tomorrow."

Beauregard reached for the isinglass-covered map Stewart had placed on the desk. Smoothing it out, he leaned over to study it but did not object when Maritza moved up close beside him where she could see it more clearly too. While he examined the map, Beauregard stroked his well-shaven chin thoughtfully; unlike most Army officers of the day, he didn't wear a full beard but only a rather large and curling mustache.

"This *could* be McDowell's actual battle plan," he said. "Even at the Academy, he was always a smart strategist and this one appears to be well thought out."

"I reached the same conclusion, sir," said Stewart. "If McDowell wanted us to *think* of this as his actual plan of battle instead of the real one, the Yankees who crossed Blackburn's Ford to determine our strength and then retreat could hardly have made a smarter move than to leave a copy where we would be sure to find it."

"Just how *did* you find it, Captain?"

"The countess here was holding it in her hand, sir."

"Captain Stewart seems to think I was sent to Blackburn's Ford by the Union commander to witness the skirmish and that I was carrying a fake battle plan, knowing I'd be captured and brought to you," said Maritza hotly. "Can you imagine anything more absurd?"

"She did have the map in her hand, sir," Stewart protested.

"Only because I had just taken it and a letter from the body of Colonel Thaddeus Morton, as he was dying from wounds sustained during the fighting."

"Morton?" Beauregard frowned. "A Thad Morton was an instructor in cavalry tactics at West Point, Stewart."

"The same, sir."

"You say he was killed?"

"While trying to rally his own men, when we opened up on them as soon as they crossed the ford."

"Where were you when all of this was happening, Maritza?" Beauregard inquired.

"Celestina and I had stopped on a knoll overlooking the ford after hearing gunfire there," she explained. "I *am* a reporter and, since I could see what was happening, I stayed to record it in my mind until I could get somewhere to write it down."

"You're a damn good reporter, I imagine, now that I remember some of the letters you used to write while you were in school in Mobile asking for money," Beauregard told her. "What I don't understand is how you knew where to be at just the right moment."

"*That* part was accidental," Maritza admitted. "When I saw Blackburn's Ford on a map on the front page of a newspaper in Washington yesterday afternoon, I remembered Colonel Morton's telling me at the reception on the Fourth of July—"

"A reception at General McDowell's headquarters, sir," Stewart intervened. "By her own admission, she was the guest of Colonel Morton there."

"Am I on trial here?" Maritza demanded. "As a spy for the North?"

"Now, Maritza," Beauregard soothed. "Captain Stewart isn't making any charges, just reporting the facts, as military law requires. Please continue with your side of the story."

With an effort, Maritza controlled her anger. "I had met Colonel Morton at a reception given by Henri Mercier right after I came to Washington to report on the war. We had dinner together once or twice and he invited me to the review and reception on the Fourth of July. It was then that he mentioned his assignment to make a feeling-out sortie at a ford named Blackburn's."

"Didn't you think that strange?"

"He wasn't very happy about the assignment and obviously didn't consider it very important. However, when I saw the same name on a map printed in a Washington newspaper yesterday, I decided to look at the place, hoping to be the first correspondent to report military action. The road between Fairfax Courthouse and Centreville was clogged with both military and civilian traffic, so Celestina and I made a wide swing through the countryside. Because of that, I almost stumbled on the ford just as the fighting there was beginning."

Her voice broke for a moment as she remembered the gush of blood from Thad Morton's shoulder and the frenzied leap of his mount across the creek, carrying his dying body beneath the low limb and jerking it from the saddle almost at her feet.

"Colonel Morton fell during the battle and was dying almost at my feet so I naturally dismounted, trying to help him," she continued. "His dying request was that I mail the letter in the breast pocket of his tunic to his mother. Only when I felt inside the pocket for the letter did I discover that the map of the battlefield was also there. I thought Captain Stewart saw me remove it."

"You had both the letter and the map in your hand when I stopped beside you, Countess," said Stewart.

"But you can't deny that I was kneeling beside Colonel Morton's body?"

"No. You could have gained possession of the map exactly in the way you have just described."

"I accept the facts as you described them, Maritza." Beauregard was studying the map again. "Right now it's important to study it and decide just how it will affect our own strategy. And since you will be reporting the battle for your paper, let me point out the preparations I have made to defeat McDowell and his army."

"You'd be doing me a favor," Maritza conceded. "I know little of military affairs."

"The battlefield I have chosen, my dear, is essentially in the form of a giant X, with the center here on the turnpike between Warrenton and Centreville. Actually, the start will probably be at a stone bridge across Bull Run, almost directly north of where we are standing." Using a pencil, he pointed to the spot on the map. "Your readers among French military leaders will appreciate the simplicity of my plan, if you include a rough drawing in your dispatch. By that time Jefferson Davis will be sitting in the White House."

"I thought President Davis wanted no conquest, merely a restoration of the old Union," Maritza protested.

"We will create a new nation where the South is dominant, as it was in the time of Washington, Jefferson, and Madison," Beauregard assured her confidently. "No longer will the country be governed by politicians in the pay of ironmongers, like Lincoln's present Secretary of War. As for Jefferson Davis wanting no conquest, he can hardly refuse to ride along Pennsylvania Avenue from the White House to the Capitol, with a victorious Southern Army marching behind him."

Beauregard stabbed with his forefinger at a spot which, judging from the scale of the map, Maritza estimated at some four or five miles almost due north of where they were standing. "Here is the stone bridge where the real fighting will start. You can see Bull Run coursing from northwest to southeast directly through the battlefield, down to where it is crossed by the railroad at Union Mills Ford. Once the fighting starts, a veritable tide of men in gray will pour across Bull Run, rolling up McDowell's puny levies along his left flank and piling them back upon Centreville and the road to Fairfax Courthouse and Washington."

"When will that be, Cousin Pierre?"

"Tomorrow afternoon, I hope, when the rest of General Johnston's troops arrive from the Shenandoah Valley. Is there anything about the plan you don't understand, Maritza?"

"Not the plan, Cousin; it's brilliant. But what is this curving line north of the Warrenton Turnpike?"

Beauregard waved a beringed hand in a gesture of disparagement and contempt. "It represents McDowell's hopes of outflanking me, but little does he know that I shall outflank him to the east before he can possibly get started on such an elaborate flanking march as that curving line indicates."

"What if he starts first?"

"He can't do it. General Jackson has already arrived with a brigade of fighting Virginians from across the Blue Ridge and others are only hours behind, as well as troops moving up from the south. We will strike the enemy with such force on his left flank and center at the beginning that the flanking Union force moving westward on this Yankee map toward Sudley Springs will be left with no place to go except toward the foothills of the Blue Ridge, where Jeb Stuart's cavalry will be waiting ready to cut them to pieces."

"It sounds like a great victory, Cousin Pierre."

"It *will* be a great victory! By God! Maritza!" Beauregard's voice had taken on a sudden note of excitement. "I'm going to give you a chance to become famous by letting you stay on this side of the battle line and report what happens from the Southern point of view."

"I'm a neutral, Cousin Pierre, acting here under my French citizenship."

"Be a neutral then; nobody's asking you to fight, just to tell what happens. This could be the opportunity of a lifetime for you to become the best female war correspondent in history."

"More likely the *only* female war correspondent in history and perhaps the only one killed in action."

"The risk is slight, I wouldn't expose you to it if it wasn't." Beauregard waved his hands in one of those expansive gestures that were characteristic of his manner when excited. "We've erected an observation tower on Signal Hill east of here, you may have seen it when Captain Stewart brought you here from Blackburn's Ford. A signal officer is stationed there all the time to watch the movements of the enemy and report with signal flares."

"How high is it?"

"Thirty feet, but the tower is erected on top of a knoll which

makes it considerably higher. With a powerful telescope, you'll probably be able to see the entire action from the platform. It's even big enough for you to use a pencil and tablet to write down the story as it occurs."

"What if the Yankees overrun the position?"

"They won't; our heaviest troop concentrations are protecting the fords across Bull Run in that area. Even if you're captured, though, you can always claim neutral status. You've already been accepted in Washington as a foreign correspondent, haven't you?"

"Yes, by the Secretary of State, Mr. Seward himself."

"Then it's settled. You can start this evening by describing the brilliant battle plan *I* have devised."

"But—"

"Don't worry about revealing military secrets. Long before your description of this battle reaches Paris the outcome will have been decided. Agreed?"

"I can't very well turn it down, can I? May Celestina and I go to Signal Hill now?"

"It's too dark to see anything worth recording tonight. I'll have someone take you to the tower as soon as dawn breaks."

There was a knock on the door and when Beauregard called, "Come in," an aide entered.

"What is it!" Beauregard demanded irritably. "Don't you see that I'm occupied?"

"An important message has arrived from General Lee and President Davis, sir. The courier is a colonel."

"Bring him in then!" Beauregard shouted. "Bring him in!"

A tall man, whose uniform was caked with dust, as if he had been riding a long distance, stepped into the room and saluted.

It was Richard Mann.

IV

The startled look in Richard Mann's eyes, when he saw Maritza and Celestina, was almost comical. It lasted only an instant, however, then his gaze was fixed once more on Beauregard as he came rigidly to attention.

"As you were, Colonel." Maritza didn't miss the frosty note in her cousin's voice betraying his dislike of Mann, but could think of no reason for it, until Beauregard spoke again.

"What trouble do you bring me from Richmond this time?" he demanded.

"No trouble, General," said Richard Mann. "Merely an answer to your query to General Lee and President Davis concerning the proposed battle plan."

"This is Colonel Richard Mann, my dear," Beauregard told Maritza. "You might even call him a minister without portfolio between the government in Richmond and the Army. Which," he added on a deliberately sarcastic note, "makes him neither fish nor fowl. This is Countess Maritza LeClerc, my cousin from France, Colonel, and Celestina, her sla—her companion."

"Colonel Mann and I met at Mobile where his plantation adjoins mine," said Maritza. "He was also kind enough to introduce me to President Davis and other highly placed people in Montgomery."

"Thank you for your kindness to my cousin, Colonel." Beauregard's voice took on a slightly warmer tone. "I'm sure it had nothing to do with the fact that both she and Celestina are two extraordinarily beautiful women."

"I *had* noticed, sir," Richard Mann said with a smile. "It is a pleasure to see the Countess and Mademoiselle Toutant again."

Beauregard had been reading the dispatch Mann had placed on the table before him, his expression growing more angry with every word. When he finished he slapped the document down on the table with a vicious gesture and fixed Richard Mann with a malevolent stare, as if he'd been an agent of the Devil.

"You know what his message contains, don't you, Colonel?" he demanded.

"Yes, General."

"Do you agree with it?"

"I understand why General Lee and President Davis have some reservations about the proposed plan of battle."

"Suppose you tell me their reasons then." When Mann looked inquiringly at Maritza and Celestina, the Creole officer added: "Countess LeClerc represents a French newspaper. She will be writing the story of the coming battle from the Southern side and the vantage point of Signal Hill."

"I thought Countess LeClerc was functioning as a neutral war correspondent, sir."

"Stop nitpicking on Maritza's status, Mann," said Beauregard. "She and Celestina are my guests; we need have no secrets from either of them. You were going to tell me why President Davis and General Lee are afraid of my battle plan."

"The President and General Lee believe your left flank will be dangerously weak, sir, unless General Johnston's troops arrive in force from the Shenandoah Valley before the fighting starts."

"They're already here," Beauregard snapped, "so that objection isn't valid."

"All of them?"

"Enough." Beauregard shrugged. "Besides, General Patterson and the Union troops under his command are afraid to leave the Shenandoah Valley."

"I hope you are certain of that, sir."

With a contemptuous gesture, Beauregard tossed the map Maritza had found to the table before Mann.

"Countess LeClerc found a Federal battle plan this afternoon, before she was captured by Longstreet's forces at Blackburn's Ford during a brief engagement a few hours ago. As you can see, McDowell plans a grand flanking movement against our left. According to my plan, by driving across the stone bridge and the other fords in the center, we can split McDowell's forces and cut them to pieces one at a time."

"It does sound feasible." Mann was studying the Yankee map. "When do you plan to advance?"

"Day after tomorrow morning, at the latest. A few of Johnston's troops haven't arrived yet."

Mann glanced quickly at Maritza, then back at the map. "How many still have to come?"

"How many what?" Beauregard was obviously irritated by the question.

"Men from General Johnston's forces."

"Less than half, they're dribbling in by train on that dinky little railroad from Strasburg in the valley." Beauregard stalked around the end of the desk and took a hat and a raincoat from where they were hanging from pegs driven into the wall.

"See that Maritza and Celestina are quartered somewhere, Mann, and get some supper for the three of you," he ordered. "I'm going to find General Johnston and discuss this note from Lee and Davis with him. Obviously I can't change an entire plan of attack in a few hours because a chairbound general in Richmond is afraid of his shadow. Lee is irritated because he resigned from the Union Army expecting to be placed in command of the Army of the Potomac. Instead, he finds me in command—"

"The President also asked me to remind you of the difference in rank between you and General Johnston—"

"It's no secret that Johnston outranks me, Colonel Mann. Or that I offered to turn over command of the Army to him, as soon as he arrived. Fortunately he readily saw that whoever directed this battle must be familiar with the terrain and, since he is not, requested me to remain in command."

"I can assure you that President Davis meant nothing derogatory—"

"President Davis has had no use for me since he was Secretary of War in the Buchanan Administration, Colonel," Beauregard said savagely. "Besides, how can anyone in Richmond be qualified to judge the situation here almost a hundred miles away? Rose Greenhow reports that Lincoln and his entire Cabinet are pushing McDowell to get started with the attack, so we can't afford to wait much longer to beat them to it—even if the rest of Johnston's troops never get here."

Beauregard was gone out the door, shouting to an orderly for his horse before Mann could say anything, if he had wished.

"There's a small guesthouse at Manassas that's used as quarters by visiting congressmen and the like," Mann told Maritza and Celestina. "I'll see that you're quartered there for the night and also try to rustle up some supper. Meanwhile, you can tell me how it is that you're a prisoner of war even before the fighting starts and also possess what looks like the enemy's plan of battle."

"Then you agree that the map is authentic?" Maritza asked as they mounted for the brief ride to the guesthouse.

"Let's say it's exactly the way I would dispose my troops if I were in McDowell's place, but don't ask me to approve of what the commander on either side is planning for tomorrow or the day after."

"That's a strange thing for a soldier to say."

"I served under Irvin McDowell in the Regular Army. He's a sensitive man, artistic, fond of music and growing flowers, plus being an excellent soldier. Now he finds himself commanding thirty-five thousand men, not five thousand of them well enough trained to form a decent battle line and obey orders."

"Then why did he choose to fight?"

"Lincoln made the choice, pushed into it by Horace Greeley and his New York *Tribune* trumpeting 'Forward to Richmond.' Plus congressmen and senators badgering him because they're more interested in making money and getting re-elected than they are in the welfare of the people or the country."

"What about Cousin Pierre?"

The tall man with the insignia of a full colonel on his collar laughed, a savage sound that seemed to rip the night air apart as if slashed with the sword he wore. "Beauregard wants to be the South's hero a second time so he can steal the job of Confederate general-in-chief from the only man fit to wear the title and the stars of a lieutenant general, Robert E. Lee. For that, your cousin will throw untrained levies against superior numbers, ordnance, and ammunition."

"With what result?"

"You saw what happened at Blackburn's Ford today. Tomorrow or the day after, you'll see a battle won by one side or the other. Either way the fields will be littered with the bodies of dead men, and the side that wins will be the one that happens to be the slowest in running away when hell breaks loose along the course of Bull Run. Right now," he continued, "my major concern is how to get you and Celestina out of here and back to Washington where you'll be safe."

"I'm not liable to ever get another chance like the one Cousin Pierre is giving me as a war correspondent," she reminded him.

"You're not supposed to report it from either side"—his voice was harsh—"especially when your own life will be in danger."

"That sounds as though you're not certain as to the outcome."

"You're never certain about battles, they're like farming. A hundred things can wreck the harvest, even after it's in the barns."

"But Cousin Pierre is so cer—"

"He's certain because the last message from Mrs. Greenhow said McDowell would move from Arlington Heights and Alexandria to Manassas by way of Fairfax Courthouse and on to Centreville."

"Exactly the way he did come," Maritza reminded him.

"Any moron could have picked that route as far as Centreville, what has General Lee and President Davis worried now is where McDowell will go from there. Now that I've talked to Beauregard, I'm even more concerned."

"Why?"

"He mentioned just now that you were captured near Blackburn's Ford. How did that happen?"

"Celestina and I were watching a small Union force under command of a colonel I had met in Washington, as they tried to ford the stream. A few did get across but when the woods on the other side suddenly swarmed with Confederate soldiers the Union troops turned and ran. The colonel I knew was killed trying to make them stand and fight. I took the map from his body."

"Judging from that incident, would you say the Northern drive is being concentrated toward Manassas by way of the fords of Bull Run south of the Warrenton Turnpike, as General Beauregard thinks?" Mann asked.

"I saw no sign of it," said Maritza. "When Colonel Morton

mentioned that his assignment at the beginning of the battle would be Blackburn's Ford, he referred to it only as a sortie. Why do you ask?"

"Beauregard still believes the Union attack will be directly against the Junction here. That's one reason why I'm worrying about getting you both out of here first thing in the morning."

"I'm still interested in becoming the first woman correspondent to report a battle from the battlefield itself," she insisted. "After all, Cousin Pierre *is* doing me a favor."

"Favor! In risking your life? All Beauregard wants is to have a description of the battle written portraying him as a hero. Charleston was a victory because the Federals at Fort Sumter were out of food and ammunition. If he wins here tomorrow it'll be because he's got men like Johnston, Jackson, Longstreet, Ewell, and a few others behind him. Then nothing can stop him from being general-in-chief, a job he isn't as well fitted for as you are. Do you want to help bring that about?"

"Of course not."

"Then for my sake go back to Washington tomorrow morning. You're worth far more to the Confederacy—and me—there than in the middle of any battlefield. Besides"—he reached over to kiss her—"I'm particularly interested in keeping you safe until all this is over and I can convince you that both of our plantations in Alabama should be joined permanently."

"The idea does grow more attractive as time goes on," she admitted, returning his kiss. "Any word about the blockade runner you were dickering for in England?"

"Captain Bulloch is leaving the details to your friend Captain Pennington Darrow. As much as I hate to admit it of a rival, too, Darrow is doing an excellent job."

"Then he's already found a ship?"

"A perfect one for our requirements and almost ready to sail, according to Bulloch's reports. The British government is nervous about letting munitions be sold directly to the Confederate government, so they're being bought instead by an agent in the Azores and shipped there in another bottom. In good time Captain Darrow will sail the new blockade runner from England in ballast. When he reaches the Azores the munitions will be transferred to the *Sprite* for the voyage to one of our ports."

"I learned another thing during a dinner party at Henri Mercier's," Maritza told him. "The Federal Navy is planning to build a base at a place called Port Royal in South Carolina, so the ships on blockade duty along the South Atlantic coast could operate from there."

"Our Navy anticipated that move too. We're building two forts covering the entrance to Port Royal Sound, one on Hilton Head Island and the other north of it." Mann looked at his watch, then stood up and, taking Maritza's hands, pulled her to her feet.

"Are you going back to Washington peaceably tomorrow?" he asked. "Or shall I hog-tie you and deliver you across the Potomac south of Alexandria by boat?"

"I'll go," she promised. "Just guide us as far as Little Rocky Run east of McLean's Ford, we'll know how to find our way around Centreville from there. But I warn you now that Cousin Pierre isn't going to like it."

"Then don't tell him."

"He'll take it out on you if I don't."

Richard Mann smiled. "Even the commanding general of the Army of the Potomac has no jurisdiction over the second in command of the Confederate Secret Service."

V

Maritza was awakened just before dawn by Celestina shaking her shoulder. As she sat up, the mutter of distant thunder could be heard.

"That sounds like a thunderstorm," she said. "We're liable to get wet before we reach Centreville."

"That's cannon thunder, not lightning thunder," said Tina.

"Then the battle's already begun. What time did it start?"

"I don't know exactly, but Colonel Mann woke me a few minutes ago and told me to get you ready to ride in ten minutes. He's out saddling the horses now."

By the time Maritza dressed and came out on the porch of the guesthouse in the as yet only half-light of coming dawn, Mann appeared. He was leading three horses, saddled and ready, and carried a small basket in which were a loaf of bread and a canteen.

"Sorry this is all the breakfast you'll have," he said. "It's bread and coffee but we'll have to eat in the saddle."

"Why all the rush?" Maritza asked. "Those cannon sound quite a distance away."

"About five miles, the distance from here to the stone bridge on the Warrenton Turnpike."

"Then Cousin Pierre was right. McDowell *is* attacking through the center, directly toward Manassas Junction."

"More likely he's trying to make us think so." Mann held her stirrup while she mounted, then vaulted into his own saddle. Meanwhile, Celestina had mounted and taken the basket to hold before her.

"I counted the number of cannon being fired per minute while rustling the food," he said. "Judging from that, I'd say considerably less than McDowell's main force is in action—which means a feint at the center while he's waiting for daylight to get into position for that march to Sudley Springs Ford we saw marked on the map you brought Beauregard."

"Sudley Springs Ford is way out northwest toward the mountains," Maritza exclaimed. "McDowell must be planning to turn Cousin Pierre's left flank just like the map showed."

"I'd give odds that you're right," Mann conceded as he led the way along the tracks of the Orange & Alexandria Railroad going eastward from Manassas Junction. "Whatever the plan, I want you and Celestina out of the area before the fighting even gets under way."

"Why are we going in this direction?" Maritza had urged her horse up beside him. "You'd find out what's happening a lot sooner by taking the road north toward Centreville."

"And put you where you'd be shot at," he said tersely. "We're heading for Signal Hill."

"Then I really can observe the battlefield while the fighting's going on?" Maritza said excitedly.

"Maybe for a few minutes, while I'm finding out what's hap-

pening myself," he said. "Captain Alexander's stationed atop
the tower on Signal Hill with the best telescope the Confederacy owns. By the time we get there the sun should be high
enough for him to see the Yankee lines and, hopefully, estimate
how many men are involved. If the number doesn't seem large
enough for a major thrust southward from the stone bridge,
your cousin Pierre has got to start moving troops westward
from the fords of Bull Run, where he hoped to launch his own
attack by tomorrow."

"Can he do it in time?"

"That's the question I came from Richmond to answer. This
is exactly what General Lee was afraid of. If Beauregard hesi-
tates, he's going to find his back being scratched sometime this
afternoon—by Yankee bayonets."

An hour of fast riding, the first mile of it along the roadbed
of the Orange & Alexandria Railroad east of Manassas Junction, and the rest through wooded copses and rolling meadows
of Piedmont Virginia, found them climbing a hill. On top of it a
rickety-looking tower made of what appeared to be a flimsy
pine two-by-four scantling had been erected to support a platform reached by a fixed ladder. Pulling the horses to a halt,
Mann handed the reins to Celestina.

"We've got some climbing to do," he told Maritza. "This is
the nearest you're going to get to a real battlefield, so you'd better come on or lose the chance."

When Maritza slid to the ground he was waiting by her saddle to catch her. Pausing a moment for a hard kiss, he seized
her hand and led her to the base of the tower. She was right
behind him as he climbed, helped by the fact that she was wearing a riding dress with a split skirt. The tall man on the platform reached down to help her up the last few rungs of the ladder at the top.

"Countess Maritza LeClerc, Captain Edward P. Alexander."
Mann made the introduction as he was crossing the platform
toward the telescope. "Have you learned anything yet, Ed?"

"It's a feint at the stone bridge while the main attack is
against our left," said the signal officer. "Glad to know you,
Countess. I was watching when you and your companion stum-

bled into that little fracas at Blackburn's Ford yesterday and were captured—"

"Not before she found a copy of McDowell's battle plan on the body of a dead officer." Mann spoke without turning his head away from the telescope. "Beauregard didn't take it very seriously last night but he'll damn sure have to take it seriously this morning, when he learns what's happening."

"He already knows," said Alexander. "I caught a glimpse of a soldier wearing one of those fancy plumed hats over beyond the stone bridge only a few minutes ago—"

"The Bersaglieri Guards!" Maritza exclaimed. "They've been all over Washington for the past month." Seeing the up-lifted brows of the signal officer, she added, "I'm a French subject, Captain, as well as an American citizen. At the moment, I'm acting as correspondent for *Le Pays* in Paris."

"She also reports to me when she can, without compromising her neutral status," Mann added.

Captain Alexander gave Maritza a deep bow. "You're risking a lot, Countess, and I for one am grateful to you." To Mann he said, "I sent a message by wigwag just now to the next tower to be passed on, telling General Johnston and General Beauregard the Yankees are engaged in turning our left."

"Good!" Mann had been using the telescope. Now he reached for Maritza's hand and clamped her fingers around the brass barrel. "Take a good look right where I've got the glass centered," he told her. "You can see Yankees to the left of the stone bridge and also north of it, where they're starting the flank movement."

Maritza had no trouble seeing what he was describing but Mann didn't give her long to look. "We'd better be going," he said in less than a minute. "I'd like to make Union Mills Ford before Ewell's troops there are ordered to move toward the stone bridge. With McDowell's forces all moving west and south, you should be safely on the road back to Washington by noon."

"Away from the battlefield where a correspondent is supposed to be," Maritza said somewhat angrily but she descended the ladder behind him.

Near the bottom of the ladder, Mann put his hands around her waist to lift her from the third step to the ground.

"I don't like this," she said, turning her head when he sought to kiss her.

"I don't like seeing you go back to Washington either, where I can't do anything to protect you," he said as they were mounting the horses again.

"Nobody's bothered Mrs. Greenhow and everybody in Washington knows she's a spy for the South."

"Only because they'd rather have her there. Have you seen Pinkerton?"

"He's been pointed out to me."

"Steer clear of him. Unless I miss my guess, he's been deliberately planting false information with Rose Greenhow, knowing it would be passed on to us."

"Like making Cousin Pierre think the attack would be directly south from the stone bridge against Manassas Junction?"

"That and other things, but we're feeding the Yankees some false information on our own, so it all probably comes out even. Let's go. We've got another hour at least of hard riding before you're safely on the road back where we all want you to be."

"Where's that?" she asked coldly, still miffed that he hadn't allowed her more time to use the telescope from the tower.

"In Washington, where you can let the French—and the rest of the world—know what's really happening in this war."

"Except for the battle that's going on now, while I'm moving away from it instead of toward it," she said pointedly. "And that's exactly nothing."

"Judah P. Benjamin doesn't think so. Neither do I nor President Davis."

"What would they know?"

"We get the New York newspapers just as you get the ones from Richmond. The tone of the propaganda cartoons, even in Horace Greeley's rag, has changed markedly in the past several weeks. The flow of scurrilous attacks against the South to foreign newspapers has practically dried up, too."

Maritza turned in her saddle to look at him in amazement. "You're not just telling me this to make me feel worth something, are you?"

"Ask your friends Henri and Cécile Mercier, or the English brigadier at the British Legation. They'll confirm what I've been telling you. You're worth a dozen Greenhows to the South but, even more important, you're worth the world to me. Which is why I'm spending a morning getting you out of Confederate territory when I should be at Portici, the headquarters of the Army of the Potomac."

"What could you do? Cousin Pierre already suspects you of being against him."

"That's one time he's right. My job here is really to help General Joe Johnston make sure your windbag of a cousin doesn't foul up the chance to win a great victory at Manassas. If the South can do that, we can convince the rest of the world that the Confederate States of America has every right to be recognized as a separate nation. Even more important, maybe they'll agree then to sell us rifles like those Enfields you brought over from England."

"Penn Darrow had as much to do with that as I did."

"You were the one who hatched the scheme and your money bought the munitions."

Maritza reached over to squeeze his right hand that held the reins guiding his mount. "Forgive me," she apologized. "I guess I let myself be carried away with the idea of becoming the most famous female newspaper correspondent in the world, like William Russell."

"Would you settle for being named the one I love most?"

"You couldn't bestow a greater honor on me than that," she told him. "I promise to behave from now on—and to obey orders."

VI

Crossing over into Union territory an hour later proved to be easy for Maritza and Celestina. The Federal Army lieutenant who, with a few blue-uniformed troops, had been guarding the ford accepted without question her story of having wandered across the battle line into Confederate territory and been captured. When she presented the certificate of accreditation as a correspondent furnished her by Secretary Seward, the Union lieutenant only glanced at it and waved her on.

"Where we goin' now, Miss Ritza?" Tina asked when they came to a dirt road crossing the now largely destroyed tracks of the Orange & Alexandria Railroad branch leading eastward from Manassas Junction.

"To Centreville." Maritza was guiding her horse down from the railroad bed they'd been following to the dirt road. "Watch that gravel. If they get caught in your horse's hoof, we'll be delayed while we dig them out."

"Where did that railroad we just left lead to?"

"Alexandria."

"And this cowpath?"

"Centreville."

"So you lied to the colonel when you told him you'd go to Washington?"

"I did no such thing," Maritza said indignantly. "There's a road from Centreville to Washington; we came that way yesterday."

"It was full of Yankee soldiers then and it's probably still full of 'em. You're going to the Yankee side of the battlefield, aren't you?"

"Centreville's no battlefield."

"Maybe not, but from the noise them cannon are making, there's a lot of fighting not far west of there."

"By afternoon the battle's likely to be all over. At Centreville I may be able to get somebody—maybe one of the wounded at that field hospital we saw yesterday being set up

near there—to tell me the whole story. Then, somewhere between there and Washington, maybe at Fairfax Courthouse, I
can stop to write one story at least of how we were captured by
the Confederates and, if I'm lucky, another about the battle itself. I can then put the copies in the mail to Georgetown the
way we usually do before turning the official dispatch in to Secretary Seward's office in Washington, putting me a whole day
ahead of Mr. Russell."

Tina shook her head slowly. "I might have known there'd be
a catch to it when you gave in so easily, after Colonel Mann
insisted that we go back to Washington. Your cousin Pierre really sold you on that idea of being the first woman correspondent to report a battle first hand, didn't he?"

"What's wrong with that?"

"Nothing, as long as you don't make it your life's work.
When this war's over, you promised that we'd settle down and
raise us some children."

"Suppose neither of us can conceive?"

Celestina laughed. "I'll settle for spendin' a lot of time tryin'
with André. I don't think you'll find either Captain Darrow or
Colonel Mann hard to take, either."

"Shut up and save your strength for riding," said Maritza.
"We've got a long way to go before nightfall."

"And on foot!"

Maritza was startled to see a tall man in the blue uniform of
a Federal Army sergeant step from the woods onto the path.
The soldier's face was scratched and bleeding and his uniform
torn in several places, as if he'd been running through under-
brush. His sudden appearance caused Maritza's horse to rear
and she had trouble bringing it under control.

"What do you want?" she demanded.

"What does a man always want from a pretty woman?" With
a smirk, the sergeant swung his Enfield rifle up to cover them.
"Get down off them horses—both of you."

"Better do like he says, Miss Ritza." Celestina had already
started to dismount.

"What are you doing this far from your unit?" Maritza asked
the soldier.

"The way I figger it, my enlistment expired yesterday and I'm going home. I'll give you one minute to get off that horse and start stripping."

Playing for time and a chance to use the derringer in its special pocket inside her jacket, Maritza dismounted. She made no move to start removing her clothing, however, although Celestina was stripping as fast as she could.

"Hoooe! You're a swell one, ain't you!" the deserter exclaimed. "Start stripping; I can handle two women, one after the other, any time. But if I have to shoot you and take the other one, a single pull on this trigger will do it."

Moving slowly, her eyes fixed upon those of the sergeant, Maritza started unbuttoning her jacket, watching for a swerve in his gaze toward the now almost naked Celestina that would, hopefully, give her time to slip the derringer from the pocket. At that range, even the small weapon could blow a hole in, if not through, a man's body.

"Come on, soldier." Tina's voice was deliberately provocative as she dropped the last of her garments on the green where she was standing. "Give me five minutes and I'll make a little boy out of you."

"Shut up, you black bitch!" The eyes didn't move from Maritza. "Hurry with that jacket, woman, I ain't got all day."

"The button is stuck." Maritza reached across the breast of her jacket, ready to grab the pistol in her pocket and remove the derringer, if the intruder's eyes swerved for one second toward Tina's lovely nude body.

"No, you don't!" The hammer made a distinct click as he cocked it, leaving the fulminate cap bare. "Just shed that jacket and toss it to me. Don't try to reach the pistol you've probably got in that pocket neither, or I'll pull the trigger.

Realizing that their captor wouldn't hesitate to kill her if she made a false move, Maritza slipped out of the jacket and tossed it toward him.

"That's better." Fumbling through the pockets with one hand, he removed the weapon. "Now there's a sweet little gun. Two barrels, too, one over the other. I never saw one exactly like that."

"It was made for me by Mr. Derringer himself."

"Well, now it's mine. You can just strip from the waist down; sorry, I don't have time to waste admiring them beautiful tits."

Kicking off her riding boots, Maritza obeyed. "Now just step out of them drawers and lay down on the grass here in front of me," he ordered, raising the barrel of the Enfield and gently letting the hammer down until it pressed upon the fulminate cap.

The dew of early morning felt cool to Maritza's naked buttocks as he laid the rifle on the grass about a yard away and started yanking at his belt. He was fairly drooling at the loveliness of the body he was about to possess and, in his haste, the belt came loose, letting the blue uniform trousers drop to his ankles—and giving her the opportunity for a move she had decided already was the only way to keep them both from being raped and probably killed.

Rolling quickly toward the Enfield lying some three or four feet away, Maritza managed to get a grip on it just as the soldier lunged for it. The pants that were now down around his ankles hampered his movements, though, and as he half fell toward the rifle she managed to get enough of a grip upon it to lift the barrel.

Cocking the hammer with her thumb, she slid her finger into the trigger guard where she could pull the trigger itself. Being heavier, the butt of the rifle stayed on the ground but the thunder of the black powder charge as it was ignited by the hammer striking the cap almost deafened her. The fact that the butt of the gun was against soft dirt lessened somewhat the shock of the recoil but the thrust against her shoulder still felt as if it was tearing her arm from the socket. She managed to hold on, however, and keep the barrel elevated, with the bayonet attached.

The rifle charge caught him full in the face, blowing off the top of his head and what had been his leering eyes. As he toppled forward his chest, too, was impaled by the bayonet, killing him instantly. His body fell across Maritza, pinning her to the ground and momentarily knocking her unconscious. She wasn't out long, however, but awoke to see a naked houri resembling

Celestina trying to pull the heavy weight of the dead man off while she cried: "Miss Ritza! Miss Ritza! You all right?"

With a mighty heave, helped by Tina's pulling, Maritza managed to throw off the body of the deserter and push herself upright. Leaning against a tree to keep from fainting again, she heard the sound of retching and saw Tina bending over a stump, vomiting and sobbing in turn as she held to it to keep from falling. More concerned with Tina's reaction than with her own, she went to put her arm around the naked girl and comfort her.

"It's all right, dear," she said. "He won't try to rape anybody else."

"I stripped in a hurry and needled him, hopin' he'd take me first and you could kill him with the little pistol—or run away. But when I saw you roll toward that rifle, I was sure he'd kill you and then rape me."

"We had one advantage over him," Maritza assured Tina. "A man is practically helpless with his pants down around his ankles."

Celestina stared at her a moment, then started to laugh, while Maritza, too, dissolved helplessly into laughter.

VII

It was nearly five o'clock that afternoon when Maritza and Celestina reined in their mounts atop a rise overlooking the road between Centreville and Fairfax Courthouse, near where a small branch called Cub Run crossed the turnpike. They had left the main road at this same point on the outskirts of Centreville yesterday morning, seeking to avoid the traffic crush created by the horde of civilians and politicians accompanying the Army, often in the very midst of the column of troops marching at route step.

At that time the meadow below looked more like the site of a carnival than a possible battlefield. Carriages, buggies, phaetons, and a host of other vehicles, including saddle horses, had been halted in the shadow of the trees. Early arrivals were visiting each other or picnicking on the grass, waiting for General Irvin McDowell's army to begin a triumphant march to Richmond and the capture of the Confederate capital.

Yesterday, too, soldiers had been wandering, many of them staggering, among the groups of civilians, accepting drinks freely offered from bottles and demijohns brought out from Washington for the giant celebration of victory. Ladies' parasols had gleamed in the bright sunlight, vying in color with their summer dresses. Children, too, had been playing ball in the open space of the meadow, while older boys and girls chased each other among the trees.

Congressmen and senators, each surrounded by his little group of admirers, had been holding forth importantly on the intricacies of military strategy—of which they knew next to nothing. Or spending time describing the retribution they would gleefully wreak upon the Southerners who had so recently formed one of the strongest blocs in the governing bodies of Congress. It was even rumored that President Lincoln would be coming out that afternoon and that he had already written a speech of praise for the conquering Union Army.

Now, a little more than twenty-four hours later, all was chaos in the meadow and on the high road; moreover, the situation seemed to be growing more disorganized by the minute. Thunderstruck by the scene below them, Maritza and Tina sat their horses in the shade of a towering sycamore, wondering whether they could believe what they were seeing. Or whether the long ride during the heat of a July day, plus their near brush with death at the hands of the Yankee deserter, had addled their brains.

The scene below was now one of chaos and pandemonium. Buggies lay overturned and broken, their drivers having sought to cross the meadow after the road became clogged, mainly with caissons being driven frantically northward away from the battle scene and competing for roadway against flimsy carriages and phaetons. Here and there soldiers, some wounded, many not, staggered away from Centreville toward Washington, leaving the battlefield behind them. The dazed look in many eyes

made them resemble zombies rather than trained soldiers of
what, only a little over a day before, had been an army
confident of winning a glorious victory. A few women in bedraggled finery and high-heeled shoes hobbled along with them,
too, camp followers retreating with what was obviously a defeated army.

"*Mon Dieu,* Miss Ritza!" said Celestina. "What could have
happened?"

"The South has won a great victory!" Maritza cried. "I've
got to find someone who can tell me more about it."

"You can't get any closer to the battlefield. Everybody's
going the other way."

"Maybe we can talk to some of those who were in the
fighting." Urging her mount down the slope, Maritza edged into
the line of stragglers moving along beside the main road, which
had been pre-empted for retreating military organizations and
equipment.

"What happened?" she called out to a private from one of
the proud New York regiments.

"They whipped us, lady." The man's voice didn't change
tone. "Whipped us fair and square."

"Where?"

"A place called Henry House Hill, but don't ask me where it
was." He would say no more, obviously too dazed by what had
happened to communicate.

Maritza was about to guide her horse deeper into the mass of
fleeing pedestrians, seeking someone who might know what had
happened in more detail, when the sound of a low whimpering
met her ears. Looking for the source, she saw a drummer boy
in the bedraggled uniform of the Bersaglieri Guards. The proud
plume was gone from his cap, his jacket was torn, and a bandage on his right foot was stained with blood and dirt. Red-
haired and freckled, he was obviously of Irish descent, like so
many troops recruited in New York. His eyes were red from
crying and from the dust that hung over the road like a clay-
colored cloud, while his cheeks were streaked with tears as he
limped along.

Guiding her mount up beside the boy, Maritza leaned down

from the saddle and reached for his hand. When he gave it to her, she was able to pull him up until his booted left foot caught in the strap holding the stirrup on that side and she could boost him into the saddle behind her.

"Where are you going?" she asked.

"Washington, ma'am—like everybody else, including the rebels."

"Is your wound very bad?"

The boy shook his head. "A big piece of shrapnel went right through my drums and a smaller one hit me in the foot. A doctor at a rebel field hospital dressed the wound and told me to get the hell out of there. Said he had a boy about my age."

"Where was that?"

"A place called Henry House Hill, south of a creek they call Bull Run."

The Zouave she had spoken to had said the same thing, Maritza remembered, and she resolved to get all the information she could out of the drummer boy.

"What's your organization?" she asked.

"Eleventh New York, Willcox's brigade," the boy said proudly. "I was the lead drummer."

"How old are you, by the way?"

"Fourteen, ma'am."

"You ought to be in school instead of in the Army."

"I was in a preparatory school in New York but everybody was excited about the war and I wanted to enlist. Told the recruiting officer I was fifteen and he took me in as a drummer. If you're from Washington, you must have seen us parading on Pennsylvania Avenue."

"Many times," Maritza assured him. "Tell me more about the battle and how you were driven from the field."

"The fightin' wasn't goin' bad at all this morning. We were beating the enemy back at a place called Matthews Hill—"

"You mean Henry House Hill, don't you?"

"That was later. Matthews Hill is north of the turnpike; Henry House is south. We'd driven them back this morning."

Maritza tried to envision the details of the map she'd given to Beauregard and managed to place the hills. Matthews Hill, she remembered now, lay northwest of the stone bridge that was to have been the center of the Southern attack.

"They had one mighty brave general, I think his name was Bee," the drummer boy continued. "I could tell from his accent when he urged his men on that he was from South Carolina; my roommate last year at school was from Charleston. Some of the rebels we captured said they were from Alabama. You ever been to Alabama, ma'am?"

Now that he was free from pain in his wounded foot and moving much more rapidly toward Washington and safety than the line still clogging the turnpike, the boy was growing more loquacious—which suited Maritza's purpose very well.

"I was born in Alabama," she told him.

"You don't talk like that fellow did."

"I've been living in France. What were you saying about General Bee?"

"General Willcox's brigade—we were part of it then—had got some reinforcements and the rebels were running, running like hell. We chased 'em up another hill and it looked like we had a clear road to Manassas and Richmond. Then I heard General Bee call to his men: 'Look, there stands Jackson like a stone wall. Rally behind the Virginians!' "

"Did you see General Jackson yourself?"

"Plain as I'm seeing you, ma'am. He sat on his horse at the top of the hill, watching us drive General Bee's men backward and paying no attention to the bullets whizzing all around him. We got almost to the top, then all hell broke loose."

"What happened?"

"Jackson had his soldiers and artillery hidden behind the hill so we couldn't see 'em or shoot at 'em until they raised up to fire. On the first volley, they mowed us down like wheat before a scythe blade and drove us back down the hill. We got together at the bottom, though, and started up again. General Willcox called in the artillery and I was drumming like mad. Then, all at once, a colonel the rebels called Jeb Stuart came sweeping across our flank with a bunch of cavalrymen riding like devils. About that time, too, an organization with the 33rd Virginia on their banners came howling across from the left side of the hill. Their uniforms were sort of a bluish gray and I guess our artillerymen couldn't be sure they weren't reinforcements. Anyway, our cannon didn't start firing until the rebels were too close and a marine battalion broke. When that happened, I tell you those rebels went through us like a knife through soft cheese."

"You say some of your regiment turned and ran?" Maritza asked.

"Everybody ran that could; that was when I lost my drums and the piece of shrapnel went through my foot. I was captured, but on the way back I could still see the one they call Jackson sitting on his horse up there on that hill. I guess he was waiting till his men could see the whites of our eyes before firing, like the history books said they did at Bunker Hill."

"Were many of your unit captured?"

"Most of what weren't killed, ma'am. I'll say one thing for the rebels, though, they treated the prisoners all right. A bunch of us wounded were taken back to a field hospital near a place they called Portici that seemed to be their field headquarters. They say Jefferson Davis himself was there but I didn't see him. I could hear some rebel generals arguin' and I remember General Jackson telling somebody that if they'd give him five thousand fresh men he could take Washington."

The boy looked back along the seemingly endless line of soldiers, civilians, *vivandières,* and equipment of all sorts, inching along the road eastward toward Washington. "I guess Jackson was right at that," he added, "but I didn't wait to see whether or not they were going to try it. When that rebel doctor at the aid station told me to get the hell out of there, I headed north. Caught a ride on a caisson as far as Centreville and then started walking."

"I'm a French newspaper correspondent and I'd like to write your story," Maritza told him. "Do you want to give me your name?"

"You mean you want to write about me?" the boy asked eagerly, then his face fell. "All you could say is that I ran like the rest of our soldiers and that wouldn't sound so good, would it? Not after the way I bragged to my schoolmates that I was going to drum my brigade into winning the war. Better just call me Jimmy, the drummer boy; that way nobody will know what a coward I turned out to be."

"You weren't a coward," Maritza assured him. "You said yourself that you drummed your company up Henry House Hill twice. How could you know a smart general named Jackson had hidden his men behind the crest where you couldn't see them?"

"We did go up that hill twice, ma'am." A proud note had come into the boy's voice. "The second time we knew the Virginians were there, too, with rifles and cannon, so maybe I'm not a coward after all."

"There weren't many heroes on your side today, Jimmy," said Maritza. "What are you going to do now?"

"Go back to New York and see if I can make up what I lost in school when I enlisted. The regiment's only got a few more weeks of enlistment anyway so they won't miss me."

VIII

With Washington less than twenty-five miles away and the long line of stragglers rife with fear that the whole Confederate Army was in pursuit, not many people were stopping as close to the scene of battle as Fairfax Courthouse. Just outside of town Maritza, Celestina, and the drummer boy they seemed to have adopted found shelter for the night in a house whose former occupants had apparently fled at news of the Confederate victory.

While Celestina was finding enough meal in the nearly empty larder to bake corn bread and cutting slices from a ham left hanging in the smokehouse, Maritza took the writing materials she carried in her saddlebags and made preparations to start writing the two stories she would file with the Secretary of State tomorrow. Before that, however, she planned to post copies of her dispatches to the address in Georgetown where she sent all her writings for the quickest possible transportation to Paris.

When the meal was finished, Jimmy was ready for a pallet in the attic, so while Celestina helped him make his bed, Maritza began to write in the light of a candle they'd found in the house. Celestina came back from the attic, pulled a chair up at the other side of the table, and started copying what Maritza was writing.

It was almost midnight when the two stopped writing but the rumble of caissons and wagons passing through the town was still plainly audible. No more cannon or rifle fire could be heard, however. From which Maritza presumed that Jefferson Davis and the other Confederate leaders Jimmy had described as meeting at the place called Portici had decided against giving General Jackson the fresh five thousand he'd asked for. Having taken a terrible beating in the early hours of the battle before the lucky stand of the Virginia troops on Henry House Hill, as Jimmy had described, the Confederate Army of the Potomac had apparently been neither ready nor eager to pursue the fleeing and thoroughly defeated Army of Northeastern Virginia.

The roads were still clogged with troops and equipment when the three rode out of Fairfax Courthouse on a rainy Monday morning. To these had been added women and children from the families of Federal troops who had been stationed in Alexandria and Arlington Heights in the months before the disastrous march upon Manassas Junction. Fearing retribution at the hands of a victorious rebel Army, these, too, were straggling along as best they could. Some carried suitcases and baskets containing the few belongings they'd been able to salvage when the head of the retreating column reached the suburbs of those towns, bringing news of the Federal rout.

Troops who had not been involved in the fighting and those garrisoning the entrenchments on the Virginia side of the Potomac were now clogging the roads too. Some even waved their enlistment papers in their hands, as they headed for the trains in Washington that would bear them home, unabashedly happy, even though many had been no nearer the actual fighting than Centreville and some not even that far.

Maritza was anxious to get the mailed copy of her dispatches to their Georgetown destination in time to reach Paris as quickly as possible with news of the disastrous defeat of the Union troops at Henry House Hill. She decided, therefore, to go cross-country northwestward to the "Chain" Bridge, as it was called. A somewhat shorter route to Georgetown, it had the advantage of being relatively free from fleeing troops and civilians.

The members of the artillery battery guarding the bridge made no resistance to their entering the city. Before noon Maritza had posted her mail in the post office and turned in their mounts at the stable where she had hired the horses. On familiar territory once he was in Washington, Jimmy had decided to catch the first train going north to New York, so Maritza gave the now ex-drummer boy twenty-five dollars, which he promised faithfully to repay, and they watched him trudge away. He was limping only a little, for they had stopped at one of the dressing stations, now established all over the city, where a lighter, fresh dressing had been put on the small wound in his foot. At the corner, he turned to wave good-by just before disappearing from view.

From the livery stable where they had turned in their mounts after reaching Washington, Maritza and Tina went to their quarters for baths and fresh clothing. By lunchtime Maritza was able to take the official copies of her dispatches to the State Department, certain that those intended for Richmond would, hopefully, soon be aboard a swift blockade runner on the first leg of the trip to Paris. As she was coming out of the clerk's office she met William H. Russell, bringing his own copies and looking considerably the worse for wear.

"You're lucky you didn't try to watch the battle, Countess," he told her. "If you'll wait a moment and have lunch with me, I'll tell you about it from firsthand knowledge."

Russell came out of the office a few moments later and they moved to a restaurant less crowded than Willard's dining room was likely to be. There he ordered whiskey and soda for himself and a glass of sherry for Maritza, before tackling a luncheon of broiled chicken and wild rice.

"I tell you, Countess, the battle called Bull Run was a farce," said the Englishman. "Two masses of untrained rabble tried to see which one could make the most mistakes. If it hadn't been for one man, the Confederates would be fighting halfway to Richmond at the Rappahannock River today instead of trying to decide what they're going to do next."

"You must mean General Jackson," she said. "I've heard a lot about him."

"'Stonewall' Jackson they're calling him now; he was given the nickname on the battlefield." Russell gave her a probing look. "By the way, where were you yesterday?"

"Somewhere between Union Mills Ford and Centreville on my way back from having been taken prisoner by the rebels."

Russell gave her a startled look. "You wouldn't per chance be pulling my leg—as you Americans say?"

Maritza gave the English journalist a quick summary of the events of the weekend, leaving out her visit to McLean House at Manassas Junction and the near brush with death she and Celestina had suffered later at the hands of the Union Army sergeant.

"I suppose you included all that in the story you just left at Secretary Seward's office," he said.

"I left two stories. One was titled, *'I Was Captured by the Rebels.'* The other was, *'A Drummer Boy's Eye View of the Battle of Bull Run.'*"

"I guess I'm getting too old for this business." Russell shook his head morosely. "I hired a buggy that was smashed west of Centreville, and rode a horse so much I can hardly sit down this morning. Yet here you come along and gain a clean beat on me with the best stories of the whole affair." Then he brightened. "But in the end you won't be any better off than I, Countess. When the censors at Secretary Seward's office get through with what both of us wrote, it will sound like a schoolboy's description of a Sunday afternoon ball game."

IX

The day after the defeat at Bull Run—or Manassas as it was called by the Confederacy—General George B. McClellan was called from western Virginia, where he'd been winning minor victories, to take command of the new Federal Division of the Potomac, including the defense of Washington itself. Meanwhile, the victorious Confederate Army of the Potomac moved forward as far as Munson's Hill, about halfway between the capital and Fairfax Courthouse. From that point their squirrel-hunters-turned-soldiers could harass the Union troops drilling on the fields around their encampments in Alexandria and Arlington Heights, while the Confederate Stars and Bars again floated in plain view of anyone in Washington possessing a telescope and a high window.

Life in the capital was much stricter under McClellan than it had been under General Sandford. Sale of liquor to soldiers was forbidden but ways were found, without much difficulty, to evade the order. The military police patrol in Washington were sharply increased and forts were started on every piece of high ground around the city. Allegedly, their purpose was to guard against a rumored invasion by the Confederates but building the forts made a lot of work and money for civilian contractors and the drain upon the Federal exchequer rapidly increased.

McClellan's taste for flamboyance and downright insolence soon made itself evident. Openly contemptuous of the aged General Winfield Scott, his superior, McClellan also largely ignored President Lincoln. Nor could Lincoln do much about it, since the colorful general, riding back and forth across the city daily in full uniform with a dozen spurred and booted dragoons accompanying him and a long black military cloak floating behind him, was a far more romantic and attention-getting sight than Lincoln. Meanwhile, much to the disgust of the shippers whose wharves had been swarming with vessels carrying supplies and munitions a couple of months ago, Confederate guns in fortifications constructed on the south bank of the Potomac downstream from Alexandria were busy shelling Union shipping on the river, effectively sealing off the city by water.

Life was relatively quiet for Maritza and Celestina, enjoying the cuisine at Monsieur Cruchet's and attending the active theater and social life in Washington. Under the sponsorship of Cécile and Henri Mercier, Maritza was invited to diplomatic receptions and was soon a regular visitor to the levees staged by Mrs. Lincoln on Sunday afternoons.

Copies of *Le Pays* reached her regularly through the mails, since Union shipping was quite active, except on the Potomac. That her stories of affairs in America were claiming the interest of French readers was proved by the appearance of her by-line more and more often on the front page of the journal. For this she was widely complimented by those of her fellow correspondents who could read French but she had no idea that they were stirring interest in another quarter. Then, shortly after the articles dealing with the Battle of Bull Run appeared, she received a peremptory summons to visit the office of Secretary Seward.

When Maritza came into the Secretary's office she was hardly surprised to find there the man who answered most often to the name of Mr. Allen but was in reality Allan Pinkerton, Seward's top agent. As Seward himself rose to greet her cordially, she saw the latest copy of *Le Pays* lying on his desk.

"I trust our summer weather here in Washington is not discommoding you too much, Countess," said the Secretary. "Many Washingtonians are happy to leave the city for higher elevations at times like these. Even President Washington, I am told, had a preference for Bath and often took the waters there."

"I was born in the deep South, Mr. Secretary, as Mr. Pinkerton has no doubt informed you, so I became accustomed very early to hot weather."

"I understand that you spent some time in Paris."

"Not so much in Paris, though we often went there. My husband's estates and Château LeClerc were on the Loire well away from the city. It was much cooler there."

"How long did you stay in France, Countess?" Pinkerton asked.

"About seven and a half years, from the time of my marriage until my husband's death."

"You have a remarkable facility with the language," Seward complimented her. "I studied it when I was younger but never seemed to get it quite right."

"You should have read more French authors as I did, Mr. Secretary," Maritza said urbanely. "One gets to know the language quickly that way and also becomes proficient in writing it."

Then, in order to needle Allan Pinkerton who, she was sure, had called the French journal to Seward's attention, she added: "I see that you have the latest issue of *Le Pays*. My own arrived only a few days ago."

"Much of it written by you, I note," said Seward.

"Monsieur Claudet gives me considerable latitude in my writing."

"To the point of turning news into fiction," said Pinkerton harshly.

"So?" Maritza's eyebrows rose in simulated surprise. "I can assure you that everything in the two articles is quite true, Mr. Pinkerton. If you will refer to your files, I imagine you will find a copy of my dispatches, since I am told that you and your censors—"

"Please, Countess, use another word," said Seward. "We have nothing to hide from our friends in France and England. Or even in America."

"Then we're both happy, Mr. Secretary."

"Of course a few of your statements could have been toned down somewhat."

"Like what, sir?"

"Where you describe a marine unit breaking under fire and fleeing at Henry House Hill, for example."

"I used the exact words of the drummer boy who described the engagement for me, Mr. Secretary. He was right on the ground and was wounded and treated in a Confederate field hospital before being released."

"Now, now, Countess," Seward said in a tone of gentle reproof. "Surely an experienced correspondent would not have accepted without question a tall tale by a New York street urchin."

"If Jimmy, my source, were what you describe as a 'New York street urchin' I certainly shouldn't have accepted his rather dramatic account without going onto the battlefield to check the facts for myself. This boy was from a New York college preparatory school and spoke better English, I suspect, than either you or I. Besides, so many military units were clogging the turnpike leading away from the battlefield at the time that it would have been quite impossible for me to breast the tide by trying to ride toward, not away from, Bull Run."

"What we really want to know, madam," Pinkerton interposed, "is just how these dispatches reached Paris."

"You must have forwarded them, as you do the stories of the other correspondents, Mr. Pinkerton. The account in *Le Pays* is almost exactly the way I wrote it, with only a few minor editorial changes made by Monsieur Claudet. I consider that a minor miracle, too, since it was written the night after the battle in an empty house at Fairfax Courthouse by candlelight." She laughed gaily. "I even stole a march on Mr. Russell of the London *Times* by not waiting until I could get back to the noisy city to write my accounts."

"They *are* brilliantly written, Countess," Seward admitted. "Our only quarrel with them is that you could have kept your facts a little straighter than you did."

"Every word was true, I assure you, Mr. Secretary," Maritza said piously, quite realizing that she was engaging in a sparring match with words against what William Russell had termed a "wily" antagonist. "Would you rather I had let Mr. Pinkerton's censors dictate what I wrote?"

"Of course not." Seward's patience was beginning to get a little thin.

"Then what should I have done? I stopped at the hotel only long enough to bathe and dress in something more presentable than a riding habit before bringing the manuscripts directly to the clerk who has always handled dispatches for foreign correspondents. In fact, Mr. Russell was coming in with his own as I was leaving and we had lunch together afterward." She turned to Pinkerton. "I want to thank you, Mr. Pinkerton, for sending them to Paris exactly as I had written them."

When neither man spoke, she asked, "Is there anything else I can tell you?"

"No, Countess," said Seward. "We would appreciate it, though, if in future writings you are a little more accurate where the actions of the United States Government and the Army are concerned."

"Believe me, sir, I was trying to be as impartial as I could possibly be."

"Perhaps, considering your Southern birth and girlhood, you could hardly be expected to be completely neutral, Countess, but in the future please try harder. We don't want our French friends to believe we've already lost this unfortunate war, when the only fighting has been several small engagements outside Washington. Good day, Countess—and thank you for coming."

"Thank you for reading my story, sir. And you too, Mr. Pinkerton. Good day."

Maritza had been invited to dinner at the Merciers' that evening. Afterward she told the French minister about her visit to the office of the Secretary of State that morning.

"It's not you they should have been angry at," Mercier told her. "But at the clerk who accidentally let your accounts of the battle go through without being censored."

Maritza didn't comment, since Henri Mercier knew nothing of the copy that was regularly mailed to the Georgetown address. "Seward doesn't dare open the mailbags containing diplomatic correspondence between myself and the Quai d'Orsay," Mercier continued, "but hardly anything else addressed to England or France goes through the mails without a thorough scrutiny. As for newspaper accounts, you should hear William Russell hold forth on that subject."

"Why would they deny losing the battle, when the Richmond papers are naming Beauregard and the one they call 'Stonewall'

Jackson heroes? Surely they know those newspapers go to France and England too."

"In this case, your account seems to have brought a considerably quicker response than the papers from Richmond ordinarily elicit."

"What do you mean?"

"It was announced officially by the White House today that Prince Napoleon will soon visit Washington."

"Surely they don't think my account of the Battle of Bull Run could have influenced that decision. It must have been made weeks ago, if he's coming soon."

"He's due to arrive in New York on August 3, so the decision for him to make the trip had to be made before your stories appeared in *Le Pays*. In fact, Prince Napoleon was probably at sea when they appeared in Paris."

"Then why was Secretary Seward upset?"

"Right now, so soon after the first Federal defeat, the appearance of an official observer for Napoleon III could hardly be anything except a warning."

"What kind of a warning, Henri?"

"That getting France to recognize the Confederacy as a nation could be the price for overlooking Napoleon's plans for intervention on the side of the *imperialistas* in the revolution going on down in Mexico. When Prince Napoleon gets to New York, I'll see that he gets copies of *Le Pays* he may have missed in his travels. The way you described the Union defeat could influence the Emperor to believe the North is not nearly so strong as he has been led to believe in correspondence between Secretary Seward and our Foreign Minister in Paris, Édouard Thouvenel."

BOOK FIVE

BOSTON

I

Although Washington was reputed—and with good reason—to have one of the worst summer climates in the country, Maritza found herself so busy during the summer and fall of 1861 that she hardly had time to be uncomfortable from the heat.

Already considered a failure by many of his own constituents, Abraham Lincoln could do little to control the flamboyant General McClellan. Having announced his intention to carry the war into the heartland of the South by attacking Richmond, McClellan, often referred to in newspapers as the "Bonaparte of Washington," continued to court recognition. He even wrote his wife, it was reported, that he could become dictator of the North almost without opposition, if he chose such a role. In any event, after McClellan's daily performances, the arrival of a real Napoleon in the person of a French prince came as something of an anticlimax.

Henri Mercier, who was in charge of arrangements for Prince Napoleon's official visit, would have preferred that the royal visitor come to Washington by way of the Potomac on a French warship, to be greeted by the marine band under Professor Scala. Because of the Confederate fortifications controlling the Potomac, however, the princely visitor had to be brought into the country through the port of New York. There, since France was believed to support the rebels, as did many residents of New York, he was welcomed by a large and enthusiastic crowd.

Having promised Henri and Cécile Mercier to help welcome the prince, Maritza could hardly escape the state dinner given for him at the White House. It turned out to be a very dull affair, however, since neither the Frenchman nor the gangly backwoods-lawyer-turned-President was particularly impressed with one another. The prince was heard to confide to Henri Mercier his conviction that Lincoln was a dullard with very little of the polish a Parisian diplomat would expect from a head of state. Lincoln, on the other hand, rather obviously considered the visiting royalty nothing but a dandy not worth cultivating except as a matter of state.

One event during Prince Napoleon's visit Maritza had to describe in her dispatches to *Le Pays* second hand from the observations of Henri Mercier. It had been arranged, at the request of Mercier, for the visitor to cross the Potomac under a flag of truce and have lunch with Generals Beauregard and Johnston in the Confederate camp near Centreville. This was done over the strong objections of Secretary Seward, who saw in the courtesy a blatant attempt by the French minister—known to be sympathetic to the Southern Cause—to help the Confederacy obtain recognition as a nation.

II

All in all, Maritza was happy to see the princely entourage take train for Chicago. When Henri Mercier returned to Washington at the end of Prince Napoleon's visit, she dined with him and Cécile at their Georgetown home. It was Indian summer by then, with the leaves starting to turn and draping the smaller city in browns, red, and yellow. She could report nothing of significance in the events of summer in Washington, however, except the tension between General McClellan and General Scott, accompanied by a steadily growing coolness between the flamboyant general and the President.

"Allan Pinkerton and Secretary of War Cameron haven't let the heat of summer lull them into tolerance where either the foreign or the domestic press is concerned," said Mercier as he handed Maritza a printed sheet. "One of your competitors for the attention of the foreign public gave me this today. I was fairly livid with indignation and I suspect William Russell and perhaps even Horace Greeley are an even deeper shade of purple."

The sheet was a printed General Order from the War Department titled: GIVING INFORMATION TO THE ENEMY. Maritza read it quickly and, when she looked up, her cheeks were flushed with anger. "This sort of censorship could muzzle the press both in America and abroad. They can't do that without throwing away the Constitution."

"Exactly that is happening, article by article," said Mercier dryly. "First Lincoln suspended the writ of habeas corpus. Now Secretary Cameron takes it on himself to keep the people in ignorance of how the war's going, even though it seems no more than a stalemate. I'd wager Secretary Seward hit the ceiling, as the Americans say, when he first saw that War Department order."

"I don't blame him—when he's been so busy denying there's any censorship here at all."

"Will you be able to keep on writing for *Le Pays?*"

"I have ways of getting the news through. Right now I'm more concerned with what Prince Napoleon will advise the Emperor about interference when he returns to Paris."

"The prince is no fool and neither are the military equerries who accompanied him," said the French minister. "I'd wager he will tell Napoleon he can accomplish more by keeping hands off in this conflict than in any other way."

"France still needs cotton."

"So does England, but you won't see Lord John Russell and Prince Albert advising Queen Victoria to interfere. If England entered the war on the side of the Federal government, in order to stop it quickly, Napoleon III would have to help the Confederacy or give up his ambition to gain control of Mexico."

"How could he seize a country that far from France anyway?"

"Mexico is torn apart right now by revolutionaries who owe large sums to France and England. Suppose one of the warring parties—say those calling themselves the *imperialistas*—requested help from France, Napoleon could then place somebody from among European royalty on the throne in Mexico City and support him with part of the French Army."

"I still don't see why everybody doesn't realize peace is better than war," Maritza commented.

"It isn't for those moved mainly by greed—for money and power. Before the fall of Fort Sumter, the United States was growing rapidly in economic and military power. England and France have colonies in the Western Hemisphere, which a strong United States Government could have taken over by stretching the Monroe Doctrine a little but, if the Union and the Confederacy keep fighting long enough, the strength of both will be exhausted. Then neither could pose any opposition to the increased influence the two countries have in this part of the world."

"Surely thoughtful men on both sides realize that," said Maritza.

"They did and they do; unfortunately none of them rule on either side. On the one hand, Abraham Lincoln will accept no peace, such as I've offered to mediate, unless the South comes back into the Union. Jefferson Davis, on the other hand, insists that reunion of the states is impossible and separate nations are the only answer. Meanwhile, schemers on both sides are very happily lining their pockets with profits, so they're naturally reluctant to see the war end and will do everything they can to oppose a reconciliation between the Union and the Confederacy."

III

With little news to report to *Le Pays* during the midsummer dog days, Maritza had offered herself as a volunteer nurse in one of the military hospitals organized by Miss Dorothea Dix and Miss Clara Barton. Her motives were not entirely humanitarian, although the wounded among both Union soldiers and Confederate prisoners naturally earned her sympathy. By talking to the patients while ministering to their needs, she quickly discovered she could learn much about the progress of the war that would not have filtered through the censorship being more and more rigorously enforced as the months drew on.

And there *was* progress. As July drew to a close and Congress prepared to adjourn, Horace Greeley of the New York *Tribune* became as much of a dove as he had previously been a hawk and called for peace negotiations. General Benjamin F. Butler, now in command at Fort Monroe, guarding the entrance to Chesapeake Bay at Hampton Roads, asked the War Department whether the nine hundred or more fugitive slaves, called "contraband," living in the area were property and could be used—as he actually was already doing—to build additional fortifications. He received no answer to what was becoming a vexing question, however, as more and more blacks fled from their former masters to become "free" in the North. That freedom, they quickly discovered, meant work or army service, neither of which most of them wanted. Union orators had assured the blacks before the war that, freed from bondage in the South, they would become fully qualified citizens of the North. But when they crossed the lines to claim that citizenship, and the vote that went with it, they could find nobody ready to grant it.

Without much real enthusiasm, President Lincoln nominated an obscure colonel named Ulysses S. Grant, along with others, as brigadier generals of volunteers, bringing the caustic comment from the President's critics in Congress that the Army already had too many chiefs and too few Indians. On August 2, also, Congress levied on individuals the first income tax in American history, three per cent on incomes over eight hundred dollars per year—and found few anxious to pay.

If the Army and the War Department were dilettante, the Navy was not. The blockade was increased, as blockade running became more and more profitable to Confederate ships' captains daring to attempt it. Meanwhile, a fleet of perhaps half a dozen ironclad gunboats was authorized by both belligerents. The maneuver received almost no mention in the press but was destined to revolutionize naval warfare.

On August 10 the first major battle in Missouri, a state

whose sentiment was almost equally divided between the Confederacy and the Union, was fought at Wilson's Creek, southwest of Springfield. It ended in a rather confused Confederate victory causing doubt and fear in the Union about the border states, which had remained loyal for the most part. Equally questionable was the loyalty of the 79th New York Volunteers, who mutinied in Washington over demands for furloughs.

Lincoln proclaimed that "inhabitants of Southern states were in a state of insurrection against the United States and that all commerce between loyal and disloyal states was immediately to be discontinued, upon pain of arrest and punishment." Five New York newspapers were almost immediately subject to legal attack and soon closed, a suspension of the Fifth Amendment of the Constitution he was sworn to defend. In another order, Lincoln merged the Federal government of Northeast Virginia, Washington, and the upper Shenandoah Valley into the Department of the Potomac, placing General McClellan in command of what now came to be known as the Army of the Potomac.

Although Maritza found that she could obtain a certain amount of information useful in her dispatches to Paris from her nursing duties, Celestina's talents were much more useful elsewhere. With an avalanche of three-year enlistees pouring into the city from all over the Northern and Western states, the demand for entertainment had risen sharply in camps, hospitals, and, of course, theaters. With her beautiful figure, lovely voice, and fund of songs, many of them bawdy, from her girlhood in Louisiana and Alabama, plus seven and a half years in France, Tina had no trouble finding occupation as a music hall entertainer. Many of the girls, particularly the chorus, supplemented their rather meager wages through becoming the mistresses, on a regular or intermittent basis, of political and military men both high and low. From them Celestina brought home a constant fund of gossip full of information and scandal on life in the teeming Northern capital.

Instead of buying the Richmond newspapers, on sale only a day later than publication, at the same newsstand daily and thus risk throwing suspicion upon themselves, Celestina and Maritza alternated both in time and place, never buying at the same stand more than once a week. It was Celestina who came back to their rooms at Monsieur Cruchet's one evening, triumphantly bearing a copy of the Richmond *Examiner*.

"Your lover made it!" she cried. "Just like I knew he would."

With fingers trembling in excitement, Maritza took the newspaper and read the account where Tina had folded it:

> Wilmington, N.C., August 20. Residents of this important port city awoke this morning to find that, during the night, a new ship had appeared at the Wilmington docks. Loaded with munitions and other articles of war, the *Sprite* resembles her namesake and is a thing of beauty both at sea and in port. Sleek, powerful, long, this swift side-wheeler was built in the shipyards of the Clyde. Its fireboxes burn anthracite coal, which is practically smokeless, and, if pursued, *Sprite* can lower its smokestacks and become almost invisible on the horizon. Captain Pennington Darrow, who commands this fine new ship, predicts that *Sprite* can and will outrun any Federal gunboat afloat, thumbing its nose at the Federal blockade.
>
> While unloading the cargo, the swift vessel is being coaled in preparation for the run with a load of cotton to one of several ports in the British colonies. It will join the blockade-running fleet now plying industriously between various blockaded Confederate ports and the harbors of English and French colonies in the Caribbean and Nova Scotia, where large amounts of munitions and other articles badly needed by the Confederacy are being unloaded daily from the hulls of English vessels.

"Aren't you going to Wilmington to inspect your property—and Captain Darrow?" Tina asked.

"Of course not."

"Mr. Russell crosses the lines whenever he wishes to report on what's happening on either side. Why couldn't you do the same for *Le Pays?*"

"Russell doesn't get his writings past Pinkerton's censorship the way I do. Besides, I'm sure both Secretary Seward and Pinkerton already suspect me of being other than what I appear to be."

"You may be right," Tina conceded. "Pinkerton's brought in more agents and is busy making lists of the spies he plans to arrest soon."

"How do you know that?"

"One of the girls in the chorus is his Saturday night mistress; they get paid so little that prostitution is the only way they can make any extra money. She says the bastard is too cheap to keep her regularly. He brags a lot about the people he's going to arrest, though, and sometimes she warns them—for a fee."

"I hope we're not on his list."

"Not yet anyway. Right now he's gunning for Mrs. Greenhow and the men who supply the information she passes on to the couriers from Richmond."

"If it's anything like what she passed to Cousin Pierre before the battle of Manassas, I'd think he wouldn't want her arrested."

"Things have changed," said Tina. "With Secretary Cameron putting out orders like that one muzzling the newspapers and General McClellan being mysterious about what he plans to do next, I guess Mrs. Greenhow doesn't know much any more. Anyway, Pinkerton's hoping to catch the whole bag at once."

"When?"

"The next time she has a gathering—and that's almost every night. He has to be sure Senator Henry Wilson isn't there, though; being chairman of the Military Affairs Committee, the senator still pulls a lot of weight in the government. If Wilson was caught in Mrs. Greenhow's bed, he could probably have even Pinkerton fired."

Tina's information proved to be accurate, as usual. Three evenings later, Maritza was returning from a dinner and, obeying an inspiration, told the driver of the hack she'd rented to drive by Sixteenth and I streets. Usually the narrow brick house in the very heart of the city, only a few blocks from the White House, was darkened at night, except for lights kept discreetly low behind rose-colored curtains. Tonight it was ablaze with light and a crowd extended halfway down the block. When the hack could go no farther because of the people jamming the street, Maritza told the driver to wait and walked the rest of the way to the outer gate, where a Pinkerton operative was on guard.

"Yer cain't go in, ma'am," he said, barring the walk to the front door with his body.

"What's going on?" Maritza asked innocently. "Everybody appears to be excited."

"Major Allen is searchin' the house. It belongs to a woman that's a rebel spy."

"I represent a newspaper. Can you tell me who's involved?"

"Half of Washington, from the stories I've heard. She must have a pretty big bed," he added with a smirk. "They say the secesh visit her at all hours of the night."

"Who is she anyway?"

The man gave her a sidewise look, then lowered his voice. "I could tell you, if it was worth my while."

Maritza took a purse from her handbag and lifted out a five-dollar bill, surreptitiously passing it to the Pinkerton agent.

"It's Mrs. Rose Greenhow," the man confided. "Most anybody in the crowd could have told you that for nothing."

"Surely you know more than her name, if you work for Mr. Pinkerton."

"They say she's got men workin' for her all over Washington, even on General McClellan's staff. Mr. Pinkerton—Major Allen—is searching the house."

Just then Pinkerton came out, followed by a half dozen agents but no prisoners. He didn't look happy and the sight of Maritza talking to the guard at the street only made his expression more forbidding.

"You do seem to get around, Countess," he said sourly. "Were you perhaps coming to visit Mrs. Greenhow tonight?"

"I only met the lady once—at a reception. Is she really a Confederate spy? My readers in France would love to hear about her; spy stories are always exciting."

"If you know what's good for you, you'll stay away from here and from anybody connected with Mrs. Greenhow, Countess," Pinkerton advised. "Now if you'll excuse me."

"Aren't you going to take her to prison?"

"She's only under house arrest for the time being, madame, so don't go writing any lurid accounts for your newspaper telling how we Yankees torture innocent people."

"If *you* don't have enough evidence to arrest her, Mr. Pinkerton, *I* don't have enough information to be worth writing about," said Maritza. "That is, unless you're letting her go because she has friends so highly placed in government that you're afraid to put her in prison."

The thrust struck home and Pinkerton's sallow cheeks flushed with anger. "I've said all I'm going to say, Countess." He lifted his bowler. "Good evening to you."

"Better luck next time, Mr. Pinkerton." Maritza couldn't resist a final thrust. "Maybe you'd better concentrate on smaller fry."

Telling Tina about the encounter later at their hotel, Maritza was surprised by her companion's reaction.

"You shouldn't have baited him," said Tina. "The girl he sleeps with occasionally says he can be real mean when he wants to. He's bragged more than once that, if the State Department and Secretary Cameron would let him have his way, he'd see every secesh sympathizer lynched."

"I just needled him a little, the opportunity was too attractive to let pass."

"Needling Mr. Pinkerton is like spittin' in the eye of a bobcat. Just because he ain't a big man don't mean his claws aren't sharp."

"You're right, I guess," Maritza agreed as she got into bed. "Both Dick Mann and Judah P. Benjamin warned me to stay out of any active spying activities."

IV

Late in September, troops manning the earthworks facing the Confederate lines at Munson's Hill suddenly discovered that those same lines were now empty. Obviously, Generals Beauregard and Johnston had fallen back, first to Fairfax Courthouse and, as developed later, all the way to Centreville and Manassas.

Confederate troops still occupied the south bank of the Potomac farther upstream, however, in the area around Leesburg, Virginia. And when a Federal force of several thousand crossed over to the Virginia side of the Potomac to assay the situation there, they were trapped by waiting Confederates between the cliffs near a place called Ball's Bluff and the river. In the resulting massacre the Federals suffered over nine hundred casualties to less than two hundred for the Confederates, almost another Manassas. Moreover, in the days following the debacle, bodies of dead men in blue uniforms floated down the river to wash up against the supports of the bridges across the Potomac, reminding the by now thoroughly concerned Washingtonians that the war was still very near them.

The affair at Ball's Bluff and the strange retreat of the Confederates before Washington—apparently for the purpose of attacking somewhere else—threw the capital and nearly half the nation into a state of panic. This situation Maritza busily reported for *Le Pays,* knowing the accounts she dutifully turned over to the State Department were being scrupulously emasculated by Pinkerton's censors but confident that the truth could still reach Paris through her connection in Georgetown.

From the music hall, where she was now a principal artist, Celestina brought home a steady stream of gossip about goings on in Washington, particularly the blatant thievery taking place in Secretary Cameron's War Department dealings with its suppliers. At Sixteenth and I streets, too, although under house arrest, the country's most famous female spy continued to ply her trade. In fact visiting tourists usually named "Fort Greenhow," as it was being more and more often called, as their first preference of sights when they got off the train in Washington.

From time to time the Richmond papers carried news of the arrival at first one and then another of the blockaded Southern ports of the now most famous of the Confederate blockade runners, *Sprite.* A startling bit of news reached Maritza on August 24, when Jefferson Davis announced the appointment of three special representatives to major European capitals. The avowed purpose of these new commissioners was to gain recognition for the Confederacy and buy supplies of war for eventual transmission through the blockade to the South. James M. Mason, a former senator, was assigned to Great Britain and Maritza's own relative, John Slidell, to France.

Celestina brought the newspapers with the announcement. "Why don't we go back to France with your uncle John?" she asked. "The way the Union Army is growing and with all the money President Lincoln is spending on equipment and munitions, this war can only end one way."

"Knowing so many people with important governmental positions in France as I do, I suppose I could help Uncle John a lot by acting as his secretary," Maritza admitted.

"Then let's go."

Maritza considered for only a moment, then shook her head. "Henri Mercier tells me the supply of cotton in France is growing shorter all the time and so is that in England. When the looms are idle and people can no longer make a living, Lord Russell and Monsieur Thouvenel will have to take some action."

"What could they do?"

"William Russell says that if worse comes to worst England and France could demand that the Southern ports be kept open to all shipping—and enforce that demand with their navies."

"Is that likely to happen?"

"Mr. Russell doesn't think the South can last that long. The Union can manufacture practically anything it needs but the South has to import almost everything, except men and food, through the blockade. Mr. Seward's job is to see that England, in particular, with its tremendous navy, has no excuse to step in on our side."

"What can Mr. Mason and your uncle John possibly hope to achieve then?"

"Probably not much," Maritza admitted, "unless the situation changes in some dramatic way that would bring the British in on the side of the South."

"I'm going to bed," said Celestina. "The music hall management wants me to teach the girls the cancan, so I'll have to start rehearsals in the afternoons."

"I didn't know you even knew the dance."

Celestina laughed. "A lot went on downstairs at the Château LeClerc that you and the count didn't know about. Good night."

V

As it happened, the political situation did change soon in a very dramatic way, one neither Maritza nor Celestina—nor Secretary Seward for that matter—could possibly have foreseen. Maritza learned about it even before Seward and the rest of Washington. Late on the night of Thursday, November 14, Celestina came home early from her nightly appearance at the music hall and burst into their room at Monsieur Cruchet's, still in the gaudy costume of a cancan girl.

"It's happened!" She was waving a copy of the Richmond *Examiner*. "Exactly the way you said it might."

"How did you get a Richmond paper the night before it usually goes on sale in the newsstand?"

"The gentleman friend of one of the music hall girls distributes the Richmond papers as soon as they arrive shortly before midnight on the same day they're published. He stopped in to see her at the music hall and brought a copy of yesterday morning's paper."

Maritza was staring at the headline, hardly able to believe what she saw.

The headline extended completely across the front page of the *Examiner:*

UNION GUNBOAT STOPS BRITISH VESSEL: SEIZES CONFEDERATE OFFICIALS

The Confederate blockade runner *Sprite,* on a run from Halifax, Nova Scotia, to Wilmington, was hailed on November 9 at sea by the British merchant vessel *Trent.* Captain Moir of the *Trent* reported that two passengers,

Mr. James Mason and Mr. John Slidell, duly accredited diplomatic representatives of the Confederate government, to England and France, respectively, were removed under threat of gunfire from the decks of the *Trent* by the captain of the U.S.S. *San Jacinto*.

The British captain asked Captain Darrow of the *Sprite* to convey news of this high-handed action of a Federal gunboat against a merchant vessel of a neutral country to Confederate authorities, and also to Lord Lyons, British ambassador to the Union government in Washington. The *Trent* expects to reach London, Captain Darrow reported, in about two weeks and Captain Moir's official report will no doubt cause international repercussions and perhaps even war between England and the government in Washington.

The report went on to give details of the seizure of Mr. Slidell and Mr. James Murray Mason, Confederate diplomatic representative to England, and former United States senators, on the deck of the *Trent* by a boarding party under command of Lieutenant D. M. Fairfax, executive officer of the Union warship. The stopping of the *Trent* at sea by means of a shot fired across its bows had been vigorously objected to by Captain Moir, who, since his ship was unarmed and lying hove to under the guns of the United States warship *San Jacinto,* could only make verbal protest against the highhanded action of the Union vessel. The report went on to say that the incident occurred in the Old Bahama Channel north of Cuba, after Mr. Mason and Mr. Slidell had boarded the English vessel in Havana for the journey to England and France, as representatives of the Confederate government. When asked where he was taking the captive prisoners, Captain Wilkes had volunteered to the master of the *Trent* that the first stop would be Fortress Monroe not far from Norfolk.

Asked why Fortress Monroe would be his destination [the account concluded], Captain Wilkes refused to answer, but there can be no doubt that his failure to bring the prisoners to Washington is caused by the fact that the lower Potomac is closed to all Federal shipping by Confederate batteries.

"What do you think?" Tina asked when Maritza put down the paper.

"There'll be a crisis, but probably not involving France. The dispatch makes it clear that this was a British vessel."

"Your uncle John was accredited as a representative to the Quai d'Orsay," Tina reminded her.

Maritza put down the paper but there was a thoughtful look in her eyes when she said, "I wonder if William Russell knows of this yet?"

"Probably not," said Tina. "The man who distributes the Richmond *Examiner* to the newsstands of Washington said the copies he gets come to Manassas on the afternoon train from Richmond. They're carried across the Potomac after dark by rowboat and stored somewhere until the newsstands open in the morning. He only brought this copy with him because of the dramatic news about the seizure of the Confederate envoys."

"Russell needs to know about this and so does Henri Mercier," said Maritza. "But how can I communicate with them at this time of night?"

"That's easy," Tina assured her. "For five dollars, any of the hotel waiters going off duty after serving late supper will deliver a message for you."

Maritza didn't waste time with inaction. "Go downstairs and get two of them while I write the notes," she told Tina.

"In this costume?"

"Use the back stairs. You know the way, don't you?"

Celestina giggled. "I ought to. I've used it often enough."

"Then get two five-dollar bills from my purse and find the messengers. I'll have the notes for Mr. Russell and Henri Mercier ready in fifteen minutes."

When Tina had departed, Maritza took note paper and wrote two identical messages addressed to William Russell and Henri Mercier:

> Have urgent news for you. Important that you join me
> for breakfast at eight o'clock tomorrow morning in the
> hotel dining room.
>
>   Maritza LeClerc

VI

William H. Russell was the first to arrive at the table Maritza had selected in the corner of the dining room. Only a few people were having breakfast that early, so the table was relatively isolated. The English journalist was scowling as he bowed and took an empty chair.

"Something's in the air, Countess," he said. "The city's alive with rumors but nobody seems to know what it's all about." He gave her a probing look. "Unless you do?"

"I know and so will the rest of Washington by this afternoon," said Maritza. "Henri Mercier is joining us shortly; he had to come all the way from Georgetown, so he'll probably be a few minutes late."

"May I ask how you came to know something nobody else seems to be sure of?"

"I'll tell you when Henri gets here," she promised. "Meanwhile, why don't we order breakfast?"

Russell shrugged and waited while Maritza gave her order to the hovering waiter, then gave his own. By that time Henri Mercier had arrived, the expression on the face of the French diplomat as perplexed as had been that on Russell's.

"If it's bad news you have, break it to me gently, Maritza," he said. "I missed my morning coffee and already have a splitting headache."

"If it's any consolation to you," said Maritza, "Secretary Seward will have a worse one than you have before the day's over."

Removing the copy of the Richmond *Examiner* from her lap, she spread it out on the table where they could both read it without difficulty.

"This could mean war!" William Russell exploded. "That warship captain has insulted the proudest part of the British Empire, its navy."

Henri Mercier's reaction was less intense, since no French vessel was involved. Nevertheless, his tone was just as serious when he asked, "How could the captain of an American ship of war possibly be so stupid?"

"Wilkes could." Unexpectedly, Russell gave the answer. "I interviewed him shortly after I came to America."

"Why him?" Maritza asked.

"He's one of the most famous officers in the U. S. Navy," Russell explained. "Twenty years ago he led an expedition to the Antarctic that mapped over sixteen hundred miles of coastline. Actually, part of that area was named Wilkes Land in his honor, though he was later reprimanded lightly by his superiors for illegally punishing enlisted men serving under him."

"In other words," said Henri Mercier, "Wilkes is exactly the sort of self-willed man who would defy the declarations of the Congress of Paris of 1854 concerning war at sea."

"The United States has never adopted the provisions of the treaty," Russell reminded him.

"Five years ago I was only twenty and concerned mainly with social affairs at the Château LeClerc and the court in Paris," Maritza admitted. "What was it all about?"

"The Congress ended the Crimean War," Henri Mercier explained. "The only provision that would apply here stated that only contraband of war was subject to capture on the high seas."

"Two diplomats accredited to neutral nations could hardly be regarded as contraband of war," she said, "so there's no precedent under international law for Captain Wilkes's action, is there?"

"None whatsoever," said William Russell dogmatically. "What are you going to do for an encore, Countess? You've already scored a clean victory over the rest of the news gatherers in Washington."

"We're in luck," said Maritza. "Secretary Seward's news conference will be held later this morning. I'm going to ask for permission to go to Fortress Monroe and interview the Confederate agents."

"By heaven, that's a good idea! I'll go with you if I may," said Russell.

"Be my guest," Maritza told him.

"The conference isn't until eleven o'clock," said Russell. "Perhaps there's time for me to inform Lord Lyons, the British ambassador, about the whole affair before it begins."

"Suppose Secretary Seward wants to hush up the fact that an American warship has thumbed its nose at your country's navy?" Maritza asked Russell. "Will you play down the incident?"

"I suppose I'll have no choice," said Russell. "The American censors have complete control over what dispatches leave Washington for foreign newspapers, but Lord Lyons can send a report in the diplomatic pouch. They wouldn't dare interfere with that."

"You seem to have pretty good luck getting information through, Maritza," said Henri Mercier. "Do you think you can do any better with a story for *Le Pays?*"

"I can certainly try. Even though none of the ships involved were French, Un—Mr. Slidell speaks French like a native and is highly placed in the Confederate government."

"I met Slidell in Montgomery but only spoke to him a few times," said Russell. "As I remember it, I wasn't particularly impressed by him but you apparently know him better than I do, Countess."

"As you know, I was born in Mobile and grew up in Alabama and Louisiana," said Maritza. "Until my marriage to Étienne LeClerc, John Slidell was my legal guardian."

"No wonder you're concerned about him," said Russell. "I wouldn't emphasize the family connection, though, Countess. Mr. Pinkerton is watching all of the foreign correspondents closely nowadays. He'll make something of the connection if he can."

Russell stood up. "If you will excuse me, I must get to the embassy and discuss this with Lord Lyons. Shall I see you later at Mr. Seward's office, Countess?"

"You can count on it," Maritza assured him. "What about you, Henri?"

"Officially, I can have no connection with your dispatches to *Le Pays,* but I can use the account in the *Examiner* as the basis of a report to Monsieur Thouvenel in Paris," said Mercier. "I would appreciate it if you would make detailed notes on what

Secretary Seward says, Maritza, so I can include that in my report, too. We must preserve at all costs the *entente* between
Britain and France, so any hint I can give our foreign minister
about the reaction of Seward and President Lincoln to this unfortunate affair will be helpful."

"I'll report to you as soon as the conference is over,"
Maritza promised.

"So will I, Mr. Minister," said William Russell. "May I give
Lord Lyons the assurance that, as the representative of France,
you will act in close agreement with him?"

"Your ambassador and I have been in frequent consultation
ever since the affair at Fort Sumter," Mercier assured him. "We
shall be even more so in the present crisis."

"But hardly to the point of going to war with the North,
would you say, Henri?" Maritza asked.

"No. Why do you ask?"

"The more I think about this affair, the more it sounds like a
plot to goad England into coming into the war on the Confederate side."

Both men looked at her in astonishment but it was William
Russell who asked, "Who could possibly have thought of such
a scheme?"

"One man high up in Richmond would know Captain
Wilkes, since he was a United States senator for quite a while.
He'd also know how Wilkes would react to information that the
two top diplomats in the Confederacy were changing from a
blockade runner to a British merchant vessel at Havana and
make certain that Captain Wilkes got the information."

"That," said Russell, "would be like waving a chunk of meat
in the face of a shark. But I still don't understand who could
have thought up such a scheme."

"Who else but Judah P. Benjamin?" said Maritza.

"You could be right!" Henri Mercier exclaimed. "Benjamin
is often referred to as 'the brains of the Confederacy'."

William Howard Russell stroked his side whiskers with long
fingers, obviously deep in thought.

"The idea may not be as farfetched as it seemed when you
first voiced it, Countess," he said. "As Attorney General, Benjamin's part in the Confederate government would seem to be

insignificant at first glance, yet in Montgomery it was no secret that he was closer to Jefferson Davis than any other man in the Cabinet. Besides, in his capacity as Attorney General he could maintain a staff of secret agents."

"Who could easily have determined from the U. S. Navy that the *San Jacinto* would put into Havana Harbor to take on coal," said Maritza. "He could also have arranged for Mason and Slidell to be carried to Cuba while the *San Jacinto* was there; it wouldn't take more than a couple of days for the blockade runner to sail from Wilmington or Charleston to Havana."

"You make it sound like a novel, Countess," said William Russell.

"More likely a real-life adventure; the ingredients are all there, Mr. Russell. If I could just interview the people involved, I might get the truth."

"You have my blessing, Countess, but I still hope you're wrong."

"So do I," said Henri Mercier. "Another war between the United States and Great Britain would be a great tragedy."

VII

The Secretary of State had reluctantly agreed, at the insistence of the foreign correspondents, to hold a conference monthly at which they could question him about the position of the United States Government on matters related to the war. The large room in which it was held was packed when Maritza entered but a gallant reporter from Brazil gave her his chair. She had just seated herself when the Secretary entered, for once not accompanied by his shadow, Pinkerton. When Maritza raised her hand to be recognized, the other correspondents gave her preference.

"Good morning, Mr. Secretary," she said. "I wonder if you've had an opportunity to read yesterday morning's Richmond *Examiner?*"

"I'm not in the habit of reading enemy propaganda, Countess," said Seward frostily. "Nor would I recommend such material to you as a source of your dispatches to *Le Pays* in Paris."

"Being neutral, I do the best I can to obtain correct information from both sides in this unfortunate war, Mr. Secretary." Maritza didn't let Seward's harsh admonition disturb her. "The incident I'm most interested in at the moment involves a United States warship on the high seas, so I thought I should bring it to your attention."

Unfolding the newspaper, she carried it up to the desk where Seward was standing, but held it so those in the room could see the front page, while the Secretary could not. Only at the last moment did she turn the sheet so his cold gray eyes could hardly escape seeing the black headlines spread across the front page. Placing the newspaper on the desk, she retreated to her seat amidst a sudden explosion of excited whispers among the correspondents gathered in the room.

Seward did not look up for at least two minutes while reading the account. When he did, the flinty gray in his eyes had turned to fires of anger.

"May I inquire where you obtained this spurious rag, Countess?"

"My companion, Mademoiselle Toutant, sings at a music hall here in the city," Maritza explained. "The man who supplies Confederate newspapers to the newsstands in Washington each morning is a friend of one of the ladies of the chorus and gave my companion this copy shortly before midnight. As you can see, it is dated yesterday morning and the front-page story was telegraphed from Wilmington, North Carolina, sometime the day before yesterday. That means the *San Jacinto,* which was involved, will soon be docking at Fortress Monroe. No doubt, too, Captain Wilkes will be telegraphing his account of what happened as soon as he reaches port.

"Meanwhile," Maritza continued coolly, "I'm sure we would all appreciate a hint from you concerning the effect the high-handed abduction of two diplomats of the Confederacy from an unarmed English merchant vessel on the high seas will have on relations between the United States, England, and France."

"Surely, Countess"—Seward kept his voice under control but only with an obvious effort—"you don't expect me to speculate on the outcome of a matter that may well be a complete fabrication."

"Suppose the account is true, Mr. Secretary?" William Russell had risen to his feet to ask the question. "What would the United States do to make reparations to my country for what appears to be a case of piracy on the high seas? Something, incidentally, that is forbidden by the Congress of Paris of 1854."

"I'm sure you know that the United States is not a signatory to that agreement, Mr. Russell."

"Then you see nothing disturbing about it?"

"If the incident did happen—and the description in a rebel newspaper is no assurance that it did—both the Navy and State departments will naturally be interested."

"What about the President?" another correspondent asked.

"A report will certainly be made to Mr. Lincoln as soon as the government has been informed officially," said Seward. "Now if there are no—"

"Since my government is involved, I would like very much to interview the persons involved in this affair as soon as the *San Jacinto* reaches Fortress Monroe, Mr. Secretary," William Russell interrupted smoothly.

"I join Mr. Russell, too, in requesting permission to go to Fortress Monroe immediately," Maritza said before Seward could speak. "Mr. Slidell was to be an envoy to France."

"Both requests are refused," Seward snapped. "Lord Lyons and Monsieur Mercier will be informed as soon as the true facts become known, so there is no need for either of you to undertake a journey to Fortress Monroe. Just how much information the ambassadors from Britain and France will care to give the press about the incident is their own affair. Good day, lady and gentlemen."

As the spare figure of the Secretary of State disappeared through a side door, the correspondents crowded around Maritza. She could tell them no more, however, Seward having taken the copy of the Richmond *Examiner* with him.

"What next, Countess?" Russell asked as they were leaving.

"I'm going to write an account of the conference for my journal. Can you give me a quote from Lord Lyons about the British reaction?"

"He's naturally very concerned but cannot make an official statement until he receives information of the incident from the United States Government."

"You can be sure Seward will put as innocent a face as he can on the whole matter," said Maritza. "I wonder how he'll manage it?"

She didn't have to wait long. Shortly after noon an "Extra" edition of the *Star* appeared on the streets but Maritza didn't need to buy a copy to know what it contained. From the open window of her suite, where she was busy writing a dispatch and making several copies, she could hear the shrill voice of a newsboy shouting:

> *"Union warship captures rebel agents. Captain Wilkes hero of the hour."*

The account in the *Star* of what it called the *"Trent* Affair" was essentially the same as the one Penn Darrow had telegraphed from Wilmington but the emphasis was entirely different. In the *Star* account, Mason and Slidell were depicted as Confederate secret agents on the way to buy munitions in England and France. The nationality of the vessel from which they had been taken wasn't even mentioned until the last paragraph of the account, where Lord Lyons was quoted as refusing to comment, pending a conference with U. S. State Department authorities.

"Can Mr. Seward sweep this whole thing under a rug, the way they're obviously trying to do?" Celestina asked when she finished reading the account.

"Not according to William Russell," said Maritza. "If Judah Benjamin is really behind this whole affair, as I'm beginning to believe, let's hope this time he hasn't overreached himself."

"What are you going to do?"

"Nothing but report the news as it develops. Right now the crowds are making Captain Wilkes a hero, if you can believe the *Star,* but there's bound to be a reaction soon when thinking people realize this is a rash act of provocation against England."

Signs of a change of heart on the part of important men in the Union government began to appear sooner than Maritza expected. The New York newspapers, much more sympathetic usually to the South than Washington, toned down considerably their version of the story which appeared the next morning. General McClellan was reported to have told Lincoln, when asked the consequences of the entry of England into the war on the Confederate side, that nothing but disaster would be the outcome.

To her surprise, Maritza was summoned to the office of the Secretary of State the next day and instructed by an assistant to report to the French people through *Le Pays* that the entire affair was in no way to be considered an insult on the part of the United States Government to that of France. The thing she needed most to discover, however, was what was being done with Mason, Slidell, and their secretaries. That she learned from Henri Mercier, when she saw him the next day at his office.

"I left the Navy Department just about an hour ago," Mercier told her. "The *San Jacinto* has been instructed to go to Boston and deliver Mason, Slidell, and their secretaries to the authorities at Fort Warren."

"Fort Warren? I never heard of it."

"Neither has anyone else to speak of," said Mercier. "I did get some information, however, at the Navy Department. Fort Warren is a relic built in the middle of Boston Harbor on what is called Georges Island after the War of 1812. It was built to guard the harbor but is now used mainly as a prison."

"In a place like that they could hide Uncle John away until the war ends or he dies from pneumonia," Maritza told Celestina later when she described her conversation with Henri Mercier.

"What can you do?"

"Go to Boston and let the government of France know what the Lincoln Administration is doing to a commissioner who undoubtedly was fully accredited to the Quai d'Orsay."

"When?"

"Tomorrow—by train. Pack enough clothes to last me about a week. I've got to find William Russell and talk to him first and also talk to Henri Mercier again."

"Do you have any idea what time in the morning our train leaves?" Tina asked as she began pulling portmanteaux from beneath the bed.

"I want you to stay here and keep track of developments while I'm gone," Maritza told her. "If Mr. Allan Pinkerton turns up trying to find out where I am, you can send him on some wild goose chase."

"I'd like to send him to a much hotter place than that," said Tina. "But I still don't like the idea of your being in Boston alone. The whole Abolitionist movement started up there and Bostonians furnished most of the money to support John Brown and his band of thugs. If they were to learn that you're really a spy for the South, you might be mobbed before the police could protect you."

VIII

William H. Russell was at the Willard Bar, holding forth in great indignation to a crowd of fellow reporters on the subject of the insult handed England by the captain of the *San Jacinto*. When Maritza sent a bellman in for him, he came out, still holding a glass of scotch and water in his hand.

"Sorry women aren't allowed in the bar, Countess," he told her. "I'll be glad to bring something out for you if you like."

"I don't have time," said Maritza. "It occurred to me that you might be interested to know where the *San Jacinto* is headed after it leaves Fortress Monroe."

"I was told it would be New York."

"Apparently that's been changed to Boston."

"Why Boston? The diplomatic maneuvering over the *Trent* affair will be done between Washington, London, and Paris. New York is a lot nearer Washington than Boston."

"Boston appears to be a little more suitable as a place to imprison the commissioners. They're putting them in Fort Warren."

Russell frowned. "I don't even remember a fort with that name."

"As far as I've been able to find out, it's one of those forts the United States built to guard its harbors after your navy sailed up the Potomac during the War of 1812 and shelled Washington. They're located in practically every important harbor from Boston to New Orleans but most of them aren't even garrisoned any more. According to a map I found of Boston, this one is located on what's called Georges Island in the middle of the entrance to Boston Harbor. It's several miles from the nearest land, which would be the eastern tip of Cape Cod."

"Good Lord! They might as well be buried in the middle of nowhere."

"I gather that's the general idea, to get them away from contact with newspaper reporters."

"Lord Lyons should hear of this. It was bad enough to take the commissioners by force from the deck of an English vessel like common criminals. Now they're to be shut up in an American Bastille."

"I'm going to Boston tomorrow to see what I can find out," said Maritza. "I wondered if you'd like to go with me?"

"I'd like nothing better, believe me, but I need to stay here in close touch with Lord Lyons." Then his face suddenly cleared. "But you can represent the London *Times* as well as *Le Pays*. I'm authorized to employ assistants when I need them."

"Good! I'll need all the help I can get, if I'm to persuade the commander of the garrison at Fort Warren to let me talk to the prisoners. While I'm gone, Celestina will know how to reach me by telegraph. If anything newsworthy happens, I'm going to count on you to notify her so she can get in touch with me."

"I'll be glad to do that of course. Good luck."

"I'll need it to get into that dungeon, but I'm going to try just the same."

After talking to Russell, Maritza went to the office Henri Mercier maintained downtown. Fortunately the Frenchman was there.

"Any more news from Fortress Monroe?" Maritza asked.

"Not since the State Department notified me that the *San Jacinto* would be going to Boston. Have you turned in your dispatch on *l'affaire Trent* to the State Department?"

"Yesterday afternoon," she told him. "I imagine Pinkerton's censors are busy cutting it to pieces, if they haven't already sent it on."

"Thank God they can't open diplomatic pouches. I sent a full report to Monsieur Thouvenel immediately. Fortunately a ship happened to be leaving Baltimore for Le Havre today, so it will soon be on its way. Meanwhile, I suppose we can only wait."

"I'm not waiting," said Maritza. "I'll take a train for Boston tomorrow morning."

"What could you possibly do by setting yourself against the United States Government?"

"I filed the first account of the Yankee defeat at Bull Run," she reminded him.

"I still don't understand how you managed it."

"Simply by being at the right place at the right time and something tells me Boston is where I should be now. Do you have a consul stationed there?"

"Yes, an excellent man named Aristide Lescaux. I'll give you a note asking him to help you in any way he can as a French citizen."

"Good! That may be the passport I'll need to get into Fort Warren."

IX

Boston in November was cold and blustery. Maritza found a porter who took her two suitcases from the train into the station when she arrived about seven, but had to wait a half hour before a hack appeared to take her to the hotel she'd telegraphed ahead to for reservations.

"Where are all the conveyances?" she asked the driver, an Irishman with a nose as red as his cheeks, who breathed an effluvium of Irish whiskey around himself like an aura.

"Sure and they'll all be carryin' people to the big dinner the mayor's stagin' this evening," he told her.

"Who is the dinner for?"

"The captain and the crew of the ship that caught them two rebels down near Cuba about a week ago. I forgot his name."

"Wilkes?"

"He's the one; the whole town's celebratin' in his honor. I hear they're a-goin' to hang them two scoundrels from the flagstaff of Fort Warren. No more than they deserve, neither, the way them rebels treat poor niggers." He turned his head. "What would you do to rich people that eat nigger babies?"

"Do they do that?"

"That and worse. Beggin' yer pardon, but they tell me that down South every planter's got himself a stable of nigger girls he keeps pregnant all the time, producin' more slaves for him to sell."

Maritza laughed. "That must keep them pretty busy."

"Yeah," said the driver. "Not that I wouldn't be happy to help 'em out at times. Them black wenches really know how to —you know what I mean."

"This place called Fort Warren, how does anybody get there? I'm curious to see what those men look like."

"A boat runs out to the fort two or three times a day, carryin' supplies and a change of guards. Better wear the thickest coat yer got, though. The wind blowin' across Massachusetts Bay strikes the fort full from the nor'east. On a day like this it ain't a fit place for man nor beast."

The driver was telling the truth, Maritza discovered when the workboat for Fort Warren left its pier about ten o'clock the next morning and headed for an island upon which loomed the outlines of a thick-walled fortress. The morning newspapers had been full of last night's banquet. Captain Wilkes had made a fiery speech, justifying his action at sea with the odd argument that the Confederate commissioners had actually been contraband of war themselves. This conclusion he based on the fact that they were on the way to London and Paris to purchase arms, thus making them liable to capture from any neutral vessel under the provisions of the Congress of Paris.

The streets of Boston were still littered with the aftermath of the giant parade held in honor of the *San Jacinto* and its crew the day before. Apparently it had led all the way from the waterfront, where the warship was now docked, to the City Hall. There, according to the newspapers, a speech of welcome and praise had been given by city officials before going on to one of the large hotels for the congratulatory dinner that had lasted until late the night before.

At the landing on Georges Island, a graveled roadway led up to the entrance to the fort, Maritza saw as she debarked with the others. The passengers had been mainly members of the garrison returning from leave, a few forlorn-looking women on the way to visit other prisoners in the fort, and a scattering of other people. Many of these looked at her curiously but did not question her reasons for going to the forbidding-looking fort in the center of Boston Harbor.

She followed the small crowd to the entrance and saw them admitted—immediately if they were in uniform or known to the guard, or upon displaying written passes if they were not. When she reached the guard post at the portals of the forbidding structure of the prison, however, the soldier on duty lowered his musket to bar her way.

"Where's your pass?" he demanded.

"I'm a newspaper correspondent for the London *Times* and *Le Pays* of Paris, here to interview two men being held in prison," she told him. "As a correspondent, I don't need a pass."

"Nobody gets in here without one unless they're in the military," said the guard. "Who was it you wanted to see?"

"Commissioners John Slidell and George Mason."

"The secesh that were landed here yesterday?"

"Yes."

The man looked perplexed for a moment. Then, turning his

head, he bawled to someone farther down the entrance corridor, "Sergeant of the guard!"

"What the hell do you want, Hagerty?" a rough voice called.

"There's a newspaper reporter out here. Wants to see them secesh that were landed here by ship's boat yesterday morning."

"Tell him to go away. Them fellers ain't seein' nobody."

"It ain't a him, it's a her—and she's from London and Paris."

"All right. Send her in."

The sergeant of the guard was redheaded and big. Maritza felt almost like a pygmy beside him, but she didn't let his size, or his scowl, intimidate her.

"Newspaper reporter, eh?" The sergeant eyed her up and down. "You're a damn handsome one, I'll admit. What's your name?"

"Countess Maritza LeClerc, Paris, France. I represent the French journal *Le Pays,* as well as the London *Times.*"

"Got any proof?"

"Certainly." Maritza handed him a note on the official stationery of the French government, which she'd taken the precaution of getting from Consul Aristide Lescaux on the way to the waterfront. "This is a request from the French consul in Boston to Colonel Justin Dimick, who, I believe, commands the garrison of this fort. I'd like to see the colonel, please."

"Whether you see him or not depends on what you want with him," said the sergeant.

"You have two new prisoners, a Mr. Slidell and a Mr. Mason—"

"Nobody talks to them two."

"Was the order issued by Colonel Dimick?"

"Yes."

Maritza took a shot in the dark. "If you will tell the colonel I'm here and show him Lescaux's note, I'm sure he'll see me."

"Maybe he will and maybe he won't," said the sergeant somewhat truculently.

"You will ask him and find out, won't you?"

The sergeant shrugged. "Follow me," he said gruffly, and turned down a damp corridor that appeared to lead into the very bowels of the fort. Maritza followed, deliberately suppressing her sense of victory at having gotten even this far.

At a door standing ajar some distance down the corridor, the sergeant paused and knocked. When a voice with a distinct Scotch burr from inside demanded, "What is it?" he answered: "Lady to see you, Colonel, sir."

"Show her in then, Sergeant. And get back to your post."

Stepping into the room, Maritza heard the door close behind her but concentrated her attention upon the man behind the desk wearing the blue uniform and insignia of a colonel in the Union Army. Middle-aged, he had a small paunch and only a fringe of almost white hair but a bristling gray mustache. His eyes, too, were bright and intelligent.

"Good morning, madam," said the seated officer. "Or is it miss?"

"I am Countess Maritza LeClerc," she said, taking a chair before the desk.

"Please excuse me for not getting up, Countess. A rebel minié ball struck my leg at Bull Run and getting up and down is rather painful." The Scotch burr she'd noticed out in the hall was still strong and Maritza felt a sudden rise of hope at the thought of what it might mean to the purpose for which she had come.

"I was captured at Blackburn's Ford myself," she said, "and a man I might have grown to love died there in my arms."

"This war never should have happened. I got my wound at a hill several miles west of where you were captured. Can't remember the name."

"Probably Henry House Hill."

"That's it. I was leading a regiment of Massachusetts militia in the attack, when a tall scarecrow of a mountain man from Virginia took a bead on my leg with a squirrel rifle. I didn't have as much chance as the squirrel usually does."

"He must have been from the 33rd Virginia, part of General Stonewall Jackson's brigade."

"How do you know so much about the battle, Countess, when you were miles away at Blackburn's Ford?"

"Foreign correspondents have a neutral status, Colonel; we cover both sides. When General Beauregard found out who I

was, he let me go and had me guided as far as McLean's Ford.
As my companion and I were riding from Centreville to Fairfax
Courthouse, we gave a lift to a drummer boy whose foot had
been hit by a piece of shrapnel on Henry House Hill. He told
me the whole story."

"He had better luck than I did, then. Wound up in a rebel
field hospital at a place they call Portici—"

"The boy's wound was treated there too. The doctor told
him to get the hell out of there, so he wasn't taken prisoner."

"Might have been the same surgeon. Anyway, he saved my
leg, even if it is stiff and sore. Afterward, I was exchanged and
the Army gave me this job where I could sit most of the time.
What can I do for you, Countess?"

"I came to interview the Confederate commissioners brought
here yesterday by the warship *San Jacinto*." She placed her credentials on the desk where he could read them without getting
up. "You will see that I'm fully accredited as a war correspondent, Colonel. My credentials are signed by Mr. Seward,
the Secretary of State. At this time, I'm also representing the
London *Times* for Mr. Russell."

"William H. Russell?"

"Yes. We're very good friends."

"Now there's a man who's handy with a word," said Colonel
Dimick on a note of admiration. "Our ancestors came from the
same part of Scotland."

"Were you born here in the United States?"

"No, in Glasgow. My parents came to Nova Scotia when I
was a little boy and lived there a few years before moving to
Boston. Great paper, the *Times,* one of the best in the world."

"About the interview—"

"That'll take some doing. That stiff-necked bas— I mean,
Captain Wilkes gave strict orders to my second in command
through his executive officer that no reporters were to be allowed to see the commissioners. He didn't even have the courtesy to come ashore to tell me, though. The politicians were
getting ready to give a parade in his honor and he couldn't wait
to be civil."

"Captain Wilkes has that reputation. Mr. Russell knows him."

"The executive officer was a nice enough guy, though. Name's Fairfax. I gather he wasn't too happy about the way the capture of the commissioners was accomplished."

"In what way, Colonel?"

"Anybody who knows much about maritime law would realize that stopping a ship of a neutral nation that's not carrying contraband is illegal. When news of this affair gets to England there's going to be hell to pay; you can count on that. If the British Navy should attack Boston, we couldn't even fire the cannon atop this hunk of bricks and mortar. They're only up there for show."

"Do you think it might come to war with England?"

Colonel Dimick shrugged. "It will unless Abraham Lincoln has the good sense to apologize to Queen Victoria and release the prisoners. If you ask me, Countess, instead of giving a banquet and a parade for Captain Wilkes, somebody should have locked him up in a nuthouse."

"Then I *can* see the commissioners?"

Colonel Dimick rubbed the stubble on his chin thoughtfully. "If you weren't a newspaper correspondent, I might . . ."

"Suppose I were a relative, inquiring about their health and safety?"

"*That* would be a different matter, but—"

"Actually I was born in the South, Colonel. I married a Frenchman when I was eighteen, accounting for my French citizenship, but before I was married Senator John Slidell was my legal guardian. I have always called him Uncle John."

Dimick gave her a keen look. "Are you conning me, Countess? No, I don't want to know the answer. If Senator Slidell is your uncle, I could hardly refuse you the right to see him now, could I?"

"Colonel, you're a dear." Getting to her feet, Maritza leaned over to kiss the older man on the top of his bald head.

"Just don't intimate in your dispatches that I knew you had anything to do with newspapers, girl." He scribbled a pass and handed it to her. "Take this to the sergeant of the guard outside and he'll show you where your uncle is. I've assigned the prisoners to the most comfortable part of this Godforsaken dungeon, but it's still damp and cold compared to Louisiana, or even Richmond, so they'll be lucky if they don't get pneumonia. Come to see me after the war's over; you'll find that a Yankee Scotsman isn't such a bad host."

"I promise to," said Maritza. "I'll even let my companion, a beautiful octoroon who was once my slave, dance the cancan for you."

"Don't know's my old heart could stand it," said Dimick with a broad smile, "but damned if I won't give it a chance. Good day, Countess."

"Good day, Colonel, and God bless you!"

X

The suite of rooms to which the sergeant led Maritza wasn't even barred, but, in spite of a coal fire burning in a small grate, it was—as Colonel Dimick had warned—damp and cold. John Slidell was dictating to his secretary when the guard opened the door and let Maritza in. For a moment he was speechless, then he jumped up with a whoop of joy and gave her a bear hug.

"By God, Maritza!" he exclaimed. "You have a habit of turning up in the damnedest places. How in the devil do you do it?"

"I'm not in league with the Devil," she told him when she could speak. "But much of the time in Washington, I'm being followed by an agent of his. His name's Pinkerton."

"Watch out for that one," said Slidell. "He's cut off some of our best sources of information about the enemy."

"I know. I was outside Sixteenth and I streets when he put Rose Greenhow under house arrest, but you may be actually better off at that. Pinkerton was using her to feed false information to Cousin Pierre Beauregard."

"I heard you saved us that time by finding a copy of McDowell's battle plans."

"I was lucky."

"How in the devil did you get into *this* place?"

"I came to visit you and to check on your welfare, Uncle John. After all, we are related."

"Thank God for it, but I heard Captain Wilkes give orders to Lieutenant Fairfax that the commander of this Godforsaken pile of rock should keep reporters from seeing us."

"Reporters, yes, but Captain Wilkes forgot to mention grieving relatives. Colonel Dimick couldn't resist letting a sympathetic niece make sure you're not dying of pneumonia and starvation in a cold, damp, Federal prison."

"Dimick's a decent enough fellow and so's Lieutenant Fairfax of the *San Jacinto*," said Slidell. "But that Wilkes is a son of a bitch in any language."

"Colonel Dimick agrees with you, which is another reason why I was allowed to see you," she told him. "He says this whole affair is likely to embroil the Union in war with England—"

"As smart as you are, I guess you've already realized that's the general idea, haven't you?"

"Let's say I suspected it. I forgot to tell you that, in addition to being a grieving relative and correspondent for *Le Pays,* I am also at the moment an accredited correspondent for the London *Times* at the request of Mr. Russell."

"The London *Times!*" Slidell turned to his secretary. "How do you like that?"

"Everything seems to be working out better than we had hoped, sir," said the young man with the short beard who had been taking down Slidell's dictation in a flowing hand. "We met at Montgomery, Countess," he continued, "but you may not remember."

"I remember very well," said Maritza graciously. "It's nice to see you again, but not quite under such circumstances."

"We're better off than we might be at that, Countess—thanks to Colonel Dimick."

"Perhaps I'd better make some notes on the circumstances of your capture," said Maritza, "before Colonel Dimick has regrets about letting me see you."

"You're right," said Slidell. "Go and ask Mason to come in for a few minutes," he told the secretary. "Tell him we have an important visitor."

James M. Mason was a rather serious-looking man of middle age who comported himself like the Virginia aristocrat he was. Maritza knew he had been a senator in the United States Congress and, like many important Virginians and North Carolinians, had also tried to settle the conflict between the North and the South without resorting to warfare.

"I've heard a lot about you, Countess," Mason told Maritza when Slidell made the introduction, "all of it good."

"Good?" Slidell exclaimed. "She singlehandedly informed the French government about the debacle at Manassas. Now she's going to marshal both French and English opinion against the North because of our capture from the *Trent*."

"In any event, Countess," said Mason, "we're grateful to you for taking the trouble to come here."

"I must hurry, gentlemen," she said, "so pardon me if I ask direct questions."

"You always did," said John Slidell. "Even as a little girl, 'Why?' was your favorite word."

"Let's come right to the point then," said Maritza. "Was your seizure on the *Trent* a mere happenstance, or was it planned?"

She saw a quick glance pass between Slidell and Mason before Slidell answered: "Happenstance, of course. Why would we want a Union war vessel to capture us, when we were headed for London and Paris to buy arms and try to convince the two governments that they should open trade with the South?"

"For a very simple reason," said Maritza. "To trap the Union government into a position where they would give enough offense to the British flag to bring England into the war on the Southern side."

Once again the quick glance passed between Mason and Slidell before Mason asked, "Whatever gave you that idea, Countess?"

"It's just the sort of trick I would use, if I wanted the English Navy to keep the sea lanes open for me to import munitions and export the cotton that's piling up on the wharves of New Orleans, Mobile, Charleston, and Wilmington."

"It's too bad we don't have you running the Confederate State Department, Maritza." Slidell laughed boisterously—and on a distinctly insincere note, she thought. "We deliberately made it known that we were on our way to Europe to negotiate help from France and England, using a neutral vessel for passage so nobody could mistake our purpose."

"Your purpose, yes, but also just where it would be most convenient for a U.S. gunboat to stop the *Trent* and take you prisoner."

"Now, Maritza, you're dreaming something up," said Slidell. "Even if he'd known what ship we were on and when it would leave, what legal excuse could Captain Wilkes have possibly used to seize us?"

"The same one he was using when he spoke at a congratulatory dinner last night here in Boston—that, since you were seeking to buy munitions in Europe, you were actually contraband of war yourselves, according to the Congress of Paris declarations of 1854."

The secretary started to laugh, but subsided at a warning glance from Slidell. "The United States is not signatory to the decisions of that Congress, Maritza."

"But the Confederacy is." Maritza saw by the surprise mirrored in the faces of John Slidell and James Mason that they had not known of this development. "The Congress in Richmond declared its adherence to all the provisions except the one against privateering, as soon as it was known that you had been taken prisoner."

"That puts the United States into an even worse position vis-à-vis England and France," said Mason on a note of satisfaction.

Maritza had obtained the answer she sought so didn't belabor the point further. The whole *Trent* affair had obviously been a plot to make sure Slidell and Mason would be seized while aboard a neutral vessel on the way to visit two neutral nations. And the belligerent Captain Wilkes was unwittingly made the scapegoat.

"If you will each tell me what you remember about the details of your capture," she suggested, "I can get the information Mr. William Russell and I need for our dispatches so they can be sent to London and Paris before Captain Wilkes hears that I'm in the fort and has me taken off."

The facts were quickly recounted while Maritza scribbled notes as swiftly as she could write. When she finished, the story was quite clear, as well as her conviction that her first evaluation of the situation had been correct.

"What will happen next, Maritza?" Slidell asked as she was about to call the guard to escort her to the boat landing for the return to Boston.

"Henri Mercier's report is already on the way to Paris by ship from Baltimore and I'm sure Lord Lyons sent his by the quickest possible method, too," she said. "The question of a possible war with England will probably depend on whether Mr. Lincoln is willing to apologize and make amends as well as release the four of you. But with so much of the country making a hero out of Captain Wilkes for letting himself be drawn into the trap of seizing you and Mr. Mason by force on the high seas, that may be a bitter pill for Mr. Lincoln, the politician, to swallow."

"Are you going to report the affair as a trap?" Slidell asked somewhat anxiously. "You would do our Cause a great disservice if you did."

"I agree that the worst thing anybody could do is insinuate that the Confederate government deliberately set out to create friction between the Union and England. But I'm also bound, as a correspondent I've set myself up to be, to report the news as I see it."

"You just said people everywhere are idolizing Captain Wilkes for seizing us," James Mason reminded her. "I wonder how many will believe you?"

"Perhaps not many," Maritza admitted. "Let's hope your imprisonment won't be too long."

"It won't," John Slidell assured her. "I told the family when we were leaving the *Trent* that I'd see them in Paris in sixty days."

In the room she had taken in a hotel near the harbor, Maritza was busy during the afternoon and evening, writing her story and making the necessary copies. The copy for the address in Georgetown, and from thence to Richmond, she mailed from Boston. The others she kept to deliver to Secretary Seward's office when she returned to Washington and the inevitable censorship.

Tired from the effort of making the needed copies without Tina's help, she slept like a log and was awakened by the cry of a street seller hawking oysters, clams, prawns, and other delicacies so prized by Bostonians. The morning paper was still extolling the virtues of Captain Wilkes and his crew. More important, it also carried the announcement that, starting that morning at ten, the public was invited to visit and inspect the famous screw sloop *San Jacinto* before it sailed to resume its regular blockading assignment.

Maritza was among the first to be admitted to the famous vessel when it was opened for inspection that morning. She examined it thoroughly, including the stateroom amidships where the famous rebels had been held during the voyage to Fortress Monroe and on to Boston. On deck again, she found a handsome officer with the insignia of a lieutenant on his uniform, answering questions for a small circle of visitors, and she joined the group.

"Are you the Lieutenant Fairfax mentioned in the newspapers as having captured the prisoners, sir?" she inquired when she had an opportunity.

"I am, madam." Fairfax bowed courteously. "May I help you?"

"I'm curious, Lieutenant, about the authority by which you boarded a neutral merchant ship at sea and removed some of its passengers."

The naval officer stiffened slightly at the question and several bystanders, who had heard it, moved closer to hear the answer better.

"Captain Wilkes was quoted in the press as saying he was acting under the provisions of the Congress of Paris of 1854," Fairfax answered.

"But the United States was not, and is not now, I believe, a signatory to those provisions," said Maritza. "So how could he act under them?"

"The Congress of Paris gave naval vessels of belligerents the right to board neutral vessels carrying contraband of war, madam."

"Just what contraband of war did you remove from the British merchant vessel *Trent,* Lieutenant?"

A crowd was now forming around the two, and the lieutenant showed a tendency to fidget. "The persons of spies—"

"Spies, Lieutenant? It was widely known in the press that Mr. Slidell and Mr. Mason were on the way to England. I have been told that, while they were waiting with their families in Havana for a ship to carry them to England, they entertained the officers of this ship at lunch. In fact, didn't they advise Captain Wilkes and, presumably yourself, that they would cross the sea soon in a British merchant ship?"

"Your information is correct, madam," said Fairfax stiffly. "May I ask what is your interest in this affair?"

"You certainly may. I am the accredited foreign correspondent for *Le Pays* of Paris. Mr. William H. Russell of the London *Times* has also delegated me to represent him in interviewing members of the *San Jacinto* staff and the prisoners."

The crowd around them had grown and when she heard a clicking sound Maritza found herself looking directly at the lens of a large black box held by a man in a bowler hat. She recognized the apparatus as a camera, having seen the famous photographer Mathew Brady using one at the Battle of Manassas.

Before the now perturbed naval officer could speak, Maritza added, "I have also been told that you personally objected to Captain Wilkes's action, Lieutenant, when you were ordered to carry it out. And that the grounds for your objection were that it might bring on war with England. Is that true?"

"I—I cannot say more, madam," Fairfax said stiffly.

"It isn't necessary that you do so now, Lieutenant. I'm sure you will have an opportunity to speak fully and freely when a board of inquiry meets to consider the highly questionable conduct of this vessel's commander in undertaking an action likely to provoke war with England. Good day, sir."

As an excited babble broke out among the small crowd that had gathered around her and Lieutenant Fairfax, Maritza walked sedately along the deck to the short gangplank and down it to the landing. Waving her parasol to call a hack, she was driven to her hotel and, two hours later, was on the afternoon train for Washington. That a picture of her questioning Lieutenant Fairfax would be in tomorrow's Boston newspaper she could be quite certain and had decided it was expedient to be back in Washington by then.

As the train started leaving the station, Maritza saw a heavy-set man sprinting along the platform obviously trying to catch it. Three cars back, he seized the vertical rod of the handle beside the steps and swung himself aboard. His face, in the brief glimpse she'd had of him, seemed familiar, but she didn't really remember where she'd seen him until he followed her off the train in Washington. It was then that she realized he'd been the agent guarding the gate to Rose Greenhow's house the night Allan Pinkerton raided it.

XI

Celestina was asleep in their room at Monsieur Cruchet's when Maritza came in shortly before midnight but came wide awake at the sight of her mistress.

"I was sure the Pinkerton agents in Boston had arrested you," she said. "Or that Captain Wilkes already had you drawn and quartered."

"A Pinkerton agent did follow me from Boston and I suspect must have followed me to Boston from Washington. I put the fear of God into Captain Wilkes's lieutenant, though. Hated to do it, too, because he was only acting under orders when he seized Mr. Mason and Uncle John."

"You didn't get to see them, did you?"

"Yes. Fix me a cup of coffee while I write out an account for

Mr. Russell. Maybe I can catch him in the morning while he's having breakfast at the Willard."

"He came to the stage door of the music hall tonight and asked whether I'd heard from you but I couldn't tell him anything. I think he really came to see the cancan; we gave our first performance tonight."

"If it's anything like the Paris version, I'm surprised not to find you in jail."

Celestina laughed. "I may be by tomorrow night. The Church Women's League is threatening to picket the hall but we're sold out for the next ten days and the management can probably pay off the police. Especially with General McClellan so busy trying to put General Scott out as commander-in-chief that he doesn't have time for anything else."

"Doesn't he still ride through Washington every day?"

"Not as often. A lonely brigadier general who took me to supper last night says McClellan doesn't know where to start fighting, and Lincoln is thinking of replacing him, if he doesn't produce that battle plan he's been talking about ever since he got to Washington."

"Sounds like the same old routine. Lay out some clothes for me while I'm writing this account for Mr. Russell. I've got to be up early tomorrow morning but I won't wake you up and you can sleep late."

Maritza found William H. Russell exactly where she expected to find him, in the dining room of the Willard Hotel holding forth to a small group of foreign correspondents. As soon as he saw her he moved to her table.

"You must have returned home late last night," he said. "I spoke with Celestina after the performance but she hadn't heard from you."

"How was the cancan, by the way?"

"Superb! Never saw better in Paris. Mademoiselle Toutant could be a music hall star anywhere in the world."

"She doesn't want that. She's in love with André, the maître d'hôtel at the Exchange House in Montgomery, Alabama— except that I believe André is now at the Hotel Spotswood in Richmond."

"I remember him well; they'll make a handsome pair. Did you learn anything in Boston, Countess?"

"The city went wild over Captain Charles Wilkes and the *San Jacinto*."

"Same here—and in New York too. When Congress convenes early in December, I hear, they're planning to give Wilkes a medal."

"Has Secretary Seward made any statements for the press about the *Trent* affair?"

"He's had nothing to say yet, which is surprising."

"Why?"

"It's well known that Seward once considered provoking England into declaring war against the United States, hoping to reunite the North and South and prevent the present war because of the threat."

"I'd heard that too but wasn't sure it was true."

"Those were his sentiments as recently as a year ago. Now that Captain Wilkes has done the provoking for him, though, Seward seems to realize what it would mean to fight the South and England at the same time. As far as I can tell, the stated policy right now seems to be one of watchful waiting, particularly until Lord Lyons and Henri Mercier can hear from their governments."

"Is there any doubt about what the reaction of England will be?"

"None whatsoever, unless an apology is forthcoming and the commissioners are released. What about France?"

"Before I left, I asked Henri Mercier the same question. He feels that France will follow the lead of England—though probably not into war."

"So all we can do is wait," said Russell with a shrug. "Which means three weeks before any answer can be expected from Paris or London and probably even longer, with the weather being what it is on the North Atlantic."

"I learned one thing in Boston," said Maritza. "The executive officer of the *San Jacinto,* Lieutenant D. M. Fairfax, was very much against Wilkes's action. He even suggested that Wilkes consult a Federal judge named Marvin in Key West, who's an authority on maritime law, before intercepting the *Trent*. Wilkes refused so the affair went through."

"So Wilkes really was acting on his own?" said Russell thoughtfully. "You'd better tell your friend Henri Mercier about that."

"Why?"

"He showed me a copy of his first dispatch to Thouvenel in Paris about the affair. In that report he stated that Wilkes's action had been taken only after receiving formal orders from Washington and that Seward had been looking for an excuse to break with England."

"I must see Henri this morning and give him the truth, that the whole affair was planned in Richmond," said Maritza.

Russell gave her a startled look. "Are you sure?"

"I couldn't prove it, but I'm sure."

Russell whistled softly. "'What fools these mortals be'— Shakespeare was right. I have it on the authority of General McClellan that if England enters the war on the side of the South the Union will be defeated."

"A lot of Southerners would like that."

"But maybe not for long. After the North was defeated, you can be sure Earl Russell and the Prime Minister of England would demand a price for giving the victory to the Confederacy."

"What sort of price?"

"One of them might be adding some of the northern tier of states to Canada, perhaps Vermont, New Hampshire, and Maine."

Maritza nodded slowly. "In less than a hundred years, England and America have already fought two wars. A third, with Napoleon III waiting in the wings to grab whatever he could on both sides of the Atlantic after both nations are prostrate from a long and bitter war, would be a major disaster."

"I quite agree," said Russell. "Are you going to reveal the scheme the *Trent* was unwittingly involved in, when you send your dispatch on the affair to *Le Pays?*"

"No. As you know, I was born in the South and my sympathies will always be there, but provoking a world war is an act I can only denounce."

"I shall keep silent too," Russell agreed. "As you say, we could never prove it anyway."

While letters moved back and forth across the Atlantic with their usual maddening slowness, made even worse by the weather, Washington continued to be quiet. Congress convened on December 2 and the House of Representatives immediately passed a resolution of congratulations to Captain Charles Wilkes, naming his conduct "brave, adroit and patriotic."

The following day, however, in his message to the new Congress, Abraham Lincoln failed even to mention the *Trent* affair. Later the President was reported by the usual "highly placed source" to have confessed: "I fear the traitors will prove to be white elephants. We must stick to American principles concerning the rights of neutrals. We fought Great Britain for insisting, by theory and practice, on the right to do precisely what Captain Wilkes has done."

Even as Lincoln spoke his misgivings, a dispatch was on its way from Lord John Russell and the British Prime Minister, Viscount Palmerston, requesting specific actions on the part of the United States Government. One of these demands was an apology to England for the insult Captain Wilkes had given the British flag. The other insisted that the two commissioners be released immediately.

The British demand reached Lord Lyons on the night of December 18. Thoughtful but firm, it reflected the mollifying touch of Prince Albert, who had died on December 14. The French note, although in full agreement with the British, was slower in arriving and, at the request of a now thoroughly aroused Secretary Seward, Lord Lyons delayed official presentation of the British decision to the United States Government. He did state that, when he presented the British note officially, failure of the United States to act upon it immediately would make necessary his departure from the country in seven days and the breaking off of diplomatic relations between England and the United States. At the request of Secretary Seward, however, Lyons delayed until December 23 but after that the clock started ticking toward the beginning of a world war.

On Christmas Day, 1861, Lincoln convened a conference of national leaders at the White House for the purpose of finding an answer to the dilemma in which the rash action of one man, Captain Charles Wilkes, had put the United States Government. Henri Mercier had made it quite clear to Secretary Seward beforehand that, should war with Britain occur—as occur it must without the action demanded in the British note presented by Lord Lyons, even then packing preparatory to departure—France would remain neutral.

The official dispatch from Foreign Minister Thouvenel in Paris, setting forth what Mercier had already told Seward, arrived at 10:00 A.M. Christmas Day and the French minister had the White House conference interrupted so the note could be delivered. Recording every report from the conference chamber as messengers brought them out, Maritza made notes preparatory to writing a dispatch for *Le Pays* that would go to Richmond via the Georgetown address.

On December 27, Secretary Seward sent a note to the British government with the requested apology. On January 1, 1862, John Slidell and James Mason, with their secretaries, were released from Fort Warren and immediately ushered aboard the English vessel *Rinaldo* at Provincetown, Massachusetts, their destination being Southampton, where they arrived on January 29.

On the day Mason and Slidell sailed, Maritza LeClerc was ordered deported from the United States and her credentials as a war correspondent revoked, on the grounds that she had filed dispatches again and again that were prejudicial to the cause of the United States in its war with the Confederacy.

BOOK SIX

WILMINGTON

I

Looking back over the past year, Maritza found it hard to believe she'd stood almost in the same position just a few days over twelve months ago, with spray from the white-capped waves breasted by the ship that bore her molding her frock against her superb body. The circumstances were much the same, too, except that the line of land visible to the west was the Atlantic coast of North Carolina at the mouth of the Cape Fear River instead of the Gulf of Mexico just south of Mobile.

The familiar, and just as stalwart, figure in the crow's nest atop the foremast with a brass telescope glued to his eye was once again Captain Pennington Darrow. And the cargo beneath the hatches was much the same as it had been on that other occasion: rifles, cannon, gunpowder in barrels, quinine against the epidemics of intermittent fever that would attack both Union and Confederate armies with the coming of summer, and even a few silks and satins to be sold to the belles of Wilmington, Richmond, and Charleston at fantastic prices.

As she watched three plumes of black smoke on the eastern horizon grow larger by the minute, Maritza didn't need her own telescope to know they came from the stacks of the three Union blockading warships that had picked up their trail not far from Cape Hatteras. Now the question uppermost in the minds of crew and passengers this late afternoon in April 1862 was simple: could the long powerful guns of those vessels come within range of the swift blockade runner *Sprite* before night fell? Or would the side-wheel paddles of the *Sprite* herself, churning in frantic haste, take it to safety within the mouth of Cape Fear and the protection of the massive guns of Fort Fisher, strongest bastion left along the whole Confederate coast?

"What do you see?" Maritza called up to Penn Darrow.

"Three of the fastest Federal gunboats in the blockading fleet." He lowered his telescope for a moment to answer. "A shell from any one of their guns landing amidships, where the powder is stored, could send us to heaven without the trouble of acquiring wings."

"Never mind heaven—can we beat them to Cape Fear?"

"We'd better," he said grimly. "Want to wager another bottle of French brandy on it?"

"I can't. Tina and I drank all we had while we were waiting for you in Nova Scotia."

His laugh floated down to her from the crow's nest where, with characteristically unconscious grace, he'd wrapped a leg around the top of the mast to steady himself while he studied the distant pursuers. Hearing it and remembering that other time, Maritza felt her pulse quicken in spite of the promise she'd made to herself on the way from Mobile to Montgomery, a promise that she would not again yield to the masculine demand the mere presence of Darrow's handsome body near hers always created.

"I've been saving a few bottles myself for this very occasion," he assured her. "We'll dine on one of Tina's epicurean feasts tonight before we broach them to celebrate our victory."

"You haven't won yet," she reminded him, bringing another shout of laughter from overhead.

"But I will, just as you outwitted that Yankee bloodhound Pinkerton and led your cousin Pierre to win a victory at Manassas."

II

Pinkerton, at least, had been pleased at the opportunity to deliver the order for Maritza's deportation to her rooms at Monsieur Cruchet's almost exactly three months ago. She'd made no objection. Even before she left Washington, Federal censorship had been slowly cutting the flow of information to the newspaper correspondents to the point where, watched night and day as she had been by Seward's beagle, the situation had ceased to be worth the risks she took. When William H. Russell became disgusted with Washington and sailed for England, Maritza, too, had soon realized the futility of staying in the Union capital any longer and almost welcomed the deportation order.

It had taken Henri Mercier two weeks to arrange for passage from New York to Paris for Maritza and Celestina on the French steamer *Angélique*. Two hundred of Maritza's own dollars, almost all the Union government had allowed her to take with her, had been needed to convince the master of the steamer to drop her and Celestina ashore at Halifax, capital and principal port of the Canadian province of Nova Scotia.

They hadn't expected to be isolated in Nova Scotia for the winter, while waiting for Penn Darrow and the *Sprite* to come and get them, however. Her last letter to Richmond, via the address in Georgetown, had been addressed to him in the care of Judah Benjamin. It had told Darrow of her intention to leave the French ship at Halifax and wait there until the *Sprite* docked with a cargo of the South's "white gold," cotton, and picked up its usual shipload of vital military and medical supplies for deposit on the docks at Wilmington.

Maritza had possessed no way of knowing two very important things when the ship's boat from the *Angélique* finally deposited her, Celestina, and their baggage on the dock near Mrs. Gilhooley's boardinghouse, which the captain had recommended for her stay in Halifax. One was that damage by a random shell from a Union blockade ship to one of her paddle wheels had put the *Sprite* temporarily into dry dock. Although she was the fastest of the South's blockade-running fleet and therefore able to make the long runs to and from Halifax, the blockade had been tightening steadily to the point where slipping in and out had become more and more difficult—even for *Sprite*.

The other event had happened even before Maritza left Washington. Early in November a large sea-borne invasion fleet, with Admiral Samuel F. DuPont in charge of many ships and a substantial land force, had attacked Port Royal in South Carolina. Its spacious harbor was easily capable of basing the entire United States fleet and therefore its capture had been a prize of the first water. The defenders had fought valiantly, it was reported, but after heavy bombardment from the sea the walls of the Confederate forts had been destroyed easily by Union troops.

With Port Royal now a major Federal base for the blockade fleet, operations of the blockade runners had been sharply curtailed. Savannah and Charleston were largely closed to them soon afterward and the Cape Fear River, with its network of channels allowing entry from both north and south, remained the only port of entry capable of handling the larger ships. As for Wilmington, it was protected by some twenty-eight miles of river upstream and had remained the single most available haven to the much-curtailed fleet of blockade runners.

Since only a few ships from the South did put in at Halifax any more, Maritza had been largely denied the Richmond newspapers, too. And when nothing appeared about *Sprite* in the arrival and departure columns, she became more and more concerned both for the vessel and for Penn Darrow.

New York and Canadian papers were easily available, however, and, familiar with the censorship techniques of the Union, Maritza could read between the lines by now. Thus she managed to obtain a fairly accurate picture of what was going on both in the North and the South.

Toward the end of March, during the seemingly interminable period while Maritza and Tina waited in the cold blustery wind and fog-wrapped major port of Nova Scotia, General McClellan had finally revealed his plan for ending the war. By this time the channel of the Potomac and the mouth of Chesapeake Bay at Hampton Roads had been cleared by a new type of warship—the ironclad, from which ordinary cannon balls bounced off largely without causing harm to the attacking vessel. With Hampton Roads now cleared by the Union Navy, McClellan boldly—for him—embarked the army he'd been training in the former Alexandria Line area and sailed down the Potomac.

The destination of the Union force had been quite apparent—the peninsula between the James and York rivers, with Richmond at its western terminus and three railroads leading to the capital of the Confederacy. The plan was for a three-pronged advance on a large scale. General Irvin McDowell, with a substantial force, was to drive southward past the old battlefield at Manassas and hold the Confederates in the Rappahannock River area. In the Shenandoah Valley, meanwhile, three armies were pitted against General Stonewall Jackson. General Nathaniel Prentiss Banks was given the task for the Union of holding—and defeating—Jackson, assisted by General John Charles Frémont advancing eastward from bases in the western part of Virginia. And General James F. Shields was with another force located near Front Royal, where he could move to help Banks in the Shenandoah Valley or eastward to support McDowell, if the need arose. At the same time McClellan would be moving up the peninsula to grip Richmond in a giant pincers and end the war.

With Maritza's own funds largely depleted by the payment to the skipper of the *Angélique* for setting her and Celestina ashore at Halifax, she'd found herself one day with only enough money to pay for a week's stay at Mrs. Gilhooley's highly respectable boardinghouse. Dressing, therefore, in her best Paris frock, she presented herself at the Bank of Nova Scotia with credentials from the Bank of England and a draft made out against the account in London. She was surprised when the teller asked her to come into the office of the bank manager, Mr. McDougal, who proved to be a grizzled Scotsman and ushered her deferentially to a chair before his desk.

"Is anything wrong with my draft?" Maritza asked.

"Nothing wrong, Countess. Nothing at all. We will be happy to cash it if you wish."

"Then why—"

"I was just wondering why you would be cashing a draft on the Bank of England, when you are already one of the largest depositors in this bank."

"I'm afraid I don't understand, Mr. McDougal. Are you saying I already have an account here?"

"A rather large one, Countess." McDougal glanced at a ledger sheet the teller had laid on his desk when Maritza was ushered into the office. "Something in the neighborhood of a hundred thousand pounds."

"But how–" Maritza stopped suddenly. "Of course, Halifax is the principal port for the Confederate ship *Sprite* and Captain Darrow, isn't it?"

"Yes, he comes in regularly about once a month. In fact, the past few weeks make up the longest period he's ever taken between voyages."

"I'm sure it would have made news if the United States Navy had captured or sunk the *Sprite*. From what I read in the papers, it's the most famous of the blockade runners by now."

"And rightly so," McDougal agreed. "When Captain Darrow sells his load of cotton at the end of each voyage, he conscientiously divides the profits and deposits half of it to your account."

"What about his own?"

"He usually finances the next shipment out of his own funds. I understand that you and he are in partnership–"

"I hired Captain Darrow in London to skipper an old brigantine with a shipload of munitions we sold later in an auction at Mobile to the Confederate War Department. The operation was so profitable that we leased the *Sprite* just before she was finished in the shipyard at Glasgow and went into partnership running the Federal blockade."

"Captain Darrow told me you furnished the capital. He also described you as a very beautiful and smart woman."

"I hope he didn't tell you I served in Washington as a spy for the Confederacy."

McDougal chuckled. "Penn Darrow is not only a very handsome man but also the very soul of discretion. He and I have become very good friends during the past half year or so. You see, in addition to acting as the banker for your partnership, I also fill the post of agent. Between voyages I locate buyers for your cotton–purchased at six cents a pound in Wilmington, incidentally, it sells on the docks here at fifty. I also arrange to purchase munitions and supplies for the voyage back to Wilmington."

"Is very much being shipped to the South from Halifax?"

"Blockade running, thanks to Captain Darrow and the *Sprite,* has become quite a thriving business here, Countess. Not only does it mean profit for the merchants of Canada, but also for those of New England."

"You mean the Yankees are shipping supplies to the South?" she asked, startled.

"I'd say half the cloth for Confederate uniforms comes from New England looms, plus a considerable amount of gunpowder, pig lead, medical supplies, and not a little finery for the ladies of Richmond and other Southern cities."

"And all the while Abraham Lincoln pretends to be so pious and long-suffering." Maritza shook her head slowly. "This war isn't being fought over slavery at all, Mr. McDougal. It's a commercial venture for the benefit of Yankee merchants."

"That's almost true, with my fellow Canadians coming in for their share," McDougal admitted. "I hope you aren't going to take your funds with you when you start to Wilmington on the *Sprite,* Countess. As your financial adviser over the past six months, even though you weren't aware of it at the time, the bank has strictly avoided dealing in Confederate currency."

"I knew the value was dropping. Is it in that bad straits?"

"I'm afraid Mr. Davis and his financial advisers are depending too much on the hope of floating major loans in England and France. With General McClellan holding Yorktown under siege, plus General Ulysses Grant's victories in the interior at Fort Henry and Fort Donelson, European financiers aren't going to look too favorably on requests from Richmond for loans."

"Then you think there's no possibility of England and France taking part in the war?"

"For England that chance evaporated when Abraham Lincoln apologized to the Queen for the *Trent* affair," McDougal assured her. "Actually, eight thousand English soldiers had already been sent to Canada just before Christmas last year, ready for an invasion of New England, if that apology hadn't been made."

III

The weeks while Maritza and Celestina waited at Mrs. Gilhooley's boardinghouse in Halifax had indeed been long and dreary. Ships bound for European, Canadian, and U.S. ports came and went—but none for Confederate harbors. Nevertheless, they had watched from the widow's walk atop Mrs. Gilhooley's boardinghouse like many others from which Nova Scotian wives had watched for the return of whalers from the far reaches of the Pacific whaling grounds long ago. And one morning in early April they'd been rewarded when an especially bright beam broke through the fog to reveal the tall masts of a vessel moving into the harbor under steam, its deck so piled with cotton bales that it appeared to have been through a snowstorm.

The ship was low, long, and sleek, its stacks belching black smoke and the side wheels churning as it moved into the harbor. Maritza almost dropped her telescope in the excitement of seeing a newcomer exactly like the one picture she'd seen of the *Sprite* in a Richmond newspaper. And as she focused the glass, the name of the ship came into view, in letters of shining metal on the side of the wheelhouse.

It was the *Sprite,* with the Stars and Bars of the Confederacy fluttering proudly at the masthead.

"There's your ship, Countess," Mr. McDougal called up from the street below where a small crowd was watching the blockade runner being warped to the dock. "She's safe and sound and loaded with what we like to call 'white gold.'"

"I must go down and get dressed," Maritza told Tina, who had been watching from the widow's walk with her. "Come help me, I look like a frump."

"Every sailor should come home to a frump like you," Tina said as she lifted the trap door in the small railed-in space atop the roof where they'd been standing. "Cap'n'll be so glad to see you, he won't notice what you're wearing. After all, the last time he saw you, you weren't exactly dressed for a masked ball."

"I was riding a horse on the shore of Mobile Bay. Remember?"

"But the night before that. Hooee!"

Maritza and Tina came out on the dock from Mrs. Gilhooley's just as Penn Darrow leaped ashore from the deck of the *Sprite*, leaving it to be tied up by the crew.

"Maritza!" he shouted and, seizing her by the elbows, swung her around in a flutter of skirts and petticoats, before setting her down and planting a kiss firmly on her lips, in spite of the fact that she was breathless from his greeting. "By God! You're the prettiest thing I've seen since I left you in Mobile six—no, I guess it was nearer nine—months ago." Turning to Celestina, he greeted her too with an enthusiastic kiss.

"Why were you so long in coming?" Maritza tried to sound vexed but found it somewhat difficult, with his arm still around her waist and his eyes shining with a light she was certain the few onlookers couldn't possibly fail to understand.

"When your letter finally reached me in Wilmington in February, saying you were being deported, the *Sprite* was in dry dock with a crankshaft cracked while outrunning a Federal cruiser off Cape Hatteras in a storm. A new shaft had been cast at the Tredegar Iron Works in Richmond, but it took more than another month to ship it down and put it in place. I left as soon as the *Sprite* floated out of that dock and was loaded with cotton."

"It's a beautiful ship," said Maritza.

"Almost the last of its kind." His voice took on a serious note. "The Federals are building new ships of war everywhere but all the South can do any more is cover old workhorses with iron plates and hope for the best."

"Couldn't you have let me know what was keeping you? Tina and I were worried that you might have been sunk with the *Sprite*."

"It's good news that you still thought enough of an old love to worry about him," he assured her with a grin. "Once I learned that, along with your stories in *Le Pays,* you were also doing some spying—"

"How did you find that out?"

"Monsieur Claudet, your editor in Paris, suspected it when your first accounts of life in Washington started arriving. They had obviously been chewed to pieces by censors but a day or two later he would get the full copy sent from Richmond, telling how all of official Washington was shaking in its shoes for fear that Beauregard would move on the city and take it."

"He could have, too."

"So you said. When he got both copies, Monsieur Claudet put two and two together. He figured the true one sent by way of Richmond was your report to Judah Benjamin and Richard Mann as a spy and wrote me in London at once. I was worried sick about you but couldn't write, of course, because a letter from England to you in Washington would have been opened by the censors and I couldn't put you to that risk."

"When do you plan to sail again?"

"Four days from now. McClellan's trying to crack a hard nut in the fortifications at Yorktown, and the Confederacy needs all the bullets, powder, and cannon balls I can land on the docks at Wilmington."

"I'm going with you and so is Tina, unless she wants to pursue the promising career she was developing in Washington as a music hall star."

"Hunh!" said Tina. "What's promising about seeing how high you can kick and how much you can show without being arrested? Or flipping up your skirts to show your behind either?"

Penn Darrow laughed. "Bet that was something to see, though. I'd be happy to pay the price of admission."

"No private showings!" said Maritza firmly.

"I was in Richmond ten days ago," Penn Darrow told Tina. "Everybody's not as strait-laced as Jefferson Davis, so plenty goes on after 'lights out!' I'm sure Tina can have all the career she wants as an entertainer." He turned to Mr. McDougal, who'd been standing a little distance away. "Have you ladies met our banker and agent?"

"Soon after we arrived. Mr. McDougal tells me you've been splitting the profits with me but financing the purchase of the cargoes for Wilmington out of your own pockets. From now on I want to take my share of the risks and you should pay yourself a salary in addition for acting as captain of the *Sprite*. Isn't that the way the other blockade runners operate?"

"Yes."

"Then we'll do the same. Let's neither of us forget that our relationship as far as this venture is concerned is strictly business."

"As far as this venture is concerned," he agreed, but the dancing light in his eyes told her he fully expected there would be another side to their relationship—and was looking forward to it.

IV

"Ahoy, the deck!" Penn Darrow's voice floated down from the crow's nest where he was directing the approach of the *Sprite* to the Cape Fear channel. "Pass the word to the engine room to sweat a little more steam out of these boilers. That middle Yankee gunboat must have been built on the Clyde; it's gradually overtaking us."

The chief engineer had a flourishing red beard but it was almost black with coal dust when his head popped out of the wheelhouse. "Another inch of steam and we may *fly* ashore," he protested.

"That's better than rotting in the Old Capitol." In Washington, the Old Capitol building was used as a central military prison, and the horror stories told by former prisoners, who escaped or were lucky enough to be exchanged, would put the reputation of the Paris Bastille to shame.

"Say hello to St. Peter as you pass by," said the engineer,

opening the door of the firebox and throwing a shovelful of coal into the roaring flames.

Maritza shivered, although the air was warm.

"You'd better go inside and put on some dry clothes," said Tina. "Don't forget that chill you had day before yesterday."

"It wasn't anything. Besides, I want to watch the run for the channel. From what Penn says, it's very exciting."

"And also very dangerous," said Tina. "I'll be happy when we dock in Wilmington."

With the steam-pressure gauge on the boiler nearing the danger point, the *Sprite* took a distinct surge forward as Darrow came down from his lofty perch.

"This is one time I wish I could reverse Joshua's feat in the Bible and make the sun sink faster. We need darkness to help us slip through." He looked closely at Maritza and frowned with concern. "Are you sure you're all right?"

"A little chilly. Nothing to be worried about."

"Your lips look blue. Here, put this on." Pulling off the jacket he'd worn aloft, he draped it about her shoulders. "I don't like that chill you had the other day, either."

"I've been trying to get her to go inside and put on dry clothes, but she's as stubborn as a mule," said Tina.

"Stand close to the firebox when we really start our run," Darrow advised Maritza. "You'll be better protected there and less likely to be chilled as it gets darker."

For the next hour the swift vessel raced toward the coastline and the channel into the Cape Fear River. Both were growing less distinct as the sun dropped lower in the sky but they could still easily see the formidable mass of Fort Fisher on the peninsula extending seaward. Penn Darrow stood beside the steam-pressure gauge, watching as the needle crept from twenty-four to twenty-five, then to twenty-seven pounds. They were already well past the danger point and into the near disaster range but he still called for more steam and the paddles of the two massive side wheels flailed the water even faster, creating small whirlpools that spun away behind the *Sprite*.

Darkness had almost obscured the land and the channel now, forcing Darrow to use night glasses. Beneath the roar of the engines, another sound was audible, too, the breaking of the sea upon the bar through which they must pass to reach safety under the guns of Fort Fisher.

"We're going in by way of New Inlet," Darrow explained to Maritza. "The Feds have a cordon of old merchant ships anchored there, bristling with artillery."

"Then why choose it?"

"Those old merchantmen can only shoot in one direction. Once past them, we'll be under the guns of Fort Fisher."

He looked at the steam-pressure gauge and spoke to the fireman and the sailor at the wheel almost in a whisper.

"Douse all lights," he commanded. "It'll be high tide over the bar in less than half an hour. We'll head through then and there'll be no stopping once we start."

From behind them came the boom of a cannon from the leading U.S. gunboat. An unseen shell splashed into the water well behind the *Sprite* but, when it exploded, sending a geyser of spray, some of the water reached the deck.

"That Clyde-built cruiser's as fast as I'd figured she'd be," Darrow muttered to himself. "But with his draft, he can't come much closer to the bar."

"Can you?" Maritza asked.

"We can go right over it in a pinch, though I'd much rather use the channel. This baby only draws a little more than half what that Yankee gunboat does." Raising his voice a little, he ordered: "Cover the binnacle and firebox."

With all lights doused, only a faint glow showed through the tarpaulin covering the firebox door near where Maritza stood. Wanting no part of the excitement, Tina had gone to their stateroom. The binnacle, too, was hooded, with just enough light for the steersman to see the compass. Penn Darrow stood beside it now, giving the course to the steersman in whispered directions. On either side forward, with one leg crooked about the rail, two leadsmen were swinging their lines in a regular rhythm and reporting the soundings in whispers just loud enough to be heard by the tall figure outlined faintly in the light escaping from the binnacle hood.

"Heave to or we'll sink you." A voice with the accent of a

born New Englander lanced out of the darkness, just as the dark mass of one of the anchored merchantmen loomed up ahead.

"A little to port," Darrow whispered to the steersman, "just enough to scrape his anchor chains as we go by."

The man at the wheel eased the spokes a little and the bow of the *Sprite* shifted just enough to graze the chains that held the merchantman in place.

"My God! They're ramming us!" the same Yankee voice screamed on a note of pure terror, forgetting, as Penn Darrow had hoped, to pull the lanyard of the cannon fixed securely to the deck.

Drummond lights suddenly searched the darkness in a frantic attempt to catch the *Sprite* in their converging beams. They lost her, however, in the pandemonium raised among the merchant ship inner cordon by the deliberate near-ramming technique Penn Darrow had used and, like a vicious narwhal, the *Sprite* shot through the channel opening Darrow had sensed rather than seen.

A blue light burst into brilliance from the Mound Battery, part of the system of guns of Fort Fisher guarding New Inlet. Seconds later the thunder of one of the massive guns from the fort shook the slender hull of the *Sprite,* outlining her momentarily in a red glare before the huge missile went whistling overhead toward the attacking Federal vessels.

"We've done it, Maritza!" Penn Darrow seized her in his arms, almost smothering her as he kissed her. Exhausted by the tension of the last half hour, standing beside him while the *Sprite* ran the vicious potential gantlet, Maritza sagged in his arms, feeling the chill of an intermittent fever seize her very bones in a moment of agony before she lost consciousness.

V

Maritza awakened to bright sunlight pouring through a window in a room she'd never seen before. It certainly wasn't her cabin on the *Sprite,* for those had been spartan quarters, since all possible space on the swift blockade runners needed to be available for precious cargo. Nor was there any motion to indicate that she might still be aboard a ship even at anchor. Instead, the room appeared to be a woman's bedroom in a cottage, the starched curtains at the windows matching the tester atop the tall four-poster in which she lay. The room was small but everything she could see was in perfect taste, showing that it had been done by the hand of a woman.

"Decided to wake up?" a male voice asked from the corner.

She turned immediately and saw a tall man turn from looking out the other window but still could hardly believe the evidence of her own ears and eyes.

"Am I dreaming?" Maritza asked. "Or is it possibly you?"

Richard Mann laughed softly and came over to the bed to take her hand. He was as tall and as handsome as she remembered his being, when she had seen him last, some ten months ago at McLean's Ford across Bull Run on the eve of the Battle of Manassas, but with one change. He now wore the single stars of a brigadier general in the Confederate Army on his gray uniform instead of the insignia of a colonel he'd worn there before.

"Didn't I warn you I'd be waiting for you when the war was over?" he asked.

"It's not—"

"Far from it. In fact, McClellan is starting to make the move he's been hinting at all winter—a water-borne invasion of the peninsula between the York and the James River—so the fighting's about to become hotter than it's ever been."

"How did you get here?" Maritza asked.

"Captain Darrow sent me a telegram before he sailed. It said that if I loved you I'd better come to Wilmington and look after you."

"Everything is all so muddled, I feel as though I've been in a dream. You did say Penn has sailed again, didn't you?"

"Five days ago, for Halifax. You've been delirious for a week."

"From what?"

"Dr. Merwyn says you were already in the midst of a bout of

intermittent fever and Tina told me you had a chill two days before the *Sprite* ran the gantlet and entered the Cape Fear. You were having another when Darrow brought the *Sprite* to anchor in the mouth of the river that night."

"Where is this?"

"Darrow has an aunt, Mrs. Dalton, in Wilmington; this is her home. When you became unconscious aboard the *Sprite,* he brought you here and got Dr. Merwyn. The doctor's been feeding you quinine and whiskey—an old army remedy—ever since."

"How could Penn leave me, as sick as you say I was?"

"He didn't have any choice, that's why he sent for me. McClellan is laying siege to Yorktown, the main barrier to the march he wants to make on Richmond from the east. Many ships from the Union blockading fleet off the mouth of Cape Fear have been sent to Hampton Roads to help McClellan. The armies defending Richmond badly need ammunition an English ship was to deliver to the docks at Halifax a week ago. And since the *Sprite* is the fastest ship in the blockade-running fleet, Secretary Benjamin ordered Darrow to sail for Nova Scotia as soon as he could take on a load of cotton."

"He still deserted me." Maritza's head was beginning to ache and her spirits, low enough after her illness, were wounded again by what she considered Penn Darrow's desertion.

"As much as I hate to admit it when Darrow is a rival, he had no choice. Besides, don't forget that neither you nor he really owns the *Sprite;* the ship was built for the Confederate government and leased to you. When Benjamin ordered Darrow to sail, he had to go but he took care of your welfare in the only way available to him, by telegraphing me to come here at once."

"If you had been in Penn's place, would you have left me here unconscious and probably dying?" she asked petulantly.

"I'd have had no choice either. McClellan is making his big push to end the war and nobody in Richmond can be sure he won't succeed. We've already made arrangements to move the government to Lynchburg or even to Danville, if the Union captures Richmond, but munitions already on the docks at

Halifax, Bermuda, and Nassau might make it possible for General Lee to stop McClellan."

"Shouldn't you be in Richmond, too, then?"

"I certainly should, but I had to be sure you were receiving the best possible medical care. Now that I'm satisfied of it, I've got to take the train back to Richmond tonight or be cashiered for a deserter."

"Where does that leave me?"

"Dr. Merwyn tells me you should be able to travel in another week. Personally, I hope you'll decide to take the train for Mobile and a long rest, preferably until the war's over and I can join you on our plantations."

"Why can't I go to New Orleans? I have more relatives there."

"Union warships under Admiral Farragut have captured New Orleans and General Butler is in charge of the city. You know what his reputation is."

"Then Mobile and Alabama will be next?"

"I don't think so. Fort Morgan is the most powerful bastion on the entire Gulf Coast now and blockade runners are still bringing in supplies from Cuba under its guns. If Farragut attacks Mobile he'll find the fort a considerably harder nut to crack than the weak fortifications that had been built on the river south of New Orleans in the hope of protecting the city from invasion."

There was a discreet knock on the door and a cheerful-looking middle-aged woman entered, followed by a plump man carrying a small bag.

"This is your hostess, Mrs. Margaret Dalton," Mann told Maritza. "And your physician, Dr. Samuel Merwyn."

"Who also saved your life," said Mrs. Dalton. "Let's not forget that."

"I'm grateful to you both," said Maritza. "Having me dumped on your doorstep unconscious must have put a heavy burden on you, Mrs. Dalton."

"Not at all, dear. Not at all. Penn told me how you risked your life getting valuable information from the enemy and how that horrible man, Mr. Pinkerton, treated you."

"How are you feeling today, Countess?" Dr. Merwyn was opening his black bag. "Obviously better, or you'd still be delirious."

"My head aches and I feel too weak to even lift a hand," said Maritza. "But I thank God I'm still alive."

"Just let me listen to your chest a moment, Countess." Dr. Merwyn had taken from his bag a wooden cone hollowed out inside and highly polished. "This is a—"

"A stethoscope!" Maritza exclaimed. "I saw one in France used by the doctor who took care of my husband during his last illness."

"Fine! Fine! You'd be surprised how many people are afraid of them." The doctor was placing the larger end of the cone here and there on her chest, applying his ear to the smaller end. "Now the back, please," he said, and Richard Mann gently pulled her over on her side so the doctor could listen in several places there too.

"Excellent!" he announced. "The pneumonia has almost cleared up and the first few doses of quinine took care of the intermittent fever. You're well on the way to full recovery."

"I wish we could handle fever that easily with the troops stationed in the swampy areas east of Richmond," said Richard Mann. "Almost every night, boatloads of quinine and other medications are ferried across the lower Potomac by speculators from Maryland. They steal the drugs from Union warehouses in Baltimore and Washington so they cost nothing, but you wouldn't believe the prices they're getting for them when they're delivered to us. Even then, we can't get enough quinine and laudanum to take care of the fever and pain of the wounded."

"If all my patients recovered as speedily as you have, my dear Countess"—Dr. Merwyn was putting the stethoscope back in his bag—"I'd soon be out of a job."

"I don't *feel* recovered," said Maritza. "I feel more as if I'd been put through a wringer."

"A natural reaction under the circumstances but, between Mrs. Dalton and that handsome servant of yours, they'll have you well in no time," the doctor assured her.

"Where *is* Celestina?" Maritza asked when the doctor had left.

"Asleep," Richard Mann told her. "She's been sitting up with you at night while Mrs. Dalton and I took turns in the daytime."

"General Mann is a wonderful hand in the sickroom, Countess—"

"Please, Mrs. Dalton, call me Maritza. After what you've both done for me, titles certainly have no place between us."

Mann looked at his watch. "The train will be leaving for Richmond in a couple of hours and I'd better be on it, if I'm to be in Secretary Benjamin's office by tomorrow morning. When you feel like traveling, Maritza, take the Wilmington & Weldon Railroad to Petersburg and hire a carriage to bring you to Richmond. Troops are pouring into Petersburg from the southwest on the South Side Railroad and you might be held up for a half day if you stayed on the train."

"A carriage would certainly be better than that," she agreed.

"I'll also leave orders with the stationmaster here before I start for Richmond tonight, to give you a sleeping car compartment when you're ready to travel," he promised.

"You and Penn are alike in one way at least," Maritza said with a somewhat wan smile. "You both think of everything."

"Where you're concerned, I try to, and I'm sure Darrow does too. You see, we both have the same ambition—to look after you for the rest of our lives."

"While risking your own in the process?"

"No more than you risked yours by continuing to spy for us in Washington, when you knew Pinkerton was desperately looking for an excuse to put you in prison. Tell me this: would you have stayed if you hadn't been deported?"

"Of course. By the way, when I left you in Montgomery, you were a colonel with no particular job except looking for supplies for the War Department. Do you have a different one now?"

He shook his head. "The supply job was a disguise. I'm second in command of the Confederate Secret Service."

"So I'm really under your command when I function as a secret agent?"

"Technically, yes. But as of now you are relieved of your duties as a spy—to name it baldly—and returned to your original status as correspondent for *Le Pays*." He reached out to take her hand. "That is, unless you're prepared to take on a different title?"

"What's that?"

"Mrs. Richard Mann."

"Dear Richard—and I could say the same for Penn—surely I'm blessed beyond all women to be loved by two men such as you. And, moreover, to be able to love them both without having to decide between you."

"The war will end someday; when it does, one of us will have to be turned away. Whichever side wins, many laws that hold true today will have to be changed but I'm sure the one against bigamy won't be one of them." He leaned over to kiss her. "You're tired and need your rest, so I won't see you again before I leave for Richmond. Good-by and—whoever your choice falls upon at the end of the war—be sure I shall understand and always love you."

VI

In spring, Wilmington was a lovely city, Maritza discovered as she sat rocking in an old Boston rocker on the porch of Mrs. Dalton's cottage about a week after Richard Mann's departure for Richmond. Although she was feeling better every day, she felt a strange sort of reluctance about starting for Richmond and the inevitable activity she knew Judah P. Benjamin would somehow talk her into once she arrived.

Today was warm with the promise of summer and in the garden setting off the cottage from the street a profusion of flowers were in bloom. Jonquils, narcissus, violets, even an occasional rosebud gave a special fragrance to the air quite different from the stink of the City Canal in Washington or the cold, bone-chilling fog that gripped Halifax most of the time.

Located about twenty-eight miles upriver on the Cape Fear, Wilmington was a center for oceangoing traffic by way of the channel leading to its mouth. Upper river traffic, carried in boats of somewhat less draft and in barges, made the river navigable almost to Fayetteville, some seventy-five miles upstream. Celestina was picking flowers in the garden; Maritza had slept so well the night before that Celestina had been able to lie on a cot Mrs. Dalton had placed in Maritza's bedroom and had slept most of the night as well. Mrs. Dalton herself came in from the vegetable garden back of the house, carrying a basket of lettuce, cabbage, and tiny sweet peas in their pods.

"You're looking better all the time," she told Maritza. "Dr. Merwyn says you can go north by the middle of the month but I'll hate to see you leave. Down here, with the ships still coming and going, we feel as if the war is far away but, from what I read in the Richmond papers, the Union Army is moving steadily closer to Richmond."

"With Yorktown having been evacuated and Williamsburg captured, it seems nothing can keep McClellan's army from taking Richmond," Maritza agreed.

"Do you think you ought to go back?"

"I'm afraid my conscience won't let me do anything else. My editor in Paris would never forgive me if I didn't describe the final hours of the war."

"I still hate to see you go back into danger," Mrs. Dalton said.

Maritza smiled. "I really won't be in danger. I've lived in Washington, so I know the Yankees—at least not many of them, except maybe that General Butler who is holding New Orleans—aren't predators. If you'll let me, I'll help you shell those peas while you tell me something about Penn. He doesn't have much to say about himself."

Mrs. Dalton went into the kitchen and came out a few minutes later carrying an empty bowl and the peas in the basket. She settled down on a stool beside Maritza's rocker and put the bowl on a small table between them.

"I'm afraid my nephew will always be a sailor," she said as they began to shell the delicate, tiny peas. "Back in Alabama as a boy, he always liked to ride the log rafts down the river to Mobile whenever he had a chance. Once I'd gone down to do some shopping and, when it was time for us to start back, I couldn't find him anywhere. Then someone mentioned seeing a boy standing on the docks watching the ships from Europe being loaded and there he was. At home, too, he was always climbing trees and swinging from ropes tied to their limbs, pretending he was setting sails or reefing them in a storm."

"Maybe that's why he's so good at handling sailing vessels," said Maritza. "The *Pride of Bristol* that we came over to Mobile in was driven only by sail."

"When Pennington got the appointment to the Naval Academy," Mrs. Dalton continued, "I'm sure he was the happiest boy—" She laughed. "No, boy isn't exactly right. He was six feet tall, handsome as a Greek god, and could outrun all the other boys his age. And the girls!" She gave Maritza a quick sidewise glance. "I don't have to tell you how they felt about him, do I?"

Maritza didn't choose to follow that line of thought but took up another. "You were saying something about his appointment to Annapolis."

"He was the happiest young man in the world. Came by here on his way to the Naval Academy to see George—my late husband—and me. When we heard a few years later that he wasn't going to be allowed to finish and get his commission—"

"Over a girl, wasn't it? At least that's what he told me."

"He was a sacrifice, that's what he was," Mrs. Dalton said indignantly. "A senator's son had a girl from the town in his room but, when he heard the guards coming, he managed to slip her into Pennington's quarters."

"Didn't Penn defend himself?"

"Very eloquently, according to my husband; George insisted on going to Annapolis and being at the hearing. He said Pennington might have cleared himself if he had named the other boy but he wouldn't do it. The whole thing had the elements of a kangaroo court anyway, so Pennington missed getting his commission by less than six months."

"Was he very bitter about it?"

"Bitter enough to give the one who was really guilty a horse-whipping afterward. The young man's father had enough influence in high places to bring civil charges against Pennington for the beating, but he escaped and came here ahead of the authorities. George managed to put him on as a stowaway aboard an English merchant steamer that was just on the point of sailing, so the law never caught up with him. The ship was caught in a storm off the Azores and the captain was washed overboard, but when the other officers were too scared to save her Pennington took over and brought the ship into port safely. He was accepted for training by the British merchant marine because he already knew more than the retired ship captains who were teaching him. In only a little over a year he had his own ship and—well, I guess you know the rest."

"I've seen him handle a ship several times in a storm and while running the blockade. He's—I guess 'magnificent' is the best word."

"You talked a lot about my nephew while you were delirious, Maritza. Are you going to marry him when the war's over?"

"I don't know." Maritza blushed at the thought of some of the things she must have said during that period of delirium.

"Pennington is everything a woman would want in a man."

"Except one thing—stability and the wish for a home and a family." Maritza's voice took on a serious note. "You said yourself he'd always be a sailor."

"Some seafaring marriages are very happy ones. All voyages don't have to be long either."

"I know, but Penn's the kind who'd choose the most dangerous and they're usually the longest."

"Whatever you do—if you marry him—don't try to change him," the older woman advised. "A man's got his own destiny to work out and when a wife tries to alter it—" She broke off. "But that's your own decision—about marrying Penn, I mean."

Picking up the bowl of peas, she got to her feet. "I'd better get these into the pot with a chunk of bacon or we won't have any supper. Nothing says a woman can't use her brain in choosing her man, you know, even though the poets tell her she should always listen to her heart."

VII

Like Rome, Richmond was built on seven hills, but there the similarity ended, Maritza decided as the carriage she and Celestina had rented in Petersburg, some twenty-odd miles to the south, rolled across the crowded bridge over the James River and onto the streets of the Confederate capital. Below the bridge she could see long lines of canal boats warped against the landings of the James River canal that lay here alongside the river, some waiting for the lock gates to open and others for them to be closed, raising the boats for the next stage of their journey.

Extending over a hundred miles westward along the course of the James River—itself produced by the union of several smaller streams deep into the Allegheny ridges far to the west— the canal had been a dream, their black driver told her and Celestina, of George Washington. The long, narrow canal boats, he added proudly, carried passengers and freight up-stream and downstream for nearly two hundred miles between Richmond and the small town of Buchanan, near where the James started cutting its way through the massif of the Blue Ridge on its way to the sea.

"Them boats has got a deck above the main cabin, ladies," the driver continued, "with another cabin just for dining. They's got a galley, too, and even a small bar, they tell me."

"Do they travel at night?" Celestina asked.

"They certainly do, miss. I hears dat passengers sleeps in the main cabin, with separate quarters for men and women, and berths three deep. If you looks upriver now, you can see one comin' downstream, pulled by three horses along the towpath."

"I'm glad we're not going west," said Tina. "Sleeping three deep sounds like a layer cake."

From the east a rolling sound like thunder struck their ears, but they could see no clouds massing for a thunderstorm.

"Them's cannon in the forts at Drewry's Bluff downriver," the driver explained.

Tina shivered. "They sound close."

"The forts is maybe eight to ten miles from here," said the driver, then continued confidently, "but don't you ladies worry about that none. I hears dat the guns in the fort is shootin' holes right through them Yankee gunboats. That one all covered with iron they call the *Monitor* can't even get within firing range of the fort. If the Yankees want to take Richmond, they've got to come some other way."

"They're getting pretty close by land, too, aren't they?" Maritza asked.

"I heered somebody say afore we left Petersburg that they're almost to a place about twelve miles or so from Richmond called White House. But General Johnston and the rest of them generals has got an awful lot of soldiers between the Yankees and Richmond."

"They're already too close for me," said Celestina.

"Don't worry, miss. General Johnston is just waitin' for the Yankees to come on where he can get a good shot at 'em. He's goin' to whup 'em just like he done at Manassas last year."

"How many men does General Johnston have on the peninsula, driver?" Maritza asked.

"The last figger I heard, ma'am, was fifty thousand."

"What about General McClellan?"

"He's got maybe three times that many; at least he did have about a month ago when he was tryin' to take Yorktown. Since then, though, Mr. Lincoln's got scared that General Stonewall Jackson might cross the Potomac, so he called back a lot of General McClellan's soldiers to guard Washington. They say General McClellan was fit to be tied."

"Did General Jackson cross the Potomac?" Maritza asked.

"Not that I read of, and I guess the newspapers would have been full of it if he had. The last I heard, he was busy chasing

Yankees up the Shenandoah Valley. General Jackson always prays before he starts fightin', they say, and once he gets goin', ain't no Yankees goin' to stop him. It's hard fightin' a man that's convinced the Lord's on his side and it sho 'nuff looks like the Lord's takin' care of General Stonewall."

"Why do you say that?" Maritza asked.

"About six weeks ago, the Yankees thought they had him trapped over at Kernstown close to Winchester. Three Yankee armies was after him that time but Jackson sneaked away before they could pin him down. He knows that valley like the back of his hand and he can hide his soldiers anywhere he wants to till they're ready to tackle the Yankees again. You can bet that's another time Abe Lincoln was yellin' for more troops to defend Washington, and McClellan screamin' his head off, claimin' he didn't have practically no army left."

"If he's only twelve miles away from Richmond, it sounds like he's got one," said Tina.

"Don't you worry 'bout Richmond, ladies. They say that in less'n a month General Robert E. Lee will be over all the soldiers in Virginia, and he's a prayin' man, too, like General Jackson. When them two get together, you're goin' to see a lot of wet Yankees, swimmin' the Potomac back to Washington."

VIII

At the Spotswood Hotel, Richmond's famous and most luxurious hostelry, the two women found the red carpet literally rolled out for them. The desk clerk handed Maritza a quill pen with a flourish and, while she signed the register, signaled for a bellman to take up their bags.

"It's an honor to have you with us, Countess," he said. "Since Mr. Russell departed from Washington, you've become the most distinguished foreign war correspondent in the press corps."

"Mr. Russell hasn't come back, has he?"

"I'm afraid not. He was very fond of the Spotswood and we

entertained him here several times, but the Federal censors finally made it impossible for him to write the truth about what was happening on the battlefields. I hear he left Washington in disgust."

"I had much the same experience," Maritza confessed, "except that they threw me out."

"That Major Allan Pinkerton is certainly no gentleman, ma'am. General Mann and Secretary Benjamin asked if they could look forward to your company at dinner this evening, if the journey from Petersburg hasn't been too wearing on you."

"Please send word to them that I shall be happy to join them," said Maritza. "Mademoiselle Celestina and I will go up now, if our rooms are ready."

"Of course; the bellman will show you. André, our maître d'hôtel, asked me to inform you that he has personally selected your dinner this evening."

Celestina had been craning her neck trying to look into the dining room, which was crowded with guests at luncheon. Her face lit up in a smile when she spotted André as she and Maritza crossed the lobby to the elevator followed by a bellman pushing a cart on which their bags were stacked. Though more elegantly furnished, the lobby of the Spotswood could have been another Willard's, or another Exchange hostelry, such as the one in Montgomery, Maritza decided as the two women crossed the teeming lobby, running the gantlet of every male eye there. They'd long ago become accustomed to that, however, and Celestina preened herself a little to stimulate the watchers.

The décor was just as ornate as that of the Willard or the Exchange, though much cleaner, and the same groups of men in top hats and cutaways, plus officers in dress uniform, were standing outside the door of the bar, which had overflowed into the lobby. The dining room, visible through its open doors, boasted snowy linen and highly polished silver, something not always found in wartime hotels. And from the crowded room the buzz of conversation and the higher notes of women's laughter were easily heard.

It was true that the uniforms were gray, where those above

the Potomac were blue. But the facings, pipings of the officers, and insignia of their uniforms were just as colorful and the sounds from the bar just as loud and boisterous. In fact nothing in the lobby, bar, or the dining room of the Hotel Spotswood in Richmond even hinted that, from the north and from the east, massive armies were even now struggling through mud and forest on the very doorstep of the city, as intent on capturing this capital on the James as were the men in gray pitted against them in its defense.

"At least this is a lot better than the last two hotels we stayed in," Tina observed as she directed the bellman in stowing their boxes and portmanteaux in the bedroom of the suite to which they had been ushered. It was surprisingly luxurious, for an American hotel, Maritza decided, boasting a small sitting room as well as a much larger bedroom, with the usual impressive four-poster.

"I hope the water's hot," said Maritza. "I'll take my bath first, Tina, then I'll lie down and take a nap while you get yours."

"I hope they have carbolic acid," said Tina practically. "While you're undressing and putting on your robe, I'll clean up the bathroom. Did you notice that the clerk didn't know how to address me when you were registering just now? I looked at the register afterward and he put me down as your maidservant."

"I'll change that tomorrow."

"Better not. We're back in the old South now and I'm supposed to know my place."

"Your place is beside me as my companion," said Maritza indignantly. "You're as free as any man down there in the lobby."

"But still black by Richmond standards."

"Surely you're not ashamed of that. You're one of the most beautiful women in the hotel."

"The second most beautiful." Tina laughed and began to open one of the portmanteaux to take out a robe for Maritza to wrap about her nude body. Dropping to her knees, she held a pair of embroidered slippers for Maritza's feet.

"I took a look at that bathroom as we passed," she said. "The tub's battered but it's certainly going to be clean. Do you want me to put out the *peau de soie* for the evening, the one with the low-cut bosom?"

"I suppose so, if you don't think it's too daring for Richmond."

"It's all right for Paris and New Orleans, so it ought to be all right here too. When I think of what the Yankees are probably doing to that lovely city of New Orleans since they captured it, I could cry." Celestina was steering Maritza toward the door to the bathroom as they went down the hall. She opened it and let her mistress step inside. "While you're gone, I'll see how much ironing the *peau de soie* needs, particularly the bodice. With that décolletage, when you walk through that dining room this evening, every man there is going to stand up and salute, that is, if he can stop looking down long enough."

IX

"*Bon soir, Madame la Comtesse.*" André was beaming when he met Maritza at the door of the dining room, ignoring several other couples who had been waiting. In black evening clothes, with a snowy white starched shirt front, he was the epitome of the veteran maître d'hôtel. "If you will follow me, please. General Mann and Secretary Benjamin are in the bar talking to the editor of the Richmond *Examiner*. I will notify them immediately that you have arrived."

Maritza followed André across the crowded dining room to a table secluded enough to be away from the closely packed tables in the rest of the large room. As always, the hubbub of conversation had died the moment she entered.

"*Madame la Comtesse* has created a sensation by making an appearance," André said with a smile. "May I say that you are looking even more beautiful than when I saw you last, at the Exchange Hotel in Montgomery?"

"Malaria and pneumonia took a few pounds off of me in

Wilmington," said Maritza. "I'm afraid that, if I'd stayed on in Montgomery and continued to enjoy that food you served us, I'd be as fat as a pig."

"*À Dieu ne plaise*—God forbid!" André exclaimed as the conversation in the room began to be resumed. "We were very much worried about you in Wilmington. Celestina wrote me at least twice a week and for a few days she wasn't at all certain you were going to live."

"Fortunately I was unconscious and didn't know how sick I was or I might not have survived," said Maritza as he seated her with a flourish at the table. "At that, I probably owed more of my recovery to Tina's nursing me at night than I did to the medicine Dr. Merwyn doused me with. Quinine and whiskey! Ugh!" She made a wry face. "It was terrible."

André laughed. "We can always tell here when a new shipment of quinine comes across the Potomac from Maryland by the increased number of men at the bar. Whether or not the drug works better when chased by a large glass of whiskey, I cannot say, but it certainly is a good excuse for a double. *Un moment, s'il vous plaît, madame.* I will tell the general and the Secretary you are here."

Moments later Benjamin and Mann, looking a little sheepish at not having met Maritza when she came in, hurried across the dining room to the table.

"A thousand pardons, my dear Countess." Benjamin lifted her hand to his lips. "You look absolutely ravishing tonight."

"I lack the Secretary's French," said Richard Mann with a smile, "but the sentiments are the same."

"You," Maritza told Benjamin in a tone of mild reproof, "have developed more embonpoint since I saw you last than is good for you."

"Blame André," said the somewhat portly Benjamin. "The Spotswood is known to set the best table anywhere in the South and he always selects fattening dishes he knows I love for me. I hardly need ask whether you have completely recovered from your illness."

"I have—thanks to a half dozen people I shall always love." She put her hand under that of Richard Maun as he seated himself. "Including a handsome brigadier general, the nature of whose duties still baffle me."

"I'm just a simple soldier doing his job." Mann squeezed the hand beneath his own. "And waiting for the war's end to claim his reward."

"Would Madame like an apéritif before dinner?" André inquired.

"Please do," Benjamin pleaded. "A reunion such as this deserves champagne at the very least."

"I have a very fine French champagne," said André. "It was delivered to Wilmington by a blockade runner only a short time ago."

"It's probably the same one Penn Darrow and I were going to broach to celebrate *Sprite*'s running the blockade," said Maritza. "Unfortunately I chose that moment to have a chill and be seized by delirium."

"It shall be brought immediately." André snapped his fingers to a hovering waiter. "The bottle of champagne I have been cooling for the last four hours, Armand," he commanded. "And now, for Madame's first dinner at the Spotswood, I would suggest roast guinea hen, a fluffy soufflé of New Orleans yams—"

"Something we're not likely to see again for a long time, now that New Orleans has fallen," said Benjamin mournfully.

"Fresh green beans," André continued, "with rolls from the Spotswood's own bakery—"

"Don't tell me the rest, please," Maritza pleaded laughingly. "I can feel the pounds going on already."

"*Madame la Comtesse* will be safe in my hands," André assured her.

X

Celestina had come back to their suite at the Spotswood Hotel sometime during the early hours of the morning and was sleeping peacefully on the cot when Maritza woke up. Without disturbing Tina, she dressed and went down to breakfast. The dining room was only about half full and she enjoyed a leisurely meal before opening the Richmond *Examiner*. When she did a startling black headline in heavy type seized her attention.

NEW ORLEANS WOMEN INSULTED BY "BLOODY BEN" BUTLER was the caption. Beneath it the text of Order No. 28, issued by the Federal commander of the Union troops occupying New Orleans, read:

> As the officers and soldiers of the United States have been subjected to repeated insults from the women (calling themselves ladies) of New Orleans in return for the most scrupulous non-interference and courtesy on our part, it is ordered that hereafter, when any female shall, by word, or gesture, or movement, insult or show contempt for any officer or soldier of the United States, she shall be regarded and held liable to be treated as a woman of the town plying her avocation.

"This action on the part of a notorious officer of the U. S. Army can only be regarded," the *Examiner* commented, "as an example of what treatment women of the South could expect at the hands of a victorious Union force."

When Maritza came back to their suite she found Tina awake and handed her the newspaper, folded to expose the news from New Orleans.

"That pig Butler!" Tina exclaimed after reading the account. "I hope one of the women 'plying her avocation' gives him a dose of the clap. What do you think that sanctimonious Mr. Lincoln would have to say about such an insult to women?"

"He'll probably make one of his back-country jokes about it. Did you enjoy yourself last night?"

"Enjoy?" Tina stretched herself like a beautiful jungle cat. "Could anybody fail to enjoy a glimpse of heaven?"

"Come now!" Maritza laughed. "They don't do what you were probably doing in heaven."

"Heaven on earth then. How about yourself?"

"I had dinner with Secretary Benjamin and General Mann. We talked mainly about the war."

"When you could have talked about love with General Mann, after getting rid of Mr. Benjamin?" Tina's eyebrows rose. "I even had a bottle of brandy sent up before I went to meet André. Nothing encourages love-making like a fine brandy."

"We drank the champagne at dinner that Captain Darrow and I were going to have the night we ran the blockade into the Cape Fear River."

"But no love-making?"

"None."

"*Quel dommage!* What a pity! You can be sure if you'd been with Captain Darrow he wouldn't have let you sleep in an empty bed."

"What's the news backstairs?" Maritza asked.

"Practically everybody expects the Federals to take Richmond before the middle of June. President Davis has sent his family to Raleigh, North Carolina, and all the important government records have been transported by train to Columbia, South Carolina, or to Lynchburg."

"That sounds bad."

"The Secretary of the Treasury has a train standing with fire under the boilers, ready to take the money in the Treasury to Lynchburg, too—or even farther south. Oh yes! They say General McClellan is having trenches dug less than twelve miles from Richmond."

"That means a siege, if he isn't able to take the city by assault."

Tina shrugged. "If you ask me, it looks as if we're in the wrong place at the wrong time. What are you going to do?"

"Write the story of what's happening for *Le Pays*."

"You don't think the Confederate authorities are going to let you describe how near Richmond is to falling into Federal hands, do you?"

"I don't know," Maritza admitted. "We do know the government looks fairly kindly on Napoleon III's ambition to rule in Mexico. The State Department might like France to realize how badly the future looks for the South and let the dispatches go through in the hope of stirring Napoleon into giving support to the Confederacy."

"If Richmond falls, that would still be a case of too little and too late."

"Maybe you're right," said Maritza.

"André says an argument's going on among the government bigwigs right now about a lot of tobacco that's been sold to foreign countries but hasn't been delivered yet. Some say it should be burned, if the government has to move, so the Yankees won't get it."

"Where is this tobacco now?"

"In some warehouses here in Richmond, according to André. At least that's where it was when Monsieur Mercier came to Richmond last March."

"Henri was here?" Maritza exclaimed. "Secretary Benjamin didn't say anything about it last evening at dinner."

"Monsieur Mercier stayed six days. André remembers serving him at the Spotswood."

Maritza frowned. "Henri is very sympathetic to the South. If he was trying to persuade President Davis to let France be the third party in negotiating a peace treaty, it could be that President Lincoln and Secretary Seward are more anxious to end the war than they've been letting people know."

"Whatever his reason for coming, Monsieur Mercier didn't get anywhere," said Tina. "The way things are going here in Virginia, the whole thing will soon be over anyway."

"If Richmond has to fall, I'm praying it will happen before General McClellan launches the final attack and thousands of soldiers on both sides are killed," said Maritza. "Which also reminds me that I can always serve as a volunteer nurse while I'm waiting for the final story to develop, so I'd better get going."

"Where?" Tina asked.

"To the office of the Surgeon General, I guess. Whoever heads the nursing service probably has an office there."

"Don't count me in on *that,* I faint at the sight of blood. I'll go into town with you if you can wait for me to dress, though. I hear Richmond has plenty of music halls, so if you see 'Mademoiselle Celestina' billed tomorrow as a 'French chantoozie' direct from 'Paris,' don't be surprised."

XI

Outside the weather was cool for mid-May, so Maritza decided to walk to the War Department, which was not far away. Sprawled on and between its seven hills, Richmond was a beehive of activity. The wide thoroughfare of Broad Street, bisecting the city, was clogged with vehicles of all sorts, and a long line of army wagons toiled up the hill from the bridge across the brown flood of the James River at the southern edge of the city flanked by the canal that crept along beside it.

From the canal came the shouts of lock keepers and canalboatmen as they locked the boats loaded with food and other supplies through to the docks for unloading. Boats going back west were also loaded but mainly with munitions and other matériel of war, no doubt intended for the Shenandoah Valley nearly two hundred miles away. There, according to the newspaper reports, General Stonewall Jackson was busily engaged in creating a diversion calculated to scare Abraham Lincoln into fearing for the safety of Washington and pulling troops away from the armies besieging Richmond.

The voices of street vendors, pulling their carts or driving their wagons, vied with the shouts from the canal area. Each morning trains of wagons brought food to Richmond from Petersburg and beyond but now they'd been more than doubled in number to supply the thousands of men being poured into the city by train daily from armies farther south, in order to strengthen those defending the capital.

From the Tredegar Iron Works, largest in the Confederacy and almost the only major fabricator of metal weapons left, a half dozen plumes of smoke spiraled upward in the morning air, marking the furnaces that were kept white hot day and night. Even the cannon from the Revolution that Maritza had seen along the streets on a former visit to Richmond had been dug up and melted down to produce the smoothbore Napoleons favored by many Confederate generals as artillery support to the infantry in battle. In the center of the James the sprawling structure of the Belle Isle Prison was crammed with prisoners of war awaiting the almost daily exchanges and already a source of lurid stories of corruption and cruelty on the part of the keepers.

As they neared the heart of the city, Maritza and Tina could see the state Capitol in its twelve-acre square. Designed by Thomas Jefferson to resemble the Maison Carrée, with which he had fallen in love while minister to Paris almost a hundred years earlier, it was lovely by any standard. Even in a time of mortal danger, the beautiful building gave to the city a grandeur and quiet dignity that was somehow reassuring to the viewer.

"Makes you feel as if you're back in France, doesn't it?" said Tina in a voice tinged with awe. "Do you think the Yankees will dare destroy it?"

"Not by intention, I'm sure, but if General McClellan chooses to lay siege to the city it can hardly fail to be the target for cannon."

"With so much land around it and a mile-long plain from the Capitol to the river, why would they want to destroy something so lovely?"

"Like all wars, this one seems to have generated a lot of hate. Even if it ends quickly, the hate will linger a long time."

"All over whether black people are any better than animals," said Tina bitterly. "It's a wonder God would ever let something like this happen."

"A lot of men fighting for the Confederacy believe they're doing God's will," Maritza reminded her. "General Mann and Mr. Benjamin were telling me last night about a general who holds prayer meetings before he goes into battle and always thanks God for giving him the victory after he's won."

"That's General Jackson. He helped the South win the Battle of Manassas. We were there, remember?"

"I'll never forget that day," said Maritza. "My conscience keeps reminding me that I played a part in it and probably caused a lot of men to die by bringing General McDowell's war plans to cousin Pierre Beauregard."

"What's going to happen if the South should win, Miss Ritza? Are they going to make slaves out of the Yankees the way we used to hear men talking about when we were in Washington?"

"President Davis and President Lincoln have both said there'll be no vengeance, if their side wins. It's going to be hard, though, for men who've seen friends and even brothers killed by the other side not to feel that they have a right to repay blood with blood."

Tina shivered. "Use another word, please; that one gives me a cold sweat."

"At least you don't have to worry which way it goes," Maritza assured her. "You're free and so is André. When it's all over you can marry and live wherever you please."

"I wouldn't be too sure of that," said Tina. "André says a lot of black people crossed the lines at Fortress Monroe, when General Butler was in command there last year. All he did was label them 'contraband' and put them to work, digging breastworks—with no pay and practically no food. A lot of them said they were much better off when they were slaves."

"I guess there're people like Butler on both sides," Maritza observed. "If you want me to, though, I'll take you and André with me wherever I go when the war is over. That way, you will at least know what kind of treatment to expect."

"I wish it was over now and we were back in Alabama—or France. Oh, look! You can see the balloons."

Three of the observation balloons with which they had become so familiar while in Washington were easily visible now high in the air northeast of the city. They could hardly be more than five or six miles from Richmond, Maritza estimated, and observers in them could spot preferred targets for the Federal artillery without any difficulty, telegraphing the information to batteries on the ground. In fact, with a high-powered telescope, she suspected that those occupying the baskets hanging beneath the huge gas bags could look right into the office windows of the Confederate Capitol.

"There's your answer to what Union gunners can do if they're ordered to shell Richmond," she told Celestina. "I don't see how the city can hold out for more than a few days with Federal artillery that close."

The mutter of cannon was plainly audible as they approached the War Department. Then a single cannon suddenly sounded louder and nearer than the others, and seconds later one of the three Union balloons collapsed when a shell struck it and exploded. The basket swung erratically as it started falling, spilling its two occupants, whose arms and legs flailed instinctively as they plummeted from the sky like wounded birds.

"I wonder if Professor Lowe was one of those." Tina's voice was tinged with horror. "I saw him once in Washington, when he was trying to convince the War Department that the government should buy his balloons. He seemed to be a very nice man."

"I imagine we'll be seeing less of the balloons now that our gunners have proved they can be hit by artillery," Maritza observed.

A horse-drawn ambulance, actually only a converted wagon with a frame over the bed covered with burlap, rolled by. Blood was dripping through a crack in the floor boards, mute evidence of the conflict being raged almost in the outskirts of Richmond and the toll it was taking in human flesh.

"Miss Ritza, let's me and you get out of here." In her disturbed state, Celestina tended more and more to revert to the patois of the Southern Negro.

"Where could we go?"

"If Mr. Davis can send his family to North Carolina where they'll be safe, you can certainly take us back to Alabama. Or we could even go with Captain Darrow to Halifax on his next trip from Wilmington and take a boat for France or London. You've got plenty of money in the Bank of England, besides what the captain put in the Bank of Nova Scotia."

"That would be like rats deserting a sinking ship."

"If the rats have got more sense than people, I'm willing to be a rat."

"And leave André?"

"He's not too happy about being in Richmond either."

"You could both cross the lines into Union territory without danger," Maritza reminded her. "Former slaves are doing it all the time and you're both free."

"And let some Yankee officer set us to digging trenches! That ain't no paradise for black folks up there north of the Potomac River. I learned that much soon after we got to Washington."

XII

Timorous, as always, about launching an attack until he could be certain of odds numbering at least three to one in his favor, the Union commander was wasting time. In full sight of Richmond, his troops could be seen digging entrenchments to which he could fall back for a siege if the final push failed to bring about the fall of the Confederate capital. Skirmishes and small battles occurred daily, while to the north, some fifty-odd miles away beyond the Rappahannock River, General Irvin McDowell slowly prepared for the march on Richmond ordered by Lincoln on May 17.

Then one day the Richmond *Enquirer* electrified the capital with the headline: FEDERAL ARMY FLEES NORTHWARD IN SHENANDOAH VALLEY. The *Examiner* countered with: JACKSON CHASES BANKS TOWARD POTOMAC AND WASHINGTON.

On Tuesday, May 20, one Richmond paper headlined: JACKSON'S ARMY DISAPPEARS while another heralded: JACKSON SETTING TRAP FOR BANKS. FEDERAL ARMY SEEKING TO ESCAPE.

With such startling news being reported almost daily from the Shenandoah Valley—a natural route into Maryland and Washington from Virginia—McClellan's fears were understandable. If Stonewall Jackson managed, by one of his astonishing feats of generalship, to sneak through Harpers Ferry and use the Baltimore & Ohio Railroad to transport his army eastward to Washington, McClellan and nearly a hundred thousand men could be left, so to speak, hanging on the vine.

With Washington threatened, Generals Frémont in western Virginia and Shields, commanding a section of McDowell's army, were now being hurried to the Shenandoah Valley. They were obviously hoping to stop Jackson in time to extricate McClellan and McDowell from what would be an untenable position, caught in a trap between two Confederate armies. And that this possibility was considered seriously by Lincoln was proved by news from Confederate spies on May 22 that the Union President was conferring with General McDowell. Furthermore, the conference was a clear indication of Lincoln's lack of confidence in McClellan and his concern over the mysterious disappearance of General Stonewall Jackson and his army, plus a division under General Richard Ewell sent by Lee to strengthen the forces taking part in the lightning Shenandoah Valley campaign.

An "Extra" edition of both newspapers on May 24 carried news of Jackson's easy victory over part of Banks's Federals at Front Royal the day before and, at last, the mystery of Stonewall's disappearing act had been solved. He had simply marched his troops through the Massanutten range at New Market to join General Ewell in a swift march northward along the South Fork of the Shenandoah River.

Hidden during the march by the towering range of the Massanuttens that extended for some forty miles, bisecting the valley from Harrisonburg to Front Royal, Jackson had suddenly reappeared at the latter town. At that point he was only a little over fifty miles from Washington and newspaper accounts the next day announced that he had cut off General Banks's main wagon train on the Valley Pike just south of Winchester, capturing close to three thousand vehicles. Racing after the fleeing Banks, Jackson paused only a day to recapture his old headquarters city, Winchester, from the Federal troops. With Banks's command now thoroughly demoralized by the swift Confederate victory, the Union general fled toward the nearest crossing of the Potomac at Williamsport and safety.

XIII

The succeeding two weeks were exciting ones, with more military activity than had happened since McClellan started preparations for the assault on Richmond. With twenty thousand of McDowell's troops under General Shields now moving toward the Shenandoah Valley, hoping to help trap Stonewall Jackson, McClellan chose to split his forces. Three corps were sent northeast of the Chickahominy River, ready to join McDowell, who was daily expected to arrive.

Learning of the change in the disposition of the forces arrayed against him, Confederate General Joseph E. Johnston defending Richmond, for once wasted no time but attacked. Successful at first, Johnston's troops were slowed when McClellan threw one Federal corps across the Chickahominy River to blunt the effect of the Southern attack at Seven Pines. Much of the early Confederate success was thus dulled, but the general result could be called at least a moderate Confederate victory.

Seriously wounded during the battle, "Fighting Joe" Johnston was carried from the field. Late that same afternoon General Robert E. Lee was ordered to take over, his first major command since he had refused the role of commander-in-chief of the Union Army roughly a year before. From the Shenandoah Valley that night came the happy news, too, that Stonewall Jackson, pursued by three Federal armies, had somehow managed to squeeze between two of them—Frémont's and Shields's—at Strasburg. Moving swiftly southward now in familiar territory, Jackson had made his escape to Elk Run Valley and safety at the lower end of the Massanutten Range. From which point he turned to smash the pursuers in two savage battles at Port Republic and Cross Keys.

The tale of Jackson's now famous "Valley campaign" formed one of the great sagas of military history. In only thirty-eight days the famous Stonewall had marched his "foot cavalry," as he called his beloved troops, six hundred and seventy-six miles. They had fought five battles and defeated three Union armies, all as large as or larger than his own, thoroughly upsetting McClellan's "grand plan" to take the Confederate capital.

"Now you can write your story of Jackson's feat," Richard Mann told Maritza when the news came. "I will personally see that it goes to Wilmington for transport to Halifax, Bermuda, or Nassau by the next blockade runner that leaves the port."

XIV

One afternoon shortly after she had filed her story on Stonewall Jackson's Valley campaign, Celestina brought Maritza a note from Secretary Benjamin, asking her to come to his office immediately. She was ushered in upon arrival and one look at Benjamin's face told her something serious had happened.

"I thought you'd want to know right away," he said. "General Benjamin Butler hanged your cousin William Mumford in New Orleans yesterday."

Maritza reached quickly for a chair and sank into it, overcome with horror.

"William was only a playboy," she protested. "Uncle Albert and Tante Marie de Montfort raised him, although he was not related to them. They loved him like a son, but he never settled down in the exporting business as they wanted him to do. When he visited Château LeClerc, Étienne had to get him out of several scrapes."

"I know," said Benjamin. "I was the De Montfort family lawyer before I went to the United States Senate."

"What could possibly have been the charges against him?"

"Treason, according to the message a friend telegraphed to me this morning, but even Butler would have had to stretch the meaning of the word to justify the charge. It seems that, when New Orleans surrendered to Admiral Farragut to avoid being destroyed by cannon fire, the U.S. flag was raised over the mint. An angry crowd tore the flag down and it was quite the thing for a day or two to wear a fragment of the flag in one's buttonhole, as Frenchmen wear the tricolor of the Legion of Honor."

"William would do that, he was very excitable. But I imagine a lot of others did the same thing."

"Butler apparently wanted to make an example of someone from one of New Orleans' oldest Creole families and arrested William. It's the sort of thing he would do."

"No wonder they call him Bloody Ben," said Maritza bitterly. "William was older than I and I had my first girlhood crush on him. He used to visit us at Mobile and I often stayed with Uncle Albert and Aunt Marie when I went to New Orleans for Mardi Gras." Her voice broke. "Now he's dead—executed by a beast."

"That's the second time Butler has gone beyond the limits of decency," Benjamin commented. "First was when he defamed the women of New Orleans and now by executing an excited wastrel. With that record behind him, who knows what he'll do next?"

Maritza was suddenly inspired by an idea. "The world needs to know what Federal occupation of a city can be like," she said eagerly. "Will you approve of my going to New Orleans and exposing Butler for what he is by denouncing William's execution as an example of the way the Union Army expects to treat the civilian population of the cities they conquer?"

"I'm not telling you to do anything, Countess," said Benjamin. "Actually, Farragut's capture of New Orleans was a bigger blow to our diplomatic endeavors than the mere physical loss of the city. It was already under blockade and all shipping to and from it had stopped anyway, so it was of no real value to the Confederacy. However, before Farragut captured New Orleans, Commissioner John Slidell was on the point of concluding some negotiations with the French government in Paris that would have been very much in our favor."

"The loan we've been hearing about?"

"That, plus the completion of several warships under construction in French shipyards. Too, Napoleon III has been very kindly disposed to acting as agent, in conjunction with Earl

Russell of England, to force a six months' armistice on the North during which the blockade would be lifted."

"Do you suppose our losing New Orleans will wreck those negotiations?"

"It will delay progress, at least, coming at a time when we were about to win a great victory here at Richmond. To say nothing of our repulsing Federal attempts to take Vicksburg and open the Mississippi to commerce while cutting off our armies beyond the river. Lord Lyons left Washington about a month ago, planning to tell Earl Russell and Viscount Palmerston that the South has already lost the war."

"Then it's more important than ever that Butler's atrocity at New Orleans be described in *Le Pays* and the London *Times,* to say nothing of other newspapers in foreign countries," Maritza urged.

"No question about that," Benjamin agreed.

"It might stimulate Napoleon to go on with his projected invasion of Mexico, too."

"That I cannot say. In fact I'm not among those who believe either France or England should be allowed to gain another foothold on the North American continent."

"In any event, the risk is still worth taking. Especially if Butler keeps up the campaign of terror he's been waging in New Orleans."

"I agree," said the Secretary of State. "But in all fairness, I must ask how much risk to you is involved."

"Not much," said Maritza. "I'll use my maiden name and visit relatives there, most probably Uncle Albert and Aunt Marie de Montfort. Of course I can't escape the possibility of running into someone who knew me in Washington but that's a risk I'm willing to take."

"Whatever you do has to be on your own decision entirely," said Benjamin. "I'm certainly not going to persuade you to take any unnecessary risks when you've already done so much to further the Cause."

Maritza needed no more convincing. Actually, she'd been committed to some act of revenge the moment Benjamin told her of the shameful execution of William Mumford.

"I'll need money, but right now most of my assets, besides my plantation in Alabama, are on deposit in the Bank of Nova Scotia and in the Bank of England," she told Benjamin. "Could you cash a draft on the Bank of Nova Scotia for me—in gold?"

Benjamin frowned. "Gold is hard to get these days but it can be done with a little"—he smiled—"shall we say finagling? Much of the Treasury's assets have been kept ready to be moved since General McClellan came so near Richmond. Besides, considering the risk you'll be taking, it's hardly fair to let you use your own assets."

"I insist on it," said Maritza. "It's one way of being revenged against Bloody Ben Butler for murdering William. I'll give you a draft on the Bank of Nova Scotia and Penn Darrow will cash it for you the next time he makes a run to Halifax."

"That's perfectly satisfactory."

"I'll also need a pass out of Richmond for myself and probably for Celestina, if she insists on going with me."

"No problem there either," Benjamin assured her.

"I presume that Richard Mann can arrange for my dispatches to be gotten out of New Orleans just as we got them out of Washington."

"He can but you'll have to convince him first that this is what you really want to do. Dick's as loyal to the Cause as the next, but this venture comes within the duties of the Confederate Secret Service. Besides, he's in love with you."

"I'll take care of that too," Maritza assured him as she rose to leave. "He suggested only a few days ago that I go to the plantation in Alabama and sit out the rest of the war. When I tell him I'm going to Mobile he'll be very pleased."

"What about New Orleans?"

Maritza smiled. "A woman never knows just how much to tell a man who loves her until she's with him, Mr. Secretary. That I'm going to Alabama may be all Richard needs to know at the moment—unless you feel you should tell him."

Benjamin shook his head. "I'm not sending you, remember? I'm only arranging to help you do something you decided you should do yourself. As far as I'm concerned, where you go or what you do after leaving Mobile is your own business. Good luck."

"Thanks," said Maritza. "If Bloody Ben Butler is everything he seems to be, I may need all the luck I can muster."

As it happened, Maritza had more trouble with Celestina than with Richard Mann—and in a way she had never expected.

"I'm going with you," said Tina, "but I'm pretty sure André will want to go too."

"Why? He was born on Martinique, as I remember it, so he's a French citizen and free to come and go as he pleases."

"A lot of the people he serves at the Spotswood don't know that. They treat him the way they would any other Southern Negro slave."

"He still has a good position and probably makes an excellent salary."

"For which he's paid in Confederate money that's going down in value every day."

"Secretary Benjamin has agreed to cash my draft on the Bank of Nova Scotia in gold. If you and André insist on going with me—and your decision makes me happier than I can tell you—I insist on paying you both a decent wage."

"That doesn't matter too much. I know you'll always do what's right. André wants us to be married and, when I tell him I'm going with you to Alabama, I know he's not going to take no for an answer."

"Then marry him by all means. French citizenship will protect you far more than I could."

Maritza had less trouble with Richard Mann than she'd expected—simply because she didn't tell him the whole truth.

"I'm glad you're going to the plantation in Alabama," he told her when she'd finished telling him of the projected trip south. "You'll be safer there than anywhere else I can imagine."

"Suppose I want to write about military activities in the South, or even write to you. How can I do it?" Maritza asked.

"Just send anything you want me to see, or to be sent abroad, to me here. New Orleans is in Federal hands but the

rest of Louisiana is far from it. And if you need to mail anything behind the Federal lines, use the Georgetown address you
used when you were in Washington. I'll eventually get whatever
you send there and pass it on to Paris and London."

BOOK SEVEN

NEW ORLEANS

I

Late June in New Orleans was hot and humid and what flowers were still in bloom drooped from the heat and lack of rain. In the early evening dusk when Maritza, Celestina, and André reached the city, the streets of the French Quarter, where most of the old families lived, were largely deserted. Spanish, French, or Acadian in descent, the Creoles—as they liked to be called—had always been an enclave inside the city but a very important one, numbering most of the richer businessmen, doctors, lawyers, and other professional people.

In 1862, New Orleans was still only partially Americanized, retaining even in war a dignity and quiet pride that set it and its native population apart. Visiting once again the city she loved most, as she rode along Dauphine Street where her uncle Albert de Montfort and his family had lived since long before she was born, Maritza began to feel a deep sense of happiness rise even through her mourning for William Mumford.

Crossing the line into U. S. New Orleans from Confederate Louisiana had been ridiculously easy for an obviously rich and highborn Countess LeClerc, simply because there was no real line. With her handsome black coachman and startlingly beautiful personal maid, she was obviously a relic of a past that would never return, yet, like a period piece in a museum, something worth preserving.

While spending a few days at the plantation near Mobile, on the way to New Orleans, Maritza had noted that, instructed by Richard Mann from Richmond, Moses had planted the acres usually devoted to cotton, now unsalable, into corn and vegetables and other grains. These not only fed the slaves still living there but also became meat for them when fed to hogs. The re-

mainder was easily sold in the market at Mobile to bring money
enough to pay taxes and keep the blacks on the plantation.

With two Federal gunboats prowling the Gulf outside the
bar, carefully remaining beyond range of the big guns of Fort
Morgan, shipping had long since come to a halt, leaving the
warehouses of Mobile stuffed with unsold cotton. The countryside, always fertile and rich, provided food for the needs of old
men, women, and children left after the young men had
marched north to fight with the Army under General Braxton
Bragg, who had relieved the once adulated but now largely disgraced Beauregard after his loss of the key city of Corinth, Mississippi, to the North.

Hiring a fishing boat whose Cajun skipper knew the creeks
and bayous between Mobile and New Orleans like the back of
his hand had been no problem. Ships from France, England,
and other countries, it was reported, were once again sailing in
and out of New Orleans, since Admiral Farragut with his warships and Commander Porter with his floating mortar batteries
had cleaned out all the Confederate fortifications along the
channel between the port city and the Gulf of Mexico. Proceed-
ing upriver, the Federal naval force had also taken Baton
Rouge and Natchez with no difficulty as General Mansfield
Lovell withdrew to save the helpless cities.

The Federal fleet had easily plowed upriver as far north as
Vicksburg, but there Confederate guns had answered back for
the first time, and Farragut had narrowly escaped disaster. With
Vicksburg on its high bluff holding on, the North was now at
stalemate while General Ulysses S. Grant prepared to launch a
land attempt at the city.

At the small village of Slidell, in a country that was as familiar to Maritza as the land around Château LeClerc had been,
she disembarked with Celestina and André. Buying a rickety
carriage and a pair of horses to pull it, she and her black servants had taken to the land along back roads leading westward
toward New Orleans.

With Maritza directing André, who was occupying the driving seat with Celestina beside him, they had no trouble making
a surreptitious entry into a city that wasn't even ringed with

pickets, proof of military Governor General Benjamin F. Butler's confidence in his own ability to hold it. Now, as the carriage rumbled through the narrow, cobblestone-paved streets of
the French Quarter, memories came rushing back upon her in a
tide that threatened to break down her defenses at the obvious
signs of decay and neglect everywhere and set her weeping for a
lovely city in its time of deep travail.

It was after dark when the carriage arrived at a familiar
home on Dauphine Street, but Maritza had already begun to feel
at home again. During the afternoon, as the carriage plodded
past canebrakes, sloughs, and clumps of cypress, she'd reveled
in the recalled memories of her childhood. Even the alligators
sunning on the banks of the streams they crossed on wooden
bridges here in the section of Louisiana that was half land and
half water didn't bother to slither into the streams like some
monsters from the distant past. They, too, were a warm remembrance, as were clumps of cypress, and pads of water lilies
floating upon the ponds and sloughs, reminding her again that,
although she was a third of the way around the world from the
French formal gardens of Château LeClerc, she was far more at
home here than she had ever been in France.

Tomorrow, or the day after, she told herself, she must go
wading again in the creek that wandered through the back yard
of the De Montfort home, as she'd done when a little girl. Or
perhaps she would pause to fish with a cane pole and earth-
worms for bait to catch plump, succulent catfish that were like
nectar and ambrosia when simmered in a tall pot with the fillets
of white meat layered between sliced onions, tomatoes, and potatoes.

When André brought the carriage to a stop before a typical
French Quarter house on Dauphine Street, Maritza did not immediately descend. The house itself was as she remembered it
from her girlhood, when she'd spent so many delightful weeks
visiting her uncle Albert and aunt Marie de Montfort. Two-
storied, the usual balcony with its wrought-iron railing and
grillwork fronted upon the street, while the door opened
directly upon a narrow, cobblestoned sidewalk called a *ban-
quette*. Behind the house she could glimpse, through the

wrought-iron gate leading by a walk paved with bricks to the rear, the garden she remembered so well. But even from the street she could see weeds growing over the edges of the walk and in the flower beds, while the iron grilles of the gate were rusting.

"This place sure has gone down, Miss Ritza," said Tina from the coachman's seat beside André. "I never remember it looking like this."

"I guess it's the effect of the war—that and the occupation of New Orleans. You two stay up there in the carriage; I'll go and see if my uncle and aunt are at home."

When Maritza knocked on the massive front door, nothing happened at first. Then the curtain partly hiding a window beside the door moved a little and, when she knocked again, it was opened a crack.

"What do you want?" asked a quavering voice which she hardly recognized as that of Tante Marie—as she'd always called her aunt.

"It's Maritza! Maritza Slidell."

The door opened a little more widely, enough for Maritza to see her aunt's face, but the emaciation eroding those once lovely features, the dingy gray of that once shining black hair, startled her. Then as the door was finally opened she stepped forward to take the frail body of Marie de Montfort in her arms.

"Tante Marie!" By now both of them were weeping. "What have they done to you? And where's Uncle Albert?"

"Albert died—of a stroke—the week after that beast hung William." The older woman clutched Maritza even tighter. "Why couldn't it have been me instead of him?"

"Mr. Benjamin learned of what happened here by telegraph at Richmond. I came as fast as I could to help you," Maritza told her.

"Nobody can help me now." Marie de Montfort wiped her eyes with her sleeve and stepped back in order to see Maritza better in the dim light of the small lamp burning in the foyer. "When God let them hang William the shock brought on Albert's stroke."

"I've come to stay awhile, Tante Marie. Celestina and her husband are with me. Can we put the horses in your stable?"

"When the Yankees came, our servants left and went north, but Tina and her husband can stay in the room over the carriage house. You must be starved," she added hurriedly, "but I don't—"

"Tina and André will go out and buy some food for dinner." Maritza turned back to the street where the other two were waiting. "Show André where to stable the horses and then come into the house, Tina," she called. "I want you to buy some food for dinner; Tante Marie wasn't expecting guests."

Putting an arm around her aunt's frail shoulders, Maritza walked with her back through the first floor of the house to the kitchen, where she lit a lamp. By that time Tina came in through the back door Maritza opened for her.

"*Bon soir,* Madame de Montfort," she said formally as she'd always done. But when the older woman stretched out her arms, Tina embraced her warmly.

"You're as beautiful as ever, Tina," said the white woman. "Almost as beautiful as your mother was."

"Nobody is as beautiful as *Maman* was, but I thank you just the same." Just then André came in and Tina turned to him proudly. "This is my husband, André, from the West Indies."

André took the frail hand Madame de Montfort extended in greeting and touched it to his lips. "I am honored, madame," he said. "Tina has spoken much of her happiness when she visited here in your lovely home."

"It's not lovely any more," Madame de Montfort said sadly. "We have no money to buy enamel for the ironwork or paint for the wood and nobody is left to cut the weeds or tend to the flower beds. General Butler"—she choked momentarily upon the words—"has levied a tax on the natives of New Orleans and takes all our money."

"I remember your flowers particularly," said Tina. "They always were the prettiest on the street."

"And will be again." Maritza opened her purse. "We need bread, some eggs, butter, coffee, sugar and cream, and anything else you can think of, Tina. Does Monsieur Fallon still operate the baker's shop at the corner, Tante Marie?"

"He does but his prices are so high—"

"We won't worry about prices tonight. Bring a couple of bottles of wine, too, Tina, if he has them. Tomorrow we will go shopping to fill the larder but tonight we'll do with that."

"It's not safe for a woman to go out on the streets after dark," Marie de Montfort objected. "The Yankee soldiers take anything they want."

"I don't think they will bother us," said André with a grin. "We're black and they're supposed to be here to free us. Besides"—he reached quickly to his boot and straightened up with a long slender knife in his hand—"I never go out at night without this."

Taking a chair by the kitchen table where her aunt was sitting, Maritza asked, "Do you feel like telling me about William, Tante Marie? Or would you rather wait until later?"

"I can talk about it now. Losing my godson and my husband in less than a month has dulled my mind to almost everything."

"What possible reason could even a beast like Butler have for hanging William?"

"Since he took control of the city, General Butler's been doing terrible things to show us he has the power of life and death over everyone in New Orleans."

"That's always been his record," said Maritza. "When he seized Baltimore he showed no mercy to anyone who resisted him. At Fortress Monroe he even persuaded ignorant slaves to leave their masters by promising them freedom, then set them to digging entrenchments with practically no pay and barely enough food to keep them alive."

"It was right after Admiral Farragut took New Orleans and had the United States flag raised over the building that once housed the mint," Marie de Montfort continued. "The people were angry because the Union Navy practically put cannon at the heads of everyone in the city and made them surrender."

"I wonder if Admiral Farragut really would have shelled New Orleans," said Maritza. "I've known quite a number of

Union officers and most of them were gentlemen. Had Butler arrived then?"

"No, he came a few days later. You know how William was, always excitable when he was with a crowd. Somebody probably said the flag should be torn down and he took it upon himself to do it. He threw it down to the crowd and they made quite a hullaballoo, jumping on the flag and tearing it to pieces."

"You sound as though you saw it happen."

"Everybody was at Jackson Square that day to see what the Yankees would do. Admiral Farragut controlled his men, though, even when some of the crowd tried to spit on them. It was only after General Butler arrived that real trouble began."

"Did William have a lawyer to represent him at the trial?"

"Trial?" Marie de Montfort's voice rose with indignation. "It wasn't a trial; it was a farce. What do they call such things in military language?"

"A drumhead court-martial?"

"That's the word. Some of the crowd who had been at Jackson Square that day and wanted to get in good with Butler testified to everything that happened, and Butler sentenced William to die without even hearing his side."

"Butler wasn't even a witness, was he?"

"No."

"Didn't Admiral Farragut intervene?"

"He had taken the fleet upstream to capture Baton Rouge and Natchez. Dr. Mercer—you remember our pastor—pleaded with Butler not to hang William for something that was done in excitement. But when Dr. Mercer told the general a scratch of his pen could free him, Butler said: 'A scratch of my pen could burn New Orleans. I would just as soon do the one as the other.'"

Marie de Montfort got to her feet and went to a cabinet in the dining room. Fumbling in a drawer briefly, she took out a newspaper clipping and brought it to Maritza.

The clipping was actually half the front page of the New Orleans *True Delta,* with a single photograph occupying most of the page. Maritza recognized immediately the building that had housed the United States mint for so many years. Hanging from one of the upper windows was the unmistakable figure of a man with a rope around his neck, the dangling arms and drooping head leaving no question about his being dead.

"No wonder General Butler's known as Beast Butler all over the South," she exclaimed. Then an inspiration suddenly struck her. "Is the paper still being published, Tante Marie?"

"Not by Mr. Tyler any more. General Butler gave him a long proclamation to publish, demanding that everybody in New Orleans take an oath of allegiance to the Union or lose their possessions. When Mr. Tyler refused to print it, Butler took over the paper and put his own editor in charge."

"Does Mr. Tyler still live on Bourbon Street?"

"Yes. Why?"

"Just something I thought of. Never mind."

Celestina and André arrived just then with two bags of food they had purchased and the wine. "Monsieur Fallon apologized for not taking Confederate money," said Tina. "I had to pay him in gold but we got the change in Union money."

"It's dangerous to even have Confederate money any more," said Marie de Montfort.

Celestina and André busied themselves making an omelet and soon the four of them sat down to the table, breaking chunks from a long loaf of typically French bread and buttering it with sweet butter.

"I haven't eaten anything so delicious since I left France," said Maritza. "Beast Butler can try to change New Orleans if he wants to, but he'll never be able to change its food."

II

Maritza was awakened by the cry of a street vendor proffering his wares in the patois characteristic of New Orleans alone. Through the open window of the bedroom she could see the tall magnolia she remembered growing in Tante Marie's garden. A half dozen creamy white blossoms hung from the limb nearest to the window and she could have reached several of them if she had wished, but she knew they soon wilted and lost their color and fragrance, once they were cut from the tree.

From some distance away the metallic rumble of iron tires upon the cobblestoned streets of the French Quarter reached her ears. Getting out of bed, she put on a filmy peignoir over the wisp of gown in which she had slept and went to the window to see what was happening. The sound grew increasingly louder but the street outside was still empty, strangely so, compared to the way she remembered it from the days before the war. Then it would have been happy with the sound of playing children and housewives chatting together in lilting French. Now it was as if everyone were locked inside the houses afraid to go out.

Finally the cause of the sound she had heard came around the corner. A tall officer in blue, booted, spurred, and riding a beautiful roan, was leading a battery of artillery through the Quarter at full speed, while a bugler following him sounded the charge. The iron tires on the wheels of the guns struck sparks from the cobblestones and the cannoneers clung to their seats to keep from being thrown from the jolting caissons.

Maritza leaned out the window the better to view this flamboyant display of military power. Seeing her, the officer drew his saber and lifted it in a salute before she remembered her state of undress and withdrew hurriedly from the window. Celestina opened the door just then and came into the room, carrying two buckets of water, one of them steaming.

"I let you sleep late because you needed it but nobody could sleep with all that noise," she said. "Madame de Montfort says the Yankee cavalry ride through the city like that every morning, just to make sure the people realize they're prisoners. It's another of Beast Butler's forms of torture."

"The men riding those caissons had all they could do to stay on them. I doubt that they were enjoying it very much."

"I was outside in the yard and saw that officer salute somebody with his saber. It wouldn't happen to be you, would it?"

"I was at the window and—"

"If you were leanin' out wearin' what you've got on now, he

saw plenty to salute." Tina pulled a tin bathtub out of a closet and started pouring water into it. "Get ready for your bath so I can wash your back before I go downstairs and fix your breakfast."

Maritza was shedding the peignoir and gown, preparatory to stepping into the tub. As she tested the temperature of the water with an exploring toe, she glanced at the pier mirror on the back of a closet door and noted with approval the familiar nude figure staring back at her.

"Stop admiring yourself and take your bath," said Tina. "You already know that body can set men crazy with passion, but you'd better be less of a show-off in New Orleans."

"Why should I dress any differently here than I did in Paris or London?" Maritza stepped into the tub, which was shaped somewhat like a large wooden shoe. As she slid down into it the warmth of the water caressed her body and the scent of the bath oil Tina had put in it filled the room.

"You're almost full Creole and your relatives here in New Orleans are *all* Creole." Tina was scrubbing Maritza's back with a soft cloth. "They'll be looking for signs that during those seven years in France, where every woman has a lover the way her husband has a mistress, you've changed for the worse."

"New Orleans was just like Paris before the war."

"It isn't any more. With you all pink and flushed after your bath, what you need right now is for Captain Darrow to be here. He'd see to it that you get what a woman your age—and mine—needs regularly."

"Why not General Mann?"

"Him, too, but it would be different."

"How?"

"I'd give you odds that, when the general makes love to you, he'll take his time, the kind you like to have around when you feel like being loved gently before you go to sleep in his arms. Men like Captain Darrow are for special occasions, something you remember for a long time and wonder when it's going to happen again."

"Shut up, you lecher." Maritza was laughing. "You're a married woman now and have no business talking like that."

Celestina chuckled. "Sort of got you stirred up though, didn't I? Just don't go shaking your bottom at the Yankees or Beast Butler will have you shut up in a New Orleans bordello."

"He'd better not try." Maritza was sober now. "If what I've got in mind works the way I think it will, Beast Butler will be sorry he ever insulted the women of New Orleans. Or dared to hang a man who was better than he'll ever be."

III

Phineas Tyler opened the door of the house on Bourbon Street about an hour later and peered out at Maritza through metal-rimmed spectacles.

"You look familiar," he said, "but I can't seem to place you, mademoiselle."

"I'm Maritza LeClerc, Mr. Tyler. When I was only a girl called Maritza Slidell, you were kind enough to publish some of my pieces in the *True Delta*."

"Maritza! Of course. Please come in." Beaming, the former publisher of New Orleans' leading newspaper held the door open for her. "I seem to remember something about you marrying a nobleman and going to France to live."

"I was married to Count Étienne LeClerc for seven years and widowed about a year and a half ago."

"Then I should address you as Countess?"

"Maritza will still do nicely. Actually, I'm here this morning as a correspondent. I write for *Le Pays* in Paris and also for the London *Times*."

Phineas Tyler smiled, a little wistfully. "I wanted to be a foreign correspondent when I finished college, but the publisher of the *True Delta* offered me a job . . ." He didn't finish the sentence.

"I came to ask a favor of you." Maritza took the clipping Marie de Montfort had shown her last night from her reticule. "You recognize this, of course."

Phineas Tyler recoiled as if from one of the cottonmouth

moccasins that infested the Louisiana low country. "I had nothing to do with that," he protested vehemently. "The photograph was printed after General Butler seized my newspaper."

"Do you know who took the picture?"

"A photographer Butler employs; I think he was a former assistant of Mathew Brady. It was printed on the order of a Captain John Clark who claims to have been the former publisher of the Boston *Courier*. Butler brought him to New Orleans for the purpose of publishing a newspaper, once he found an excuse to take over one. Unfortunately that turned out to be the *True Delta*."

"What else can you tell me about Butler?"

"What can I not?" Tyler's voice choked momentarily with indignation. "You've heard of the infamous Order No. 28, I suppose?"

"Yes. Butler is being condemned by decent people, even in the North, for insulting Southern womanhood."

"That was just the start. A Creole merchant refused to sell shoes to a Yankee soldier, so Butler had his provost marshal sell everything at auction, keeping the money."

"In the name of the United States?"

"Allegedly, but nobody doubts that the money wound up in his pockets or those of that scalawag brother of his, Andrew Jackson Butler, he's placed in charge of the commissary department. A woman who dared to laugh when a funeral procession of an officer from Butler's command passed her window was condemned to the prison on Ship Island for two years. Another brave woman, who wore the Stars and Bars in defiance of Federal occupation, is confined there too. I hear the prison is running over with prisoners condemned by Butler without legal trial and fed mainly on bread and water."

"It sounds as if he fully deserves the nickname 'Beast,'" said Maritza.

"The name is too good for him. He has put a tax on everybody who supported the Confederate government and uses the money, in his words, 'to relieve the suffering of the poor.' I have it on good authority, though, that much of the money goes into the pockets of Butler and his henchmen, mainly that brother. If anyone dares oppose him, he gives them the choice of taking an oath to support the United States Government—which means obeying Butler and his whims—or losing everything they possess."

"Do many swear allegiance?"

"Quite a lot. In fact I did myself rather than see our life's savings taken—what we don't have in Confederate bonds, which Butler has declared worthless. Any oath given to an outlaw in uniform who can have you shot, merely by saying the word, couldn't be held against you by a just God."

"You did right," Maritza assured him. "I'll not hesitate to do the same if he requires me to swear allegiance."

"That would be the wise course, but I must be wearying you with my complaints."

"I *did* come for another purpose," said Maritza. "I want you to help me expose Beast Butler to the people of France, England, and the civilized world for what he is. If his actions become enough of a scandal, President Lincoln will be forced to remove him."

"They're more than a scandal already. Nobody knows exactly how, but Butler seems to have so much political influence in Massachusetts and other Union states that even Lincoln is afraid to do anything to stop him. As for Farragut and Grant, they're having enough troubles trying to capture Vicksburg. The last I heard, they were at work digging a canal around it."

"This photograph." Maritza picked up the clipping again. "Do you suppose I could obtain a print?"

"I imagine there was only one, and that was used to make the cut for the newspaper."

"Wouldn't the original print be on file at your office?"

"At Captain Clark's office, yes. He's in charge now."

"Probably in the same file where you kept other prints published in the paper when you were in charge?"

"Yes. I suppose so."

"How much trouble would it be to steal that print from the files?"

Phineas Tyler gave her a startled look. "Trouble—or danger?"

"Either, or both."

"It wouldn't be much trouble, I could put my hands on the file blindfolded. But it would mean breaking into the newspaper office and Butler would like nothing better than to order anyone caught stealing the photograph shot." He blinked at her from behind his spectacles. "What would you do with it if it came into your hands?"

"Include the print with my story for *Le Pays* and the London *Times* on the hanging and what Butler's doing to New Orleans. I would title the story, 'The Beast of New Orleans.' "

"You'd never be able to send anything like that by mail from New Orleans," he warned. "Butler has all mail censored and cuts anything the slightest bit critical of him from the dispatches of the Union correspondents who came here with him. He even opens the diplomatic mail pouches of the consuls here; most of them have made protests against the way he has been treating people from other countries."

"Butler would never see what I would be sending," Maritza assured Tyler. "I got stories out of Washington for almost a year and the Federal censors never saw even one of them. My description of the Mason-Slidell affair got the two commissioners released from Fort Warren."

"How would you— No, don't tell me." Tyler took a deep breath. "Somebody ought to print the truth about what Butler's doing here and I suppose it's my duty as a newspaperman to help."

"Do you still have a key to the *True Delta* building and also to your office?"

"Yes. Butler and Clark demanded them all but I held one set back."

"What are we waiting for then?" said Maritza briskly. "I remember from last night that the moon rises late."

"I hate to see you take the risk."

"I hold French citizenship from my marriage. Butler would have to send me to a military prison, if I'm caught, and I've had pretty good luck getting people out of those. Shall we meet here at ten o'clock? I'll bring candles and matches."

"Ten o'clock!" Phineas Tyler's voice was firm. "God help us if we're caught."

"God, yes, but Lincoln too. Napoleon III is preparing to invade Mexico and Secretary Seward is quite familiar with the fact that I'm a close friend of Henri Mercier, the French minister, and his wife. Besides, I'm well known at the French court, so I hardly think Abraham Lincoln would risk incurring the displeasure of France by having me shot."

Her business with Phineas Tyler completed, Maritza couldn't resist the impulse to visit Jackson Square and the Place d'Armes. The heart of the city, they adjoined the wharves that lined the river bank for a full mile. At Maritza's request, André drove the carriage slowly while she and Celestina looked eagerly for the sights that had characterized New Orleans ten years ago, the last time she had visited it with Étienne LeClerc. But where everything had been gaiety then, and the shops around the square packed with New Orleanians and visitors, most of them were closed today.

The gutters, on the other hand, were clean, with none of the refuse almost universal in the old days. Beast Butler, it seemed, admired cleanliness—perhaps because he'd heard that it kept down yellow fever and malaria, scourges that had visited New Orleans many times in the past. The "poor" he'd hired were busy with brooms, mops, and buckets—at the expense of the monied citizens of the city—cleaning it up.

André stopped the carriage where Maritza could see a ship that seemed to have a familiar look to her, berthed at one of the wharves. Just then a splendidly caparisoned vehicle accompanied by a half dozen mounted troopers whirled around the corner and came to a stop before the customhouse on Jackson Square.

"That must be the Beast himself," said Celestina in a sibilant whisper, as a man in a splendid uniform decorated with gold lace at collar, cuffs, and shoulders started to descend from the carriage.

Benjamin Butler, Maritza saw, was far from being a pretentious-looking man. His head was large, much more so than the proportions of his body required. The slanting forehead and his almost total baldness intensified the receding character of his brow so as to make it almost non-existent. Not tall, he walked with something of a waddle instead of the military stride expected from a major general.

Maritza couldn't see his eyes but she'd been told they didn't match, giving him an appearance of subtlety and trickery that had earned him the nickname of "Old Cock Eye" long before he also acquired the even more appropriate sobriquet of "Beast." In practically every respect, she decided, General Benjamin F. Butler was one of the most unpleasant-looking individuals she'd ever seen.

Accompanied by a clerk, who ran to open doors before him, Butler entered the customhouse. There, Maritza had been told, he held court every morning, settling all questions as judge without jury or counsel and, it was maintained, according to no laws found in Blackstone.

The carriage drove off and an unnatural quietness—for New Orleans—descended upon the city, as if most of the population was afraid of being either seen or heard. Even the roustabouts loading bales of cotton on the sleek merchant vessel which had attracted Maritza's attention were not shouting their usual musical chanty as they worked. The French tricolor rippled in the river breeze from the mast of the vessel, while farther down the wharf was a more solid ship, flying the flag of England. Still another with the Dutch emblem at the masthead was tied up farther away. Both, Maritza could see, were loading hogsheads of sugar.

"It looks as if the Beast has opened the port," Tina observed. "Isn't that the French ship *Angélique* that took us to Nova Scotia?"

"That or its sister," said Maritza. "Drive closer, André, and stop near the end of the gangplank. I can't make out the name."

When the carriage came to a stop, Maritza still couldn't read the name of the vessel because of its proximity to the wharf to which it was moored. Descending from the carriage, she walked up the gangplank to the deck, dodging the roustabouts who were loading five-hundred-pound bales of cotton into the hold of the vessel.

"Le capitaine?" she said to a crew man who was handling the hoist. *"Est-ce qu'il est ici?"*

"Oui, madame. Dans la kiosque." The wheelhouse door he had indicated was open and Maritza stepped inside.

"Can I help you, mademoiselle?" a broad-shouldered officer who'd been studying a chart asked.

"I am Comtesse Maritza LeClerc. Isn't this the *Angélique?*"

"A thousand pardons, *Madame la Comtesse.* I am Capitaine Boncours and this is the *Andromeda,* a sister ship of the *Angélique*—a natural mistake, considering that the two ships are so much alike. What can I do for you, madame?"

"I am a correspondent, writing of America for *Le Pays.*"

"But of course! I have read your writings with interest. Your analysis of *l'affaire* Mason-Slidell was a masterpiece."

"Thank you. I was surprised to see you loading cotton, since the port of New Orleans has been closed for some time."

"It was opened only a month ago to foreign shipping," he explained. "We are taking out the first shipload of cotton from New Orleans in about two years."

"For the account of the United States Government, no doubt?"

"No doubt," Boncours agreed dryly. "But the manifests are signed by Colonel Andrew Jackson Butler."

"The general's brother?"

"I believe so. He is also selling the sugar you see being loaded on the British ship as well as the Netherlander."

Maritza had a sudden inspiration. "I've been thinking of buying some cotton for resale myself. Would you be able to take it to France as a cargo, perhaps on your next voyage?"

"Mais non, Madame la Comtesse. No ships leave New Orleans except through Monsieur Butler. He has—what do you call it in English?"

"A monopoly?"

"Exactement."

Maritza nodded slowly. "I had heard that such was the case. It will be a profitable voyage, I'm sure, for the owner of the cotton as well as the owner of the ship and for yourself."

Captain Boncours's teeth flashed in a smile. "One has to

look after one's interest, *Madame la Comtesse.* Surely you agree to that?"

"*Oui,*" said Maritza. "I understand fully why you couldn't ship my cotton, but could you perhaps carry a small packet to France containing my next dispatch for Monsieur Claudet, editor of *Le Pays?* I would pay you well."

"Please have no thought of pay. It will be my pleasure to serve you in any way I can."

"Will you be sailing soon?"

"Tomorrow morning, at dawn."

"I will send my coachman with the dispatch for Paris before you cast off. He is black but was born in Martinique, so he is a citizen of France."

"Have no fear. Your package will be delivered in person to Monsieur Claudet in no more than three weeks at most, probably even sooner."

"Thank you, Captain Boncours. On your next voyage to New Orleans, it will be my pleasure to entertain you and your officers at dinner."

"I shall look forward to that occasion every day I'm gone," said Boncours gallantly.

"*Au revoir,* then, Captain. Until our next meeting."

IV

Maritza was dressed in black with a black mantilla over her hair when she left Madame de Montfort's house shortly before ten o'clock that evening. She walked swiftly through the deserted streets of the French Quarter to Phineas Tyler's home, although only an occasional light showed in the houses separated from the street by the narrow *banquettes.* She had to walk very carefully on the cobblestones in the almost Stygian darkness, however, to keep from tripping.

At Tyler's house, no lights were showing when she traversed the narrow walk with its wrought-iron gate leading to the garden in the rear and the back door. She knocked three times and the door was opened at once by Tyler, who stepped out into the yard and shut it behind him.

"It's only another hour to moonrise, so we'll have to work fast," he said in a whisper. "Did you bring the candles and matches?"

"Yes—and this, in case we need it." Maritza took the small derringer from her pocket.

"I have an aversion to firearms," Tyler protested.

"I don't. Let's go."

Keeping to back streets, they traversed the few short blocks to the newspaper office without rousing any dogs, their greatest fear. Tyler easily opened the back door with his key and let them into the building.

"You'd better light one candle," he advised. "Ordinarily, I could find my way here in the dark but they may have moved things around. We could fall over something and perhaps break a leg, besides revealing our presence."

Carefully, Maritza scratched a sulphur match into flame and lit the candle, placing it in a small candleholder she'd also brought with her. Hiding the light as best she could, she walked close behind Tyler, while he made his way through the building, dodging the silent presses and composing desks until they came to what had been the publisher's office.

Another key opened the filing cabinet and Tyler started looking through the most recent photographs stored there. Nor did he have to go very far. Taking out the photograph showing William Mumford's body hanging from a window of the building housing the United States mint, he quickly arranged the others as they had been before and closed the filing cabinet, locking it. Only a few more minutes were required to make their way back to the door they had left unlocked, in case they needed to escape in a hurry.

"The Lord was with us." Phineas Tyler drew a deep breath of relief as he stepped out into the darkness and handed Maritza the print he was carrying. Then both of them froze when a loud voice from farther down the street struck their ears.

"You there! Advance and give the password."

"Come on!" Maritza seized her companion's arm. "He can't see us in the dark at this distance."

Crossing the street, they ran to the far end of the block, reaching it just as the man who had hailed them appeared at the other end. He was swinging a lantern in one hand while holding a pistol in the other and the shot broke the silence of the French Quarter like the shattering of a crystal. Not a light showed, however, as the bullet ricocheted off an iron railing above their heads and went whining off into the distance. Maritza and her companion didn't hesitate and, before their pursuer could load again and fire, they had reached Phineas Tyler's house.

"You'd better come in," he told Maritza as the back door was opened from the inside by his wife.

"I'll be all right," she assured him. "Don't show a light and he'll never know which house you came from."

She was gone, clutching the photograph as she ran like a shadowy wraith through the blackness of the night. Their pursuer fired his pistol once more before she reached the De Montfort residence and slipped in through the back door.

"Who was shooting?" Tina asked in a whisper.

"A night watchman, or a night patrol. I got just a glimpse of him but I could see that he was in uniform."

"Did you get what you went there for?"

"Yes." Maritza laid the photo on the table. "Make sure all the shades are drawn, I've got to write one or two more paragraphs on the story André will take to Captain Boncours at dawn. I wish I could do it but anyone who saw me out at that hour would be sure I was returning from an assignation and I'd wind up by having General Butler label me a prostitute."

"André doesn't mind taking the dispatch to the ship. He likes adventure."

"Make sure he has his certificate of French citizenship with him, in case there's any trouble."

"He can take care of himself, Miss Ritza. Do you think it's safe to light a candle yet?"

"Not for a while. We'd better get into night clothes first.

Then if the watchman starts knocking on doors we can be properly indignant at being aroused from bed."

An hour later, in a nightgown, while Tina held a blanket over the street window to further hide the flame of a candle, Maritza hurriedly finished the dispatch for *Le Pays*. Placing it and the photo between two pieces of cardboard, she sealed the package carefully for protection and covered it with isinglass against moisture damaging the photographic print before putting it in an envelope and addressing it to Monsieur Claudet in Paris. Tina took it then and, slipping out the door, flitted undetected to the room over the carriage house where she and André slept.

Maritza had anticipated having trouble getting to sleep after the excitement of the evening. Instead, the exertion of escaping from the night watchman and getting the dispatch ready for André to take to the *Andromeda* left her so tired that she slept immediately. She only awakened when Tina brought her a cup of the typical black New Orleans coffee at eight the next morning.

"Is André back yet?" she asked, sipping the coffee which, according to New Orleans custom, was heavily sweetened.

"Not yet." Tina's concern was betrayed by her tone. "I think I should go to the wharves and see whether the ship has sailed."

"I'll go with you," said Maritza at once. "Help me dress and we'll leave right away."

If anyone at the docks was surprised to see two extraordinarily beautiful young women walking along the waterfront—where ladies of quality almost never went any more—they did not accost them. The *Andromeda* was gone and moored in its place was a steamship flying the flag of the United States, while a clerk stood at the foot of the gangplank, checking off articles from the ship's manifest as they were brought ashore. To Maritza's surprise, the cargo was not being taken to nearby warehouses, as was usually done, but was simply trundled on carts and wheelbarrows a short distance along the wharf. There it was loaded into a small, stern-wheeled river boat, such as was used for traffic along the tributary waterways to the Mississippi.

Leaving Celestina on the dock, Maritza approached the clerk, careful to step close enough to read the items listed on the manifest he was checking.

"Excuse me, sir," she said. "Was there not a French vessel here yesterday?"

"Yes, the *Andromeda*. She sailed at dawn."

A dock worker came down the gangplank, pushing a cart piled high with packages of what looked like medicine. From where she was standing, Maritza had no trouble reading the word "quinine" stamped on the packages and the same word was on the list the clerk checked off on the manifest.

"I'm glad to see we shall have plenty of quinine this summer, when the fever season opens," she said to the clerk. Then, not being certain of the latter's politics, she added, "Before General Butler came to govern New Orleans, we had almost none. The rebel government of Louisiana was sending nearly all that came through the port to the troops."

The clerk smiled knowingly. "Troops will get most of this, too, madame—rebel troops."

"How could that be when the United States Government is in control of New Orleans?"

The clerk looked at her sharply. "You must be new to the city, madame?"

"I returned two days ago, after some years in Paris where I was married to a Frenchman."

"You know little of what is happening to the port of New Orleans then?"

"Only what I saw yesterday and the day before. A merchant ship from France was loading bales of cotton—that was the *Andromeda*. Two others from England and Holland, I believe, were also loading hogsheads of sugar. Now that General Butler has opened the port once more, trade by sea should improve the condition of the city and its people."

"To say nothing of the size of General Butler's pocketbook," said the clerk.

"I do not understand," said Maritza in her best French-accented English.

The clerk looked around and, when he was certain that no

one appeared to be watching them, spoke in a lower voice. "The way it works is this, madame. The commissary—"

Maritza frowned, still in pretended ignorance. "Commissary? I do not understand."

"I'm speaking of Mr.—some call him Colonel—Andrew Jackson Butler, the general's brother. He's the commissary general for U.S. troops in Louisiana, even though Congress didn't confirm him when General Butler named him to be in charge of army supplies."

"How can he operate then?"

"Very simple. He orders quinine for the troops here and General Butler signs the order. Knowing how common intermittent fever is in New Orleans in midsummer, the commissary general in New York does not question the size of the order but sends the quinine directly."

"I remember the fever well." Maritza pretended to shiver. *"Mon dieu!* What a shaking I had when I contracted it."

"I, too, have had the shaking fever and I wouldn't want so beautiful a lady as yourself to experience it again." The clerk was checking a cartload of quinine packages being rolled off the gangplank and, reaching over casually, picked up one of the small packages and handed it to Maritza, who immediately secreted it in the pocket of her gown.

"Merci, m'sieu—"

"Lateau. Aristide Lateau."

"You are of French descent too, then?"

"Acadian—which is the same thing."

"I am Acadian too—on my mother's side!" Maritza exclaimed. "Which makes us, shall we say, kindred?"

The clerk smiled. "Or kinfolks, as we Southerners say." Then he sobered. "Speaking as a kinsman, I would advise you to leave New Orleans as soon as you can, madame. Only by serving as a lackey to General Butler—as I have been forced to do in order to support a wife and two children—have I been able to live decently, if not very proudly."

"You were speaking of the quinine," Maritza reminded him.

"Oh yes. It is only one of General Butler's many ways of

trading on the misery of the Southern people in general, as well as here in New Orleans."

"How could that be, M'sieu Lateau?"

"You see, the Army pays for quinine in New York and ships it here for the troops."

"Is that not a troopship into which it is being loaded now?"

"A troopship, yes—but not for carrying troops at the moment. When it's loaded, it will sail upriver, ostensibly carrying medical supplies to the U. S. Army troops at Baton Rouge. Somewhere—the place varies from time to time—it will sail up a tributary stream to a landing in the part of Louisiana controlled by Confederate General Mansfield Lovell and his forces, which means everywhere except along the Mississippi and the city of New Orleans. There the cargo of medicines will be unloaded and cotton bales taken aboard in exchange. What's more, the transaction will have the approval of Mr. Lincoln and Mr. Seward."

"Are you certain?"

"As certain as I am that Andrew Jackson Butler is commissary general without commission, and that the quinine will be bartered at roughly ten times its cost to the Confederate Army for cotton, at perhaps five cents a pound. The cotton, in turn, will be brought to New Orleans and loaded on foreign ships bound for the looms of England and France, at ten times the price paid in medical supplies."

"And the money for all this?"

Lateau shrugged. "On the books, it buys supplies for the troops here, but those are actually being paid for with money gained from the sale of properties of various kinds seized from the residents of New Orleans and sold by General Butler."

"You have proof of all this?"

"Who needs proof?" Lateau said with a shrug. "When even Abraham Lincoln knows of it, who would object?"

"No one, I suppose."

"Recently the State Department sent a civilian investigator, a Mr. Reverdy Johnson, from Maryland to look into Butler's reign here. Johnson concluded that a state of fraud and corruption has been built up by Butler that is, to quote him, 'without parallel in the history of the country.'"

"Did the government do anything about it?"

"Why should they when they're part of it? Besides, a movement is afoot to force the inhabitants who haven't already sworn allegiance to the United States Government to do so—on pain of losing their property and perhaps going to jail if they don't. Then we'll have rigged elections and there'll be a pair of senators from Louisiana in the U. S. Congress and several representatives."

"I suppose General Butler will be that senator?"

Lateau grinned. "Not if the *people* have to elect him. Right now, New Orleans is under martial law and the government of the United States doesn't extend much beyond the boundaries of the city. Take away the soldiers and the population would vote to rejoin the Confederacy, even if it would mean having the port closed again for shipping."

"I take it that this isn't likely to happen."

"Vicksburg is holding out now and might for some time. But when Grant and Farragut mount a joint effort to take the city, a lot of people are going to die needlessly defending it because those two won't give up the attack until Vicksburg is taken." The clerk's tone had become bitter. "As bad as General Butler's rule has been here in New Orleans, and even though he and his brother are making a personal fortune, it's better than being buried in *la Cimetière des Hérétiques*."

Maritza understood the reference to the once fashionable Girod Cemetery of Christ Episcopal Church, established when the Creole burial places called St. Louis Nos. I, II, and III had begun to overflow. No longer fashionable, Girod Cemetery— now called *la Cimetière des Hérétiques*—was still a cheap place to be buried, especially for those who were not Catholic.

The last cart was trundled down the gangplank and the clerk checked it off and closed the file containing the manifests.

"What will this ship carry when it is loaded?" Maritza asked the clerk as he was moving down the wharf toward another vessel. "Cotton?"

"Cotton goes in foreign ships, so the few Confederate raiders now at sea won't bother them," he explained. "This one will be loaded with hogsheads of sugar for New York. They're starving for it up there, I hear, and we've got more than we can use."

"So life goes on, even in wartime," said Maritza as she was telling the clerk good-by. "Can you direct us to the office of the French consul?"

"Of course; it's just off Jackson Square. Count Mejan is usually there at this time of day receiving complaints against General Butler from French people in the city, but even he can do little for them."

"I know Count Mejan. He was entertained at our château in the Loire Valley several times while my husband was alive."

"Don't expect Mejan to do much, if you get into any trouble, madame," Lateau warned. "Monsieur Charles Heidsieck, who heads the French champagne company, was arrested in the United States while looking after his Southern accounts. Butler claimed he was engaged in treasonable activities and imprisoned him in Fort Jackson prison. Heidsieck was released only after Henri Mercier, the French minister in Washington, appealed directly to Secretary Seward."

"I'm a friend of Monsieur Henri Mercier, and I also know Secretary Seward," Maritza assured him. "Perhaps I shall have better luck in New Orleans than the others."

"I pray so, madame," said Lateau. "But stay away from General Butler. His wife returned to Massachusetts toward the middle of June and he has started holding office hours for ladies at his home in the early morning. If you've read Order No. 28 you have some idea of the esteem in which the general holds your sex."

V

As Maritza and Tina were crossing Jackson Square a squad of soldiers came marching around the corner of Canal Street and headed for the local jail, where those accused of crimes were held until Butler could pass judgment and pronounce sentence.

Stumbling in their midst were two prisoners, a man and a young girl. The man's face was bloody from a cut over his right eye that almost closed it, while the girl was disheveled and weeping. A small crowd of people had gathered at the sound of the soldiers' booted feet on the pavement but made no attempt to interfere.

"What did they do?" Maritza asked a distinguished middle-aged man who was standing at the edge of the crowd.

"One doesn't have to do anything to be arrested in New Orleans these days, madame," he said. "Actually, they were caught reading a Confederate newspaper that contained an article denouncing *l'Animal*."

"That's what they call the general here," Tina said in a low voice intended for Maritza's ears alone. "I heard someone using the term when we were buying food the other night at Monsieur Fallon's store."

"Merci, m'sieu," said Maritza, and the bearded man blinked.

"You speak French like a native, madame. Are you perhaps recently from Paris?"

"No, but I spent six years in the Loire Valley."

"In what city, may I ask? My name is Legrand; I have relatives in the area."

"I lived in the country," said Maritza, "at Château LeClerc."

"But of course." The speaker gave her a deep bow. "You can be none other than Comtesse Maritza LeClerc, the Cassandra of *le journal Le Pays*. I am honored to be in your presence, *Madame la Comtesse*. Will you be describing New Orleans as it is today for your readers abroad?"

"New Orleans was my home as a girl, m'sieu. I came here to visit a relative recently bereaved, Madame de Montfort."

"Quel dommage! Her husband, Albert, was a friend; we enjoyed a glass of wine together several times a week." He shook his head sadly. "It was a most unfortunate affair, as are many other things these days. If Mr. Lincoln only knew—"

"I believe he does, M'sieu Legrand," said Maritza. "Only this morning I learned that the Federal government sanctions the sale of medicines to the Confederates—at a considerable profit."

"You can be sure the profit goes to *l'Animal* Butler, and to *les politiciens*."

"So I have heard," Maritza agreed. "Now if you will excuse us, M'sieu Legrand—"

"Of course." He bowed again. "Be assured that the secret of your presence in the city will not be revealed by me to anyone."

"Merci! Bon jour, Monsieur Legrand."

"Do you think he will betray you to *l'Animal?*" Celestina asked as they moved toward a stationer's shop that was open, in contrast to many of the other establishments that lined the square.

"I think not, but in wartime one never knows who is an enemy and who is a friend."

"That's not limited to wartime," said Tina bitterly. "Someone who saw us at Madame de Montfort's may already have betrayed us to *l'ennemi.*"

"Let's hope not. Actually we have done nothing except to cross into U.S. territory. Besides, our passes were signed by Governor Pettus of Mississippi and, from what we learned this morning, there seems to be regular traffic in both directions all the time."

"Are you going to see Count Mejan?"

"I think not. He'd only insist that I leave New Orleans immediately and I couldn't very well ask for his protection later, should we really need it, if I don't obey him now." They were entering the stationer's shop and Maritza spied a small pile of the New York *Tribune* on the table near the door. "Let's see what Mr. Horace Greeley has to say about the war."

A clerk had started from the back to serve them but, seeing Maritza pick up the New York paper, her steps slowed. With obvious reluctance, she took the price of the paper from a silver dollar Maritza handed her and gave her the change.

"Do you perhaps sell foreign journals, mademoiselle?" Maritza asked.

"Only rarely. The gen—the administration frowns upon them."

"Not even French journals like *Le Pays,* when so many of the people are French?"

"We did sell quite a number of copies before the city was captured, but the authorities have forbidden the sale of everything except the New York and Washington papers—besides the *True Delta,* of course."

"Do you have a copy of that?"

"I'm sorry, they were sold out this morning." The girl smiled for the first time. "Many people buy it to use—" She didn't finish the sentence, but the meaning was easily apparent.

"*Merci, mademoiselle,*" said Maritza with a smile. "No doubt the New York *Tribune* would serve the same purpose with equal efficiency."

"*Certainement,*" said the clerk.

"I wish we could find out whether André is in the general's jail," said Maritza as they were leaving the stationer's shop. "I'm afraid he may have been caught with the package for France before he could reach Captain Boncours on the *Andromeda.*"

"I'm as concerned as you are, but you can't afford to go there and ask," said Tina. "That would connect you with the story and be playing right into the hands of *l'Animal.* Maybe there's a better way."

"What is it?"

"I can look and talk like *une prostituée* when I want to, and the general has put that label on most of the women of New Orleans anyway. Why don't I go to the jail and demand to know whether they arrested my pimp?"

"It might work, but I hate to see you take the risk."

"What risk? The worst thing that could happen would be for the jailer to take advantage of me right there in the jail. And one good *coup de pied* in the right place with my heel will stop his interest in *la fréquentation* for at least a week."

"Make a try, then, but be careful. I'll meet you at Tante Marie's house later on."

Celestina disappeared around the corner in the direction they had seen the two prisoners being taken that morning and Maritza started back to the De Montfort home. She arrived there to see André, grinning broadly, sitting in the kitchen and

eating an enormous breakfast Madame de Montfort had prepared for him.

"Thank God you're safe," she told him, sitting down at the
table and pouring herself a cup of coffee from the pot that was
kept simmering there most of the day. "When did you get
back?"

"A few minutes ago, madame. There were—complications."

"You didn't lose the package?" she asked quickly.

"No, madame; it's on its way to France. I went to the ship
and gave the package with the photograph and your story to
Captain Boncours, just in time, too; the hawsers holding the
ship to the landing were being loosened. As I was about to
leave the ship, however, a messenger arrived from Mr. Andrew
Jackson Butler, with a large amount of money—"

"How much?"

"I'd already given the package to Captain Boncours and I'd
never seen the clerk before so I figured he probably wouldn't
know me and pretended to be working as a deck hand. I heard
a few words like three hundred thousand dollars, and again the
Banque de France, while Captain Boncours and the clerk were
talking. My guess would be that Mr. Andrew Jackson Butler
and the general are sending money out of Louisiana to be deposited abroad, just as a safety measure."

"I'd heard rumors to that effect."

"Anyway, the clerk didn't leave until they were ready to take
down the gangplank and I didn't think it was a smart idea for
me to be seen leaving after him, so I stayed on the ship. Downstream, when we were well out of sight of New Orleans and
reached a narrow place in the channel, I stripped and put my
clothes in a waterproof Captain Boncours lent me, then dived
over the side and swam ashore."

"You took a terrible chance, that river always was full of
alligators."

"Maybe they don't like black meat." André laughed gaily.
"Anyway, I swam ashore without any difficulty and soon found
a Cajun village not far from the channel. I speak French freely
and one man there had been to Martinique and recognized the
places I told him about in order to establish my identity, so I

had no trouble getting help from the Cajuns. They have no love for Beast Butler, either."

"Thank God you got back safely."

"It was nothing—except that I had to walk several miles and in the heat that was not particularly pleasant. Madame de Montfort has fixed me an excellent breakfast. Where is Tina?"

"She went by the jail to see whether or not you had been picked up by Butler's men on some charge. She was going to pretend to be a prostitute looking for her pimp."

André grinned. "With her ability as an actress, she could play that role very well indeed."

"I'm still worried about her."

"Don't be. She'll turn up here sooner or later."

Tina turned up, not much more than a half hour after Maritza had gotten back to the house. When she saw André she ran to throw herself into his arms. Marie de Montfort and Maritza left the two lovers to their reunion. When they came back Tina was pouring herself a cup of coffee.

"What happened at the jail?" Maritza asked.

"It was nothing. All I had to do was make an engagement with the head jailer for tomorrow night—"

"Over my dead body," said André.

"Really, he was a very handsome fellow," Celestina said impishly. "He even gave me a bottle of fine French wine from a wine store the general pre-empted a couple of days ago because the proprietor refused to take the oath of allegiance to the United States."

VI

New Orleans drowsed in the summer dog days of July and early August. The summer heat was so intense that even the malignant energy of General Butler seemed to be sapped to the point where he was unable to plan more burdens for the rebellious citizens of the city. Not so, however, the rest of the Confederacy, Maritza learned from copies of the Mobile and Montgomery newspapers smuggled into New Orleans almost daily.

Activities in Virginia, Kentucky, and Tennessee were reaching a fever pitch toward the end of August, with every evidence of Confederate victories both present and future. New York papers were on sale freely in New Orleans, too, but their accounts usually differed as much from the Confederate-slanted newspapers as night from day. Experienced in extracting the truth from such propaganda accounts, however, Maritza was able to reconstruct with considerable accuracy what was happening farther north.

In Virginia, General McClellan's ambitious attempt to capture Richmond by advancing up the peninsula between the York and James rivers had been turned into a shambles when Stonewall Jackson's lightning sweep through the Shenandoah Valley practically destroyed three Federal armies. Disturbed by the threat to Washington, Lincoln had almost wrecked McClellan's campaign on the peninsula by sending troops to the valley to protect the southeastern gateway to Washington.

General Irwin McDowell, commanding the troops around Culpeper that were supposed to help McClellan in the final conquest of the Confederate capital, had been replaced by General John Pope late in June. Pope, in turn, had immediately announced his intention to let his army live off the land, leaving civilians to make do as best they could, an order that had enraged Southerners almost as much as those of Bloody Ben Butler in New Orleans. Meanwhile, General Henry W. Halleck had been recalled to Washington from the South by Lincoln and given the post of general-in-chief, a demotion for McClellan, who had been forced to withdraw after spending several months within the sound of Richmond's church bells.

As both sides prepared for another bloody conflict, the scene of expected battle had shifted to the area just south of Culpeper, close to the old battleground of Manassas. The Federals still outnumbered the Confederates by a large margin but an important factor had been added to the Southern military power, when General Robert E. Lee was given command of all Confederate forces in Virginia. With generals like Stonewall Jackson, A. P. Hill, James Longstreet, and others serving him,

Lee had become a formidable foe of the luckless Federals, almost on the doorstep of the White House, where they'd been only a little over a year earlier.

While Grant and Farragut were still trying in vain to capture Vicksburg and open the Mississippi for its entire length, Maritza learned, Confederate Generals Braxton Bragg and Kirby Smith were routing Federal armies in central Kentucky and Tennessee. This movement, calculated not only to restore these border states to Confederate control but also to take Federal pressure off northern Mississippi and Alabama, was moderately successful.

About the same time—and much to General Butler's chagrin —Baton Rouge, some seventy-five miles upstream and under Union domination since shortly after the fall of New Orleans, was under attack. Confederate troops under the command of General John C. Breckenridge pressed the city and a small skirmish ensued before Butler's troops finally drove the Confederates back.

Shortly afterward too, Butler was forced to withdraw the brigade he had sent to Baton Rouge in the beginning, lest they be trapped and destroyed by the semi-guerrilla forces operating all along the lower Mississippi. Thumbing their noses at the unhappy Butler, these forces had fortified Port Hudson, just north of Baton Rouge, blocking the Mississippi one more time. A subsequent attempt by the U. S. S. *Essex* to destroy the fortifications at Port Hudson had ended in what might be called a draw.

Meanwhile, guerrilla bands operating along the Mississippi made it practically impossible for much water traffic to pass upstream from New Orleans, or to reach it from farther north. Thus Butler found himself virtually isolated in New Orleans, with shipping confined to the hundred-odd miles between the Queen City, as it was called, and the Gulf.

Pressed on all sides, General Halleck in Washington ignored Butler's frantic pleas for more troops, for the good reason that Halleck didn't have any to send. But, in characteristic fashion, Butler reacted by enlisting three infantry regiments of Negroes which he had personally freed, and two companies of artillery.

The act was calculated to further inflame the South but at the same time it ensured the ending of Butler's reign of terror in New Orleans.

None of this seemed to trouble the man now generally known over the South as the Beast. To help raise funds to pay his black troops, as well as the brigade he'd been forced to withdraw from Baton Rouge after the attack by General Breckenridge, Butler figured out a scheme by which to harass a substantial segment of the population of New Orleans.

The new plan for raising funds required that all foreigners residing in the city or its environs—the rest of Louisiana still being strongly attached to the Confederacy—must register with the military authorities. In addition they were required to list all properties and monies belonging to them. The consuls representing the foreigners immediately set up a howl, protesting to their respective envoys in Washington, to none of which Butler paid any attention.

Maritza was among the first to register, accompanied by Celestina and André. At the customhouse, Butler's headquarters, they stood in line for a short time before reaching the desk of a perspiring captain of the U. S. Army, who was trying vainly to cope with the babble of protests leveled at him in several languages.

"Your name?" he asked automatically without even looking up from the printed form he was filling out, when Maritza took her place before the desk.

"Countess Maritza LeClerc."

The officer, whose nameplate said "Capt. Alton Rogers," looked up sharply and blinked when he saw two startlingly beautiful women and a lithe black man standing before the desk.

"Please sit down, Countess." His voice took on a note of interest. "Are these your slaves with you?"

"I have no slaves, Captain. My companions are Monsieur André Maurois and Madame Celestina Maurois, his wife. They are in my employ."

"I'll get to them later." Captain Rogers' attention was centered on Maritza. "Where were you born, Countess?"

"In New Orleans."

Captain Rogers looked surprised. "But we are registering only foreigners, madame."

"I am a citizen of France by marriage, Captain—to the late Count Étienne LeClerc." Maritza reached into her handbag and took out a paper. "Here is my marriage certificate."

"Did you grow up in New Orleans?"

"In Mobile, but I have relatives here and before my marriage I often visited them. When I returned to the United States after the death of my husband a little over a year ago, I visited Nova Scotia, Boston, and Washington before coming here to make sure my relatives were safe."

The captain's eyebrows rose slightly. "Where are you living now, Countess?"

Maritza gave her aunt's address and was relieved to see that it meant nothing to the Federal officer. "Do you have property here in the city?" he asked.

"Only my personal effects and a small amount of money."

"May I ask how much?"

"About five hundred dollars. My funds are on deposit in Paris, London, and Halifax. Whenever I need money Count Mejan, the French consul, arranges for my drafts on the Bank of France to be turned into United States currency."

"A convenient arrangement, wouldn't you say?" Rogers said with a knowing smile.

"Under the circumstances, yes."

"Very well, Countess—" He stopped as a familiar figure bore down on his desk across the crowded room, where three lines of people were being registered.

"How is the registration going, Rogers?" General Butler asked loudly while still a dozen feet away.

"Very well, General." By that time Butler was standing behind the table upon which the captain had been writing. "I was just finishing with Countess LeClerc—"

"A countess?" Butler's eyebrows rose quizzically. "We are honored."

"Thank you, General." Maritza, too, rose. "You are too kind."

Butler bowed. "At this time of the morning my orderly always prepares a pot of excellent New Orleans coffee for me in my office. I would be honored if you would join me there."

"Of course. Am I not under your command?"

"Only technically, Countess. Even then I must watch my steps carefully, or Count Mejan will be writing Monsieur Mercier and he will be protesting to Secretary Seward." Butler opened the door of his office and stood aside for her to pass, his rather large potbelly making the space so narrow that Maritza couldn't help brushing against him as she entered the room.

"Ah! Good! The pot is boiling!" Closing the door behind him, Butler indicated the wing chair beside the desk.

"Smithers," he called to the orderly, who was standing stiffly at attention, "bring another cup and saucer at once, our best china."

Maritza recognized the monogram on the china immediately, since it had once belonged to a Creole friend. When she saw three spoons, she was reminded that one of the stories told about Butler in New Orleans credited him with stealing the spoons of those who entertained him in the hope of better treatment, resulting in the addition of "Spoons" to his many other nicknames.

"Sugar?" he asked, pouring a cup for her.

"Please."

"You'd be astounded by the price sugar brings in New York, Countess." Butler was spooning the sweet into her cup. "The transports that brought the troops here, when we took New Orleans, were supposed to return to New York in ballast. We had no way of getting sand without an enormous expense, though, so I loaded them with sugar. Saved the government many thousands of dollars, too, but now they won't even send me enough troops to scour the banks of the Mississippi and destroy the rebels that are harassing shipping."

"What can you do?" Maritza asked casually as she sipped the strong coffee.

"When General Grant and Admiral Farragut capture Vicksburg, vessels of war will be able to pass freely up and down the

river. I doubt if the guerrillas will be able to operate very much
longer then."

"How long do you think the war will go on, General?"

"Certainly no longer than the end of the year. If I were in
command in Virginia, it would be over in three months.
McClellan failed to take Richmond because he didn't have the
courage to press the attack, but now that the President has replaced him with Halleck our troops will soon be moving on
Richmond from the north the way they should have done at the
start." Butler gave her a probing look. "Are you going to stay
in the United States when the war is over, or return to France?"

"I haven't decided."

"Take my advice and stay, Countess. With cotton selling in
Mississippi for ten cents a pound while bringing seventy cents
in New York or Boston, and even more in England and France,
fortunes can easily be made for those with capital."

"How could it be shipped from New Orleans to foreign ports
with the blockade growing in strength daily?"

"There are ways." Butler's right eye, always drooping a little, closed in a conspiratorial wink. "One stroke of my pen to a
shipping permit will let a vessel leave New Orleans for any port
in the world."

"It must be a great burden to possess so much power. I don't
envy you, General!"

"People vilify me because I cleaned up the city and put the
poor, who were formerly on the dole, to work, paying them out
of funds confiscated from rebels and those who had bought
Confederate bonds. Mark my words, Countess. Before the next
presidential election the people of Louisiana will have taken the
oath of loyalty and become a state of the Union."

"Is that your aim?" she asked.

"Mine and President Lincoln's. You have no doubt noted
how willing the people are to sell their cotton and sugar in the
New Orleans markets, although they were told to burn it all
when I took over. My brother Andrew handles the family's
business. He tells me he has no trouble finding cargoes for all
ships visiting the port." Once again he gave her that scabrous

wink. "I don't have to tell you what a profit can be made on such shipments."

"If your brother has the concession to ship from New Orleans he must be getting rich," Maritza observed in as casual a tone as she could muster.

"He has no complaints." Then Butler dropped his bombshell. "Neither will you, if you co-operate."

Maritza gave the plump, balding man behind the desk a quick appraising look. Was he propositioning her romantically? Or merely in a business way? Either question needed answering.

"Don't get me wrong, Countess." Butler apparently realized how his words might be interpreted. "What I propose is strictly a business arrangement for our mutual benefit."

"Could you give me some more details about what you have in mind, General?"

"Just this. You're a native of New Orleans, according to the information you just gave Captain Rogers. You also belong to the nobility of France by marriage so you must have—shall we say 'Open Sesame'?—with the upper-level French population here."

"I know many people among the oldest and best-known families in the city," Maritza admitted.

"My wife is back home in Massachusetts for the summer—partly to escape the threat of yellow fever and malaria here in New Orleans. She has been very much hurt that the better class of people in the city—the class, I might say, from which we both come in Massachusetts—has snubbed her. If you, with your standing, were kind enough to invite her to a few social functions when she returns in the fall, your Creole friends would immediately realize her charm and breeding and would accept her socially."

"What could I expect in return?"

"I'm glad you understand me, Countess. As I told you just now, any shipments of purchases from the port requested by you would gain my approval, with only a small commission being paid to my brother's company to cover bookkeeping."

"I take it that by 'bookkeeping' you mean arranging for them to be overlooked by U.S. customs?" Maritza asked.

Butler smiled, reminding her of a potbellied fox. "I see that I've not underestimated your intelligence, Countess. What do you think of the proposition?"

"May I have time to consider it?"

"Of course. Besides, if you have only five hundred dollars in your possession now, as you stated to Captain Rogers on the questionnaire of registration, you will want to arrange for the transfer of funds through Count Mejan from your deposits in France or England before entering any commercial transactions."

"That is true, but I'll also need a pass."

"That's no problem," said Butler, "but one thing more. As you probably know, I neither speak nor read French very well, while you probably do both fluently."

"It was the first language I learned as a child."

"Good. I have been informed by the State Department in Washington that the French fleet will soon visit New Orleans. I'm fairly certain it's being sent here to survey the port in relation to the wish of Napoleon III to intervene in the revolution now going on in Mexico. The Confederacy has already given its approval to Napoleon's plans."

"Officially?" Maritza asked, startled by the statement.

"Not yet, of course. It's still only a scheme in the cunning brain of Judah P. Benjamin, but we have spies at the Quai d'Orsay who are fully as knowledgeable as that scoundrel Slidell who represents the Richmond government there. They tell us Napoleon has unofficially intimated that he would be willing to intervene on the Confederate side by retaking New Orleans and opening it to the Confederacy in return for a free hand in Mexico."

"That is all very interesting, General." Maritza tried to look bored and patted back a yawn with her handkerchief. "But what part could I possibly play?"

"I need an interpreter, Countess, someone who could draw out the officers of the French fleet when it arrives. Can you think of anyone who could do that better than a beautiful woman like yourself, who also belongs to French nobility?"

"You have a point there, General." Maritza was careful to keep the excitement she felt out of her voice and manner.

By now she was certain Butler was not the fool many people in New Orleans believed him to be, so she must think the whole question out carefully before agreeing to join forces with him. Her real purpose, of course, was to unmask Butler and his brother, but if she accepted the offer she would, so to speak, be walking on eggs. On the other hand, the chance to gain invaluable information for Richard Mann and Judah Benjamin concerning both Napoleon's schemes for Mexico and those of the Union for thwarting intervention by France on the side of the Confederacy was far too important to be turned down.

"When do you expect the fleet to arrive, General?" she asked.

"In a week or less. I'd much rather not have them here but the State Department doesn't look with favor on my forbidding them the port. Fortunately the French fleet will be coming here from Martinique, where there's always yellow fever in summer, so I plan to place the ships and their personnel aboard them in quarantine during their stay."

"That was clever."

"None of your Creole friends could possibly object to your visiting the French fleet and even having dinner with Admiral Reynaud, who commands it, when he invites you," Butler continued. "And you would certainly be doing your government a signal service by helping ferret out the plans of Napoleon III in this hemisphere."

"How can I refuse? As you just said, I would be doing my government a signal service."

Outside the customhouse, Maritza found Celestina and André waiting anxiously. "Why did the general keep you so long?" Tina asked. "We were afraid you'd been arrested."

"Believe it or not, he was propositioning me," Maritza said gaily. "And I accepted."

VII

During the week that followed, all of New Orleans was agog with excitement over the coming of the French fleet. The French part of the population saw in its presence in the port a possible chance to air their grievances against Butler. Confederate sympathizers dared to hope the admiral of the fleet would train the guns of the ships on the city, as Admiral Farragut had done, and demand its surrender in the name of Jefferson Davis.

Because of Butler's quarantine, naming the danger of yellow fever being brought from Martinique as the cause, the ships were anchored in the stream instead of approaching the dockside. That afternoon Maritza received a beautifully written invitation to dinner aboard the flagship from Admiral Reynaud, brought by an officer from Butler's staff with the information that Butler's carriage would call for her at eight o'clock.

"I don't like your even sitting at the same table with that beast," Marie de Montfort protested while Celestina was helping Maritza dress. "People will be talking."

"My invitation is from the French admiral, Tante Marie. Besides, I intend to use this dinner for my own purposes."

"I won't ask what they are," said her aunt. "Obviously you didn't return to New Orleans, with everything the way it is here now, just because you were born here."

"I came to see you, Tante Marie; that's all you need to know. How do I look, Tina?"

"Like Rex's Queen at Mardi Gras but watch that Butler. He may be a general but he's also a man whose wife's been away in New England all summer."

"I can handle the general. Whatever else he may be, he loves his wife."

"So did the banker who fathered me," said Celestina with a shrug. "I'm talking about lust, not love."

Maritza laughed. "If he starts lusting, I'll take it out of him with a *coup de pied*—in the right spot."

Butler's carriage, as ornate as that of a European nobleman, was at the curb when Maritza came down the steps and was handed into it by a footman in uniform.

"Good evening, General," she said, taking her seat beside Butler.

It was hard for her to keep from laughing at the splendidly uniformed travesty of an officer seated on the plush-covered cushion of the carriage. Prodigal with gold braid, gold-fringed epaulets, and gold buttons, the tunic was buttoned so snugly over his protruding stomach that the coattails flared out on the seat beside him. The sword buckled to a broad belt was ensconced in a gold embossed scabbard, with a handle, similarly embossed, protruding and a golden tassel swinging from it.

"Good evening, Countess," said Butler. "I wish my wife could see your gown. She's always been partial to those from Paris."

"Perhaps I can start a *maison de couture,* if I should decide to remain in New Orleans," said Maritza as the carriage rattled over the cobblestoned streets toward the waterfront. "I'm sure many dressmakers in Paris would be glad to come to New Orleans if they had the opportunity."

"Say the word and you'll have a license to operate," Butler assured her. "I've done everything I could to encourage business here, but so many of the people have rebel sentiments that they'd rather spend their time cursing me and the prosperity and improved health conditions I've brought to New Orleans than do an honest day's work."

At the waterfront a crowd of people had gathered to admire the French ships anchored in the river. The admiral's barge was waiting at the landing when Maritza stepped down from the carriage. Catcalls and some curses followed her and Butler as they crossed the levee and descended a few steps to board the barge. The general only shrugged them off, however, and Maritza ignored them.

At the ship they were met at the top of the boarding ladder by the admiral's aide and escorted to the main cabin where Reynaud himself awaited them. He bowed over Maritza's hand and touched it with his lips before turning to greet a scowling Butler. Maritza wasn't surprised to find that Admiral Reynaud spoke perfect English, it being the second language of educated Frenchmen, but Butler quite obviously was.

"In the name of the United States Government, I welcome you to New Orleans, Admiral Reynaud," Butler said formally and Maritza quickly translated for the benefit of the half dozen other officers in dress uniform waiting to be introduced, in case some of them were not entirely familiar with English.

"It is a pleasure to be in your city, General Butler." Admiral Reynaud smiled. "I can assure you that we have no yellow fever aboard."

"Considering that there has been only one case in New Orleans this summer, and that brought by a ship that failed to report touching at Havana," said Butler, "I am sure you can understand my quarantining vessels that come here from islands where fever is rampant, Admiral."

"Your record is undoubtedly a tribute to your efficient quarantine measures," Reynaud conceded. "I hope, however, that they will not prevent me and some of my officers from visiting the city tomorrow."

"I shall personally conduct you through the fortifications," Butler assured him. "You will no doubt be impressed by them."

"No doubt." Reynaud courteously failed to mention the fact that, had he come on a warlike mission, the guns of the anchored fleet could have overcome the puny defenses of New Orleans with probably no more than an hour of intensive shelling.

A group of officers from other ships of the fleet had come over to the flagship for the dinner. When they were introduced, Maritza was pleased to find among them an acquaintance from France, Captain Jacques de Lesseps, commander of the frigate *Rochambeau*. The dinner was elaborate, typically French, and uniformly delicious, as were the wines that freely accompanied each course. Mellowed by wine, Butler soon lost his pique at Admiral Reynaud's having greeted Maritza before him and became surprisingly affable.

The dinner finished, Captain de Lesseps invited Maritza to take some air on the deck rather than breathe in the cloud of cigar smoke accompanying the passing of brandy in the cabin. Since Admiral Reynaud spoke and understood English so well, her services as an interpreter were not required, so Butler made no objection to her leaving the group. Moreover, he was deep in conversation with the admiral, trying to draw him out on the purpose of the French visit.

"I'm surprised that you would be with General Butler," said De Lesseps as they were strolling along the deck of the flagship in the cool breeze from the river.

"Why?"

"I read your article about him in *Le Pays*."

"When did you see it?" Maritza asked.

"At Martinique less than a week ago. Is he really the scoundrel you described?"

"When not on his good behavior, like tonight, he's worse."

"I noticed that you didn't sign this article, as is your custom," said De Lesseps. "But anyone who has followed your writings would recognize your style immediately."

"Fortunately General Butler doesn't read French," Maritza informed him. "Besides, most of the French population of New Orleans hate him, so he has forbidden the sale of any French newspapers in the city."

"You can at least be thankful for that."

"Is it true that the French government has forbidden the newspapers to mention his name?"

"I don't think it has gone quite that far," said De Lesseps. "What really puzzles me is how you can associate yourself with such a man."

"The answer is simple. First, I want revenge for the death of a good friend—by hanging from the window of the custom-house."

"I saw that photograph with your article. It was horrible."

"The other is to keep certain people informed of what's happening in New Orleans."

"Secretary Benjamin!" De Lesseps exclaimed. "Of course, your sympathies would be with the Confederacy, since you were born in the South, but you're taking a very long chance when you ally yourself with a bitter enemy, hoping to outwit him."

"If I can learn what mischief he will be up to next I can probably save friends in New Orleans and even elsewhere a lot of heartache."

"It's dangerous enough for a man, but for a woman—" De Lesseps shook his head wordlessly. "My admiration for you and what you are doing is boundless, but my fears—"

"I know exactly what risks I'm taking, Captain. General Butler and his brother are buying cotton from planters who grow and sell it for ten cents a pound by still using slave labor. The Butlers then sell it abroad at seventy cents and he has offered to let me take a flyer in cotton or sugar, both of which are very, very profitable. If I can prove to Washington that Butler is getting rich by being military governor of New Orleans, Abraham Lincoln will yank him out of his job and, hopefully, out of his uniform, too. In any event he will be disgraced."

De Lesseps nodded slowly. "You're still as much in danger of your life as the Confederate soldiers who are probably crossing the Potomac River right now into Union territory—"

Maritza frowned. "What do you mean? The last report I read said the Confederate Army was still skirmishing somewhere around Culpeper."

"That battle has already been fought and ended—with a rout of the Federal troops near Manassas for a second time. General Lee is now leading the army that drove McClellan and Pope almost to the streets of Washington in an invasion of Maryland somewhat farther west. Do you mean you hadn't heard of it?"

"General Butler lets the newspapers print only what he wants printed," said Maritza. "He also forbids the importation of anything other than the New York papers into New Orleans. No doubt he held those up when they started reporting any movement of Lee into the North. How did you learn of this new invasion?"

"We stopped at Mobile the day before yesterday," De Lesseps explained. "The Southern papers that were brought aboard there were full of Lee's daring to invade Union territory."

"Did they say how far he has gone?"

"It's been several years since I was in the United States so I'm not certain of some of the names," De Lesseps admitted. "I remember their saying that your famous General Stonewall Jackson was on the point of taking Harpers Ferry." He glanced into the dining room where Butler and Admiral Reynaud were apparently engaged in a mild argument.

"The Mobile paper was predicting the fall of Harpers Ferry at any moment, with Jackson forging on to join Lee in Maryland at a place called"—De Lesseps paused—"I forget the name but it was something like that of a rifle model."

"Sharps!" Maritza exclaimed. "Sharpsburg! Étienne and I stopped there once when we were traveling through Maryland."

"That was it," De Lesseps confirmed.

"Sharpsburg is just across the Potomac from Virginia and only a little south of Hagerstown."

"I remember seeing it on a map."

"What a victory that would be!" Maritza exclaimed. "Then Lincoln would have no choice except to agree to a negotiated peace and let the South go its own way, ending this horrible killing. Do you think General Butler knows about the invasion of Maryland yet?"

De Lesseps shrugged. "If he does he's making a good job of concealing it. I doubt that Butler's accustomed to drinking cognac, so the admiral has probably got him drunk enough now to tell him everything he knows about Union plans."

"Which is why the fleet visited New Orleans in the first place, isn't it?" Maritza asked shrewdly.

"One of the reasons. I imagine you already know something of the trouble the Empress Eugénie has talked Napoleon III into getting himself involved with in Mexico."

"Only that he's hoping to put Mexico under French rule."

"The situation has gone much further than that now. England, France, and Spain financed a series of revolutions several years ago in Mexico with large loans. When Benito Juárez briefly came into power, he defaulted on those loans, so a combined fleet visited Vera Cruz some time ago to extract payment. When they saw what a job it would be to invade Mexico, England and Spain withdrew. France's loans were the largest, however, and by that time Empress Eugénie had persuaded Napoleon to make Mexico a monarchy with one of her relations, probably the Archduke Maximilian of Austria as Emperor. It isn't going to be easy but, if the Confederacy remains willing to allow a puppet monarchy to be set up below its borders, both countries could help each other."

"By France seizing New Orleans and at least part of Texas?"

"Probably nothing so drastic. Confederate Commissioner Slidell has done a good job in Paris arranging for loans to the Confederate government. He has even managed to get a few fast cruisers commissioned in French shipyards, but if the Confederacy should lose—"

"How can we lose with General Lee invading the North?"

"Invading and conquering are quite different, particularly when you're outnumbered five or six to one at least. We French hope the South will win and are staking a lot of money on that possibility, hoping to have a friendly power on the border of Mexico. But we must also be ready for any eventuality."

"Such as?"

"The United States is building a powerful navy, something it has never had before. If General Lee meets defeat at Sharpsburg and General Grant reduces the fortifications at Vicksburg this fall, the Confederacy could collapse. That would leave France in the position of having an unfriendly United States on the northern border of Mexico, with a navy powerful enough by then to seriously hamper our operations in supplying the troops."

"Why are you telling me this?" Maritza asked, although she was already certain of the answer.

"Because I'm sure you'll get the information to Secretary Benjamin by the quickest possible method."

Maritza laughed. "When I came back to America, I never dreamed I'd become an agent of international intrigue. Now that I'm in it, I find the whole thing tremendously exciting—and what little I'm able to do very rewarding."

"Just watch Butler," De Lesseps advised as voices emerging from the main cabin warned them the evening was almost over.

"You may have him fooled now but if he ever suspects your real purpose in being in New Orleans it could be your body that will be dangling from the window of the New Orleans customhouse."

VIII

While Butler's footman, who was waiting with the driver of the general's carriage at the waterfront, helped boost the staggering military governor of New Orleans aboard his vehicle, Maritza bade good-by to Admiral Reynaud and his staff. When she got into the carriage the already snoring Butler slumped against her but, with the help of the footman, she pushed him into the corner, holding him there while the carriage clattered across the cobblestones of the boat landing toward the former home of General David E. Twiggs, which Butler had expropriated for himself.

"You'd better get the general to his house before you take me home," Maritza told the driver. "I'll wait while you and the footman put him to bed."

The driver shrugged. "Even though he's a general, he should've known better than to try to drink a Frenchman under the table with cognac."

At the former home of Confederate General David E. Twiggs, Maritza held the doors while the two soldiers carried the still snoring Butler upstairs to his bedroom. Since that operation took a good fifteen minutes, she was afforded an unexpected opportunity to ransack the general's unlocked desk in the downstairs parlor.

She didn't have to look far to find what she'd hoped for: a sheaf of manifests showing cotton, sugar, and other supplies bought for the personal accounts of Butler and his brother. The manifests even carried the names of the ships upon which they had been sent out of New Orleans, as well as the prices the shiploads had brought elsewhere, all of it representing a handsome profit to the Butlers without the knowledge of the United

States Government. Hearing the heavy footsteps of the carriage driver descending the stairs, she quickly thrust the incriminating documents into the bosom of her gown and pulled the lacy wrap she'd worn over her bare shoulders across to hide them.

"I'm glad the footman is going to stay with him," she told the driver as they went out the door. "In his condition he could fall out of bed and hurt himself."

"A lot of people in New Orleans—and in the Army, too—wouldn't be sad about that, ma'am," said the driver. "I'm from Massachusetts like he is, but that sure don't make us brothers."

It was about ten o'clock when the carriage stopped before the De Montfort home and Maritza stepped down to the stone mounting block. Everyone there was waiting for her return to hear her account of the evening's events.

"André was about to go to Jackson Square to see about you," Tina scolded her. "How could you stand being with the Beast all that time?"

"Admiral Reynaud monopolized the general. He speaks English fluently, along with most of his officers, so they talked after dinner while I enjoyed the night air with Jacques de Lesseps, an old friend."

"I remember him coming to the château once while we were there," said Tina.

"He's a distant relative of Étienne's." Maritza drew the sheaf of manifests from the bosom of her gown and put them down on the kitchen table where a candle was burning. "Look what I found at the general's house."

Tina glanced through the pile and whistled softly. "If you could get those papers to Mr. Benjamin or General Mann, they could see that Secretary Stanton and Mr. Seward got copies of them too. That would be the end of Bloody Ben."

"That's exactly what I have in mind," said Maritza. "Get some pens and plenty of ink, Tina. We're going to copy these manifests tonight. When we've done that I'll try to figure out some way to get them back in the general's desk before daylight."

"Don't worry about that, *Madame la Comtesse*," André said with a grin. "Before I became a maître d'hôtel, I had some experience as what is sometimes called a 'cat burglar.' Just draw me a sketch of the room where the desk is and the original copies will be there long before dawn."

"Good!" said Maritza. "Let's get busy, Tina."

By two o'clock that morning Maritza and Tina had finished making several copies of the manifests, with their damning proof that both the general and his brother were getting rich by cheating people who had no choice except to sell what they raised at whatever price the cheaters chose to pay. André took the originals, with the sketch Maritza made of the first floor of General Twiggs's house showing the desk, and disappeared.

"It was as easy as crawling into my own bed," he reported, no more than a half hour later. "It probably never occurred to the general or his orderly that anyone would dare to rob the house. The downstairs windows were up and I slipped out a screen with my pocketknife. Everything you took is back in its place, madame. No one could ever suspect that the papers had been tampered with."

"Thank you, André," said Maritza gratefully. "Now you and Tina had better get to bed. Tomorrow I want you to take this material to the nearest post office and personally see it put into the mail for Richmond."

As it happened, the information Maritza had gained from the stolen manifests removed any need for her to engage in buying and selling contraband sugar or cotton. However, in order to have a safe conduct out of New Orleans if the need arose, she decided to obtain the pass Butler had promised to give her.

At the customhouse several days later she was ushered into Butler's office and found the general in excellent humor.

"I've been intending to inquire what you learned from your friend Captain de Lesseps the other night about France's plans in Mexico, Countess," he said.

Not knowing how much Butler already knew, Maritza decided to stick to the truth. "Napoleon is being urged by the Empress Eugénie to set up a monarchy there."

"We've known that for some time," said Butler. "Who's to be the puppet emperor?"

"Archduke Maximilian of Austria, I believe."

"Never heard of him, but the French will get nowhere down there anyway. Disease always kills white men in places that know nothing of sanitation and cleanliness and the French are no better at that than the Mexicans. You should have seen the filth right here in New Orleans when I took over, but look at the city now. The streets and gutters are clean, thanks to my employing the poor, and there's been almost no disease."

"The city is far healthier than it was when I was a small girl," Maritza admitted.

"Healthier than it's been since it was founded," Butler corrected her. "Now what can I do for you, Countess?"

"You may remember suggesting, when I was registering with the other foreigners in New Orleans, that I might be interested in making some investment in foreign trade—sugar or cotton, for instance."

"So I did. Sugar is more profitable, though harder to obtain, now that the growers realize what profits can be made."

"I would appreciate having a pass into Mississippi for myself and my two servants, in case I decide to try to buy some cotton or sugar over there."

"That's simple; the governor and I have an understanding. What do you propose to buy?"

"Sugar—if I can find enough to make it worth my while."

"An excellent decision, Countess. My brother and I have leased a steamer which should arrive with supplies soon. Have the sugar you buy brought here and we'll ship it to New York for sale to your account—with only a small commission paid to my brother for hiring a portion of the ship's hold."

"I understand that. Count Mejan is arranging for the transfer of the funds for payment."

"That Mejan causes nothing but trouble." Butler grimaced with distaste. "He's always sending bad reports about me to his government."

"Do you open his diplomatic pouches?" Maritza asked, astounded.

"Of course. I can't have lies about me sent through official channels to other countries."

Maritza drew a long breath of relief at having been saved

from what could have been disaster, if she had entrusted any of her own dispatches intended for *Le Pays* to the French consul instead of having André mail them at the Cajun village some distance away. Meanwhile, Butler reached for a sheet of paper and scrawled a pass on it, affixing his signature and sealing it with the seal of the United States Government.

"I'm doing this on the condition that you'll not forget our bargain, Countess," he said as he handed over the precious document. "When my wife comes back, we will arrange for you to entertain in her honor."

"Do you know when she will be returning?" Maritza asked.

"In another month, I hope. The weather in New Orleans will be cool enough by then for her comfort."

"I shall look forward to meeting her." Maritza forced a smile to cover the lie.

As Maritza was passing through Jackson Square she paused at the stationer's shop to buy several copies of the New York *Tribune* that had come in that very morning on a vessel from New York. Emblazoned across the top was a banner headline that made her heart feel suddenly as heavy as lead. Dated September 18, the headline read:

LEE'S ARMY ANNIHILATED BY McCLELLAN AT ANTIETAM
Confederates Fleeing Across Potomac at Boteler's Ford

Jacques de Lesseps had been correct in his information, Maritza realized—except that the daring invasion of Maryland he had ascribed to General Robert E. Lee had already ended in disaster, if you could believe the Union-slanted account. With the army that had defended Richmond against attack on the peninsula now destroyed, McClellan would no doubt move swiftly to cut off the Confederate forces before they could return to the safety of the area just south of Washington, leaving the Confederate capital practically undefended.

A second issue, dated September 22, contained the long-expected Emancipation Proclamation Lincoln had apparently

finally been convinced by his associates to announce. Brief, but
to the point, it read:

> On the first day of January in the year of Our Lord one
> thousand, eight hundred and sixty-three, all persons held
> as slaves within any state or designated part of a state, the
> people whereof shall then be in rebellion against the
> United States, shall be then, thenceforward and forever
> free.

In still another issue of the newspaper, Lincoln had issued
another proclamation in which he suspended all constitutional
privileges of habeas corpus and provided for military trial of
"all rebels and insurgents, their aiders and abettors within the
United States, and all persons discouraging voluntary enlistments, resisting militia drafts, or guilty of any disloyal practice,
affording comfort to Rebels, against the authority of the United
states."

With those two proclamations, Maritza decided, Abraham
Lincoln had finally closed effectively the door leading to any
possibility of reconciliation between the Confederate States of
America and the United States Government.

IX

Maritza's having attended the dinner aboard the French fleet
with Butler, even though as a translator, aroused some preju-
dice against her in the French community of New Orleans.
Mindful of future plans to turn upon the hated governor with
some of his own treatment, she decided, therefore, not to engage in the commercial venture Butler had offered her for selling Louisiana and Mississippi sugar on the markets of New
York. Too, the Richmond papers, reaching New Orleans un-
derground, so to speak, within less than a week after publication in the Virginia capital, were becoming more and more vitriolic in their denunciation of New Orleans' private Beast.

The normally gentlemanly Jefferson Davis had even gone so far as to proclaim:

> Now, therefore, I, Jefferson Davis, President of the Confederate States of America, in their name do pronounce and declare that said Benjamin F. Butler to be a felon deserving of capital punishment. I do order that he shall no longer be considered or treated simply as a public enemy of the Confederate States of America, but as an outlaw and common enemy of mankind, and that, in the event of his capture, the officer in charge of the capturing force do cause him harm to be immediately executed by hanging.
>
> And I do further order that no commissioned officer of the United States, taken captive, shall be released on parole, before exchanged, unless the said Butler shall have met with due punishment for his crimes. All commissioned officers in the command of said Benjamin F. Butler will be entitled not to be considered as soldiers engaged in honorable warfare, but as robbers and criminals, deserving death; and that they and each of them, whenever captured, be reserved for execution.

Butler's reaction to this damning document was to have it posted throughout New Orleans, with the warning that any person or persons attempting to put Jefferson Davis' order into effect by betraying him should be summarily given the treatment Davis had ordered for him.

"Do you think President Davis will have that order carried out?" Tina asked when they first read the copy André brought them.

"It's not like him," said Maritza. "Butler's actions are enough to anger even the statue of Andrew Jackson in the square. Still, by placing his officers under the same indictment as himself, Butler may well have gone too far. With luck, Lincoln may have to remove him in order to keep up the morale of the Army's officer corps."

"I still wish you didn't have to associate with him," said Tante Marie.

"I'll steer as clear of Butler as I can, but don't forget my position here." Maritza put her hand over the older woman's reassuringly. "As Jacques de Lesseps said, if Butler found me out he'd have me hanged before sundown. My job is to accumulate as much evidence against him as I can."

Judging from the steadily increasing critical accounts of Butler's operations in the New York newspapers that arrived almost daily now on the ships actively trading at the port of New Orleans, the general had finally gone too far in many ways. Two days after the 1862 congressional elections gave Abraham Lincoln the solid support he needed for prosecuting the war, Generals Benjamin F. Butler and George B. McClellan were both relieved from duty with the U. S. Army. Butler's comeuppance was long overdue, of course. McClellan's punishment, however, was for a more recent event, his failure to stop General Robert E. Lee and the main Confederate Army in Virginia from escaping to their old haunts east of the Blue Ridge after their bloody defeat at Sharpsburg and Antietam Creek.

Butler's replacement was General Nathaniel P. Banks, Stonewall Jackson's old whipping boy from the north end of the Shenandoah Valley. McClellan's was the unlucky General Ambrose E. Burnside, even then in the process of being soundly whipped at Fredericksburg by Lee's Four Horsemen of the Apocalypse: Jackson, Longstreet, D. H. Hill, and J. E. B. Stuart.

BOOK EIGHT

MANATEE

I

It was nearing Easter when Maritza, Celestina, and André crossed the rusting railroad bridge over the James River to Richmond on the daily train from the South. In the long view through the soot-blotched windows of the coach, the environs of the Confederate capital hadn't changed remarkably since she'd left Richmond for New Orleans. Smoke still belched from the tall stacks of the Tredegar Iron Works but, on closer inspection, from the dingy seats of the railroad car in which they sat, passengers could see evidence of decay everywhere, even in the rust-covered iron of the bridge.

The barren fields through which they had passed on the rail journey from Mobile to Richmond had been mute evidence that Abraham Lincoln's Proclamation of Emancipation for all slaves, wherever held, had already slowed food production throughout the South to a near halt. The ragged uniforms of the soldiers, and particularly the worn leather of their shoes—when they had any—was depressing, too, as groups gathered at train stations wherever they passed, awaiting transportation northward to the long since blood-soaked battlefields of Virginia. Or perhaps westward to the equally gory fields around Vicksburg, where General Grant was under heavy criticism from Congress for his failure to capture the city that was still effectively blocking all water transport on the Mississippi. In fact, to Maritza, it seemed that everything touched by the bloody fingers of war was slowly dying.

The decision to leave New Orleans, once the menace of Butler the Beast was removed, had not been an easy one. The governing hand of aging Union General Nathaniel Banks was relatively light where Butler's had been a mailed fist. Though no commerce flowed on the Mississippi from north of the Confederate fortifications at Port Hudson, the waterways south of there and New Orleans itself were often jammed. Through an unofficial arrangement with the Federal captors, foreign commerce had been re-established and even that with Northern port cities was being resumed to a considerable degree. New Orleans newspapers were being published again, too, when they could obtain newsprint, though monitored closely by Federal censors. And the population, even those who had defied Butler, were allowed to move about freely, so long as they undertook no activities that could be called sabotage.

Actually Maritza would have preferred to remain in New Orleans at least until winter was over in Virginia. It had been Celestina, restless with inactivity and reading the papers from cover to cover, who had discovered a story in an issue of the new *True Delta*. Telegraphed from Washington, the account detailed the raid by Pinkerton detectives on an address in Georgetown that was quite familiar to Maritza, led there when neighbors reported large amounts of mail being carried in and out of an otherwise innocent-looking home.

The owners of the Georgetown house, according to the report, had managed to escape the detectives but not in time to remove or destroy files of addresses to and from which letters had been moving daily. The account also stated that the authorities confidently expected the files to reveal the names of leading members of the Confederate spy network in and around Washington.

Maritza was certain her own name would be in the files and that Pinkerton would soon put together the seeming coincidence of articles describing Union-related events for the past several months in New Orleans appearing intact in *Le Pays,* after being thoroughly cut to pieces by Federal censors. The imminence of the expected warrant for her arrest gave her no choice except to leave the warmth, the brilliance of the flowers, and the relative peace of New Orleans.

Escaping from the city had been relatively easy, since the lines between the Federally controlled metropolis and the remainder of Louisiana—still forthrightly Confederate—were no longer rigidly observed. In order to avoid suspicion, Maritza had taken nearly a week to remove from the Banque de Louisiane the fairly large amount of gold deposited there by means of a draft on the Bank of Nova Scotia against just such a hurried departure as she was now being forced to make.

No one had even bothered to stop the wagon and its black driver that André had hired to take them to the Cajun village of Slidell. There they'd had no trouble hiring a boatman for the journey eastward through the watery maze that separated the Gulf of Mexico along this coast from the mainland itself. A three-day sail in the somewhat cramped space of the boat had brought them to Mobile Bay, guarded still by the massive guns of Fort Morgan, and the city of Mobile itself at its head.

At her plantation a few miles from the city, Maritza had found Moses and most of the field hands busy plowing the rich dark soil for planting corn. The grain was much more valuable now as food for soldiers and civilians alike than the cotton being shipped through the blockade only from Wilmington, North Carolina. And then only by daring men like Penn Darrow, who was well on the way to becoming a legend in his own day.

While Celestina was happily greeting companions from her girlhood days and proudly introducing her handsome new husband, Maritza sat on a log by the cornfield, discussing recent events with Moses.

"What made you decide to plant corn this year, Moses?" Maritza asked.

"Cunnel Mann—he's a ginrul now—said we ought to plant somethin' we can eat, and maybe even spare some for other folks."

"Did he write those instructions to you?"

"No'm. He told me that when he was heah, a couple of months ago."

"General Mann was here?" Maritza asked, startled.

"Yes'm. Mr. Jeff Davis was in Mobile right after Christmas and the ginrul was with him. He didn't stay long though; seems like he's in charge of guardin' some purty important peepul up in Richmond."

"That's part of his job."

"You goin' to marry him, ain't you, oncet this war's over?"

Maritza smiled. "Did he tell you that?"

"He said he hoped you would and it shore makes sense, with both of you owning plantations alongside each other."

"I don't know, Moses. He's asked me to marry him but we've agreed not to decide until the war's over."

"Folks 'roun here's sayin', now that Mr. Lincoln done freed the slaves, it ain't gonna go on much longer."

"Right now the only slaves Abraham Lincoln can free belong to Northern people, Moses. Slaveowners in the South don't recognize the authority of the government in Washington any more."

"That's what I bin tellin' black folks that gets all 'cited 'bout freedom. I was up North once, afore the war, and I couldn't see we was bein' treated any better up there than you and Ginrul Mann was already treatin' us down here."

"I wanted to free all of you when I first came back from France and England, but General Mann said that would only make trouble for all of you with the people around here that didn't want to free their slaves."

"He was right—then. Lately, though, some of the young bucks bin talkin' 'bout the Yankees givin' black men uniforms and guns."

"General Butler did that in New Orleans."

"We heard 'bout it. The ones that's talkin' say the Yankees'll let 'em keep everything they can take away from Southern white folks."

Maritza felt a sudden chill at the old Negro's words. That particular fear, she knew, had been in the minds of Southerners even before John Brown attacked the Federal arsenal at Harpers Ferry before the war began, seeking guns with which to turn Southern Negroes loose upon their former masters.

"It hasn't come to that yet, Moses, but it may before the war is over."

"That'd be stealin', Miss Ritza. An' stealin' ain't right."

"They've got a different name for it in wartime, Moses—it's called seizure." She stood up. "I guess we'd better be getting back to Mobile. I'm going to leave some money with Lawyer Anderson in case you need it for the crop. If any of the young bucks, as you call them, want to go North, be sure and pay them for the work they've done before they leave. They won't find the Yankees as generous as General Mann and I have been."

"Tell the ginrul we's lookin' after his plantation the same as we's lookin' after your'n—and that I'm prayin' this'll all be over soon."

"We're all praying for that, Moses."

Maritza wasn't surprised to see the tall figure of Richard Mann standing on the station platform when she descended from the coach at Richmond in midafternoon. She'd telegraphed ahead from Danville that morning, during a delay of several hours while troop trains were being shifted about and sent out of the railroad yards ahead of the passenger coaches, which in fact were only part of a long freight train. Mann was eagerly examining the small groups of passengers descending from each of the half dozen cars allotted for their use. When he saw Maritza his face lit up and he came striding along the platform toward her.

Overcome with a surge of feeling she hadn't dreamed she would experience at the sight of him again, Maritza found herself running toward him without volition, hurling herself into his extended arms. The ecstasy of feeling them about her, the crushing pressure of his mouth upon hers, was greater than any she remembered experiencing before and she yielded herself utterly to it, ignoring the staring passers-by. In fact she didn't even notice the small bearded man with the decidedly Jewish countenance and smiling eyes who was watching them from a few yards away.

When finally Richard Mann released her, Maritza was too breathless to speak or even to hear anything for a moment, save the furious pounding of her heart. Mann, too, was almost at a loss for words while he held her back to look at her, his eyes shining.

"You're here at last," he said in a choked voice. "When I heard you were in New Orleans—"

"Welcome to Richmond, Countess."

At the sound of a familiar voice, she turned to see Judah P. Benjamin standing a few feet away. Flustered, and conscious now that the tumultuous greeting by Richard Mann and her equal response had knocked her trim Parisian chapeau almost off her head, she held out her hand to Benjamin while Mann was still holding her half encircled within the crook of his right arm. In a gesture of Old World courtesy, Benjamin lifted her hand and pressed it to his lips.

"You're like a ray of sunshine after a summer storm, Countess," he told her and, turning, also lifted Celestina's hand to give her an equally courteous greeting before shaking hands with André.

"The lovely Celestina and the incomparable André," he added. "How nice to see you both again."

"You're very kind, Mr. Secretary," said Tina. "André and I are very grateful for your welcome."

"A welcome well deserved indeed for all of you." Benjamin turned to give a cold stare to a knot of bystanders who had been watching the brief scene in openmouthed astonishment, sending them scurrying away. Meanwhile, Maritza had adjusted her hat and, taking the arm Richard Mann held out to her, they started along the platform to where several carriages and hacks waited. When they reached the line of waiting conveyances, Benjamin stopped beside a barouche drawn by a lithe bay mare.

"I must be getting back to work," he said.

"Won't you have dinner with us tonight, sir?" Mann asked, but the Secretary of State shook his head.

"Two is company, especially when they're in love. If you're not too tired tomorrow morning, Countess, I would like to see you in my office around eleven. I'll send my barouche for you."

II

At the Spotswood Hotel, Maritza found her suite ready and, at her request, a room was found in the staff quarters for Celestina and André. For the first time since they'd left Mobile, she was able to enjoy the luxury of a bath, while Tina unpacked what baggage she'd been able to bring out of New Orleans at the time of their hurried departure. After the bath she put on a dressing gown and slept until it was time to dress for dinner with Richard Mann.

Maritza had made many friends during her previous stay in Richmond before going to New Orleans, and their journey through the crowded dining room to their table was like a triumphal procession. Besides, she was widely known from her descriptions of the regime of General Butler, which had been printed under her by-line in one of the major Richmond papers, as well as elsewhere throughout the South and, of course, in Paris and London.

"You always were the most beautiful woman in any room you enter," Richard Mann told her proudly. "Now you've become a reigning celebrity and every man in the room envies me."

"In a two-year-old Paris gown that was the best dress I could take from New Orleans? I don't deserve it. Besides, it's the women who are envying *me*."

"I doubt that," he said. "Lately I've spent so little time in Richmond, hardly anyone knows me any more—which may be just as well considering the sort of job I have to do."

"Things really aren't going very well, are they?"

"On the Virginia battle fronts the genius of General Robert E. Lee—plus Jackson, Longstreet, and a few others—is worth ten thousand men. Elsewhere . . ." He shrugged. "Espionage gets harder every day, too. When our mail center in Georgetown was raided by Pinkerton's men, I was nearly out of my mind about you but had no way to reach you."

"Celestina read all the newspapers we could get and saw the

story in a Mobile paper. We started making preparations to leave right away."

"You were lucky at that. If Pinkerton could have caught you it would have been quite a victory for him."

Maritza shivered involuntarily. "Will it ever end?"

"Since Lincoln issued his Proclamation of Emancipation, the South is more determined than ever to fight on to the end."

"But are the prospects of victory any better?"

"If we were doing as well on land as our new raiders, the *Alabama* and the *Florida,* are doing at sea, I'd feel a lot better about our prospects. They're sinking Union shipping right and left but unfortunately nothing they capture or destroy changes the critical shortages of everything we need, even to live. By the way," he added, "Mr. Slidell—I think you call him Uncle John —has been doing a very fine job in Paris. He's arranged a large loan and even has a French shipyard building some ironclad vessels that might let us open ports like Charleston again to our shipping."

"Is there any prospect of France coming in on our side?"

"I think Napoleon III would be glad to open the blockaded Southern seaports tomorrow to French shipping if he could be sure of support from England. The nearest we came to actually getting England in on our side, though, was the Mason and Slidell capture. You did a fine job with that one and the whole South owes you a debt of gratitude. If Lincoln and Seward had delayed one more day at the end of '61 in apologizing, the English would have been ready to declare war."

"Is the blockade complete now?"

"Everywhere except Wilmington; it's the main life line of the whole Confederacy now. Your friend Darrow is doing a yeomanlike job with the *Sprite,* incidentally, and making a lot of money for you both."

"What good will it do?" Maritza said disconsolately. "There'll soon be nothing to buy."

Richard Mann put his hand over hers on the table. "I shouldn't have insisted that we have dinner together tonight, when you must be worn out completely from that long train ride."

"I'm not that tired; it's just a reaction, I suppose, to leaving a peaceful city like New Orleans and coming here where the signs of war are all around us. In New Orleans and in Mobile, too, the flowers were in bloom and there was almost no real evidence that anyone was at war."

"I know how you feel; it was spring in eastern Tennessee when I left there a few days ago."

"Why did you have to go there?"

"They're having trouble with the Conscription Act. Out of more than twenty-five thousand conscripts, only about six thousand are actually in uniform. The rest gained exemption through political influence, claims of being in an essential occupation, or by hiring someone to take their places."

"What could you do about it?"

"Nothing, really. The only consolation is that our agents in the North tell us Lincoln is having even more trouble with his conscription program. We know of near riots in Chicago and several other places where they've tried to enforce it."

"Moses said 'yellownecks' have been raiding plantations near Mobile."

"That could be. Mississippi is next door and it's been a headache almost from the start of the war. Governor Pettus has allowed trading with the enemy ever since New Orleans was captured, and the deserters called yellownecks are everywhere down there. President Davis even went to Alabama to prove to the people that they are not in any great danger from the enemy; the inhabitants of Mobile had been protesting to him that they were not being protected properly."

"All the Federal activity I heard of while I was in Mobile was a few raids on saltworks along the coast."

"That's all the furor amounted to but we do need salt badly, too, so the loss of even one saltmaker's kettle is a defeat in a way. There's good news from Charleston, though. Your cousin General Beauregard is in command once again. A few days ago he drove off a Federal attack trying to take the forts in the harbor. Several enemy ironclads were damaged so badly that we hear they'll have to be sent to New York for repairs."

"Good for Cousin Pierre! Is the port of Charleston open then?"

"No. The Federal blockade fleet stays beyond the range of our cannon, but the attack on Charleston is said to have cost the Union a hundred million dollars. I can hear a lot of Yankee businessmen screaming about that and the taxes they'll have to pay for somebody's stupidness in trying to take the city, when all those heavy guns are in place facing seaward."

"I wonder what the war is costing the South, besides the suffering and loss of life?"

"The last figure I saw was sixty million dollars a month but some people in the Confederacy are still getting rich. Farmers are charging four hundred dollars for a ton of hay, three dollars and a half for a pound of butter, and sixteen dollars for a bushel of potatoes—all of it grown by slave labor the rest of us are fighting for them to keep." Mann's tone was bitter for the first time.

"I could see signs of that on the way north from Mobile," Maritza agreed. "Still, what can we do except pay?"

"You could marry me and join our plantations into one—managed by you."

Maritza smiled and squeezed his hand. "Are you offering to take me away from all this?"

"I'd send you back to Alabama tomorrow if I could—as much as I love you and want you. I could tell this afternoon on the train platform that you want me as much as I do you, so don't deny it."

"I'm not denying it." Maritza had the grace to blush. "If we hadn't been in such a public place, I'm afraid I would have been as eager as you obviously were to do something no lady is supposed to do until she's properly married."

"I've got the answer to that," he said promptly. "A justice of the peace lives right here in the hotel and does a thriving business marrying people who don't have much time."

Maritza looked at her wineglass, as if hoping to see some secret answer revealed in the pale amber fluid, but found none. Then she looked up and shook her head gently.

"I've never taken the easy way out of anything and marrying

you now would be doing just that," she told him. "I really came back for the same reason you stay in the Army, when you could resign honorably on the grounds that you could do more good for the Cause in Alabama, raising corn for the armies and cattle to furnish them both meat and hides from which to make shoes."

"I guess we're both bound by chains we can't break until they're broken for us," he agreed. "When Pinkerton's men raided our Georgetown mail center they got the names of several people who were working with us while holding responsible positions in the Union government. One of them has already been hanged and another is in the Old Capitol, awaiting trial. If I quit now, I'd be defaming their memory."

"I feel the same way," said Maritza. "It looks as if you have no choice except to do what you're doing and you heard Mr. Benjamin say he had something in mind for me."

"No more spying," he said urgently. "Promise me you won't let him talk you into that."

"No more spying. I had enough of that with the threat of Bloody Ben Butler hanging over my head all those months in New Orleans."

III

A half dozen people were waiting in the anteroom to Judah P. Benjamin's office the next morning but the clerk at the desk ushered Maritza in as soon as the secretary to whom Benjamin had been dictating left. The Secretary of State stood up at once and came around the broad desk to greet her warmly.

"I trust you enjoyed an excellent dinner last evening and a good night's sleep, Countess," he said. "After that long train ride, you were entitled to both."

"Plus a proposal of marriage," Maritza said with a smile.

"Did you accept? Richard Mann is a fine catch."

"I'm here to do a job, Mr. Secretary, not to find a husband. I should warn you that he made me promise I wouldn't let even your eloquence talk me into keeping on with the role of Confederate spy I've been playing these past two years."

"It *is* just about two years since I asked you to go to Washington, isn't it? And what a job you've done, young lady! Warning Beauregard of General McDowell's change of strategy in time to save us from defeat at First Manassas. Making sure the whole world knew of Captain Wilkes's seizure of Mr. Mason and Mr. Slidell on the high seas, almost bringing England into the war on our side as a result. And exposing Ben Butler for the Beast they named him in New Orleans, plus a lot of other contributions."

"Then you aren't going to ask me to be a spy once again?"

"Not at all. Besides, you're much too famous now for that. What I plan to offer you is the job of writing the true story of the Confederacy."

"Surely everything that's happened has been reported in the newspapers and must also be in the official reports."

"That's exactly what President Davis and I want to avoid."

"I'm afraid I don't understand," she admitted.

"Newspaper accounts are always either censored to keep the truth of defeat from being revealed, or biased enough to make a small successful skirmish sound like the rout of a large enemy force."

"How would I tell the wheat from the chaff?"

"By using that excellent brain inside your beautiful body," said Benjamin with a grin. "We have files of Northern newspapers in the archives, along with Richmond papers and official reports filed by the generals after battles. I'm sure you'll find the accounts fascinating—particularly the Battle of Sharpsburg that we call Antietam."

"Why that particular one?"

"When Lee invaded Maryland some high officer involved took the battle plan and wrapped it around a package of cigars he stuck in his pocket. Somehow the whole thing fell out, when the officer was going through Frederick, Maryland, on the way to Sharpsburg and Antietam Creek. It was found by a Union soldier with the good sense to take it to his commanding officer, who gave it to General McClellan. If 'Little Mac' hadn't known

Lee's exact battle plan in advance, the invasion could have ended differently, with Lee plunging northward to outflank Philadelphia and New York."

"For want of a shoe . . ."

"Exactly—but when you're dealing with human beings, you're always plagued by human errors." Benjamin's tone turned to a serious note. "There's never been a war quite like this, Countess. Who would have thought an obscure teacher at the Virginia Military Institute named Thomas J. Jackson would turn out to be one of the two or three military geniuses of our time. He's only a step behind Napoleon I or Robert E. Lee and I'm not even sure of that."

"I remember Jackson's Valley campaign," said Maritza. "It was fantastic."

"Whipping three armies—each larger than his own—in less than six weeks and forcing McClellan to give up his Peninsular campaign when he was only twelve miles from Richmond was quite a feat."

"How soon will the Yankees make another try?"

Benjamin shrugged. "Who can tell? We're expecting another big push to begin any day."

"You don't seem to be much disturbed at the prospect."

"McDowell, McClellan, Pope, and Burnside have all made a try at it and Joe Hooker will be next. They might have had a chance, too, last spring, if Lincoln hadn't gotten cold feet and withdrawn so many of McClellan's troops because he was afraid Stonewall Jackson would attack Washington through Maryland. What they don't seem to know is that we've got a secret weapon here in the South that's stronger than any of them."

Maritza gave him a startled look. "You've done a good job of keeping it hidden so far."

"Actually, it's not hidden at all." Benjamin looked like a mischievous, and rather plump, elf, with his gamin grin. "The name is Robert E. Lee. If Lee had accepted the position of general-in-chief of the Union forces when Lincoln and General Winfield Scott offered it to him right after your fiery cousin Pierre captured Fort Sumter before Major Anderson had time to surrender of his own accord, the war would probably be over now."

"Do you really have that much confidence in General Lee?"

"Robert E. Lee is one of the great military geniuses of all time—which is another reason I want you to write the true story of the war from the viewpoint of the Confederacy."

"What would I emphasize besides the feats of Generals Lee and Jackson?"

"Perhaps the miracle that made a fat Jew, who wasn't even born on the North American continent, into first a U.S. senator and then the second most influential politician in the Confederacy. Another thing makes this war different and may account for the South having been able to do so well with such a small fraction of the population and even less resources. By far the greater number of those now guiding the Confederacy were leaders in the United States Senate or the House of Representatives before secession. When the country split along the northern border of Virginia it was more than a geographical division; the North lost many of its most promising statesmen—"

Maritza smiled. "Present company included?"

"If that's the way you see it after you do your preliminary research, yes. It's very important that your account reflect the exact truth."

"A lot of people will be writing the same story, once the war is over, and they're all bound to differ."

"Some of them have already started," said Benjamin. "I've an idea your friend Beast Butler has someone busy with the job of whitewashing him. Which reminds me—he's been pestering Lincoln to put him back on duty ever since he was removed from his command in New Orleans. He even worked out a plan that might end the war pretty quickly."

"Butler didn't strike me as being any kind of a genius—except in torturing innocent people."

"We have it on good reports that Butler has asked Lincoln to put him in command of the Federal Army of Tennessee and give him seventy-five thousand men. With them, he guarantees to march clear across the country to Savannah, cutting the South in two."

"That would be a disaster!"

"More than likely the end of the Confederacy," Benjamin agreed. "Before much longer, that bulldog named Grant is going to take Vicksburg. When he does, the whole Trans-Mississippi Department will be severed from us. If Butler could put his favorite scheme into action at about the same time, the South would be cut into four parts and supplies to Richmond and the rest of Virginia and the Carolinas would be sharply curtailed. You can imagine how long we could hold out then."

"If it's such a good plan, why didn't they let him try it?"

"For the same reason that has destroyed the careers of four Northern generals so far and, we hope, will soon destroy a fifth —Lincoln's abiding fear that some enterprising Confederate leader will take Washington. Butler wanted the seventy-five thousand troops to come from those defending Washington, so Lincoln never even considered giving them to him."

"Lincoln's probably right," said Maritza. "Stonewall Jackson might have been able to take Washington at the end of the Battle of First Manassas, if Cousin Pierre hadn't been too jealous to let him do it."

"We'll never know," said Benjamin. "I was in favor of letting Jackson try, but President Davis and the two generals—Johnston and Beauregard—were afraid."

"So a chance to win the war at the very start was lost?"

"As you just said, 'For want of a shoe.'" Benjamin shrugged. "Can I tell President Davis you will take the job?"

"I'll take it." Maritza picked up her handbag. "But I get the impression that there's a reason beyond what you are telling me. If I'm right, I would like to know what it is."

"I should have known better than not to tell you everything," Benjamin admitted with a wry smile. "My reluctance was because the real reason might sound a bit as though President Davis and myself were tooting our own horns and that's not what's involved at all. You see, we can't depend on this war's lasting much longer; Hooker might suddenly become the man of the hour in the North before the month is out by capturing Richmond. Besides, Grant is on the verge of taking

Vicksburg and a very capable general named Sherman is beginning to make a name for himself in the Southern Theater."

"You don't paint a very promising picture for the future of the Confederacy."

"I'm a realist, Countess, and so is General Lee. Jefferson Davis is too sick to be of much value to the government any more, except as a symbol of our defiance of the North—a job he does very well indeed. That means somebody has to face the facts, even if it means taking an unpopular stand, and I seem to have been elected. That's why I'm about the most disliked man in the government to some people."

"Such as?"

"John Beauchamp Jones, for one, and unfortunately you're going to have to deal with him a lot in writing your accounts. Jones is very jealous of his position as a chief clerk in the office of the Secretary of War. He was formerly the editor of a newspaper, the *Southern Monitor,* I believe, in Philadelphia. He's writing his own story of the war which you can count on to be as biased and vitriolic as Jones himself is—especially against Jews. You're going to have to call on him for access to the War Department archives but don't make the mistake of mentioning my name."

"How am I going to account for my authority, then?"

"I'll get you a letter of introduction signed by Jefferson Davis. That will take care of Jones."

"I also take it that there's some urgency about getting started on my story of the war," said Maritza. "May I ask why?"

"Do you remember last year when McClellan was so near Richmond that we had a locomotive and several cars ready, with steam up in the boiler, waiting to carry the government, the archives, and what was left in the Treasury out of the capital?"

"Yes."

"Well, there's another engine out there in the yards now, all ready to pull out for Lynchburg or Danville, if Hooker succeeds in putting Richmond under siege. When, as, or if the Confederacy falls, you can be sure Lincoln and the other politicians in the North aren't going to let the true story be published of how near the Confederacy came to winning the war with far less troops and resources than the Union. Nevertheless, both President Davis and I, along with a lot of other people in the government, think there's a strong need to keep the record of the South as something we can use to lever more concessions out of the Federal government, if we're defeated. Besides, there are future generations to think of and I'm counting on you to make the story so interesting that it will not be allowed to die out in the history books as a small engagement."

"If Richmond does fall, am I to take what I've written by then with me?"

"Absolutely. Moreover, I hope you can reach England and see that the real truth is published for all the world to know, not just some biased account such as John Beauchamp Jones is writing day by day, a lot of it so fantastic that even a Southerner would hardly believe it."

"I'd better get busy then, but the first thing I've got to do is find a house for the three of us to live in."

"Three?"

"Myself, Celestina, and André. Tina writes a beautiful hand, particularly in French. She can copy my first draft of the story as I write it. André is one of the best handymen you ever saw, too, besides being a wonderful cook."

Benjamin came around the desk to see her to the door. "I'll see that a special position is created for you as archivist, with access to any information you may need. Unfortunately there won't be much salary with the position."

"That's of no importance. I've got more than enough money on deposit in the Bank of Nova Scotia, the Bank of England, and the Banque de France."

"Were you able to bring anything with you out of New Orleans?"

"I converted everything I had on deposit in the Banque de Louisiane into gold before we left New Orleans."

"Congratulations!" said Benjamin. "Gold is getting scarcer by the minute here, so you'll be getting richer every day, merely by keeping it safely locked up somewhere."

IV

Maritza wasted no time in beginning the task Benjamin had asked her to undertake. Before she could start, however, present events began to move so rapidly that she could do little but send dispatches covering them to France practically every day.

She was fortunate in being able to rent a small furnished house in Richmond itself, near the War Department, where much of her sources would be obtained. The day after her visit to Benjamin's office a letter was delivered to her there by messenger. The stationery was that of the President of the Confederate States of America. The message itself was terse and to the point:

> Countess Maritza LeClerc is hereby appointed to the position of archivist on my personal staff. It is my wish that all members of the government and the armed forces cooperate with her to the highest degree.
>
> Jefferson Davis, President
> April 30, 1863

While Celestina and André, whose quarters were at the back of the house overlooking the small vegetable garden, were busy cleaning in the wake of some sloppy previous renters, Maritza dressed carefully and walked to the War Department and the office of the chief clerk, Mr. John Beauchamp Jones. The usual group of people were waiting in the anteroom but, when she presented the letter from Jefferson Davis, she was at once admitted to Jones's private office.

The man behind the desk, a somewhat spare and stern-looking individual of middle age, kept her waiting for more than a minute—a trick of petty bureaucrats the world over—then looked up and handed her back the letter which had been brought in to him by the clerk outside in the anteroom.

"What can I do for you, Countess?" he asked on a somewhat frosty note.

"I am writing an account of the war for a publisher in France, Mr. Jones—Monsieur Claudet, editor of *Le Pays*." Having been told Jones, himself the author of several books, was keeping a diary he no doubt expected to publish, she didn't intimate the real purpose of the assignment Judah Benjamin had given her. "Mr. William Russell of the London *Times* has also asked me to keep him posted on events over here." It wasn't quite the truth, but near enough, she hoped, to impress Jones. "Incidentally, I read your *Wild Western Scenes* when I was in school. It was fascinating."

"You speak English very well, Countess." Jones had mellowed considerably at the praise of his book about the American West, published almost twenty years earlier.

"I was born in Mobile and spent my early life there and in New Orleans," Maritza explained. "I hold American citizenship although I was married to a French nobleman, who is now deceased."

"You have my sympathy."

"Thank you, Mr. Jones. You are most kind."

"Aren't you also the author of the newspaper accounts published here about the reign of General Butler in Louisiana?"

"Yes."

"Was he really the beast you pictured him to be?"

"Worse, Mr. Jones. Besides tormenting the people of New Orleans, he and that rascal brother of his made a fortune buying cotton and sugar at distressed prices and selling high in New York and elsewhere."

"It's no more than the farmers down there deserve for selling it to them," said Jones acidly. "Trafficking with the enemy is the same as treason but that doesn't excuse Butler's actions, of course."

"We're certainly in agreement there, Mr. Jones. May I have your permission to dig into the military reports for the past two years from time to time?"

"Of course, considering the authority you brought with you," said Jones. "Besides, I'm sure we both want the world to know the truth about this cruel war thrust upon us by Yankee Abolitionists."

"Thank you, Mr. Jones."

"My wife is away but will soon return. When you're settled

in your new residence, I'm sure she would like to call upon you."

"I would love to see her, Mr. Jones." Maritza could recognize a quid pro quo when she saw one. "May I suggest a Sunday afternoon? The rest of the week I'll probably be moving from office to office gathering information."

As it happened, Maritza had no opportunity to write about the past for several weeks. On May 1, General Joseph Hooker moved seventy thousand of his estimated hundred and fifty thousand Federal troops across the Rappahannock and Rapidan rivers west of Fredericksburg and set up headquarters at a town called Chancellorsville, composed of only a few houses. Meanwhile General Lee, leaving General Jubal Early on Marye's Heights across the river from Fredericksburg to hold back many times that number of Federal troops, had moved rapidly westward to place his main force south of the Union Army under Hooker.

At a nighttime conference in the piny woods at the southern edge of what was called the Wilderness, a large forested area lying west of Fredericksburg, Lee and Jackson decided upon a daring maneuver. With twenty-six thousand men, half of the available forces, Jackson would perform a maneuver he liked best. By means of a wide flanking march—later known in history books as the "Grand Flank March"—he proposed to place his troops opposite Hooker's largely unopposed right flank.

Starting early the next morning, Jackson marched all day, reaching the Orange Turnpike, which transected the area, just before dusk. At six o'clock Jackson struck the Federal XI Corps who, quite unaware that Confederate troops were anywhere near, were busy butchering cattle and cooking steaks for their supper. Many of the Federals had no time even to unstack arms before their entire right flank was sent reeling eastward toward Chancellorsville in an utter rout.

It was then that tragedy struck. While riding through the woods in the gloom of approaching darkness attempting to locate the various units making up his force, which had been scattered in pursuit of the retreating Federal troops, Jackson and his staff were mistaken for Federal cavalry and fired upon by

Confederate soldiers. Struck in the left arm and several other places by minié balls, Jackson was borne from the field on a litter but was dropped accidentally when some firing broke out nearby, bruising and perhaps breaking his ribs. At a nearby field hospital Jackson's left arm was amputated that night at the shoulder by Dr. Hunter McGuire, his personal physician. The next morning, apparently recovering satisfactorily, he was transported by ambulance to a small house at Guiney's Station, a few miles away.

Maritza wrote her account of the Battle of Chancellorsville in Richmond, utilizing War Department reports, questions put to the walking wounded and, a few days later, to thousands of prisoners guarded by a few ragged Confederate soldiers as they marched to Libby and Belle Isle prisons. No one could question that the North had once again been dealt a body blow in this fifth major attempt to take Richmond and that still another Federal general had lost his chance to make history. A few days later, however, on May 10, any joy the South could take in still another victory in Virginia was swept away by the death of General Stonewall Jackson from pneumonia following the injury to his chest, when he'd been dropped while being carried from the battle area in the darkness.

For twenty-four hours the body lay in state in the Capitol, while thousands passed in silent tribute. Later it was taken by train to Lexington, Virginia, home of the Virginia Military Institute where Jackson had been a professor, for burial. As correspondent for *Le Pays,* Maritza accompanied the funeral train and remained in the lovely old Shenandoah Valley city of Lexington until the burial of Jackson was completed. She returned by train to Richmond the following day in order to put her dispatch covering the funeral into the mail and start its trip to Europe—where Jackson was easily the best-known general of the entire Confederate forces.

Working from the reports filed by the individual commanders available to her from the Confederate archives at the War Department, Maritza was able to reconstruct much of what had been happening that spring in the states of Tennessee,

Kentucky, and Missouri, where sentiment had been divided more or less evenly at the beginning between those supporting the Confederacy and staunch adherents of the Union. After taking New Orleans, Baton Rouge, and Natchez without much resistance to the massive guns of his naval force, Admiral Farragut had been painfully reminded of how difficult it was to capture a strongly fortified height when the Confederate guns at Vicksburg sank a number of his ironclads trying to pass the city on the river. Occupying a high bluff, largely surrounded by swamps, and heavily gunned, Vicksburg was literally a fortress, to be taken only by siege and assault.

Unfortunately for the Federal cause, too, instead of being able to concentrate on Vicksburg, its armies had been tied down by a two-pronged invasion of Kentucky by forces under the command of Confederate Generals Braxton Bragg and E. Kirby Smith. When the Confederates captured Lexington, Kentucky, there'd been a mad scramble to save Louisville and Cincinnati, Ohio, leaving few troops for use against Vicksburg at the moment.

A second Confederate offensive in northeastern Mississippi was contained by one of General Grant's commanders, Major General William Rosecrans, but both actions delayed Grant in sending a large army to surround Vicksburg and conduct a joint action with naval forces waiting north of Vicksburg on the river. And when he finally got around to making his big push against Vicksburg, he was stopped again and again by the swamps and bayous around the city.

By April 1863 thirty-two thousand Confederates were occupying the earthworks surrounding Vicksburg, a formidable force indeed but—fortunately for Grant—rapidly running out of food and other supplies. Bringing his troops down the Mississippi by boat, Grant crossed the river south of Vicksburg and put it under siege in the late spring of 1863, determined to hang on until the now starving city was taken.

Faced with the loss of Vicksburg, unless Federal forces could be diverted from the Mississippi area, Jefferson Davis and Robert E. Lee chose to make a diversion. If successful, it would create a threat to Washington that Abraham Lincoln could not ignore and lead to a frantic withdrawal of troops from other sources, the same sort of action that had stopped McClellan only twelve miles from Richmond the year before.

On the last day of June 1863, his army enlarged with all the troops he could draw from eastern Virginia, North Carolina, and surrounding areas, General Robert E. Lee started an invasion of Maryland and Pennsylvania, following much the same route he had used before the Battle of Antietam. Crossing the Blue Ridge through the low passes opposite Winchester, Virginia, he used the Shenandoah Valley and the Cumberland Valley north of the Potomac River to drive into the lush farmlands of central Pennsylvania as far as Chambersburg and Carlisle, only a few miles from the capital at Harrisburg.

Worriedly following Lee and his Confederate Army, now dangerously near the very heart of Pennsylvania with the strong possibility of by-passing Washington and taking Philadelphia and Baltimore, President Lincoln removed General Hooker and gave command of the Union forces to General George G. Meade, who promptly moved in pursuit of Lee.

The Battle of Gettysburg, scheduled to go down in the annals of military history as one of the greatest and most romantic military operations of all time, marked the deepest penetration of the North by Southern forces and, indeed, the climax of the bloody war. Fought in the low parallel ridges, open fields, and knobby hills around Gettysburg, the battle ended with Lee's retreat southward to the Potomac crossings, having lost twenty-eight thousand men to Meade's twenty-three thousand. Had Meade pursued, the Confederate Army of the Potomac could have been destroyed before it could cross the river.

Like other Union commanders before him, however, Meade delayed and on the night of July 4, Lee's men staggered and waded across the Potomac to a measure of safety on the Virginia side. That same morning, with Vicksburg strangled by the noose thrown around it by Grant and Admiral Porter, now commanding the naval forces, General Pemberton accepted Grant's terms of unconditional surrender and marched his starving troops out of the city on the Mississippi.

Grant's victory gave him full command of most Federal
forces east of the Mississippi, other than Virginia. At the same
time it earned him a new nickname, "Unconditional Surrender"
Grant. And with the defeats at Gettysburg and Vicksburg coming on the same day, the South had sustained a mortal wound
indeed, one from which it would never recover.

V

Richmond was a city in mourning, with supplies of almost everything short and often non-existent. When people started riot-
ing in the streets, breaking into the stores to seize food and
whatever else they could carry with them, the Confederate capital seemed slated for self-destruction, until a pale and wan President Jefferson Davis left the sickbed where he was now forced
to spend much of the time. Quieting the rioters more by his
presence and his obvious courage, even in pain, than by offering any solution to the lack of food, Davis still managed to end
the riot.

Writing an account of the dramatic event for transmission to
France, Maritza was not surprised when it was not passed by
the Confederate censors. Reports from the diplomatic front indicated that Commissioners John Slidell and James Mason
were now at a delicate stage of the negotiations to obtain loans
with which to buy ships and military supplies from England
and France. Coming on the heels of Stonewall Jackson's death,
the surrender of Vicksburg, and the stunning blow of Lee's defeat at Gettysburg, any apparent weakening of Southern morale
like the "bread riots" could disrupt all progress on the diplomatic front, since neither nation could have wanted to back an
obviously doomed Confederacy.

One item—obtained from reports by Richard Mann's agents
in New York—was encouraging to the depressed Confederate
government. While the people of Richmond were engaged in a
mild riot over bread, New York City was the scene of a bloody
insurrection over the enforcement of the Draft Bill passed by

the U. S. Congress on March 3 of that year but only now being
enforced. The city had long been a center of seething discontent
on the part of the two hundred thousand Irish immigrants, most
of them poor, against the Negroes pouring in in response to
Lincoln's Emancipation Proclamation, and the registration of
eligible men for conscription set off the explosion in mid-July.

During the succeeding days, mobs raced through New York,
burning, pillaging, and hanging unlucky blacks from lampposts
along Fifth Avenue. The riots raged for nearly a week, with
more than a thousand reported killed, and only ended with the
appearance of two regiments of veterans from the battle at
Gettysburg, placing the city practically under martial law. Similar but much less violent demonstrations also occurred in Boston and even as far north as Portsmouth, New Hampshire—all
of which Maritza reported to Paris without any difficulty from
the Confederate censors.

Meanwhile General Lee managed to lead his battered and
weary remnant of an army safely across the Potomac, even
though General Meade waited with a considerably larger army
to the east toward Frederick, Maryland, and Washington.
Slowly, harassed by cavalry raids and small skirmishes, the
Confederate Army of the Potomac escaped destruction and returned to its old haunts in central Virginia east of the Blue
Ridge, but trains poured into Richmond daily carrying
wounded to the hospitals.

The rest of the year 1863 was marked by sporadic scenes of
fighting, but none of major importance except the campaign in
eastern Tennessee. There a Federal battering ram, commanded
first by General Rosecrans and later by Generals Sherman and
Thomas, was aimed at Chattanooga, a key point in the area.
Impressed by Grant's victory at Vicksburg, Lincoln appointed
him commander on October 16, 1863, of practically all Union
armies operating east of the Mississippi and south of Virginia.

The Battle of Chickamauga, fought just south of Chattanooga had ended with a Federal army retreating to that city,
where they were practically encircled by Confederates. Hurry-
ing to Chattanooga, Grant supervised the opening of a supply
line to the beleaguered Federal troops, then sent an assault

force under Sherman against Confederate forces heavily entrenched on Missionary Ridge just east of the Tennessee city. When the Federals charged straight over the ridge to take it and Chattanooga, too, Confederate forces had to drop back into Georgia. The road to Atlanta lay before General Sherman, although he would be many months reaching the Georgia capital, the most important Confederate center south of Richmond.

Writing her dispatches covering the continuing action for French readers, and recreating between times the story of those first two glorious years of Confederate history from her own memory, the Army reports, and newspaper accounts, Maritza was fully occupied that fall and winter. The recurring illnesses of President Jefferson Davis left much of what might be called legwork in the government to Judah Benjamin. As the right hand of the Confederate Secretary of State, Richard Mann was almost constantly on the go too. When he was in Richmond he and Maritza usually dined quietly at the little house she had rented, sometimes on catfish André caught in the James River, with "hush puppies"—balls of corn meal, egg, and onion dropped into deep fat and fried until crisp. Occasionally Mann would bring back a few bottles of wine bought from Marylanders who nightly crossed the Potomac in small boats with goods stolen from Federal supplies. The four of them would enjoy the wine, but all too often Mann's visits were for no more than one or two days. Farewells were tender, for Maritza never knew when the next news about him would be the announcement of his death in action or from the guns of a Northern firing squad.

Occasionally she received an accounting, mailed from Wilmington by Penn Darrow, of monies deposited to her account in Halifax. Richmond newspapers regularly carried lists of the blockade runners arriving at Wilmington and the *Sprite* was mentioned more often than any of the others, showing that Penn Darrow had lost none of his skill and daring in running the Federal blockade. Occasionally, too, Maritza would receive a note from him accompanying the deposit receipts, but he was obviously too busy ferrying cotton from Wilmington to Nova

Scotia, and bringing supplies and weapons back in return, to take time for writing.

With the intense military activity of Vicksburg, Gettysburg, and Chattanooga—plus the presidential campaign now getting under way with General George McClellan running on the Democratic ticket in opposition to Abraham Lincoln—occupying the attention of both sides, one event went almost unnoticed, the landing of a French army at Vera Cruz in June 1863. The unannounced, but nevertheless thoroughly planned, intention of Napoleon III to turn Mexico into a colony of France had now become a fact.

Neither the North nor the South, however, could do much about this French invasion of the North American continent. Nor did either try, except for an abortive expedition to Sabine Pass, Texas, by General Banks to guard the Louisiana border against any attempt fostered by Napoleon III to turn Texas into a republic closely supporting his Mexican dream. The South, having invited France to intervene almost from the beginning, could certainly not object. Lincoln was very much against this bold breach of the Monroe Doctrine represented by the presence of French troops and, it was rumored, the arrival soon of a European-born ruler in Mexico, but he could hardly fight France and the Confederacy at the same time.

At the start of 1864 Union forces totaled six hundred and eighty-three thousand, while the Confederate armies were down to a mere hundred and ninety-five thousand. Both forces were now largely armed with a new rifled musket, the Springfield .58. Though still loaded from the muzzle, the weapon was accurate for massed intensive fire at five hundred yards, making it a murderous instrument of war against the massed charges of infantry in vogue during combat between the now vastly unequal forces.

In March 1864, General Ulysses S. Grant was placed in command of all Federal forces. Meade's Army of the Potomac numbered a hundred and nineteen thousand strong and faced Lee's sixty-four thousand in Virginia. Sherman's Military Division of the Mississippi pitted ninety-nine thousand against sixty thousand commanded by the veteran General Joseph E. Johnston. Small Federal units also faced still smaller Confederate forces on the Red River in Arkansas, at Fortress Monroe in Virginia, and in the Shenandoah Valley.

In May 1864, Sherman started southward toward Atlanta, while Grant and Meade chose to penetrate the Wilderness once more, hoping to drive Lee back toward Richmond. In four Virginia battles during the spring, at Wilderness, Spotsylvania, North Anna, and Cold Harbor, Grant did manage to drive Lee steadily southward but with terrible losses. Fifty-five thousand men, seven thousand of them in one terrible day at Cold Harbor, was the casualty total that summer for the North.

While Union newspapers screamed for Grant's removal because of the casualty toll and McClellan used it to condemn Lincoln during the presidential campaign, Grant managed to surprise Lee by swinging around east of Richmond by way of White House, where McClellan had been stopped two years earlier. Crossing the James on pontoon bridges, he attacked Petersburg by June 15, cutting the main rail line between Richmond and the South, and placing the Confederate capital virtually under siege except for a single railway track leading westward toward Lynchburg.

Restless at Richmond, and with Richard Mann away, Maritza took a train for Lexington when it was rumored that the cadets from V.M.I. were being pressed into service by Confederate General Breckinridge to help stop Federal forces under General Sigel sweeping southward through the Shenandoah Valley. Writing practically from the battlefield, she chronicled the saga of the two hundred and forty-seven cadets who fought like veterans at New Market on May 15, stopping Sigel with a loss of only ten cadets.

A few days later Maritza boarded a transport on the James River Canal near Lexington along with the young soldiers. Placidly they floated through lock after lock as the canal descended while traversing the Blue Ridge passage of the river, arriving at Richmond to reap glowing applause. Her descriptions of the New Market victory earned plaudits for her from fellow reporters throughout the South, as did another feat. Hiring a horse and riding furiously the twenty-odd miles between Richmond and Petersburg, she managed to reach the smaller city shortly after Federal troops exploded a powerful mine beneath part of the earthworks defending Petersburg, leaving a giant crater through which they planned to pour, seizing the town.

Maritza's description of the abortive Federal attack following the explosion, when over four thousand blue-clad soldiers died in the depths of the bomb crater, while the Confederate defenders on the rim poured a deadly fire into their ranks, earned her further plaudits. In fact, by now she had become almost the female counterpart of William Russell.

Maritza was barely back from Petersburg when news began to pour into Richmond of a fantastic feat by Confederate General Jubal Early with about ten thousand troops in the Shenandoah Valley. When Federal General David Hunter, now commanding the forces in the Shenandoah Valley area that had taken part in the Battle of New Market against the V.M.I. cadets and others, threatened the rail and supply center of Lynchburg, Early moved swiftly. With the gallant V.M.I. cadets again part of a fighting force, he drove Hunter back into West Virginia and, to his surprise, found himself on the Valley Turnpike with no major Federal forces opposing him.

Moving rapidly northward, still with only about ten thousand men, Early crossed the Potomac and raced eastward toward Washington, to the utter consternation of Abraham Lincoln and the rest of the capital's inhabitants. A one-day battle with some six thousand Federal troops under General Lew Wallace slowed Early long enough for Lincoln to send Grant at Petersburg a frantic message for help in protecting Washington. Embarked at City Point on the James River near Petersburg, the Federal troops sent by Grant made a quick voyage to Washington by boat, arriving to find Early in the suburbs busy causing a panic in both Baltimore and the capital, as well as crippling Lincoln's desperate political campaign against General McClellan, who was trumpeting that the war was a failure and should be ended.

Unfortunately for the South, Early did not have enough

strength to remain and deal a body blow to Washington. Instead, he was forced to begin the long retreat back to the Shenandoah Valley, seeking safety in Stonewall Jackson's old haunts near Elk Run Valley and Staunton. Meanwhile, Grant detached General Philip Sheridan with forty-eight thousand men to chase and destroy Early, an operation that, in spite of the considerable difference in numbers in favor of the Union, took almost the rest of 1864.

In spite of Confederate successes at New Market, the daring race northward to the very edge of Washington by Early, and the tragic effects for the Union troops besieging Petersburg, when the mine they exploded under the fortifications turned out to be more of a trap for them than an actual danger to the Confederates in that city, Maritza could see the end steadily approaching in reports from the South.

Following the dramatic Union victory at Missionary Ridge, Sherman had started fighting his way steadily southeastward from Chattanooga toward Atlanta, finally taking that city on September 2 after considerable losses. On November 12 he set fire to the Georgia capital before starting to cut a fifty-mile-wide swath through the very heart of Georgia, destroying almost everything in his path by burning and pillaging in a maneuver more reminiscent of the tactics of Attila the Hun than of modern warfare.

Several weeks before the burning of Atlanta, Richard Mann seemed to disappear from the face of the earth and no one appeared to know where he was, or would tell Maritza, whose anxiety for his safety increased daily. Oddly enough, she finally did learn what he was about from a totally unexpected source on November 27 in a copy of the New York *Tribune,* which she bought regularly at a newsstand that sold Yankee newspapers only a few days after their printing in New York. The black headline was spread across the page:

REBEL AGENTS TRY TO BURN NEW YORK. ATTEMPT FOILED BY PROMPT FIRE DEPARTMENT ACTION.

On November 25, two days earlier—according to the story that followed—a group of about two dozen Confederate secret

agents had slipped undiscovered into New York. In their baggage they had managed to bring in a large supply of the chemicals used to produce Greek fire. Registered in hotels all over
the city, they waited for the night decided upon for the daring
attempt, then mixed the chemicals to start fires aimed at destroying the very heart of the city, including Barnum's famous
museum, which was open in the evening. Only prompt action
by the regular and auxiliary fire departments called in from the
farthest environs of the city's suburbs had kept the many small
conflagrations from spreading to engulf the entire heart of New
York. Everything, it was now reported, was under control,
however, with several of the perpetrators captured by the police.

Reading the account and noticing particularly the mention of
Greek fire, Maritza remembered the time Mann had taken her
to a theater in Montgomery, where a magician had apparently
created fire out of thin air. He had mentioned then having studied how to use the so-called Greek fire at West Point and she
did not doubt for a moment that he was involved deeply in this
particular attempt to damage the confidence of New York inhabitants in the Union, usually at a lower point than in any
other major city north of the Potomac.

Farther down on the page a brief mention appeared of a
large seaborne expedition being fitted out at Fortress Monroe
and Norfolk. Its announced intention was to silence the guns of
Fort Fisher, closing the port of Wilmington, North Carolina,
and the last haven for Confederate blockade runners such as
the *Sprite*.

VI

"You knew Richard was leading that attempt to burn New
York City," Maritza accused Judah Benjamin when she saw
him later that day at the War Department.

"I plead guilty to the accusation, Countess, but Richard
made me promise not to tell you."

"Why?"

"You're sometimes a rather impulsive young lady," said Benjamin. "Maybe Richard figured you'd go riding off to the rescue if you knew what was going on."

"The least he could have done was to take me with him," Maritza complained. "'I tried to burn New York' would make a wonderful headline for the newspaper."

"You're quite famous enough, my dear. I'm sure our friend William Russell has repented more than once having left Washington and asking you to report on special events to the London *Times* in his stead."

Maritza smiled. "Russell would never admit it if he has. Is there any hope yet that Uncle John Slidell or Mr. Mason will be able to float a loan abroad to continue the war?"

Benjamin shook his head sadly. "Our only real hope was for General McClellan to win the presidential election on an 'End the War' platform. Unfortunately Sherman torpedoed that possibility when he burned Atlanta and started eastward for Savannah, destroying everything in his path."

"I hear General Sherman has sworn to be in Savannah by Christmas."

"He'll probably get there. War suddenly loses all its glamor when it involves burning cities like Atlanta and destroying the property of civilians. By the way, how far have you gotten with your story?"

"I've almost caught up, just as the fighting seems to be winding down to the end. What worries me now is whether Richard got away from New York safely after he and his agents set the fires."

"I can reassure you there," said Benjamin. "A telegram this morning said most of the others escaped by train into Canada after they set the fires."

"How will Richard get back from there?"

"Our Copperhead friends west of the Mississippi will help him and his team of agents escape southward; you can count on that. Also, General Jo Shelby and General Kirby Smith's forces are still pretty well intact in the Trans-Mississippi area. By the way, have you seen Captain Pennington Darrow?"

"No. Is he in Richmond?"

"The *Sprite* landed in Wilmington yesterday but it doesn't look as if the Cape Fear mouth can be kept open much longer. Admiral Porter and your old friend Beast Butler are organizing a seaborne invasion at Fortress Monroe and Norfolk to take Fort Fisher and Wilmington."

"I just read that in the New York *Tribune,*" said Maritza. "How long have you known about it?"

"Almost a week."

"Penn Darrow shouldn't be coming to Richmond then. He needs to be taking the *Sprite* to sea where she'll be safe."

"I think he intends to do just that, but not before he talks to you."

"About what?"

"Let him do it his way. All of us owe him that much for the yeoman job he's done of running the blockade again and again with munitions, when a single shell amidships could have blown him and his crew to kingdom come."

Maritza didn't have to wait very long to see Penn Darrow. He was sitting in the parlor of her small house when she arrived after visiting Benjamin's office. Boots off, and with his feet propped upon a footstool in front of the fireplace, Darrow was holding a glass of whiskey in his hand from which came the distinctive aroma of mint, though how André had managed to find enough to make a julep Maritza couldn't understand.

An obviously admiring Celestina stood ready to tend to Darrow's every need and from the kitchen came the aroma of one of André's finest dishes, slabs of Virginia ham broiled in a skillet, while biscuits were waiting to be put in the oven where a baking dish of *pommes de terre lyonnaise* already rested.

Darrow looked just as handsome as he had the day they had first auctioned the munitions on the deck of the old *Pride of Bristol* in Mobile Bay—and just as sure of himself. He leaped to his feet as Maritza came up to the fireplace to warm herself after the cold walk from Benjamin's office, startling her by taking her in his arms and kissing her thoroughly before she could protest. For a moment she felt her body respond to the purely masculine allure of his own, as she'd experienced it on more than one occasion years before. Then she gently pushed him away, lest her own reaction to his presence betray her.

"I didn't expect you so soon," she told him as she removed the bonnet she had worn against the cold breeze from the river and, quite unconsciously, patted her hair back in place before a mirror.

"How did you know I was coming?"

"Judah Benjamin told me the *Sprite* landed yesterday at Wilmington and you'd soon be coming to Richmond. With an invasion fleet preparing to sail against Wilmington and Fort Fisher, it would seem more appropriate for you to be down there getting the *Sprite* ready to go to sea where she'll be safe."

"My crew is busy making those preparations, but I couldn't leave without bringing you a personal invitation to be aboard. After all, we *are* partners."

"Why would I want to go back to Halifax when you let me freeze there through almost an entire winter?" Pulling a Boston rocker up before the fire and kicking off her shoes, Maritza put her small feet beside his considerably larger ones before accepting the julep Tina handed her.

"This time the *Sprite*'s destination won't be Halifax. When we leave Wilmington for the last time we'll be heading for a new land."

Maritza stared at him incredulously. "Don't tell me *you're* running from Beast Butler."

"Not Butler but a very smart admiral named Porter, said to be amassing a flotilla of some sixty warships to bombard the entrance to Cape Fear and Wilmington. He's already proved he knows how to do it on the Mississippi."

"Would you be able to get in and out of the port any more if they destroyed Fort Fisher?"

"Not a chance," said Penn Darrow. "Once the Federal fleet controls Fort Fisher, they'll steam upriver and take Wilmington itself without any difficulty. Cutting the main rail connection between the Confederacy and the outside world will be a catastrophe almost as bad as losing the Battle of Gettysburg."

"I take it you're leaving then?"

"As soon as we can get ready."

"I thought you were one who believed in taking chances to win your objectives," she said a little acidly.

"That's why I'm here." Penn Darrow's voice was sober now. "I came to give you a chance to leave the South before your plantation and everything else you own is destroyed."

"Don't tell me you're going to France—or England?"

"No. Either country would intern us and the *Sprite* for what's left of the war. Actually, that couldn't be much longer but what I'm offering is a lot better than internment."

"Stop talking riddles, then."

"There speaks the Maritza who risked a fortune on a load of munitions for the *Pride of Bristol*," he said approvingly. "A group of Southerners hardheaded enough to see the handwriting on the wall, something those here in Richmond don't seem to be able to do, are taking measures to protect themselves. The re-election of Abraham Lincoln, plus closing the port of Wilmington, is going to sound the death knell of the Confederacy. This group plans to buy the *Sprite* from the Confederate government; in fact they've just about finished making arrangements."

Startled, Maritza asked, "If blockade running won't be profitable any longer, why would they do that?"

"The government of Brazil has offered large tracts of land where they can grow cotton to Southerners wishing to leave before the debacle ends. The price of land in that part of Brazil is so low that they're practically giving it away as an inducement to build up a flourishing cotton industry there."

"Brazil's a big country," said Maritza doubtfully.

"The best land for cotton appears to be not far from São Paulo. One of Brazil's largest cities, it's surrounded by some rich agricultural country that should be ideal for growing cotton, corn, and the other things Southerners have been producing since America was established. It's an ideal spot to start another Southland, where the Yankees won't be in control and we Southerners can go our way in peace."

It was an intriguing prospect. Remembering the wide sections of the South through which she had traveled on the way from New Orleans to Richmond, once fertile and rich with cot-

ton and other crops but now wasted and weed-grown, Maritza
felt a strong attraction for what Darrow was offering. Besides,
now that General Sherman had added a new and horrendous
dimension to warfare by the swath of utter destruction he had
cut through Georgia's heartland, no one could tell how many
more thousands of acres in the South would be similarly destroyed.

"How about it?" Penn Darrow inquired.

"You make it sound attractive," she admitted.

"Then why wait? With luck, the *Sprite* will sail day after tomorrow before Porter and Butler can launch their attack on
Fort Fisher."

"My capital is tied up in Nova Scotia, London, and Paris."

"Not any more," he assured her. "Before I left Halifax, I
persuaded the manager of the Bank of Nova Scotia that, since
we were partners, he could issue a gold certificate for your
share made out to you and let me bring it to you." From his
wallet he took an impressive-looking piece of paper. "It's worth
a fortune and the National Bank of Brazil in São Paulo will be
happy to cash it for you in gold."

"Dinner is served," André announced proudly from the door
of the small dining room at just that moment, and Maritza got
to her feet.

"We can talk about it at dinner," she said. "Are you carrying
a load of cotton to Brazil?"

"No," he told her. "This time we'll be carrying only people
and cotton seed for the new crop."

VII

The delicious meal was topped off with small glasses of a
French brandy Penn Darrow had brought from Halifax as a
Christmas gift. While Tina and André cleared the table and
washed the dishes, Maritza and Darrow returned to the parlor
and made themselves comfortable before the fire that was burning briskly from a log André had put on.

"How large a plantation are you going to buy in South America?" Maritza asked Darrow as she sipped the fragrant liqueur.

"Not any."

"Why?" she asked, startled.

"I've been a lumberman and seaman all my life and there'll be fortunes to be made in both fields in a new and growing land like Brazil. Did you know that it's as large as—perhaps even larger than—the whole United States?"

"Lately my studies in geography have been mostly limited to the eastern United States."

"Once the war ends and the country starts to recover, there'll be a wide field for fast packet ships like the *Sprite* carrying passengers and mail back and forth across the oceans, as well as fleets of large merchant ships hauling lumber and other things Europe needs," he said confidently. "We've already got the capital between us to start such a merchant and shipping empire and, before long, we could be to the oceans what the Vanderbilts and the Goulds already are to the railroads. We'll summer at Saratoga and winter at St. Augustine, stopping off at Pinehurst for spring and fall. You'll love it, and of course we'll go to Europe after a few years for the grand tour."

"I've already made the grand tour, Penn."

He gave her a startled look and she realized it had never even occurred to him that the entrancing picture he was painting could possibly fail to be what she would want.

"But—"

She touched his lips gently with her index finger, silencing his protests. "Dear, dear Penn. Why would any woman fail to want what you're offering her? To say nothing of your handsome self as a bonus?"

"I'm damned if I know," he exploded. "You certainly wanted something like that when we met in London almost four years ago."

"I did—or thought I did," she admitted. "Especially when a very romantic, exciting, and handsome sea captain named Pennington Darrow went with the whole package."

"Then—"

"A lot has changed since. For one thing, I'm four years older."

"So am I, but that hasn't made any difference in what I want out of life."

"Don't let what you want ever change, Penn. You're one of the few men I know who are fully equipped to enjoy this glittering world you've obviously been dreaming about. The past four years for you has been a time of excitement, putting yourself and that beautiful *Sprite* against what looked each time like insuperable odds—and winning."

"*You've* been successful too," he reminded her. "Your name is just as well known in today's newspaper world as William Russell—and that's saying a lot."

"More than I deserve. Much of what I've accomplished has been because opportunities just seemed to fall in my lap, which may be why they've lost their allure. I've crossed and recrossed the South these past three and a half years and seen the land laid waste, but the spirit of the people has gone on burning as brightly as it did before. Their spirit and their pride in the land and its beauty are something men like General Sherman may have been able to dampen for a little while but certainly could never destroy."

"When the Union wins, Abraham Lincoln is going to give the land to the slaves to do with what they wish."

"Then I'll cash this gold certificate and what I have invested in London and Paris to buy back my plantation and Richard Mann's property that lies beside mine. A spirit that's carried the Southern people through a war with the odds so long against them isn't going to die when their armies are finally forced to surrender. While you and those who go to South America with you are starting new lives for yourselves in a new land, we back here will be starting anew in the old one."

"But you'll have nothing—"

"We'll have as much as our ancestors did when they settled here in the first place."

"Aren't you forgetting that it took generations to get where the South was when your cousin Pierre Beauregard fired the first gun at Fort Sumter?"

"I'm not forgetting, Penn. And I'm perfectly aware that it'll take more generations than mine, and even more dedication and spirit than it did for our forefathers, to restore the land to what it was before. We can still do it, though, and that in spite of the Beast Butlers, the Shermans, and even the Bulldog Grants. America wouldn't have been whole without the South; that's why the war really had to be fought. Whatever his faults, Abraham Lincoln understood that perhaps even better than Jefferson Davis. And, I'm sure the part Southerner from Tennessee named Andrew Johnson who's Vice-President of the Union understands it too."

He studied her for a moment, then shook his head gently but admiringly. "I can't help believing you're making a terrible mistake, Maritza. But damned if I don't admire you more for your decision than I admire myself right now for what, until less than an hour ago, I thought was an excellent one."

"It's still a good one—for you." She leaned over to kiss him lightly on the lips, a kiss which he understood meant farewell. "But I'm afraid it comes almost four years too late—for me."

He looked up at the clock on the mantel. "My train leaves for Wilmington in less than an hour and we've got only a few days before that Federal armada will be appearing off Cape Hatteras on the way to the mouth of Cape Fear. I'd better be going, if I'm going at all."

"I shall pray that you find everything you've dreamed about in Brazil, Penn," she told him in parting. "You've risked your life more than enough times running the blockade to deserve all that and more. Good-by."

When the door closed after him Maritza turned and stood for a long moment with her back to it. She didn't doubt that she had made the only choice her conscience would let her make. Yet, somewhere deep in her soul, a small adventurous part of her couldn't help regretting the decision and feeling a little sad at letting him go.

"I guess you know you've just sent a man away who could have made you happy," Tina's accusing voice broke the silence in the room.

"Happy while I was in his arms, I'm sure, Tina. Perhaps

happier than I could be with any other man I know or ever will know. Now more than ever before, the South is going to need leaders both white and black, and the job of conceiving them, bearing them, and rearing them to manhood and to womanhood is going to be more important for both of us than any other destiny we could hope to have."

"You'd better get started soon, then," said Tina. "I'm already a couple of months ahead of you."

VIII

On December 21, with the prospect for Christmas never more bleak in the history of the states still making up an almost moribund Confederacy, General Sherman captured Savannah. Sparing the beautiful old city established by Lord Oglethorpe on the banks of the Savannah River, the Union Army headed northeast for Columbia, the capital of South Carolina.

Ahead of Sherman, with an occasional pause for a brief skirmish that slowed but did not stop the Union juggernaut, General Joe Johnston's steadily weakening forces retreated. A ragged and weary group of men, they had lost all hope of keeping Sherman from joining Grant at a slowly starving Petersburg, although they could still slow him occasionally by brief skirmishes.

On Christmas Day, 1864, ragged, limping, bearded, and saddlesore, Richard Mann knocked on the door of Maritza's small house in Richmond. Tina opened it and shouted for Maritza, who came running downstairs to seize him in her arms, grime, nettles, and all, weeping in her happiness and scraping her soft cheeks against his rough beard as she kissed him over and over. Only when she released him did he see the plump, smiling, bearded man who was their Christmas dinner guest and greet Judah P. Benjamin, as the Confederate statesman came forward to grip his hand and murmur a prayer of thanksgiving in Hebrew.

While André took Richard Mann upstairs for a bath and lent

him a razor to shave off the accumulation of several days' stubble, Maritza and Tina bustled around, resetting the table for three. They also poured another julep, for which André had performed his usual magic in finding the ingredients, for the unexpected guest. When Mann came back downstairs half an hour later André had also brushed his uniform, improving his appearance considerably.

"Thank God you're back safely, Dick," said Benjamin, handing him the julep as Maritza came in from the dining room to join them.

"Let's drink to that and your never being away again, Richard," she said.

"You'll have no objection from me," said Mann as they touched glasses. "I rode all the way from Farmville since midnight so I could get here for Christmas."

"Did you see any of Sheridan's cavalry along the way?" Judah Benjamin asked. "Rumors have been pouring in that he's heading east to join Grant, after smashing the remainder of Jubal Early's forces in the Shenandoah Valley."

"I came through Lynchburg, with the idea of planning a route of escape for the government, if Sherman succeeds in joining Grant at Petersburg," said Mann. "Is President Davis still planning to make Charlotte the site of government if Richmond falls?"

"With Sherman apparently headed for Columbia, South Carolina, I'm afraid it will have to be farther from Richmond than Charlotte," said Benjamin. "Some people are saying Columbus, Georgia, would be the best—with somewhere in the Trans-Mississippi area, maybe even Texas, second best."

"We've got to give up one day," said Maritza. "Why not tomorrow?"

"Admittedly, the Confederacy is down," said Benjamin, "but it's not quite ready to be counted out yet."

"How did you get away from New York?" Maritza asked Mann.

"It was surprisingly easy. The New York authorities had been warned that we would try the burning; it's no secret that the Union has agents within our spy rings just as we have agents among theirs. After Sherman burned Atlanta on November 14 and 15, I guess nobody in New York figured we would try to burn the city ten days later. What they didn't know was that we were already on the way. Once we got the fires going, so much confusion was created that most of us made it to the railroad station and caught a train to Albany as we had planned."

"If you'd let me know what you were up to, I would have gone along," Maritza said.

"That's why I didn't," he assured her. "Looking back on it, I guess the whole attempt was foolhardy at that, but most of those making up the group were like me. We hadn't seen much real action during the war, so we jumped at the chance to play the hero."

"You're heroes, even if your mission did fail," Benjamin assured him. "Just having the courage to go through with it has earned you that commendation."

"If you could have been waiting with us for hours in that railroad station at Albany, until a train came that we could take to Canada, you might not have felt so heroic," Mann conceded wryly. "Newsboys were all around us shouting about the attempt to burn New York and the pursuit of the spies who carried it out. Sitting there, never knowing exactly when a heavy Pinkerton hand would land on your shoulder, wasn't exactly conducive to feeling very heroic."

"After you got to Canada," said Maritza, "how did you find your way back home?"

"Enough Confederate sympathizers are located throughout Illinois, Indiana, and Ohio that as recently as only a few months ago Captain Thomas Hines was almost able to marshal a hundred thousand men to strike out for the Confederacy in a rebellion against Abraham Lincoln and the Union. We had lists of sympathizers all along the way and they passed us from one town to another. Most of us were able to work our way eastward through the southern part of West Virginia where sentiment for the Union never has been very strong anyway." Mann turned to Benjamin. "Is the situation around Richmond and Petersburg really as bad as we heard it was out in Ohio?"

"Worse," said Benjamin.

"What about foreign intervention?"

"All hope we had of help from France ended last April, when Maximilian of Hapsburg landed at Vera Cruz to become Emperor of Mexico. Of course it's in name only, with Napoleon III the real ruler, but Benito Juárez is fighting the French troops effectively all the way. If Maximilian lasts a year on that throne in Mexico City it's going to be a miracle."

"Is England supporting France in this attempt?"

"Earl Russell is keeping hands off, both in Mexico and the Confederacy. Unfortunately we lost our best friend in London when Prince Albert died and I guess Russell figures the Confederacy and France are both in the process of destroying themselves, so all England has to do is wait and pick up the pieces."

"Dinner is served," André announced, and they went in to another of his *exploits de cuisine*.

When dinner was over Benjamin pleaded the need to do some work and departed, as did André and Celestina to their own quarters, leaving Richard Mann and Maritza alone.

"Penn Darrow was here about a week ago," Maritza told him.

"I read in a Lynchburg paper that the *Sprite* had evaded the invasion fleet that's trying to take Wilmington right now. Darrow will never get back into the Cape Fear and Wilmington again, though."

"He doesn't plan to. A group of rich Southerners bought the ship and have employed him to take them to South America."

"Brazil! I was approached some time ago by friends who are part of that scheme."

"What did you think of it?"

"For those willing to leave the South, it makes sense. The war can only end one way, with Sherman burning his way through the Carolinas as he did across Georgia. By leaving when they did, Darrow's passengers will be able to get a cotton crop growing this year in an area where labor is perhaps even cheaper than maintaining slaves. The price is certain to be good, too, because cotton has become scarce in London, without any blockade runners to speak of getting through."

"Penn wanted me to go with him—as his wife."

"The paper I saw on a newsstand, as I rode into Richmond this morning, said the Federal invasion fleet off Fort Fisher is being withdrawn because General Butler failed to carry out the land operation according to plan. There might still be time for you to hire a boat and join the *Sprite* at Havana."

"I refused to marry him, Richard. Don't you understand what I'm telling you?"

"I understand and, if I can be sure you know just what you're giving up, marrying you will make me the happiest man in the world."

"The girl you met on the deck of the old *Pride of Bristol* nearly four years ago, when you came to bid on a shipload of munitions, would probably have married Penn Darrow when he was here and be on the way right now to Brazil."

"I've been afraid of that ever since," he confessed.

"I'm not that girl any longer, Richard. I'm a woman with roots in the land my father and my mother lived on back in Alabama and Louisiana. I want our children to grow up in that land in the South—not the Confederacy but the southern part of a United States that has been joined together once more. We're going to have to rebuild down there but I want it to be together —if you want me."

"If I want you!" His arms about her and his lips crushing hers were an answer beyond words. "I've wanted you every minute since you stepped out on the deck of the *Pride of Bristol*. We'll not only rebuild, when the fighting's over, but we'll create something better than we ever had before."

IX

Maritza and Richard Mann were married quietly on January 1, 1865, in the pastor's study of St. Paul's Episcopal Church, with the distant mutter of the guns at Petersburg the only music. It was the same church where President Jefferson Davis and many highly placed members of the Confederate government worshiped. The only witnesses to the vows were Judah P. Benjamin, Celestina, and André. The wedding supper was hosted by Benjamin at the Spotswood Hotel.

There was no time for a honeymoon. In fact, with men in ragged and fading gray—as well as blue—dying daily, often by the hundreds, hardly more than twenty miles away at Petersburg, neither bride nor groom wished for one. Richard Mann's clothing and military equipment were moved that afternoon by André into the small house in Richmond from the boardinghouse where he had been living on his infrequent brief stays in Richmond.

For the beleaguered Confederacy, events were moving with appalling swiftness as the war wound down to the inevitable end. On January 15, Fort Fisher fell, closing the port of Wilmington, last refuge of the blockade runners. The city itself, located some twenty miles upriver, was captured by Federal troops a few days later.

On February 6, General Robert E. Lee—who had once refused the appointment of general-in-chief of the Union armies in order to serve Virginia—was finally given the post he should have had the day after Beauregard captured Fort Sumter, general-in-chief of the Confederacy. Unfortunately the appointment came much too late, with Grant steadily closing a ring of steel around Petersburg and Sherman burning a fiery path through South Carolina.

Meanwhile, political negotiations designed to end the war before the South suffered the humiliation of utter defeat were going on with frantic haste. On January 29, Vice-President Stephens, Senator R. M. T. Hunter, and James A. Campbell, Assistant Secretary of War for the Confederacy, but formerly a member of the Supreme Court of the United States, headed for Washington.

The refusal of Lincoln to recognize Napoleon III's puppet government in Mexico under Maximilian had brought a brief spate of hope that France would take offense and join with the South against the North. But with a motley bunch of guerrilla fighters led by Benito Juárez now threatening the entire French attempt at building an empire on the American continent, nobody with any grasp of international relations could take that possibility seriously. When the "commissioners" returned from Washington with news that Lincoln was even more adamant than before that only one government could exist within the territorial outlines of the United States, all hopes of staving off defeat vanished.

Working daily to bring her story of the war up to date, winnowing the wheat of truth from the chaff of rumors, Maritza saw Richard Mann only occasionally. Sheridan was moving southeastward from Charlottesville, which he had captured easily on March 3, obviously aiming to join Grant in the final push on Petersburg that would shut off any escape from Richmond by the high officials of the Confederate government.

Early March found Sherman and his army in the Carolina sand hills between Columbia and Raleigh, his whereabouts revealed only when pillars of smoke suddenly began billowing up over the countryside. Late in March, Sherman turned up at Goldsboro, North Carolina, southeast of Raleigh, and within easy distance of the capital of the state. That same day, dusty and tired, Richard Mann rode into Richmond and dismounted to hand the reins of his horse to André at the hitching post before the house.

"Is Mrs. Mann at home, André," he asked, "or at the War Department?"

"She's at home, sir. Just came in a few minutes ago."

Maritza was in the living room and came forward eagerly to kiss him. "You've been gone nearly a week," she complained. "What sort of a way is that to treat a bride of three months?"

"Blame General Sherman, darling. I've been busy trying to figure out which way he'll go next."

"The papers say he's at Goldsboro. Is General Johnston anywhere near?"

"Near enough to slow the Federals a little but not strong enough to stop them. Not many crops will be planted in eastern Carolina this spring."

"What a pity—with so many going hungry, in uniform and out."

"How soon can you three be ready to start south?" he asked.

"Are we all going home?" It was more a cry of joy than a question.

"Not all, I'm afraid. Only you, Celestina, and André."

"Leaving you here to the end?"

"That's my job—to guard the members of the Cabinet and the President, until the government is located somewhere safer than Richmond."

"Where could that possibly be?"

"Texas, probably. If Sherman turns west and takes Raleigh, Durham, and Greensboro, all access by rail to the deep South will be cut off any day now. Right now, you three should have a good chance to make it home to Alabama, if you leave right away. I've already arranged to get you a special military pass for use on the railroad."

"I'm not going without you," said Maritza firmly.

"I could be shot at sunrise for deserting if I left now."

"Didn't you hear how General Johnston's troops have been deserting by the hundreds as he retreated through the Carolinas?"

"That's common knowledge, but I'm an officer. Moreover, I'm charged with guarding the safety of one man."

"The President?"

"No. Davis has a guard of his own but he's in poor health and could probably never stand the hardships of trying to escape anyway. If Judah Benjamin wasn't a Jew, he could have been President of the Confederacy a long time ago, but he's still its brains. My job is to guard him."

"Then so is mine and don't try to talk me out of staying behind," said Maritza firmly. "When you leave, I leave with you, but not before."

He gave her a long probing look, then smiled and leaned down to kiss her. "I suppose I already knew you'd say that. Be sure and keep everything ready to leave at once; when the time comes, we'll go by train. Guard that manuscript you've been working on, too. Benjamin said you wouldn't leave ahead of us and told me to tell you to hang onto that story with all your might. The South may lose the war but the world is going to know we couldn't be conquered."

"They'll know it," she promised. "I'm going to keep on writing that story to the bitter end."

"Listen carefully, then," he told her. "General Lee has been quietly making preparations for a retreat westward toward Danville, if Grant succeeds in breaking the ring he's been welding around Petersburg. Lee will be trying to join up with General Johnston somewhere in North Carolina but, when the retreat starts, the government must get out of Richmond fast, so a train will be waiting with steam up. If I can't reach you, I'll manage to send word ahead of time. Even if I don't, get to the train with Celestina and André and stay on it. I'll join you somewhere along the way."

"Celestina's almost five months' pregnant," Maritza protested.

"I've already talked to André and advised him that they might be better off staying here even after the Federals take over Richmond. He says they'd rather go to our plantations in Alabama, so I've given him the necessary military passes and tickets, just as you will have."

"What about Secretary Benjamin?"

"You and he will be together. Stay with him and I'll find you somewhere along the way."

"Do you have any idea when this flight from Richmond will start?"

"It could be next week or it could be tomorrow. I just want you to be ready."

"Where will you be until then?"

"Probably watching Phil Sheridan. We were at West Point together and I know something of how his mind works, so I may be able to warn General Lee which way Sheridan will take his cavalry. Right now, they're the greatest hazard Lee has to fear, once he starts retreating westward."

"Be careful, darling." Maritza put her arms around his body and held him tightly for a long moment before letting him go.

"I've been a widow once and I have no wish to be one a second time."

X

Abraham Lincoln's second Inauguration Day as President of the United States on March 4, 1865, was rainy and cold. Deep mud was everywhere throughout Washington and a damp and not very enthusiastic crowd of listeners gathered before the Capitol steps when the time came for the administration of the oath and the inauguration address.

Vice-President Andrew Johnson was ill and took the oath earlier in the Senate chamber. Because of a fever, Johnson had fortified himself with whiskey before entering the chamber and had taken too much. After the brief ceremony he'd indulged in a rambling speech that said nothing but did earn him an undeserved reputation as a drunkard. By the time Lincoln appeared on the open-air platform to speak, however, the sun had come through, adding a touch of beauty to the otherwise drab occasion.

The inaugural address was conciliatory but firm. Less conciliatory and considerably firmer was the telegram sent to Grant on Lincoln's orders in answer to Grant's report of a request from General Lee for a meeting to discuss "the possibility of arriving at a satisfactory adjustment of the present unhappy difficulties by means of a military convention."

Rather obviously Lincoln had recognized that Lee, no slaveowner himself, was tired of Jefferson Davis' intransigence when it came to the question of slavery. Fearing that military minds might reach an accommodation not entirely in accord with the political situation, Lincoln had ordered Secretary of War Stanton to wire Grant an order saying:

THE PRESIDENT DIRECTS ME TO SAY TO YOU THAT HE WISHES YOU TO HAVE NO CONFERENCE WITH GENERAL LEE UNLESS IT BE FOR THE CAPITULATION OF GENERAL LEE'S ARMY, OR ON SOME MINOR AND PURELY MILI-

TARY MATTER. HE INSTRUCTS ME TO SAY THAT YOU
ARE NOT TO DECIDE, DISCUSS OR CONFER UPON ANY
POLITICAL QUESTION. SUCH QUESTIONS THE PRESIDENT
HOLDS IN HIS OWN HANDS; AND WILL SUBMIT THEM TO
NO MILITARY CONFERENCES OR CONVENTIONS. MEAN-
WHILE YOU ARE TO PRESS TO THE UTMOST YOUR MILI-
TARY ADVANTAGES.

The telegram was smuggled to the Richmond papers by Confederate secret agents and was allowed to be reprinted verbatim
by Confederate censors. The uncompromising message to the
Union general naturally doused the hopes of the "peace party"
within the Confederacy. More than that, it pointed up a sharp
turn away from Lincoln's promise, on a previous Inauguration
Day, not to disturb slavery in states where it already existed.

That Lincoln's own plans for rebuilding a defeated South
might not have been as harsh as Secretary of War Stanton's telegram to Grant implied was revealed—at least in the opinion of
General Sherman—after a high-level conference of Union generals at City Point on the James River, to which Lincoln had
come by steamer. In Sherman's opinion, Lincoln was prepared
to treat the rebellious South generously with no severe re-
prisals.

Lincoln would even be pleased, thought Sherman, to see
Jefferson Davis make his escape to some foreign country where
he could live out his life in peace. Meanwhile the handful of
Confederate soldiers left with arms to bear would be allowed to
lay them down and go home in peace as citizens of a reunited
nation.

"I know I left his presence with the conviction that he had in
his mind, or that his Cabinet had," Sherman avowed, "some
plan of settlement, ready for application the moment Lee and
Johnston were defeated."

Thus, as March came to an end with spring already beginning to warm that part of the land not torn by shot and shell,
and also preparing to burst the remaining dogwoods into
bloom, there was even a hopeful air astir in the South. In Richmond on April 2, President Jefferson Davis was at St. Paul's
for the Sunday morning service. He looked pale and drawn

from his long illness but was able to kneel in prayer, even though the sound of increased cannonading from the south could only mean Grant was launching another attack.

The nature of that offensive and its importance was shortly revealed to the worshipers at St. Paul's in Richmond, when an aide brought a message to Davis that caused the President to leave the church immediately. Even then, however, most of the worshipers didn't realize the truth that Petersburg was being evacuated that very morning on the orders of General Lee. Or that its former defenders were already marching westward toward Burke's Station where the Richmond & Danville Railroad, leading into the Carolina Piedmont and beyond, joined the South Side Railroad from Petersburg to Lynchburg and a junction with the Orange & Alexandria leading to the Virginia & Tennessee line. Supply dumps had already been accumulated at these points for future use and Lee's hungry troops were eager to reach them.

Worshiping at St. Paul's, Maritza was surprised to see Richard Mann appear suddenly among a small group of men at the outer door. Since he towered above the others, she was able to see his signal to her and understand that he meant for her to leave immediately. As soon as she came out he took her arm and led her aside.

"I've sent word to Celestina and André to start loading your baggage ready to take it to the train," he told her. "The government will be leaving late this afternoon or early evening."

"Has Petersburg already fallen?"

"Not fallen—abandoned. Lee broke out after some hard fighting and is headed for Burke's Station. The government is being moved to Danville tonight and probably on to Greensboro, so Benjamin will be with it that far at least."

"What are you going to do?"

"My agents and I will be riding ahead of the train and what's left of Lee's army, watching for Sheridan's cavalry. He's certain to try to stop Lee and might also attempt to capture the government train, but he won't harm you or Celestina. With a passport from Martinique, André will be safe too."

"When will I see you again?" she asked.

"God only knows." He bent to kiss her good-by. "And I'd
rather He'd devote Himself to keeping you safe."

XI

Richard Mann caught up with Maritza on April 12, at Greensboro, North Carolina, where a Confederate government was
briefly in operation. Ten days had passed since the start of
General Lee's retreat from Petersburg and the exodus of the
Confederate government from Richmond southwestward to an
as yet undetermined location. During that time the thirty thousand men under Lee's command had undergone hardship and
heartbreak, one after another and often both simultaneously.

First, a food train expected to be waiting at Amelia Courthouse, some thirty-five miles away, had failed to be there when
they arrived. Plodding westward still, the weary and hungry
men in gray had then headed for Farmville, another twenty
miles distant, where rations were supposed to have been sent
from Lynchburg. The food was there all right but so was part
of Grant's army. In a rear-guard attack at Sayler's Creek on
April 6, eight thousand Confederates and most of Lee's supply
wagons were lost.

Staggering on westward, Lee expected to find ration trains at
Appomattox Station, another twenty-five miles away, but as
they approached Appomattox the fires of burning supply
dumps were visible ahead, dousing all hope. Meanwhile Sheridan's cavalry had been racing along parallel to Lee's line of retreat, seeking to keep him from turning south toward North
Carolina. Attacking whenever they could isolate a small contingent of the Confederate rear guard, Sheridan had worn down
the gray columns and now Lee and his men were out of food
and almost out of ammunition.

Concerned for his troops, Lee finally sent a note to General
Grant, whose army was coming up fast behind Sheridan, asking
for terms of surrender. Grant replied graciously, demanding
only that Lee's troops lay down their arms, give their parole

not to fight any more, and go home. Some were even allowed to take their horses so they could put in a crop that year to feed their families next winter. In Washington, an almost livid Secretary of War, Edwin M. Stanton, was objecting to any leniency, urging instead that all the leading officers and officials of the now dying Confederacy be indicted for murder. Lincoln, however, agreed with Grant and Stanton was foiled, for the moment at least, in his vengeance. The surrender at Appomattox took place on the morning of April 12, even as General Joseph E. Johnston, with Sherman now turning eastward to smash his weary and desertion-depleted army, was at Greensboro begging permission from Davis to surrender his own army. This event took place on April 14, two days later, near Durham, North Carolina.

Ostensibly the two surrenders ended the war but, in reality, another conflict, vicious, filled with hate and the desire for vengeance, was just beginning under the leadership of Secretary Edwin M. Stanton. And there the Secretary got an unexpected windfall when, on the evening of the fourteenth, while attending a victory performance at Ford's Theater, Abraham Lincoln was shot and killed by a radical malcontent actor named John Wilkes Booth.

The assassination saddened a nation celebrating in victory. It also enabled Secretary of War Stanton to all but elbow aside a stunned Vice-President, Andrew Johnson, and practically set himself up as dictator. A public, ready to believe the false accusation that the death of President Lincoln was the culmination of a plot by Jefferson Davis and other higher-up members of the Confederate government, seized upon the opportunity thus afforded to loose the floodgates of hate and give Stanton his way.

Maritza and Richard Mann heard the news of the assassination when they came down for breakfast in the dining room of the hotel that was serving temporarily as the Confederate White House, after the nearest thing to a honeymoon they'd had time to celebrate since their marriage. Judah P. Benjamin was dining alone, while reading a newspaper, but beckoned to them to join him.

"Did you see this?" he asked, pushing the newspaper across the table.

"When we came through the lobby," Mann told him. "We're both still stunned."

"I can hardly believe yesterday brought three disasters," said Maritza as Richard seated her at the table.

"Three?" Judah Benjamin lifted his eyebrows. "I can count only two—the surrender at Appomattox and the decision to let Johnston surrender at Durham Station here in North Carolina."

"Don't you think turning a raging beast like Edwin M. Stanton loose on a defenseless South is a disaster?" she asked.

Benjamin nodded slowly. "Now that you mention it, I do. The South has no greater enemy than Stanton and neither do I. He'll never rest until he has Jeff Davis and Judah Benjamin either in a Federal prison or swinging at the end of a rope."

"Would you do the same to him, if the situations were reversed?"

"Probably not," said Benjamin, with the gamin grin she knew so well. "But I'd love to bring back an old Jewish custom of stoning a criminal in a corner of the village wall."

"What is President Davis going to do now?" she asked.

"I stopped by his suite on the way to breakfast but all the talk there was of continuing the war in the Trans-Mississippi area."

"Is that possible?"

"Hardly, when we can't even cross the river in anything larger than a rowboat," said Richard Mann.

"I'm heading south toward Florida, hoping to find a boat that will take me to the Bahamas before Stanton flays my hide and nails it to the barn door," Benjamin confessed. "I was just planning how to do it when you two came in."

"We'll go with you as far as Florida," said Richard Mann promptly. "Once you're safely at sea, we'll head for Mobile and home."

"You don't have to, you know," said Benjamin, then chuckled. "Just help me figure out a way to disguise this physiognomy of mine into looking like something else besides Father Abraham."

"We *want* to go," Maritza assured him. "Secretary Stanton's agents are likely to be looking for you to try an escape through one of the small ports along the east coast. Why don't you head for the west coast of Florida instead and fool them?"

"A capital suggestion," said Benjamin. "Fortunately I know just the man to help us, too—Colonel H. J. Leovy. He's from New Orleans and owes me a few favors. Even more important, he used to hunt and fish in Florida and will know just where we need to go."

"Can you reach him?" Maritza asked.

"He was here in the hotel last night; we had a drink in the bar together." Benjamin wiped his mouth with a napkin and stood up. "You two finish your breakfast while I go out and look up Leovy. The sooner we get a start south, the quicker I'll be out of Stanton's reach and you'll be on your way back to Alabama. By the way, I hope you turned that draft on the Bank of Nova Scotia into gold, my dear, as I advised you to do before we left Richmond. Nothing greases the reluctant palm like the feel of a small gold piece and we're going to have to grease a lot of 'em before we get to Florida."

"Do you think President Davis will be able to escape?" Maritza asked Richard as they were hurriedly finishing their breakfast. "He looked mighty frail on the train coming here from Danville the other day."

"He'd be a lot better off to give up now."

"With Lincoln dead and Stanton in control?"

"Davis had many friends in the Senate before the fighting started, besides being Secretary of War in President Buchanan's Cabinet," he explained. "I'm sure he's still got enough friends in the Washington government to keep Stanton from treating him too badly."

But there, as it turned out, Richard Mann was wrong. One day less than four weeks later—while fleeing from Federal troops searching for him and eager to obtain the price Stanton had set upon his head—Jefferson Davis was seized near Irwinville, Georgia, on May 10. Less than two weeks later he was a prisoner in Fortress Monroe.

Meanwhile Judah Benjamin, Colonel Leovy, who was serving as guide, Maritza and Richard Mann were little more than twenty-four miles away, heading for the Suwannee River and Florida. Benjamin was disguised as a French gentleman named Monsieur Bonfal. With his beard now long, his eyes partially hidden by goggles, and wearing a large cloak, he was unrecognizable to any except previous intimates—and these he scrupulously avoided.

Four days later Benjamin's party crossed the Suwannee River in Florida at Moseley's Ferry and headed southward, making for the river and town of Manatee. There loyal Confederates conducted him to truly magnificent temporary quarters while a boat was found to take him to the Bahamas or Cuba. The quarters were in the Gamble mansion, located near the Manatee River, about thirty miles south of Tampa and the center of a thirty-six-hundred-acre sugar plantation.

XII

"That's the most fantastically beautiful place I've ever seen—even including the Château LeClerc!" Maritza cried when the buggy in which she and Richard Mann were riding rounded a curve in the dirt road that wound beside the Manatee River. A tidal stream, it emptied into the Gulf of Mexico near the southern entrance to Tampa Bay. By common consent, they traveled in a buggy that stayed about a half mile ahead of the one in which Judah Benjamin and Colonel Leovy were riding, the purpose being that, if the buggy with Maritza and Mann were captured, Benjamin and Leovy would have enough time to take cover in the dense piny woods through which the road ran and perhaps thus escape capture.

Benjamin had received an invitation from Confederate Captain Archibald McNeill to hide at the Gamble mansion, near Manatee, Florida, until he could hire a boat to take him to the Bahamas or to Cuba. During the war McNeill had been the deputy commissary agent for the Manatee section of Florida's immensely important cattle industry. The herds feeding on

Florida's vast grasslands had supplied meat to two Southern armies by annual drives northward to the railhead of a line that ran westward across the Florida Panhandle, connecting with other lines leading up into Georgia, Alabama, and Mississippi. The Great House rose from a luxuriant tropical garden which had obviously suffered from neglect during the war and the rapid growth of vegetation in the warm, damp climate of Florida's Gulf Coast, giving it much the appearance of a somewhat bedraggled tropical paradise.

"I visited here once during the years before the war," said Mann. "That's why I urged Benjamin to accept Captain McNeill's offer to use the mansion as a refuge until he could arrange transportation out of the country."

"We'll build a house like it on my—our plantation in Alabama," said Maritza. "But what is it made of?"

"A type of construction peculiar to Florida, a shell brick known as 'tabby.' Some of the houses in St. Augustine built with it over two hundred years ago are as sound as the day the Spaniards quarried those blocks out of the shells and sand packed into a solid mass resembling concrete on Anastasia Island."

"Étienne and I visited the island when we toured the South a few years before the war started. He was very proud that Frenchmen were the first to settle America at Fort Caroline in 1564, even if the Spanish did destroy it and most of *them* a couple of years later."

As they approached the mansion, which stood within sight of the Manatee River, Maritza glanced behind them, a habit she'd formed since they had left Jefferson Davis and some others of the former Confederate Cabinet members on May 3 between the Savannah River and Washington, Georgia, and struck out southward on their own. To her vast relief, the buggy in which Benjamin and Leovy were riding was in sight.

"I'd better go up to the house first and see whether any Federal troops are waiting for us," Richard Mann said as he reined in their horse by a white, wooden picket fence, where a gate gave access to a brick-paved driveway leading up to the house.

"Let me go," Maritza objected. "They wouldn't harm a woman."

Their host, Captain McNeill, had seen them approaching from the watching point on the upper veranda, however, and opened the front door to greet Maritza.

"Where's Mr. Bonfal?" he asked, referring to the pseudonym Benjamin had decided to adopt.

"About a half mile back. My husband and I have been staying ahead to flush out the enemy if they're around."

"They're around all right," said McNeill as he and Maritza walked down the brick driveway to the gate. "A gunboat has been patrolling the river for the past few days, which means somebody must have betrayed our plans."

"It's happened several times already," said Mann as he greeted McNeill. "Fortunately we've been warned on each occasion in time to change our route. Were you able to locate a boat?"

"I found one yesterday," said McNeill. "A shrimp fisherman from Tampa is willing to take a passenger and drop him off in the Bahamas."

"Thank goodness for that," said Maritza.

"The boat owner insists on being paid in gold, though."

"Fortunately that's no problem."

"Are you and General Mann going with Mr. Bonfal?"

"No farther than here," she said firmly. "We have a large plantation of our own not far from Mobile and we badly need to get back there to start a crop for the fall."

Benjamin and Colonel Leovy arrived just then and two black servants took the horses and the buggies to the stables. The inside of the Gamble mansion, Maritza discovered, was as massive and majestically beautiful as the outside. The walls themselves were like those of a fortress, several feet thick, with windows of thick glass. The beams supporting the ceiling were massive, having been hewn from individual cypress logs, and the floor boards, also of cypress, were large and thick.

"This place must have cost a fortune to build," said Maritza.

"And to keep up with no slaves to do the work," said McNeill dryly. "I've done my best to control the vegetation but you can tell by the thickness of that canebrake at the back that we've hardly been able to stay ahead of the undergrowth."

Benjamin was given a bedroom at the front of the house, where he could watch the nearby river through a small telescope. Mann and Maritza were quartered in the back, as was Colonel Leovy. Dinner was enlivened by Benjamin's wit and seeming lack of apprehension about his capture. If he was concerned, he showed no sign of it, although the morning issue of a Tampa newspaper delivered that afternoon had contained bad news. A massive Federal man hunt was under way across the entire South, ordered by Secretary Stanton in the determination to capture Benjamin, last important figure in the Confederate government still at large.

After sleeping as best she could on the ground or in barns on cushions of hay during the trip southward, Maritza slept better than she had for at least a month. When she came down to breakfast in the morning she saw Captain McNeill and Richard Mann in the yard outside talking. Calling to them to join her in a cup of coffee—another unheard-of delicacy in Richmond—she took a seat on the wide veranda where the breakfast table had been set. The weather was warm in this almost tropic region and from the nearby river came the hoarse croak of frogs, broken now and then by the coughing grunt of an alligator.

"Where in the world did you find coffee, Captain?" she asked McNeill as she was pouring cups of the rich black brew for them.

"The last year of the war, cattle raisers in Florida discovered that they could get more for their beef by shipping the animals to Cuba from Punta Rasa—it's near Fort Myers about a hundred miles south of here. Coffee was plentiful in Cuba, of course, so we had no trouble bringing it in when the ships returned for another load of cattle."

"Do you think the Federals will arrest Richard because he was close to the top in the Secret Service?" Maritza inquired.

"My guess would be that he won't have any trouble since he remained in uniform," said McNeill. "According to the terms General Grant gave General Lee, all he will have to do is give his parole to the captain of the gunboat that's patrolling the rivers emptying into Tampa Bay."

"I heard those General Sherman gave General Johnston in North Carolina were even more liberal than Grant was with Lee," said Mann.

"That's true, but it didn't last," said McNeill. "The Tampa morning paper says Secretary Stanton made Sherman send for Johnston again and dictate a less lenient set of conditions for him to sign. From what I hear, Stanton would have demoted Sherman to private for being so generous to a defeated enemy, if he wasn't already such a hero in the North after burning Atlanta and then marching through Georgia like a hurricane."

"Now that it's over, it all seems like a bad dream," Maritza commented.

"It won't be over for us until we get Secretary Benjamin safely on that boat and away from the United States," Richard Mann reminded her.

"I still find myself wondering if it really happened."

"A lot of men lost their lives proving that it did," McNeill told her. "The latest casualty figures I saw were three hundred and fifty thousand for the North and a hundred thousand less for the South. But more died from disease in the South, so the losses are probably about the same. The casualty total altogether may even top a million down here but, since the North had plenty of medical supplies, they came out a good deal better as far as disease was concerned."

Maritza shivered. "I know something of that. Malaria and pneumonia almost got me in the spring of 1862."

"The quicker we can all forget about the war and go back to work the better." McNeill's tone was somber. "Unfortunately men like Secretary Stanton aren't going to let the South forget they started the whole thing any time soon."

"Hasn't President Johnson assured everyone that Lincoln's plan for the end of the war will be carried out?" Maritza asked.

"Yes. But how do we know what that plan was—now that Lincoln is dead?"

Both men stiffened as a low throbbing noise suddenly became audible from downriver.

"That sound comes from the engines on the gunboat that was here yesterday," said McNeill urgently. "Get Secretary Benjamin and hide with him in that thick canebrake behind the house. Someone may have seen your buggy yesterday and warned the captain of the gunboat that you are in the locality."

Benjamin didn't have to wait to be sent for. From his bedroom window on the second floor of the house he had been able to see the gunboat with his telescope while it was still at least a half mile downriver. Maritza and Richard Mann met him at the foot of the stairs.

"I'm going to hide in the canebrake but there's no real need for you two to run," he told them. "Richard can give his parole and assure the gunboat captain that he came here because his wife was visiting at the Gamble mansion. There'd be no reason to hold either of you then."

"We're going with you," said Maritza firmly. "In that disguise, I doubt that anyone would recognize you. If they do find us but don't realize who you are, I can always claim you're my husband."

"Maritza's right, sir," Richard Mann advised. "You could claim to be a Frenchman traveling with his wife, since both of you speak French fluently."

While they were talking the gunboat, a small one, had come into view, plowing upstream on the river that flowed quietly from a cypress swamp some distance away. If Benjamin was to make his escape, it would have to be within the next few minutes.

"All right," he said. "I hope you're not carrying arms, Richard. That would be all the excuse the captain of the gunboat would need to put you before a firing squad."

"I'm unarmed," Mann assured him, but nobody had asked Maritza so she decided to keep the small derringer she always carried with her.

They left the house not a moment too soon. Even as they worked their way with difficulty into the protection of the thickly grown canebrake they heard the captain of the Federal vessel give the order to bring the warship to a stop at the dock that had once served as a loading point for cotton and other products from over three thousand acres making up the plantation.

As the three fugitives waited in the protection of the tall and densely packed clump of bamboo canes, they were so close to the house that they could hear the tramp of feet upon the heavy cypress floor boards as a group of marines, who had been aboard the gunboat, searched every room and closet. They found nothing to arouse further suspicion, however, and after perhaps a half hour of searching the lieutenant commanding the detail gave the order to break off the search.

Through a small opening in the canebrake where someone had cut a few of them, probably for fishing poles, the fugitives could see the smartly uniformed marines leave the house and form up in the yard of the brick-paved driveway. A half dozen who had been poking through the barns and other outbuildings now came around the corner of the house and joined the others. Watching them, Maritza dared to hope the danger posed by the search was over, until one of the marines shouted, "Hey, Lieutenant! Can't you at least let us have some target practice? I'm tired of shooting nothing but alligators and turtles."

"Send a volley into that canebrake, then," the officer said. "It's the only place we haven't searched and breaking a way through those bamboos would be pure hell in this heat."

"Drop!" Richard Mann whispered urgently to the other two, as the formation of about a dozen marines raised their Springfields.

The three of them hit the dirt an instant before a shower of minié balls, fired at waist-high level, crashed through the canes. The reverberation of the volley was loud enough to drown out Richard Mann's involuntary cry of pain, as he suddenly gripped his leg some six inches above the ankle. Mowed down by the minié balls, the tops of the cane stalks were falling all around them when a small gray rabbit darted from the clump of bamboos and sped across the barnyard toward another clump and safety.

"That's a damned smart rabbit," said one of the marines in a tone of disgust. "He knowed we couldn't load and shoot again in time to get him, so he chose that time to skedaddle."

"Detail, reload," came the order from the marine lieutenant.

While the marines rammed powder, wadding, and lead down the barrels of their rifles with practiced efficiency, Maritza held her breath, certain that the Federal officer was going to order another volley through the canebrake. Instead, apparently satisfied that the volley would have flushed out any other prey, as it had the rabbit, he gave the order to "Shoulder arms," and the column marched smartly back down to the dock beside the river. There they reboarded the gunboat, which shortly disappeared upstream and out of sight, removing, at least for the moment, the danger of Benjamin's capture.

"Is it bad?" Maritza asked Richard Mann anxiously as she bent over the now freely bleeding leg.

"I think both bones are shattered just above the ankle," he managed to say. "Isn't that just my luck, after going through four years of war without a scratch, to be the target after it was over for one marine who was a lousy shot."

XIII

"It's bad news, I'm afraid, General." The speaker was a plump doctor named MacGregor, who had been called in from the nearest town by Captain McNeill to attend Richard Mann's wound. "That leg has got to come off a little below the knee."

"Get on with it, then," said Mann between clenched teeth. "The saw couldn't hurt any worse than the leg is hurting now."

Maritza had looked up from where she was applying a bandage to the wound, the shock she felt at the medical verdict rendering her suddenly speechless.

"What did you say, Dr. MacGregor?" she asked finally.

"I was telling your husband that I'll have to amputate his leg."

"Why? Look at his foot; the circulation is intact or the skin wouldn't be pink, as it is. That means only the bones are damaged and they'll heal."

"You don't understand, madam. During the war we amputated all compound fractures because otherwise they became inflamed and gangrenous. By that time the wound was suppurating so badly that the patients often died from gangrene. The only way to prevent that is to take off the leg first."

"Wartime was different, Doctor," said Maritza. "I worked as a volunteer nurse in hospitals and I talked to enough army doctors to know you're probably right—for the battlefield."

"Then why—"

"The war has ended and so, thank God, have battlefield conditions. This wound came from a stray bullet while my husband was lying on the ground beneath some bamboos with nothing but sand around. If it's treated the right way there's no reason why it should suppurate at all."

Dr. MacGregor had stiffened at her last words and a flush of anger suffused his cheeks. "Did you go to medical school, Mrs. Mann?" he asked.

"No, but I spent seven years in Europe, Doctor, during which my husband and I visited several of the leading clinics there. My husband raised blooded livestock and was seeking a way to treat broken limbs in horses without killing them. Did you ever hear of Dr. Semmelweis in Budapest?"

"I'm afraid not, madam."

"Semmelweis stopped the spread of puerperal fever in the Maternity Hospital of Vienna by teaching students and doctors to wash their hands and instruments in a chloride of lime solution. In London a surgeon named Lister has recently started doing the same thing, using carbolic acid."

MacGregor shrugged. "I've had no time to waste abroad studying foreign treatments in medicine."

"You'd be well advised to do so," Maritza snapped, irritated by the assumption of superior knowledge on the part of a physician, who obviously had little formal medical education beyond the usual apprenticeship.

Dr. MacGregor puffed up like a blowfish when scratched on the belly. "Madam, if I am to be in charge of this case the patient—and the family—must follow my instructions."

"I'm afraid that means you're discharged, Doctor," said Maritza coolly. "You're not going to amputate my husband's leg until a more modern treatment has been tried that has a good chance of saving it."

"If you will tell me what doctor you are going to, Mrs. Mann, I will send him a summary of my findings," MacGregor offered. "But I should warn you that I'm the only doctor for forty miles. Anyone who takes over the case will have to come down from Tampa."

"The wound needs to be treated as soon as possible, so we'll just have to make out the best way we can," said Maritza. "Will you sell me some laudanum to relieve my husband's pain?"

MacGregor hesitated. "Opium is hard to come by, so the tincture called laudanum is quite expensive. I'll have to charge you ten dollars in gold for it."

"I'm prepared to pay you in gold, Doctor."

"In that event . . ." The portly doctor opened his medical bag and took out a small bottle of a faintly amber-colored liquid. "You can give him twenty to thirty drops in water every four hours for pain."

"Thank you, Doctor." Maritza handed him the coin and started adding thirty drops of laudanum to a small amount of water in a glass. Lifting Richard Mann's head, she gave it to him to drink.

"When is he going to amputate, Maritza?" Mann asked.

"He's not going to. I'm taking over the treatment myself."

"I trust you," Richard Mann assured her and closed his eyes as the laudanum began to take effect.

"Could you spare me a small bottle of chloroform?" Maritza asked Dr. MacGregor.

"Of course, and there'll be no charge for that." The doctor hesitated, then added: "Would you mind telling me how you plan to treat this injury?"

"First of all, I'm going to wash the wound out thoroughly; that's why I'll need the chloroform."

"Who is going to administer it?"

"My husband, the patient. I've read descriptions of ether parties in various parts of the country. When Richard inhales enough chloroform to bring on at least partial unconsciousness, he'll drop the cloth pad he holds over his nose and thus can't get too much."

"That's very clever." MacGregor's pique at her challenging his medical knowledge seemed to be evaporating.

"Before I start I'm going to have two boxes made so one can slide inside another," Maritza continued. "One end of the outer box will be padded so it can press against Richard's pelvic bone. The smaller one will slide inside it with his shoe attached to the end by means of a twisted loop of rope to make a Spanish windlass. That way, the leg will be held immobile while traction is applied to the lower part by using a wooden peg in the loop of rope to twist it. I assume that you're familiar with the use of what's called a Spanish windlass."

MacGregor nodded. "I can see how you can apply traction with the leg in the box splint. But how do you prevent suppuration in the wound?"

"In two ways, I hope, Doctor. A sea captain I knew once told me that wounds suffered aboard ship usually heal well without suppuration; most sailors even believe sea water is a healing agent. I do know from visiting Dr. Semmelweis' clinic at Budapest that chloride of lime solution applied as a wet dressing will also promote healing very effectively by keeping down suppuration. As soon as I can put my husband's leg into a splint I'm going to see about hiring a fishing boat to take us to Mobile. I'll be able to transport my husband with his leg in this splint and also treat it with sea water and lime solution en route."

"You should have been a doctor, madam," said MacGregor admiringly. "If you don't mind, I'll stay and see how you do all this."

"I'll be happy to have your help," said Maritza. "After all, I'm not a doctor and I've never used this treatment before, so I can only assume that it will work."

"You describe it so logically that I'd be willing to bet it will," said MacGregor. "What do you want me to do first?"

"Find someone to make the boxes," said Maritza. "When they're ready, maybe Captain McNeill can find some lime solution around here for us to use. Dr. Semmelweis even performs abdominal surgery successfully without suppuration, by washing the instruments and the hands of himself and the assistants in it."

While Maritza was ministering to the needs of Richard Mann, with the full co-operation now of Dr. MacGregor, a conference of war had been going on in another part of the Gamble mansion between Judah Benjamin, Captain McNeill, and Colonel Leovy. In the early afternoon the Federal gunboat patrolling the area came back downstream but did not stop. Nevertheless, its presence crystallized the convictions of those concerned most with the escape of Benjamin, now that Maritza and Richard Mann were out of the picture. She learned of the decision late that afternoon, when Richard's leg had been placed in the sliding splint built from cypress boards by the black carpenter of the plantation, now freed but, like so many former slaves, unwilling to leave his old home.

Upon examination and under the light chloroform anesthesia, Mann's wound had proved to be a clean shattering of the heavy bone called the tibia, the main weight barrier in the lower leg. The smaller fibula beside it was only splintered slightly by the impact of the bullet, which had laid open a trough of flesh across Mann's leg about six inches above the ankle. Under traction by means of a Spanish windlass and the stabilizing properties of the splint, the bones were easily pulled down into as nearly normal a position as was possible with the tibia shattered into several pieces by the bullet.

The splinting completed, Maritza had placed over the wound a dressing of clean linen, browned slightly according to the current medical custom over an open flame in the kitchen stove. Fortunately, too, a bag of chlorinated lime—used as a bleaching agent in refining the sugar from the sugar cane of the plantation —had been left over from the last crop and was found while they were looking for boards from which to make the splint. Preparing a solution, roughly as strong as that used for bleaching, Maritza flushed out the wound with it before applying the dressing of salt-scorched linen and soaking it, too, in the lime solution.

"You'd make a good doctor right now, Mrs. Mann," said Dr.

MacGregor admiringly when it was finished. "Are you and your husband going to live in this area, now that the war is over?"

"We're from Alabama. As soon as Richard is able to travel we'll go back to the Mobile area, where we have a large plantation."

"I hope you'll find something left besides raw earth. The South is swarming with Yankees, claiming as their own land plantations that were previously owned by men killed in battle or by disease. There's not going to be much help from the Federal authorities either to anybody who was active in the Confederacy."

"I'm sure our plantations have been safe," Maritza assured him. "Money was left with my solicitor in Mobile to pay wages to the Negroes, who used to farm the area as our slaves. It's still home to them and I think they'll stay, now that they've been freed."

"I hope you find everything in order." MacGregor held out his hand. "Please forgive me for speaking sharply to you earlier this afternoon. From now on you can be assured that I shall use your treatment for compound fractures in my practice—giving you the credit, of course."

"You don't have to bother about that. The credit really belongs to some dedicated doctors like Semmelweis. He was hounded out of Vienna because he insisted that physicians should wash their hands before delivering babies."

By the time Maritza and the old doctor had finished taking care of Richard Mann dinner was being served—supper in this semitropical clime. While she was eating from a tray and feeding Richard, who was now awake from the chloroform but still groggy from the pain-killing preparation of opium called laudanum, Judah Benjamin explained the results of the conference that afternoon.

"Because of the close proximity of a Federal gunboat and the relative prominence of the Gamble mansion," he told Maritza and Richard, "it has been decided that I should move across the Manatee River to the home of a Captain Frederick Tresca, located a little nearer town."

"Why him?" Maritza asked.

"Before the war Tresca ran a freight sloop between Cedar Key on the coast north of Tampa to Key West and, more recently, he ran the blockade from Florida to Nassau," Captain McNeill explained. "Most important of all, Tresca knows the Gulf Coast of Florida like the back of his hand."

"Will he help Mr. Ben—Mr. Bonfal?"

"I rode into town while you and Dr. MacGregor were treating your husband this afternoon," McNeill told her. "Tresca has agreed to take Mr. Bonfal to Nassau—for a price, of course."

"Which I will cheerfully pay," said Benjamin. "The only thing I don't mind about the whole deal is that I won't be able to see Secretary Stanton's face when he learns I'm safe in England or France."

"The thing we've got to watch is the possibility of someone selling Mr. Bonfal out because of the price that's on his head," said McNeill. "Fortunately, though, we don't have to worry about Captain Tresca or his crewman, H. A. McLeod. McLeod was a sailor for the Confederacy and helped sink a lot of Yankee ships. If the war could have gone on, he would no doubt have helped sink a lot of others."

"I'll say good-by, my friends," Benjamin told Maritza and Richard. "I owe my progress this far toward escaping Stanton mainly to both of you. With Richard wounded, you'll have all you can do from now on to take care of him, though, Maritza, so it wouldn't be fair to burden you with my problems."

"Write to us when you get to England." Maritza put down her tray and stood up to kiss the ex-Secretary of State for the Confederacy good-by. "Do you have the manuscript I gave you just now?"

"It's safe," said Benjamin. "As soon as I arrive in England, I'll make arrangements for it to be published there, and in France as well. You've done a wonderful job of telling the world about the glorious record of our Cause. Even if Stanton somehow manages to catch me I'll arrange to send your story on to London. Have you decided what you're going to do next?"

"If Captain McNeill can put up with us, we'll probably stay here for a few weeks, until Richard's leg has healed enough for us to transport him easily."

"You're welcome here for as long as you want to stay," McNeill assured her. "I don't think the Federals will bother you, either. It's Mr. Bonfal they want badly, but I think we're going to be able to foil them there too."

"How do you propose to get home?" Benjamin asked her.

"By the easiest way of all—water. It's a straight course north by west from here to Mobile. With Captain McNeill's help, I can probably hire a fishing boat or a shrimper to take us there."

"We'll have no trouble doing that," McNeill assured her. "But don't plan to leave until your husband is safely well."

XIV

On a hot July morning Maritza tightened the lines leading to the bridle of the horse pulling the buggy in which she and Richard Mann were riding, stopping the vehicle in the shade of a massive water oak growing beside the road. Six weeks had passed since they'd hidden with Judah Benjamin in the canebrake behind the Gamble mansion near Manatee, Florida. Although Richard was not yet able to bear weight upon the tibia shattered by a Yankee bullet that day, the bone was healing well and he was able to be on crutches. A wrapping of crinoline soaked in heavy starch was stiff enough to give his leg all the protection it needed now, as long as he didn't try to walk. As for the skin wound where the minié ball had entered, it had healed before they left the Florida coast, thanks to the suppuration-preventing quality of the chloride of lime Maritza had used on it.

"It's beautiful, Richard!" Maritza's voice held a note of awe at the beauty of the rich white coverlet of exploded cotton bolls hiding the black fecund earth from view, making the field look like a blanket of snow for as far as they could see from where she had brought the buggy to a stop. "Truly beautiful," she added once again.

"Moses and the others didn't let us down, thanks to your having the forethought to leave money with Anderson to pay them." He leaned over to kiss her. "You deserve even more credit for standing up to Dr. MacGregor when he wanted to amputate. Because you can be as stubborn as you are beautiful, I've got both legs instead of one. Give that bone a few more weeks and I can throw these crutches away, then we can truly start a new life together."

"I've got news for you." Maritza laughed softly as she slipped an arm around his waist and squeezed it. "That new life got started some time ago, around three months by my calculations."

AUTHOR'S NOTE

Readers of my historical novels, particularly those dealing with the American Civil War, already know that I follow the course of the historical events upon which they are based as closely as a fictional story will allow. This is particularly true of *The Passionate Rebel*. The diplomatic maneuverings by which the Confederacy sought to gain help from England and France in the unequal conflict were fully as involved as those depicted in the story and the Mason-Slidell incident occurred almost exactly as it is depicted.

Little has been written about the remarkable exploits of the Confederate Secret Service and only a few of them could be incorporated in the novel for reasons of length. However, those appearing here are depicted almost exactly as they happened, including the attempt to burn New York, the activity of Copperheads in the Middle West, and the attempts to outwit Beast Butler in New Orleans.

I hope readers of Maritza's adventures will find her quite as fascinating as I did while writing about her.

FRANK G. SLAUGHTER, M.D.

Jacksonville, Florida
December 1, 1978

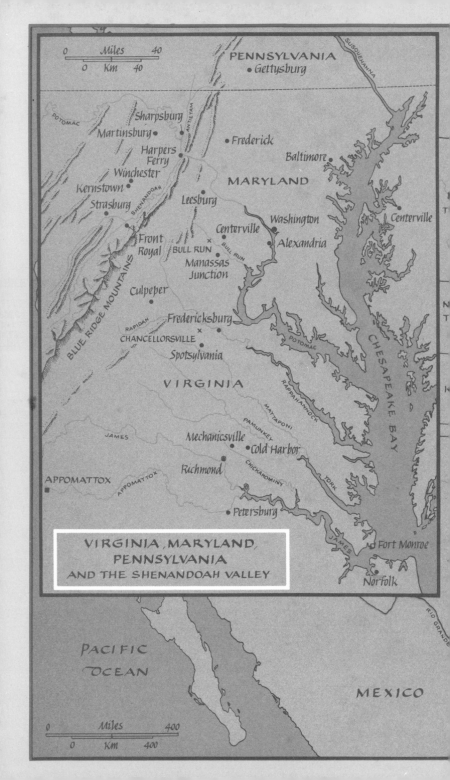

VIRGINIA, MARYLAND,
PENNSYLVANIA
AND THE SHENANDOAH VALLEY